# THE STORM RUNNER

# THE STORM RUNNER

## J.C. CERVANTES

**RICK RIORDAN PRESENTS**

DISNEP • HYPERION   LOS ANGELES   NEW YORK

Glyph illustrations by Justine Howlett

Copyright © 2018 by Jennifer Cervantes
Introduction copyright © 2018 by Rick Riordan

First Edition, September 2018
1 3 5 7 9 10 8 6 4 2
Printed in the United States of America
FAC-020093-18215

This book is set in 11.85-pt Aldus Nova Pro, Bradley Hand ITC/
Monotype; Cocotte, Genplan Pro/Fontspring
Designed by Maria Elias

Library of Congress Cataloging-in-Publication Data
Names: Cervantes, Jennifer, author.
Title: The storm runner / by J. C. Cervantes.
Description: First edition. • Los Angeles ; New York : Rick Riordan Presents,
Disney Hyperion, 2018. • Summary: To prevent the Maya gods from battling each
other and destroying the world, thirteen-year-old Zane must unravel an ancient
prophecy, stop an evil god, and discover how the physical disability that makes
him reliant on a cane also connects him to his father and his ancestry.
Identifiers: LCCN 2017048842 • ISBN 9781368016346
Subjects: • CYAC: Maya mythology—Fiction. • People with disabilities—
Fiction. • Fathers and sons—Fiction. • Maya gods—Fiction.
Classification: LCC PZ7.C3198 St 2018 • DDC [Fic]—dc23
LC record available at https://lccn.loc.gov/2017048842
Reinforced binding

Follow @ReadRiordan
Visit www.DisneyBooks.com

*For Mom, my* Seer
*And for those who don't feel like they belong*

# WELCOME TO THE VOLCANO

Zane Obispo has a pretty sweet life.

Since last year, he's been homeschooled, which means the other kids can't pick on him anymore. He gets to spend a lot of his time out in the desert of New Mexico, wandering and exploring with his faithful boxer-dalmatian, Rosie.

His mom loves him like crazy. His uncle Hondo is a fun housemate, even though he's maybe a little too addicted to pro wrestling and Flamin' Hot Cheetos.

As for the neighbors, Zane only has two: friendly Mr. Ortiz, who grows top secret chile-pepper varieties in his garden, and Ms. Cab, who works as a phone psychic and pays Zane to help her out. What's not to like?

And did I mention the volcano in Zane's backyard? That's right. Zane has his very own volcano. He and Rosie spend a lot of time climbing around on it. Recently, they even found a secret entrance that leads inside. . . .

Yep, life is good!

Er, except that Zane was born with mismatched legs. One has always been shorter than the other, so he walks with a limp and uses a cane. He's learning to deal, though, and is a crazy-fast hobbler.

Oh, and also . . . Zane just got accepted to a new private school. He doesn't want to go, but his mom is insisting. Class starts tomorrow.

Then there's the accident—Zane sees a small plane crash into the mouth of his volcano. He was close enough to glimpse the pilot's face . . . and either it was a very good Halloween mask, or the pilot was an alien zombie monster.

On top of all this, there's a pretty new girl in town—Brooks—who warns Zane he's in mortal danger. But Brooks doesn't exist, according to the school records. And how does she know who he is, anyway?

Soon, Zane discovers that nothing in his life is what he thought. There's a reason he was born with a limp. There's a reason he's never met his father—a mysterious guy his mom fell in love with on a trip to the Yucatán. Something very strange is going on in Zane's volcano, and Brooks claims it's all tied to some ancient prophecy.

How much do you know about the Maya myths? Did you know the Maya have a goddess of chocolate? (Dude, how come the Greeks don't get a goddess of chocolate? No fair.) The Maya also have shape-shifters, demons, magicians, giants, demigods, and an underworld that may or may not be accessible from the back of a local taco shop.

J. C. Cervantes is about to take you on a trip you will never forget, through the darkest, strangest, and funniest twists and turns of Maya myth. You will meet the scariest gods you can imagine, the creepiest denizens of the underworld, and the most amazing and unlikely heroes, who have to save our world from being ripped apart.

Maya myth and magic is closer than you think. In fact, it's right in our backyard.

Welcome to the volcano.

Welcome to *The Storm Runner*.

"Believing takes practice."
—Madeleine L'Engle

To Whom It May Concern,

Here it is. The story you forced me to write, with the details up to the bitter and unhappy end. All so I could serve as your poster boy for what happens when <u>anyone</u> defies the gods.

I never wanted any of this. But you didn't give me a choice. I ended up here because of some sacred oath I didn't even take, and because I made you so mad you wanted me dead.

I guess you got what you wanted.

Personally, I think you should be thanking me, but gods never show gratitude, do they?

I just want you to know I don't regret any of it. I'd do it all again, even knowing where I ended up. Okay, maybe I do have one regret—that I won't get to see your shocked faces when you read this. Anyhow, delivery made. See you on the other side.

Zane Obispo

# 1

·

**It all started when Mom screamed.**

I thought she'd seen a scorpion, but when I got to the kitchen, she was waving a letter over her head and dancing in circles barefoot. After a year of being homeschooled, I was going to get to go to school again. Did you catch that word? *Get.* As in, someone was *allowing* me to learn. Stupid! Who put adults in charge, anyway? But here's the thing: I didn't want to go to some stuffy private school called Holy Ghost where nuns gave me the evil eye. And I for sure didn't want the Holy Ghost "shuttle" to come all the way out to no-man's-land to pick me up. Mine was the last stop, and that meant the van would probably be full when it arrived. And *full* meant at least a dozen eyes staring at me.

I smiled at Mom, because she looked happy. She took care of sick people in their homes all day, and she also let her brother, Hondo, live with us. He spent most of his time watching wrestling matches on TV and eating bags of Flamin' Hot Cheetos, so she didn't wear smiles too often.

"But..." I didn't know where to start. "You said I could be homeschooled."

"For a year," she said, still beaming. "That was the agreement. Remember? A single year."

Pretty sure that *wasn't* the agreement, but once something was in Mom's head, it was superglued there. Arguing was useless. Plus, I wanted her to be happy. Really, really happy. So I nodded hard and fast, because the harder I nodded, the more excited I'd look. I even threw in another smile.

"When?" It was September, and that meant I'd already missed a month of classes.

"You start tomorrow."

*Crap!*

"How about I start in January?" Yeah, you could say I was super optimistic.

Mom shook her head. "This is an incredible opportunity, Zane."

"Doesn't private school cost a lot?"

"They gave you a scholarship. Look!" She flashed the letter as proof.

*Oh.*

Mom folded the letter neatly. "You've been on the waiting list since..."

She didn't finish her sentence, but she didn't need to. *Since* referred to the day this jerk —a jerk whose face was seared into my brain—had mopped the floor with me at my old school, and I'd sworn never to set foot in any "place of learning" again.

"What about Ms. Cab?" I asked. "She needs my help. How am I going to pay for Rosie's food if I don't work?"

My neighbor, Ms. Cab (her real last name is Caballero, but I couldn't pronounce it as a little kid and the nickname stuck), was blind and needed an assistant to help her do stuff around the house. Also, she worked as a phone psychic, and

I answered the calls before she came on the line. It made her seem more legit. She paid me pretty good, enough to feed my dog, Rosie. Rosie was a boxmatian (half-boxer, half-dalmatian) and ate like an elephant.

"You can work in the afternoons." Mom took my hand in hers.

I hated when she did that during our arguments.

"Zane, honey, please. Things will be *mejor* this time. You're thirteen now. You need friends. You can't live out here alone with these..."

*Out here* was a narrow, dusty road in the New Mexico desert. Other than my two neighbors, there were tumbleweeds, rattlesnakes, coyotes, roadrunners, a dried-up riverbed, and even a dead volcano. But more on that later. Most people are surprised when they find out New Mexico has so many volcanoes. (Of course, *mine* was no ordinary act of nature, right, gods?)

"With these what?" I asked, even though I knew what she was thinking: *misfits.*

So what that Ms. Cab was a little different? And who cared that my other neighbor, Mr. Ortiz, grew weird varieties of chile peppers in his greenhouse? Didn't mean they were misfits.

"I'm just saying that you need to be with kids your age."

"But I don't like kids my age," I told her. "And I learn more without teachers."

She couldn't argue with that. I'd taught myself all sorts of things, like the generals of the Civil War, the number of blood vessels in the human body, and the names of stars and planets. That was the best thing about not going to school: I was the boss.

Mom ruffled my dark hair and sighed. "You're a genius, yes, but I don't like you hanging out only with a bunch of old people."

"Two isn't a bunch."

I guess I'd sort of been hoping Mom would forget our deal. Or maybe Holy Ghost (who named that school, anyway?) would disappear off the face of the earth in a freak cataclysmic accident.

"Mom." I got real serious and made her look me in the eyes. "No one wants to be friends with a freak." I tapped my cane on the ground twice. One of my legs was shorter than the other, which meant I walked with a dumb limp. It earned me all sorts of nicknames from the other kids: Sir Limps-a-Lot, McGimpster, Zane the Cane, and my all-time favorite: Uno—for the one good leg.

"You are *not* a freak, Zane, and . . ."

Oh boy. Her eyes got all watery like they were going to drown in her sadness.

"Okay, I'll go," I said, because I'd rather face a hundred hateful eyes than two crying ones.

She straightened, wiped her tears away with the back of her hand, and said, "Your uniform is pressed and waiting on your bed. Oh, and I have a present for you."

Notice how she dropped the bad news with something good? She should've run for mayor. There was no point in my griping about the uniform, even though the tie would probably give my neck a rash. Instead I decided to focus on the word *present*, and I held my breath, hoping it wasn't a rosary or something. Mom went to a cabinet and pulled out a skinny umbrella-size box with a silver ribbon tied around it.

"What is it?"

"Just open it." Her hands twitched with excitement.

I ripped open the box to get to the present that we didn't have money for. Inside was a wad of brown paper and under that, a shiny black wooden cane. It had a brass tip shaped like a dragon's head. "This is . . ." I blinked, searching for the right word.

"Do you like it?" Her smile could've lit up the whole world.

I turned the cane in my hands, testing its weight, and decided it looked like something a warrior would carry, which made it the coolest gift in the universe. "I bet it cost a lot."

Mom shook her head. "It was given to me. . . . Mr. Chang died last week, remember?"

Mr. Chang was a rich client who lived in a grande house in town and sent Mom home with chow mein every Tuesday. He was also a customer of Ms. Cab's—she was the one who'd gotten Mom the job to take care of him until he died. I hated to think of Mom hanging out with dying people, but as she always said, we had to eat. I'd tried eating less, but that was getting harder and harder the older I got. I'd already reached a whopping five foot nine. That made me the tallest in my family.

I ran my hands over the brass dragon head with the flames flying out of its mouth.

"He collected all sorts of things," Mom continued. "And his daughter said I should have this. She knew you—" She stopped herself. "She said the dragon symbolizes protection."

So Mom thought I needed protection. That made me feel pretty miserable. But I knew she meant well.

I rested my weight against it. It felt perfect, like it was made for me. I was excited to cruise around with this much cooler cane instead of my dumb plain brown one that screamed *I'm a freak*. "Thanks, Mom. I really like it."

"I thought it would make going back to school . . . easier," Mom said.

Right. Easier. Nothing, not even this warrior dragon cane, was going to make my being the new kid any easier.

It was a low point, and I didn't think things could get any worse. But boy, was I wrong.

That night, as I lay in bed, I thought about the next day. My stomach was all twisted in knots, and I wished I could turn into primordial ooze and seep into the ground. Rosie knew something was up, because she let out little groans and nuzzled her head against my hand, soft-like. I petted the white patch between her eyes in small circles.

"I know, girl," I whispered. "But Mom looked so happy."

I wondered what my dad would say about the whole thing. Not that I'd ever know—I'd never even met the guy. He and Mom hadn't gotten married, and he'd bounced before I was born. She'd only told me three things about him: He was superbly handsome (her words, not mine). He was from Mexico's Yucatán region. (She'd spent time there before I was born and said the sea is like glass.) And the third thing? She loved him to pieces. Whatever.

It was all quiet, except for the crickets and my guts churning. I clicked on the lamp and sat up.

On my nightstand was the Maya mythology book Mom had given me for my eighth birthday. It was part of a five-volume set about Mexico, but this book was the coolest. I figured it was her way of showing me my dad's culture without having to talk about him. The book had a tattered green cover with big gold letters on it: *The Myths and Magic of the Maya*. It was filled with color illustrations and stories about the adventures of different gods, kings, and heroes. The gods sounded awesome, but authors lie all the time.

I opened the book. On the endpapers was an illustration of a Maya death mask made of crumbling jade, with squinted lidless eyes and square stone teeth like tiny gravestones.

I swear the face was smiling at me.

"What're you looking at?" I huffed, slamming the book closed.

I tossed off the covers, got up, and peered out the window. It was all shadows and silence. There was only one good thing about living on the mesa: it was a hundred yards from a dead volcano (aka the Beast).

Having my own volcano was about the most interesting thing in my short life. (Up until that point, that is.) I'd even found a secret entrance into it last month. Rosie and I were hiking down from the top, and about halfway down I heard a strangled gasp. Naturally, I went to investigate, half expecting to find a hurt animal. But when I parted the scraggly creosote branches, I discovered something else: an opening just big enough to crawl through. It led to a whole labyrinth of caves, and for half a second I'd thought about calling *National Geographic* or something. But then I'd decided I would rather have a private place for Rosie and me than be on the cover of some dumb magazine.

Rosie leaped off the bed when she saw me slip on my sneakers.

"Come on, girl. Let's get out of here."

I went outside with my new warrior cane and limped past Nana's grave (she died when I was two, so I didn't remember her). I crossed the big stretch of desert, zigzagging between creosote, ocotillo, and yucca. The moon looked like a huge fish eye.

"Maybe I could just *pretend* to go to school," I said to Rosie as we got closer to the Beast, a black cone rising a couple hundred yards out of the sand to meet the sky.

Rosie stopped, sniffed the air. Her ears pricked.

"Okay, fine. Bad idea. You have a better one?"

With a whimper, Rosie inched back.

"You smell something?" I said, hoping it wasn't a rattlesnake. I hated snakes. When I didn't hear the familiar rattling, I relaxed. "You're not afraid of another jackrabbit, are you?"

Rosie yelped at me.

"You *were* afraid, don't try to deny it."

She took off toward the volcano. "Hey!" I called, trying to keep up. "Wait for me!"

I'd found Rosie wandering the desert four years ago. At the time, I figured someone had dumped her there. She was all skin and bones, and she acted skittish at first, like someone had abused her. When I begged Mom to let me keep her, she said we couldn't afford it, so I promised to earn money for dog food. Rosie was cinnamon brown like most boxers, but she had black spots all over, including on her floppy ears, which is why I was sure she had dalmatian in her, too. She only had three legs, so she got me and I got her.

When we got to the base of my volcano, I stopped abruptly. There, in the moonlit sand, was a series of paw prints—massive, with long claws. I stepped into one of the impressions and my size-twelve foot took up only a third of the space. The paw was definitely too big to belong to a coyote. I thought maybe they were bear tracks, except bears don't cruise the desert.

I kneeled to investigate. Even without the moonlight I would've been able to see the huge prints, because I had perfect eyesight in the dark. Mom called it a sacred ancestral blessing. Whatever. I called it another freak-of-nature thing.

"They look big enough to belong to a dinosaur, Rosie."

She sniffed one, then another, and whimpered.

I followed the trail, but it ended suddenly, like whatever creature the prints belonged to had simply vanished. Shivers crept up my spine.

Rosie whimpered again, looking up at me with her soft brown eyes as if to say *Let's get outta here.*

"Okay, okay," I said, just as eager as she was to get to the top of the volcano.

We climbed the switchback trail, past my secret cave (which I'd camouflaged with a net of creosote and mesquite branches), toward the ridge.

When we got to the top, I took in the jaw-dropping view. To the east was a glittering night sky rolling over the desert, and to the west was a lush valley dividing the city and the flat mesa. And beyond that? A looming mountain range with jagged peaks that stood shoulder to shoulder like a band of soldiers.

This was pretty much my favorite place in the world. Not that I'd ever been outside New Mexico, but I read a lot. Mom always told me the volcano was unsafe, without ever really saying why, but to me it had always felt quiet and calm. It also happened to be where I trained. After the docs had said there was no way to fix my bum leg, I spent hours hiking the Beast, thinking if I could just make my shorter leg stronger, maybe my limp would be less noticeable.

No such luck. But by walking the rim's edge I learned how to be a boss at balancing, and that's a handy skill when you get shoved around by kids at school.

I set down my cane and began teetering along the rim of the crater while holding my arms out to my sides. Mom would kill me if she knew I did this. One slip and I'd tumble fifty feet down the rocky hill.

Rosie cruised behind me, sniffing the ground.

"How 'bout I pretend to be sick?" I said, still stuck on how to get out of Holy Ghost school. "Or I could release rats into the cafeteria. . . . There can't be school if there's no food, right?" Did Catholic schools even have a cafeteria? The only problem was, my ideas would only buy me a day or two.

A low rumble rolled across the sky.

Rosie and I both stopped in our tracks and looked up. A small aircraft zoomed over the Beast, turned, and came back.

I stepped away from the crater's edge, craning my neck to get a better look.

I waved, hoping the pilot could see me. But he didn't come near enough. Instead, he started zigzagging like a crazy person. I thought maybe he was borracho until he circled back perfectly for another run. This time he came in tighter. Just when I thought the pilot was going to pull up, he pointed the plane's nose toward the center of the crater. The wings were so close to me I could practically see the screws holding them together. The plane's thrust shook the ground, sending me stumbling, but I caught myself.

Then something started glowing inside the cockpit. An eerie yellowish-blue light. Except what I saw had to have been some kind of a hallucination or optical illusion, because there was no pilot—there was a *thing*. An alien head thing with red bulging eyes, no nose, and a mouth filled with long sharp fangs. Yeah, that's right. An alien demon dude was flying the plane right into the Beast's mouth! Everything happened in sickeningly slow motion. I heard a crash, and a fiery explosion rocked the world, big enough to make even the planets shake.

I did a drop roll as flames burst from the top of the volcano. Rosie yelped.

"Rosie!"

And before I knew it I was tumbling down, down, down away from the Beast, away from my dog, and away from life as I knew it.

# 2

••

**When I opened my eyes, the sky was a sea of** black and the world was muffled, like I had cotton balls stuffed in my ears.

I rolled over with a groan and saw that I'd tumbled about twenty yards down from the rim. My head was pounding and, after a quick inventory, I found two scraped wrists and a bleeding elbow. Then I remembered: Rosie! Where was she?

I got to my feet, frantically scanning the dark. "Rosie! Come on, girl." I was about to climb back up to the top, when I thought I heard her cry near the base. "Rosie!" Quickly, I hobbled to the bottom of the trail, feeling woozy and light-headed.

When I got there, I squatted to catch my breath. That's when Mom showed up. She fell to her knees in front of me and death-gripped my shoulders. Her eyes were flooded with tears and she was spitting out all kinds of Spanish—mostly "Gracias a Dios"—which she always did when she was freaked.

"I heard the explosion!" she cried. "I went to check on you and you weren't in your bed and"—she gripped me tighter—"I told you *not* to come out here. Especially at night. What were you thinking?"

"I'm okay," I said, slipping onto my butt. I looked up at the Beast, blacker than a desert beetle. How long had I been knocked out? "Have you seen Rosie?" I asked hopefully.

But Mom didn't answer. She was too busy thanking the saints and squeezing me.

My heart started to jackhammer against my chest in a terrible panic. "Mom!" I shrugged her off me. "Where is she?"

A second later, Rosie was there with my cane tucked in her mouth. I took it from her and she began licking my face and pawing me like she was making sure I was really alive. I pulled my dog to me, hugging her broad chest, burying my face in her neck so Mom wouldn't see the tears forming. "I love you, you stupid, stupid dog," I whispered so only Rosie could hear.

It didn't take long for the ambulance, cops, fire trucks, and camera crews to show up. Was everyone here just for me? Then I remembered the creepy guy who had crashed. He definitely needed more help than I did. Within a few minutes the paramedics checked me out, bandaged my cuts, and told Mom I had a bump on the head and should get a CT scan. That sounded expensive.

"I'm fine," I said, standing to prove it.

I could read the paramedic's doubtful elevator eyes taking me in and stopping on my cane.

"I've got a straw leg," I told him, leaning against my cane, thinking that sounded better than *freak leg*.

Mom shook her head.

"What's wrong with your leg?" the paramedic asked.

"His right leg just hasn't caught up with the left one yet," she said.

The truth was, nobody knew. Not a single doctor had been able to tell us "definitively" why my leg hadn't grown properly, which meant I could probably be on one of those medical mystery shows if I wanted to. I'd for sure rather be a mystery than a definition.

I was glad Mom didn't say anything about my right *foot*. It was two sizes smaller than my left one, which was why Mom always had to buy two stupid pairs of shoes every time I wore out a pair.

The cops were next. After I told Officer Smart (real name, no lie) what happened, she said, "So the plane just crashed into the crater."

I nodded, keeping a tight grip on Rosie, who was dancing in place and whining as she stared at the volcano. "We're safe now, girl," I told her in a low voice.

Smart continued with the questions. "Did the plane look like it was in trouble? Did it make any weird sounds? Was there any smoke?"

I shook my head. There'd been no signs of distress, but I recalled the pilot's glowing red eyes and long fangs. I must have imagined them. . . .

"Well?" Officer Smart asked.

"I don't remember." The less I said, the better. If I told them what I'd seen, they'd really think I needed a head scan. "What happened to the pilot?" I had to ask.

Smart glanced at Mom like she was looking for permission to tell me the awful truth.

"We haven't found anyone," Smart said. "There's a search crew on the way."

I didn't see how anyone could have survived crashing into . . . *Hold on. Search crew?* My body stiffened. What if they found my cave? It would be all over the news and all kinds of explorers would show up, thinking it was *their* volcano.

A car pulled up, and a second later Mr. O and Ms. Cab got out. They crossed the night desert slowly. She was wearing her big Chanel sunglasses to cover her nonworking eyes, and he had on his wide-brimmed cowboy hat, as usual, to cover his baldness. They looked like an old married couple, but unfortunately for Mr. O, that wasn't the case. He was always asking me questions about her: *What's her favorite color? Does she ever talk about me? Do you think she'd go out with me?* So one day I finally asked Ms. Cab if she'd ever be Mr. O's girlfriend. By the look she gave me, you'd think I had asked her to leap into a fire pit. I never told Mr. O about it, because I knew it would make him feel fatter and balder than he already did, and he hadn't given up. He was always working on some scheme to get her to go out to dinner with him. I respected the guy for that.

"Zane!" Mr. O said as he led Ms. Cab by the arm. His brown eyes were huge with worry. "I saw the explosion. Are you okay? Did the fire catched you?"

"It's *catch*," Ms. Cab mumbled as she pushed her glasses up the bridge of her nose.

*I must've drop-rolled just in time,* I thought.

Mom patted my shoulders. "Thank the saints, he's safe now."

"No good comes from stepping out of your house in the middle of the night, Zane," Ms. Cab said. "What were you thinking?" She turned her head toward the volcano, and even behind her sunglasses, I could see her scowl. Her hands went to the Maya jade pendant dangling from a leather cord around her neck. She'd told me once that a protector spirit lived inside the jade. Seemed a pretty lame (and claustrophobic) place to live.

Smart asked to speak alone to Mom, and they wandered out of earshot.

Before I could wonder what that was about, Ms. Cab took me aside. "I've told you, this place is muy peligroso. You shouldn't spend time here."

"It's not dangerous," I argued. *At least it wasn't before tonight,* I thought.

"Evil lurks here, Zane." Ms. Cab adjusted her sunglasses. "I can sense it. You must stay away."

Ha. If she only knew I'd found a way inside! Good thing her psychic abilities were hit-and-miss. It would seriously stink if she could see *everything*.

"Did you predict the plane crash?" I asked. "Did you know it was going to happen?"

Rosie chose that moment to break free. She took off running toward the volcano. Even with only three legs, she was a little rocket. I went after her, taking long strides, wishing I could break into a run. Still, I was a crazy-fast hobbler. "Rosie!"

"Zane!" Mom called after me.

I jumped from shadow to shadow to slip past the searchers. I headed around to the other side of the mountain, in the direction Rosie had gone. When I got there, the coast was clear—no one else was nosing around there yet. Smoke curled from the top of the Beast as if it were awake. Rosie stood at the base, barking like crazy. I picked my way toward her, wondering what had gotten her so worked up, and was finally able to grab her collar. Then my eyes followed hers until I saw what she saw.

I didn't think I'd hit my head *that* hard. I froze, thinking what I was seeing had to be a hallucination.

I still wasn't sure what exactly had been in the cockpit when the plane was coming straight toward me: An alien? A monster? A drunk pilot in a really good Halloween costume? Whatever *it* was, it had to have been killed in that crash. Yet here the dude was, behind a scrub brush a mere twenty feet in front of me, hunched over and digging like a wild animal. In the flesh, it was even more hideous than before, and it for sure wasn't an alien or an award-winning costume. It . . . it looked like one of the monsters from my mythology book, except this guy was a whole lot uglier. The monster's skin was a pasty bluish gray in the moonlight. It didn't wear any clothes, but it didn't need any. Its bloated body was covered in patches of dark hair. Cauliflower-like ears drooped down to its bulging neck. It turned and looked at me straight on with its huge lidless eyes. Standing up to its full freakish ten-foot height, it hobbled toward me, dragging its knuckles across the ground. How the heck had this dude fit in that tiny plane?

It hissed something at me that sounded like *Ah-pooch*. Or maybe it was *Ah, puke*. My mind was reeling too much to be sure.

I opened my mouth to scream, but nothing came out.

A giant black owl with glowing yellow eyes circled just a few feet above my head. It swooped so low, I had to duck to avoid its talons.

Mom caught up with me then. "Zane, what's wrong with you? Why did you run off like that?"

"Mom, get back!" Why wasn't she screaming?

The monster opened its awful mouth and yellow slime oozed out.

Rosie howled like a banshee. I gripped my cane, ready to stab the thing in the eye. Anything to keep it away from Mom.

In the same moment, the monster groaned and disappeared into a thin trail of smoke that curled into the sky.

My heart double-punched my ribs. "Did . . . did you see it?"

"See what?" Mom felt my forehead. "You're scaring me, Zane. Maybe we should get that scan."

"I'm fine. Really. It was just . . . a coyote."

Except I wasn't fine. Not even close.

I patted Rosie to calm her—no, both of us—down. At least my dog had seen the monster, too. But why hadn't Mom?

"Necesitas rest," she said. "Let's get you to bed."

The second my mom left my bedroom, I checked my Maya book. I found an illustration that looked pretty close to the creature, down to the hairy knuckles and bulging eyes. I read the caption twice to be sure. "A demon of Xib'alb'a, the underworld," I whispered to Rosie. "But how can that be? These are just stories, not real life. . . ."

She pawed my leg and whimpered.

"Yeah, I'm creeped out, too, girl."

I slid the book beneath my bed and hopped under the covers. Rosie groaned.

"Right. Get rid of it."

I retrieved the book, then got up and went to my dresser, where Mom made me keep a vial of holy water. I splashed some on the picture of the demon, then shoved the book under a pile of dirty clothes in my closet and shut the door.

Once I was back in bed, Rosie settled against me and I could feel her heartbeat thudding, telling me she was still scared.

It was impossible to fall asleep. Seeing the plane crash had been terrible, and thinking Rosie could've been burned was pretty bad, too. Seeing that evil thing had been . . . well, beyond horrible.

And then there was the weirdness with Mom. Why hadn't she been able to see the demon, too? *What if it had attacked us?* I wondered. *Could Rosie and I have protected her?*

I squeezed my eyes closed, but I couldn't escape the terrifying image.

But something else terrified me even more: knowing that with my bum leg I'd never be able to run fast enough to escape the monster.

# 3

•••

**When I climbed onto the Holy Ghost shuttle**
the next morning, I had a pounding headache and bleary
vision. Weird dreams will do that to you, especially when
they're about your dog talking to you, telling you things like
*You're in danger.*

Yeah, danger from a brain-drain at lousy Holy Ghost
Catholic School. There were eight kids on the van. That
was sixteen eyes. Rosie had come with me to the end of the
road, and when I got on the bus, she sat on her haunches and
crooned. It made me feel ten kinds of miserable. But even
worse were the kids' whispers.

*What's wrong with his leg?*
*What's up with the cane?*
*What happened to his dog's leg?*
*The freak probably ate it.*

I loosened my dumb plaid tie and untucked my white
button-down shirt, keeping my gaze on the long stretches
of desert outside. Over breakfast I'd tried to tell Mom I had
post-traumatic stress disorder from the plane crash, and I
almost had her . . . until Ms. Cab came over to wish me good
luck. She told Mom I looked "superb" in my new uniform and
convinced her that I needed to be in school to get my mind

off crazy things. Right. Because hanging with nuns all day would somehow erase the monster's face from my memory.

It took twenty minutes for the shuttle to get to school, ten minutes for me to get my schedule, and five minutes for me to get sent to Father Baumgarten's office. I had promised Mom I'd try my best to make friends and stay out of trouble, but when the *freak-probably-ate-it* dude knocks you into the lockers and elbows you in the gut "by mistake," and a bunch of stupid lookie-loos crack up, any self-respecting guy would launch his cane at the dirtbag's head. *Accidentally*, of course. It was either that or risk getting knocked around all year. No one was laughing after that.

I was sitting outside Father Baumgarten's office, tapping my cane against the floor, staring at the pope's framed picture on the wall, and trying to figure out how I was going to explain whacking a dude with my new cane to Mom, when the most beautiful girl on the planet (maybe in the universe) walked over and sat next to me. She smelled like rain, and her skin pretty much glowed. She had on a pair of black leggings, a zipped hoodie, and short lace-up boots that appeared to have seen a century of battle. I guess you could say she looked like an assassin-for-hire who took really good care of her skin. Where was her uniform? I wondered.

"Hey," she said, pushing a piece of dark hair behind her ear.

My stomach did a somersault. Okay, so I wasn't used to talking to beautiful girls. Reality check: I wasn't used to talking to *any* girls. I tucked my cane at my side and waved slightly, saying nothing, because my voice was stuck in my throat.

"I'm Brooks," she said without blinking.

My uncle Hondo had once taught me to act cool around girls by looking distracted. I nodded in her general direction and then turned my attention to a poster on the wall about something happening in two days. There was a picture of Father Baumgarten wearing clownish green sunglasses and a huge openmouthed smile.

TO ALL SOLAR ECLIPSTERS: YOU'RE INVITED TO THE GREAT AMERICAN TOTAL ECLIPSE. SHOW YOUR SCHOOL PRIDE. 5:00 P.M. VIEWING GLASSES PROVIDED IN OFFICE.

"Do you have a name?" Brooks asked.

*Yes.* More nodding. *I just need to wrestle it from my twisted tongue.*

"Are you always this rude?"

*No. Never. Only when pretty brunettes talk to me.* I turned to her, cleared my throat as casually as I could, and forced out, "Zane."

"You're new."

"First day," I said. "What about you? How come no uniform?"

Brooks smiled, and it was a million watts of wow. "Impressive," she said. "First day and already at Baumgarten's? That has to be some kind of record."

I sat up straighter. "So what'd you do?"

She leaned back, super relaxed, as if she didn't have to go face the principal.

"I'll tell you later," she said, and my heart sort of skipped a beat. *Later?* That meant she was going to talk to me again. *Yes!*

I looked down at the yellow folder she was clutching in her lap. She had drawn something on it. Not little doodled hearts, or her name in block letters, or cute kittens. No, she'd sketched a monster with hairy knuckles and bulging eyes. I almost fell off my chair. *Wait. Could that be the same one from last night?* I blinked to make sure I wasn't head-tripping. Nope, the monster was still there, every detail the same. I was about to ask her about it when Father Baumgarten opened his door and waved for me to come inside.

*Crap!* I'd been so busy falling into Brooks's orbit, I'd forgotten all about my stupid cane. After seeing me hobble into Baumgarten's office, she for sure wouldn't want to tell me anything later.

I did the only thing I could think of. I pitched my backpack across the floor, stood up, and pretend-tripped across the threshold. Okay, so it wasn't the smoothest move, but I'd rather she thought of me as a klutz than as Sir Limps-a-Lot.

The results of my visit with Baumgarten were ten rosaries, detention for a week, a call to Mom, and an apology to the jerk I'd torpedoed with my cane. It was a miserable first day, *except* for Brooks. She'd made it all worth it. Unfortunately, she was gone by the time I'd recited my last rosary, and I didn't see her for the rest of the day.

I wondered why she had that underworld demon sketched on her folder. *Maybe she has the same Maya book as me,* I thought.

Things got even weirder that night. After dinner, I fed Rosie out back before coming in to hang out with Hondo and two of his buddies and watch the big wrestling match between the Strangler and Demento. Good thing Mom was working late or she would've strung Hondo up by his toes for breaking her rule about not drinking beer or smoking cigars in front of the kid.

Hondo licked his orange-stained fingers before offering a half-empty Cheetos bag to me. "Want some?"

You'd think with his eating, drinking, and smoking habits he would've been a wasteland, but here was the thing about Hondo: he was twenty-one-ish, looked seventeen, and was built like a tank—boulder-size biceps, abs of steel, and hands of iron. He'd always wanted to be a wrestler, even won a gold medal in high school, but then his dream got "hijacked" (another way of saying he couldn't afford college) and he went to work as a custodian at the bank. I'd asked him once what he would've studied if he'd gone to college. He'd smirked and said, *Business, so I could become a tycoon and* own *the bank instead of clean it.*

After I got pummeled at school two years ago, he taught me lots of wrestling moves, like the Double Leg Takedown, the Wheelbarrow, and the Gutwrench, but most of the time he was pinning me in the dirt and mimicking a roaring crowd like it was some big deal to beat me, the Freak.

"That junk food's gonna kill you," I told him now.

One of the guys snorted, popping a handful of orange synthetic food puffs into his mouth. "We eat them with salsa. That's what, at least one serving of vegetables, right?"

I rolled my eyes. "Tomatoes are a fruit."

Hondo just shrugged. "There are worse ways to die."

How come people always said that? "Like what?" I asked,

picking up a couple of empty beer cans and tossing them in the trash. "What's a worse way to die?"

Hondo stuffed a Cheeto in his mouth and said, "A vat of acid that eats off your flesh. *That* would be worse."

Then the doorbell rang. I went to the door, thinking it was another one of Hondo's sloppy friends. But it wasn't.

It was Brooks.

"Wha...what are you doing here?" I asked, stunned. How did she know where I lived?

She looked down at my cane. Studied it for so long, I thought I might liquefy into the shag carpet. Then her dark eyes found mine and she said, "That's a supercool cane."

"I have a..." My mind went into hyper-speed, riffling through all the words that could describe my leg but not define me: *freak, bum, broken.*

"I know all about you," she said. Then she leaned closer and said, "I told you we'd talk later. It's later now."

# 4

••••

## I did the only thing I could think of.

I slammed the door in her face.

What can I say? She threw me off guard. I mean, who just shows up on your doorstep without warning? And what was I supposed to do, let her into Hondo's beer, chip, and wrestling cave? No chance. My heart slammed against my chest and my head felt like it might float off my body.

Then came another knock. Okay, so she was persistent. I stepped back.

"Don't just stand there!" Hondo barked. "Answer it!"

But before I could react, he was on his feet. The TV announcer screamed something about Demento going down. In response, Hondo's friends hollered a few choice words I can't repeat even to you gods.

If I could've pulled a Houdini disappearing act right then, believe me I would have, but Hondo was fast, and before I knew it, the door was wide open. Hondo blinked, staring at Brooks like he was as shocked as I was that a girl was standing on our doorstep.

"You selling something?" he asked her.

Brooks shook her head. "I'm here to see *him*." She gave me a narrow-eyed glare.

Hondo socked me in the arm. "Where are your manners,

Zane? Invite her in." He held the door open until Brooks stepped inside. Then he went back to the match and I went back to melting into the carpet.

"Uh, we were just watching some TV," I mumbled to her. "Do you like Cheetos?"

Brooks looked around. That's when I noticed that when her eyes moved, the amber and yellow flecks in their irises did too, like bits of gemstone in a kaleidoscope.

She lowered her voice so only I could hear. "I need to talk to you . . . alone."

One of the guys laughed and threw a chip at my head. "Didn't tell us you have a girlfriend."

I wanted lava to erupt from the volcano and swallow me whole.

And just when I thought things couldn't get any worse, I heard the back door slam. Mom was home early. Which was never a good sign, especially when I'd gotten detention and Hondo had turned the living room into a wrestling arena.

The guys scrambled to turn off the TV and retrieve sofa pillows from the floor while Hondo swept crumbs and ashes off the table, as if that would make the place look neater.

I made a move to escape out the front door, but it was too late. Mom was already standing in the threshold of the kitchen with fists on her hips and a scowl on her face. Her eyes looked tired as she took it all in . . . until they reached Brooks, and then they lit up. "Zane," she said as she came over to us, kicking an empty beer can out of the way. "Who's your guest?"

"Uh . . . er . . . this is . . ."

Brooks introduced herself, holding out her hand like she'd gone to some fancy finishing school.

"So nice to meet you," Mom said, tucking a stray hair behind her ear and flashing a smile that made you feel like nothing in the world could be broken. "I apologize that the house is a mess," she said. "My brother is a caveman and has no manners."

Hondo didn't say a single word. He was waiting for Mom to erupt.

Brooks let out a light laugh. "It's okay."

I could tell she didn't know what else to say. *Was* it okay? How could she stand there looking so casual, like she was used to this sort of chaos? And, more important, *why* was she standing there? How the heck had she found me?

"We're going to talk outside," I finally said to Mom.

She shook her head and smiled again, and I knew behind that plastered grin was a big fat lecture about my getting detention. So the school had already called her. *Crap!* "Another day," she said to me. Then to Brooks: "Zane has a few chores. I'm sure you understand. Maybe you can come back some other time?"

"Mom . . ." I started to argue, but then her gaze hardened. The conversation was over.

I walked Brooks out to say good-bye. That's when I noticed she didn't have a bike parked outside. The mesa was a few miles from town, so how'd she get to my house?

"Meet me here tomorrow," Brooks said. "After school. Time's running out."

"What do you mean?" I asked. "And oh, before you go, tell me . . . why did you draw that demon on your folder?"

"Just be here," she said. Then she started running down the bumpy dirt road. I stayed on the porch, watching her long brown hair bounce on her back as she pounded the earth with those combat boots. I didn't take my eyes off her, and as the darkness swallowed the last of the light, she vanished like she'd never been there at all.

Mom let Hondo have it. The guys left. Hondo sulked, and I got dish duty for the rest of my life. But Mom never stayed mad, no matter what I did, so later that night she came into my room and asked about the kid I'd nailed with my cane.

"Why'd you do it?"

I rubbed Rosie behind the ears, wishing I could just forget the whole thing. "He tripped me."

"And you threw your cane at him."

"Pretty much."

Mom nodded thoughtfully, as if she totally understood that I had to take a stand or end up with a fat lip like last time. "And the girl?"

"Just met her today. At school."

"I'm so happy to see you making friends," Mom said. "She seems nice, and she's very pretty."

My cheeks got hot.

Mom patted Rosie on the head. "No more breaking the rules, Zane. You could lose your scholarship."

*Maybe that would be a good thing,* I thought. Except that

Mom had worked so hard to get me into that school, and I didn't want to disappoint her.

She held her hand out. "Deal?"

We shook on it. "Deal."

By the next day, the story about the plane crash had made the front page of the local paper. They even printed my name as the eyewitness. Kids on the bus asked me if it was another alien invasion like at Roswell, or if there were any blood or guts. I just shook my head, trying not to think about it. But you know what? I liked getting attention for something other than my limp.

At school I looked for Brooks everywhere—in the halls, the lunchroom, the gym. I even poked my head into the girls' bathroom and called her name. That earned me a wad of wet TP in the face. She was nowhere to be found. So I went into the front office and asked the secretary what had happened to the girl who was in there yesterday.

She looked up from her computer and blinked, annoyed that I'd interrupted her. "Girl?"

"Her name's Brooks. She was here to see Baumgarten."

"*Father* Baumgarten." The secretary pressed her skinny lips together and focused back on her computer screen. "We don't have a Brooks at this school."

I leaned over the counter, sure she was wrong. If she'd just give me her attention . . .

"Can you please double-check?" I asked as nicely as I could. I even smiled. I remembered my promise to my mom. No breaking the rules. No getting into trouble. Did pestering the school staff count?

"Look, I know every student in this school," the lady said, "and there is no one here named Brooks."

*Don't do it, Zane. Don't do it.* But my mouth was way ahead of my brain. "What's *my* name?"

She gave me a dumbfounded look. And I didn't stop there. Oh no, I had to go in for the kill. "You said you know every kid's name in this school," I said. "What's mine?"

She pushed back her chair, stood, and walked over to me real slow like she wanted to me to sweat, or maybe she wanted to give me a head start. But I stood my ground and just kept on smiling.

I wasn't smiling a second later when she made me write the Hail Mary twenty times on Post-it notes.

That afternoon, Mr. O picked me up after detention, since the bus didn't wait around for rule-breakers. He drove an old Cadillac, the big gas-guzzling, V-8–engine kind. It was black and looked like an undertaker's car, but he loved it. When I got in he was belting out some Spanish love song that was on the radio, repeating the word *amor* over and over. The window was wide open, and a group of kids on the corner busted up laughing.

Mr. O was so lost in amor-land he didn't even notice. Me? I shut my eyes and visualized knocking them in the teeth.

"Did Ms. Cab agree to go out with you or something?" I asked after we were in the clear.

The guy was grinning ear to ear. "Not yet," he said. "But I am very close to sharing my discovery with you."

Mr. O kept a little greenhouse in his backyard and grew all sorts of different chile peppers. He was working on something top secret that he couldn't tell me about yet, but he'd promised I'd be the first to know. I had to admit, I was curious.

"How close?" I asked.

Mr. O gave me a sidelong glance and waggled his bushy eyebrows. "Tonight."

When we pulled up to my house, Brooks was sitting on the front porch, scratching at the sand with a twig. She was wearing all black again, but this time it was a pair of jeans and a wide-necked sweatshirt. My heart ricocheted off my ribs. (Note to the gods: You better never let her read this.)

"New amiga?" Mr. O said.

"Just some girl," I said casually, raking my hand through my hair. "Thanks for the ride. See you tonight." I hopped out of the car and went over to her.

Brooks stood and looked at me with a deadly serious expression. When she did, the amber flecks in her irises shimmered. "You're in danger, Zane. Big danger," she said, tossing the stick to the ground.

"Hello to you, too."

"The plane crash, it was a . . ." She hesitated, her eyes roaming the darkening sky like she was searching for the right word. "A sort of . . ."

"Demon from Xib'alb'a?"

She looked surprised for a moment, but then she quickly recovered. "Right. But there's much more to it."

Hearing her confirm the impossible made my stomach plummet. So I hadn't been hallucinating....

"How the heck did it fit into that plane, let alone fly it? Is there some kind of flying school for demons?"

She gave me an *are-you-all-there?* look. "That doesn't even *matter* right now."

"What could matter more?"

Brooks let out a frustrated groan. "How about that you're in danger?"

"Yeah, you already said that, and I sort of figured that out when a *demon* crashed into my volcano." I kicked a rock across the dirt.

"*Your* volcano?"

"Yeah. In case you haven't noticed, it's in my backyard, and I'm the one who..."

Her eyebrows shot up. "Who what?"

I wasn't ready to tell her about my secret entrance. I'd wait to see what she had to tell me first.

"And why did you lie to me?" I said. "You don't go to my school."

"I never said I did."

*Good point.* "Then how come you were in Father Baumgarten's office?"

"I just told you you're in danger and you're thinking about the principal?"

Technically, I was thinking about *her* at the principal's office. "Where are you from, anyway?"

In the dimming light, I could see Brooks's nostrils flare. She had six freckles across the bridge of her nose. Her jaw

clenched, and she took a deep *you're-annoying-me* breath. I
knew that look. I'd seen it on plenty of faces in my short life,
but it had never really mattered until now. Because now it
was Brooks. I still couldn't believe this gorgeous girl was at
*my* house. And for the second time in two days.

"Are you always so irritating?" she said, crossing her arms.
"I'm trying to tell you something important...."

I tried not to lean on my cane. I'd rather be considered irritating than different. "Okay, back to the demon. Your drawing was just like what I saw. Have you actually seen one in
the flesh?"

"Yeah. So?"

"My mom couldn't see it." I didn't know if I should be
relieved (that I wasn't going loco) or freaked (that the demon
was real). "But if you have, that means I'm not losing my
mind."

"Losing your mind...Uh-huh," she said. "This is going to
be harder than I thought." Brooks looked over her shoulder.
The TV blared through the open windows. Hondo was watching wrestling again—I could hear the grunts and groans and
body slams.

Brooks lowered her voice. "Can we talk somewhere else?"

I didn't get why she was so tense. I mean, we were out in
the middle of the desert with no one around. Who did she
think was listening in, the FBI?

"First, I definitely think you should tell me about the
demon pilot and *exactly* what you mean by danger," I
insisted. "Like, is it *you're-going-to-die* kind of danger, or

*a-storm's-coming* kind of danger?" I was really hoping it was the latter.

It was a risk. I mean, she could've reached her boiling point, thrown up her hands, and stalked off. But, to my relief, she stayed, standing there as if deciding what to tell me. Or maybe *how much* she was going to tell me, because she looked like the kind of girl who had a million secrets.

"I think I should show you," she said, "because what I have to tell you . . . well, you probably won't believe me. But you have to promise you're not going to freak out."

Whenever someone makes you promise you're not going to freak out, it's usually time to freak out. We headed through the gate to the backyard. I was glad Mom didn't have any of my underwear hanging on the clothesline. Now *that* would've been humiliating.

As we turned the corner, Rosie lifted her sleepy head from the shady grass and something came over her. Her eyes zeroed in on Brooks with a creepy laser focus, and in a millisecond she was charging us, barking like a lunatic.

"Hey, Rosie," I said, stepping in front of Brooks to shield her with my body. "Calm down!"

But Rosie was possessed. She was like a completely different dog—a hungry, snarling monster, foaming at the mouth.

From behind me, Brooks gripped my shoulders so hard I was sure she had hands of iron. "You didn't tell me you have a dog!"

"You never asked."

Rosie froze within a foot of me and Brooks and growled

like I'd never heard. Her hackles were raised, sharp and pointy. And who knew she had fangs that long?

I backed up to protect Brooks, and then the impossible happened. There was a sudden swish of air next to me and when I turned, Brooks disappeared.

# 5

---

**Okay, maybe *disappeared* isn't the right word.**

Brooks changed into something else. To be more exact, the air shimmered gold and blue, then green. She went from being a girl to being a giant hawk in two blinks.

I gasped. At first I thought it was all a dream, or maybe I'd hit my head harder than I thought the other night and I'd only imagined her coming to my house, and the hawk circling overhead was just an ordinary bird (even though it was three times the normal size). It also occurred to me yet again that I'd taken a one-way trip to loco-land.

Since I was busy looking up at the sky completely dumbfounded, I didn't see Rosie's rubber ball underneath my feet. I slipped on it and fell backward, landing on my butt with a thud that did nothing to shake off my shock. Did Brooks see that? Probably. Hawks have keen eyesight. I searched the pecan tree where the hawk—Brooks, whatever—had perched, and yes, it was staring down at me from a high branch.

Rosie licked my cheek to make sure I was okay, then cowered next to me and whimpered, hiding her face under her paws. I loved her for making an effort to protect me, but she wasn't very good at it. She was about as intimidating as a fifty-pound loaf of bread.

"Brooks?" The pitch of my voice hit a new high.

She just stared at me with those golden eyes like she was waiting for me to do something. But I was too shocked to do anything but stand there frozen in place. I'd seen plenty of hawks soaring over the desert, but never one that looked like Brooks. She had a hooked upper beak, chocolate-brown wings with white speckles, and her chest was a light tan color. But it was the black around her eyes that set her apart and made her look sort of mythical—in addition to the fact that she was also muy grande.

"I think Rosie's done being crazy," I said, hoping Brooks wasn't going to stay a hawk, because that would seriously stink.

The air around her shimmered like before—gold and green and blue—and right before my eyes, she shifted back to human form.

My heart pretty much stopped.

"What the . . . ? Who *are* you?"

She remained sitting on the tree branch and sighed. "I'm a *nawal*."

"A na-what?"

Rosie whined again and nuzzled my leg. I patted her head.

"There are lots of words for what I am, but basically? I'm a shape-shifter." Brooks pronounced *shape-shifter* in a tongue-twisted way that made me think she wasn't used to saying the word.

I knew what a shape-shifter was from my Maya mythology book: a human that could change into an animal. In some parts of Mexico, they were called *brujos*, and some people even thought they were thieves who drank human blood. Great! Nice to meet you!

But reading about a shape-shifter is totally different from seeing one in person. Or *in animal.*

"You, er . . . you don't drink blood, do you?" I had to be sure.

Just then, Hondo threw open the back screen door. "Why was Rosie making all that racket?"

"Uh—no reason. We were just playing."

Hondo scratched at his stubbly chin and smiled. "The Strangler won, kid. We should've bet on him. Best headlock I ever seen. You want me to demonstrate on you?"

*Oh God, not in front of Brooks.*

"I think I might be getting sick," I lied. "Maybe later." He looked disappointed, either that he wasn't going to get to drop me or I wasn't sharing his excitement, so I added, "Strangler's the best!"

Hondo's eyes were on the dark line of the horizon and thankfully not on Brooks, who was still hanging out in the tree. The last bit of sunlight was fading from the sky. "Yeah," he muttered. "The best." He shrugged and said, "I gotta get to the old salt mine. See ya." Then he went inside, slamming the door behind him.

I turned back to the tree. Now Brooks was walking along the rickety branch like there wasn't twenty feet of air between her and the skull-crushing ground. "Can you not do that?" I really didn't want her to splat all over my backyard.

"No."

"No what?"

"No, I don't drink blood, and whoever told you that is an idiot."

"No one told me," I said. "It's in a book."

"Then whoever wrote it is an idiot."

"Except that in the last two days, *two* mythical creatures from that idiot book have appeared."

She sighed. "Never mind. So who's the Strangler?"

"A wrestler on TV. Look, Rosie's fine. So, can you please come down?"

"She doesn't like me."

"She's just protective of *me*. And to be fair, she's never met a shape-shifter before."

"Her teeth look pretty sharp."

I squatted next to Rosie. "Are you done barking at Brooks?" I tugged on her collar to make it look like she was nodding. "And are you going to be on your best behavior?" Another nod. "See?" I said to Brooks, throwing her my most convincing smile.

Brooks didn't look convinced. "What happened to her leg?"

"I found her like that," I said with a shrug. I didn't like talking about Rosie's missing leg. It reminded me of my theory that her previous owner had abused her. When I first saw Rosie, she was all bones and no spirit, and I'd wanted to pound the person who had abandoned her. I made a promise to her then that no one would ever hurt her again.

"She's fierce," Brooks admitted. "I like that."

Brooks had asked enough questions. Now it was my turn. "So where are you from, anyway?"

"A place."

"You want to be more specific?"

"It's not on any map, or at least none you've seen."

I gazed up at her. "What is it, like, some bird place?"

"You're impossible."

"You're the one up in the tree." I needed a different tactic. That's what the FBI does when they question a criminal who's not talking—they come at him from a new angle to throw him off-balance and then *boom*, they go in for the kill. Theoretically, that is. "So have you always been a shape-shifter?"

Brooks frowned. "I'm not here to talk about me."

"Fine," I said, exasperated. "Then come down."

"I'll meet you at the base of the volcano."

"There? Really? You can't just talk to me here?"

"Don't you want to find out what's going on?" And just like that she turned into the hawk again and flew away.

Show-off!

It would take me a little longer to get to the volcano, since I couldn't fly, and of course there was my bum leg. Rosie and I hurried as fast as we could, because apparently Brooks had something *incredible* to tell me. The whole way there I tried get a handle on the weirdness of it all. I mean, turning into a hawk was so *not* normal. The more I thought about it, the more I wanted to backtrack home. I didn't even know Brooks, or what exactly a nawal was, and now she wanted me to go back to where the demon had confronted me? What if she was on the creature's side and trying to lure me into a trap? I mean, she did sort of dress like an assassin. . . .

"What do you think, Rosie? Should we trust her?"

Rosie grunted in response.

"Here's the deal," I said. "I don't know whether to keep going or turn back. You decide."

Rosie barked and kept trotting forward.

My dog was an exceptional judge of character. If Rosie was willing to give Brooks the benefit of the doubt, I decided I could give it a shot, too.

When we reached the base of the volcano, Brooks was waiting there, looking up at the crater like she was wondering what was inside. Rosie treaded up to her, sniffing cautiously. I thought Brooks might freak and turn into a hawk again, but she didn't. She squatted and held her hand out gently for Rosie to smell.

Rosie whined, sniffed, retreated. She did this a few times while Brooks waited patiently and I held my breath. I suppose I wanted Rosie to like Brooks because . . . well, just because. With one last whine, Rosie got close enough to Brooks to get a chin scratch, and my dog's eyes rolled back with pleasure.

I let out a long whoosh of air.

"Hey, girl," Brooks said, smiling. "You're a little champ, you know that?"

Rosie ate it up, rolling onto her back so Brooks could rub her belly. Then her lips went up in her signature smile. (Yep, that's right. You gods probably wouldn't know this, but dogs can smile.) Rosie raised her eyebrows and grinned so wide her eyes looked like slits and we could see all her pearly whites.

Okay, enough chumminess. Brooks had dragged me back to the volcano—not exactly the place I wanted to see up close, at least not for a very long time—and she'd turned into a bird right in front of me, and she'd said I was in danger. It was time for some answers.

But before I could ask my first question, Brooks said, "Rosie, like most dogs...they don't trust me at first. They sense my...that I'm..."

*Part animal?* I wanted to say, but I knew it would sound worse out loud, and I also didn't want to make her say it. "Well, she likes you now," I said.

After a small stretch of silence, I had to ask, "Are you even human?"

"Yes....I mean, mostly."

*Mostly* was good. A lot better than *barely*.

"We need to get moving." Brooks patted Rosie once more, then began climbing the narrow trail.

"I don't think we're allowed up there," I said. "That's the crash site, and there's an investigation..."

"I thought you said this is your volcano."

"It is." I already hated the way she twisted things around. "But where exactly are you going? To look for the demon?" If so, I was outta there.

"There has to be a way inside...and since this is your volcano, I thought you could show it to me."

I wiped my brow. I'd never even talked about the secret caves, much less shown them to anyone. But they might impress her, and that was important to me for some reason. "There might just be a hidden entrance...."

"I knew it!" Brooks pressed her lips together. "Will you take me there?"

I was about to negotiate—I still needed Brooks to give

me more info—when Rosie barked and took off toward the caves. Traitor!

With a light laugh, Brooks quirked her left brow and said, "Okay, then, come on. Do you want to know the truth or not?"

How much truth could a person handle in one day? I hurried alongside her, wishing I didn't have to use my cane, but she didn't seem to care.

Thankfully, the entrance was only halfway up the Beast, but it was around the back, so it took some time to get there.

Brooks's footsteps crunched along the ashy gravel as we followed Rosie, but otherwise she was quiet.

"So can you change into anything you want?" I asked. I was starting to realize how awesome her shape-shifting ability was. I mean, seriously, who wouldn't want to change into whatever they wanted whenever they wanted? Definitely a hundred on the amazing scale.

"I can only change into a hawk, at least for now. I'm still learning, and when I get nervous I can't really control it. It just sort of happens."

The switchback trail was steep and rocky, bordered by clumps of wayward weeds that, in the dark, could definitely be mistaken for hairy sea creatures.

After some moments of silence, Brooks finally asked quietly, "So you don't think I'm weird?"

"*Weird?* Well, yeah."

Brooks stopped and turned to look at me.

I quickly added, "But in a *good* way. I think you're about the most interesting person I've ever met!" I know, I know, I should've played it cool, but it slipped out.

Her eyes crinkled around the edges and I could tell there was a smile waiting there.

"How come you were at Baumgarten's if you don't go to my school?" I asked.

"I thought it would be better to meet you somewhere... you know, public. It wouldn't be as creepy as me showing up at your front door." She continued hiking.

"Right." Not creepy at all. And she'd shown up at my front door anyway.

"So how come we're climbing up here?" I asked. "I mean, I'd rather not run into Señor Demon again. He looked pretty vicious."

"You ask a lot of questions. And officially, he's a demon *runner.*"

Oh good. That sounded a whole lot better.

"You don't have to worry about the demon runners, Zane," she went on.

There was more than one? "But you said, and I quote, 'You're in danger, Zane. *Big* danger.'" What danger could be bigger than those ten-foot, knuckle-dragging monsters?

Brooks nodded thoughtfully. "You are, but not from those demon runners. They... they need you."

"Why the heck would they need *me*?" Rosie barked like she wanted to know, too. "And why would you go to all this trouble to search for *me* of all people?"

"It's what I've been *trying* to tell you. There's a prophecy—a very big prophecy that was told hundreds of years ago—and, well..." She took a big breath. "You're part of it."

# 6

.

*"Me?"*

If there'd been a Rewind button, I would've pressed it just to make sure I'd heard her right. I mean, it's not every day you find out you're in the middle of some ancient prophecy and demon runners want to be your buds. "How could I be a part of anything? I wasn't even alive hundreds of years ago."

"That's why it's a *prophecy,* a divination. *Seeing* the future."

"Yeah, I know what it means. I'm a psychic's assistant, you know."

Although Ms. Cab's psychic gift was third-string quality lately. She'd never warned me about getting into dumb Holy Ghost. And how come she hadn't seen Brooks coming?

On the other hand, she *had* told me that the volcano was dangerous, complete with lurking evil. It made me wonder how much she knew.

I gripped my cane. "So is that why you're here? To tell me about this prophecy?"

"That and some other stuff. But first tell me what happened the other night. I need to hear it in your words."

"Why?"

"To compare notes."

Hold on. I was the one who had all the questions. Why

was she demanding answers from me? Yet again I couldn't shake the feeling that she was trying to trick me.

"I'll make you a deal," I said. "I'll tell you what happened if you promise to give up what you know. As in, everything."

She hesitated, like she wasn't used to making deals, then said, "Fine."

So I spilled the entire story, down to the nasty hair on the demon's back and the way he dragged his bulging knuckles on the ground. I tried to sound casual, but retelling the whole thing sent shivers down my legs, and I sort of wished we weren't hiking at dusk. "And then it hissed something like 'Ah-Puck.'" My best imitation sounded more like a wheezing old man.

Brooks grabbed my arm, stopping me in my tracks. "The demon runner actually said Ah-Puch's name?" She pronounced it *Ah-Pooch*.

"Ah-Puch is someone's name? It sounds like some kind of insult," I said. "Who or what is Ah-*Pooch*?"

I leaned on my cane as a sudden gust kicked up the sand. I rubbed a few specks from my eyes, and when I looked back at Brooks, she was gazing into the darkness toward the hidden cave as if she could see it. But that was impossible. It was about thirty yards ahead, and so well camouflaged by branches that any hiker would pass by without noticing it.

"There are two things I need to tell you," she said. "Both are likely to freak you out. This part is the least freaky."

*Only two freaky things? Great!* I braced myself. "Okay."

"Ah-Puch is the Maya god of death, disaster, and darkness.

His nickname is the Stinking One. Maybe because he smells like puke. He ruled over the lowest level of Xib'alb'a, the underworld—the darkest, worst, creepiest place anywhere."

Being the god of death wasn't enough? He had to be lord of *three* things? My mind played those awful words in a loop. *Death, disaster,* and *darkness.*

Brooks frowned. "Zane, you okay?"

*Okay?* I was definitely *not* okay! There was a picture of the god of death in my holy-water-soaked Maya book. I recalled a split skull and bulging deranged eyes. Man, I hoped my memory was wrong. "So this Puke guy, he's like what, a myth?" I asked hopefully.

"Myths are real, Zane. Well, most are. And gods are very real—an important part of the universe and its balance. Long ago, Ah-Puch got into a war with some of the other gods and lost."

*Gods. Balance. War.* Okay, this was bigger than I could ever have imagined. My mind was spinning so fast I didn't know what to focus on first. "Gods . . . are *real*?" I tried to remember the other gods listed in my book. There were too many to keep track of, and on top of that, their names were impossible to pronounce.

"Of course they're real," she said nonchalantly.

"Which . . . which gods did he fight?"

"Let's see, there's Nakon, god of war, and Ixkakaw—"

*"Eesh-ka-kow,"* I repeated. "She's the goddess of chocolate." Her name came to me because it was fun to say, and because who doesn't love chocolate?

Brooks's eyebrows shot up in surprise. "How'd you know?"

"That book. You know, the one you said was written by an idiot?"

"Hmm . . . Anyways, it doesn't matter which gods Ah-Puch fought. What matters is that he lost and the gods imprisoned him, some other god stole his throne, and then the gods made sure he got a taste of his own medicine."

"Medicine?"

"Torture, dismemberment, that sort of thing."

Now I *did* feel sick.

"So where's this hidden cave?" Brooks asked.

"But you haven't told me everything." I knew in my gut there was more.

She looked around. "Let's get inside. I promise I'll tell you the rest."

I studied her face for an eye twitch or a jaw clench or anything that would tell me I shouldn't trust her. "How do I know you're not going to knock me over the head with a rock and drag me to that demon runner?"

Brooks's nose flared. "I wouldn't need to get you in the volcano to do that, Zane." She inched closer. "But if you don't want to know the truth about your destiny, then . . ." She shrugged.

*Destiny?* My guts churned. "If I show you," I said, "you have to swear that no matter what, you'll never, ever, ever tell anyone about this cave."

Brooks's brows came together. "Zane, I'm a nawal. Our word is stronger than steel. I promise, your secret is safe with me."

I walked over to the opening, squatted, and removed the branches to reveal the crawlspace.

"I really don't think we should go in there right this second," I said.

"How come?"

"Well . . . because it's *dark,* a murderous *demon* might be waiting in there, and, oh yeah—*we could die!*"

"I have to see it." Brooks peered over my shoulder into the darkness. "To make sure this is the right place."

"I could wait here," I said, trying to be chill. "Act as the lookout."

"I get it. You're scared."

I didn't like the way she was looking at me. "I've been in there loads of times," I said with a casual shrug. But that was before all this talk about prophecies and demons and death. "And I'm not scared."

"Yes, you are."

*"No, I'm not!"* I was totally scared.

"Hate to tell you, but it's going to get a whole lot worse than this."

"Right, the second freaky thing. You still haven't told—"

Brooks plunged ahead, crawling into the dark space.

"Wait!"

She glanced back over her shoulder, and her eyes locked with mine. I definitely didn't want to go in that dark cave where a demon might be lurking. But I couldn't let her go alone. That would make me the biggest wimp of all time. *Ugh!*

Rosie looked up at me with her big brown eyes and let out a little groan like she was saying *You can't be serious.*

But this was *my* volcano, and if we were going to go monster hunting, then I should lead the way. If we had to get outta there fast, I knew the route by heart. "Come on, girl," I coaxed Rosie as I got down on my hands and knees. "You've done this before."

Brooks allowed Rosie and me to pass in front of her. "How far do we have to crawl?" she asked.

"Just up ahead there's a chamber where we can stand, and then we can walk the rest of the way." I clutched my cane as I crawled on all fours through the tight rocky passage. "What exactly are you looking for?" My voice hung in the cool air. "You said you had to be sure this is the place?" I had a gnawing feeling that whatever Brooks was searching for was the same thing the demon runner had been digging for.

A sudden light illuminated the corridor.

I looked over my shoulder. Brooks was holding a mini flashlight that hung from her neck by a black cord. Seeing my surprise, she smiled and said, "I'm always prepared."

A minute later we came to a twelve-by-twelve chamber where three tunnels branched off in different directions. I got to my feet, wiping my hands on my jeans.

"This place is so cool," Brooks said, standing. "Which passage do we take to get to the center of the volcano?"

"First things first. We had a deal," I said. "I gave up my story, and now it's your turn to spill the rest. You said something about a prophecy?"

"Right. Okay, there was this Great Soothsayer—the first seer of all time. She was very powerful, and her prophecies were never wrong."

"Is that the second freaky thing?" Dumb question, I know, but a guy could hope.

Brooks tucked a stray hair behind her ear. "Like I told you, Ah-Puch was imprisoned. The gods placed him in a magical artifact they created to make sure he never got out."

"Okay..."

Rosie sniffed the ground eagerly.

Brooks pointed to the tunnel where Rosie had wandered to. "Let's take that one."

"It leads to a dead end," I said. "That one over there leads to another chamber. But maybe if you told me what we were looking for, I could point us in the right direction."

With a breathy whisper, Brooks said, "He's in here."

I felt woozy. "The demon runner?"

"Ah-Puch."

"WHAT?" The cavern spun around me. Everything felt so big and real and out of control all of a sudden. Inevitable, like the hands of a clock, turning in a direction I couldn't stop. "How do you know?" With a quick whistle, I called Rosie to my side.

"It's perfect, right? Stick the god of death in some artifact laced with magic and bury it in the depths of a volcano that the gods themselves created," she said. "Did you really think it was an accident *you* discovered this entrance? It's destiny, Zane. It tells me the prophecy is real, and it's happening."

Rosie broke free of my grip and took off down the corridor that led to a larger chamber. "Rosie!" I hurried after her, catching her in a few strides. "What's gotten into you, girl?" I tried to tug her back to the first chamber, but she resisted.

Brooks was right behind me, shining her flashlight down the narrow curved passage. "How far does this go?"

"About fifty yards, but I already told you it's a dead end, and I'm not about to go looking for some god of death and darkness that you think is hidden in this volcano because of some dumb old prophecy."

"Zane, why do you think the demon runner crashed here?"

"Because they don't know how to fly planes?"

"Because Puke's stupid demon runners are loyal pack dogs whose only mission is to serve him, and somehow they learned he was here—" She smacked her palm against her forehead. "That's it!"

"What? What's it?"

"You cleared the opening to these caves, right? That allowed Ah-Puch's distress signals to reach his demon runners." Her voice was way too eager. "That's how the demon runner knew to come here!"

*So this was my fault?* I wondered miserably. I swallowed the fat lump in my throat as I recalled the creepy tracks I'd seen the night of the crash. I told Brooks about them and added the obvious: "The demon runner . . . he must have tried to find an entrance on foot, and when he couldn't, he flew the plane into the crater, thinking it would open the volcano so he could find his jefe. Seems like a stupid plan, if you ask me."

"They aren't known for their intelligence," Brooks said. "I mean, they *are* the lowest-level demons. Their pea-brains are mush compared to a regular demon that can talk to you in full sentences."

I didn't think I wanted to meet a regular demon if it could *talk* to me. Sweat trickled down the back of my neck. "You don't think that demon runner found its way in here, do you?"

My brain had gone from first to second gear so fast I hadn't noticed Brooks nudging me down the tunnel.

"It's very likely that it found its way inside," she said matter-of-factly.

Great. And with my luck, we were heading straight for its giant fangs. I hoped it had already eaten dinner.

"But we would've seen the demon's tracks outside and I didn't see any, so I bet we're totally in the clear," I said, trying to convince myself.

"Except they don't always walk, Zane."

I remembered the way the demon runner had vanished into a trail of mist. Rosie groaned like she remembered it, too.

The hairs on my arms stood straight up. "Let's assume the worst." My voice came out in a shaky whisper. "Say the demon runner got inside and found this 'magical artifact.' Do you... do you think he let Puke out?"

Brooks's breathing filled the space as she tugged me along. "They don't have the power to do that."

"Then why go to all the trouble to find their boss?"

"You ready for the second freaky thing?" she asked.

My stomach clenched and I tried to prepare my mind— what little of it was left. "Bring it."

"The Great Soothsayer foretold something called the Prophecy of Fire."

"Okay...."

"She saw..."

I ducked into the narrowest part of the passage. "Saw what?"

"You."

I spun to face her. "Me?"

"Zane," Brooks said slowly, "you're the one who's going to set Ah-Puch free."

# 7

**I pushed her flashlight out of my eyes.** "Hang on! I don't care how powerful this soothsayer person was, she was dead wrong. I'd never be stupid enough to let some ugly, hairy, war-hungry monster free!"

"Uh-huh." Brooks raised one eyebrow. "Well, I never said Ah-Puch was hairy, and the soothsayer was punished for making that prophecy, so I'm pretty sure she was right. I mean, think about it. Why would she risk death for a lie?"

"Death?"

"The gods killed her. I guess they didn't like what she had to say."

"Which was what, exactly?"

She lowered her voice to a hush. "That a powerful innocent with ancient blood would be born, and he would release the great god of death, and evil would be unleashed during a solar eclipse."

*Solar eclipse?* I thought, with growing dread. *There's supposed to be one* tomorrow.

"How exactly does that describe me? That could be anyone." I wasn't powerful. Not in the least. And what was up with *innocent*? I wasn't Bambi!

Brooks twisted her mouth. "All the clues lead to you."

"Says who?"

"Don't worry. I'm going to help you find Ah-Puch's little hiding place. And once I get my hands on the artifact, I'll take it far away, and you won't have to be the guy who ruined the world. Sound good?"

"But maybe the demon runner already took it." I was rooting for this big-time.

"That's impossible."

Of course it was. "Why?"

"The demon runners *want* you to release Ah-Puch. They'd never take the artifact away from you. Plus, Ah-Puch can only be released at the same place he was buried."

(You gods really tried to cover all contingencies, didn't you?)

"What . . . what happens if Ah-Puch gets free?" I asked. "He'll cruise back to hell? To reclaim his kingdom and be a king or god of the dead or whatever, right?" My voice echoed through the tunnel.

"Doubt it. When he got locked away, he swore to take revenge on his punishers. After that, he would destroy the whole world."

Okay . . . No way I was going to let *that* happen. "Do you even know what the artifact is?"

"It could be anything. A rock. A statue. A piece of glass." She looked around. "Don't worry. You'll know."

Heat rushed into my face. "Maybe I'd rather *not* know."

"Don't look so freaked," she said casually.

Sure, why worry? An ancient god of the dead was locked

away in some magical object (which could be anything) in a volcano in my backyard and I was prophesied to let the guy out. Absolutely nothing to fret about.

"And what do *you* have to do with all this?" I asked, thinking it was about dinnertime or study time or any time that would get me out of here.

"It's my quest."

"Quest."

"To prove myself."

"To who?"

She tugged on her sleeve and shook her head. "Let's just say it's a big deal and I have to succeed, but that doesn't matter. Right now, all you need to know is that the artifact's magic will call to you in some way. You're the only one who can answer it. Understand now?"

"Well, then let's just leave Puke in here to rot. I'll pretend none of this ever happened. No need to go looking for the guy."

Brooks wrinkled her nose, and I could tell I wasn't going to like whatever she was going to say next. "That's not how this works. You don't exactly have a choice. Once the magic calls, you'll answer."

"Calls? Like 1-800-MAGIC?"

"Like you'll sense it somehow." Brooks searched my face. "You'll know when the magic summons you . . . I think. You won't be able to resist. Even if you tried to, the demon runners would capture you and force you to free Ah-Puch."

"All I *know* is that we shouldn't be here." My stomach felt like it was churning in a blender. I hated that I wasn't being given a choice. Whatever. I'd show that ancient soothsayer *and* Brooks they had it all wrong. I'd block any call that came in from stupid magic.

A terrible guilt gnawed at my insides. Why'd I have to open that stupid pathway into the volcano?

"Why should I believe you?" I blurted out. "How do I even know you're on the right side of things?"

Brooks's face fell and I could tell I'd touched a nerve. "You're right to wonder," she said. "How could you know I'm a good guy?" Her eyes met mine in the dim light. "As a nawal, I'm naturally loyal. It's in my DNA. We're meant to serve the higher good."

Higher good? I had no idea what she was talking about.

"Zane, think about it. If I wanted Ah-Puch to get free, I'd want you to find him and let him out. But, like I told you, I want to take the artifact away!" She came closer, her face tense and determined. "I come from a world you . . . you couldn't possibly understand. Why can't you just thank me for helping you?"

I didn't know why, but her words stung. I pivoted and continued into the darkness. "Actually," I said over my shoulder, "since I'm the only one who *can* hear the magic call, I think you mean that *you* should be thanking *me*."

Rosie huffed as she padded alongside me.

I patted her head. "You said it, girl. This is nuts."

We came to a sharp downward slope that opened up into a larger, cavernous space. I'd been here before during my cave explorations, but this time the smell of something rotten choked the usually earth-scented air. My gut was screaming *GET OUT!*

About twenty feet down was an uneven sandy floor about fifteen feet wide. It branched off into a narrow passage that I knew came to a dead end.

Brooks looked around cautiously. "Holy K," she whispered.

"K?"

"It's for Kukuulkaan, supreme god of coolness?" She took in my blank stare and sighed. "Never mind."

Rosie sniffed the ground and whined.

I followed Brooks down the rocky path, nearly stumbling on loose gravel.

"Okay, nothing's calling me," I said cheerfully. "You have the wrong guy. Mistaken identity. Happens all the time. You hungry? Wanna go back for dinner now?"

Brooks looked around anxiously. "Are you sure you don't sense anything?"

"Very."

"Like sixty percent, or closer to a hundred?" she asked.

An eerie moaning sound came from the tunnel to our right.

"Um, make that negative zero percent sure," I said. "Did you hear that?"

*Clunk. Clunk. Clunk.*

"Or that?"

My eyes darted across the dark space. We definitely weren't alone. Something was down that tunnel.

Rosie began to dance in place. I hooked my thumb under her collar. "Calm down, girl," I whispered.

A grunt echoed and was followed by the familiar and disgusting odor of vomit. "You smell that?" I whispered.

"Yup," Brooks said in a hushed tone. "A ways back." And with that, she rushed into the tunnel.

"Brooks!" I hissed, trailing her.

When I reached her, she was standing frozen. At the end of the ten-foot passage crouched a demon runner with its back to us. I couldn't tell if it was the same one from the other night. Its bluish flesh was translucent, with black ropy veins twisting beneath.

The weirdest thing? The monster was wearing a pair of big over-the-ear headphones.

"Demons listen to music?" I whispered.

Thankfully, it hadn't heard or seen us yet.

Brooks sounded like she might start hyperventilating.

I realized the demon was creating an opening in the wall by methodically removing rocks one at a time and stacking them on the ground. It must have been really tedious work. I hoped the creature's playlist was a good one, as in calm easy-listening.

Brooks began to back away slowly.

Rosie whimpered, and the demon runner turned its head toward us. It might've been my pilot friend, I wasn't sure. Its eyes were big and fiery, and the clumps of hair on its body were blacker and coarser up close. It looked like a giant angry Brillo pad.

With a pounding heart, I carefully stepped back too, tugging Rosie along. She barked frantically, trying to break free.

The demon growled, sniffed the air, and took a step toward us, then another, matching my pace as it turned its head to one side like it was studying me.

"Uh, we were just leaving," I said shakily.

The demon kept coming. I so badly wanted to turn and bolt, but I worried that any sudden movements would send this thing into killing mode.

We backed into the chamber. "Move out of the way, Zane," Brooks said, sidestepping me.

The demon emerged from the tunnel. Brooks hollered, "Take that!" Her flashlight's beam turned red and she shone the light on the creature's face. It writhed and screamed as its skin sizzled. And here I'd thought the smell couldn't have gotten any worse.

Rosie snarled.

Brooks drew closer to the demon runner, really letting it have it with her flesh-eating flashlight. Then the beam flickered, dimmed, and died completely.

Seriously? Didn't she know you always have to check the batteries before going demon-hunting?

She smacked the flashlight against the palm of her hand as the demon shook off the pain—and its headphones—and came at us again.

"Brooks, hurry! We gotta get out of here."

She clambered back up the way we'd come, passing me on the slope, because she was faster on her feet.

Loose rocks tumbled down after her, hitting my cane. I lost my footing once, then again, cursing my stupid leg, but I managed to keep my balance. The demon's shrieks of "Ah-Puch!" bounced off the cave walls, making me shudder.

Rosie was going crazy, slipping and sliding as she climbed ahead of me. I kept stumbling, maybe because of sheer panic, or the fact that the demon was only steps away and its skin was now slick with some kind of yellow ooze.

"Zane Obispo," it hissed. "Zane Obispo."

Hearing that, I tripped and nearly fell. How did this monster know my name?

"Hurry!" Brooks cried as she rushed on toward the tunnel that led out of here. "Don't let it touch you—its slime is poisonous!" Then she morphed into a hawk. Her flashlight dropped to the floor.

In that moment I knew I wasn't going to make it out of there. I figured maybe I could distract the demon runner long enough to give Brooks and Rosie a bigger head start.

Once I reached the top of the path, I pressed my back against the wall and shielded Rosie behind my legs. I extended my cane in front of me, wishing it were a monster-killing sword.

Rosie barked and howled, then slipped out from between my legs. Using her powerful back haunches, she leaped right into the beast's chest, sinking her teeth into its throat.

"ROSIE!"

The beast staggered and tried to rip Rosie off with its slime-covered hands. Her jaws maintained their tight grip.

"Don't touch her!" I screamed.

Brooks swooped in to help. She clawed at the monster's eyes, her cry of *kee-eeeee-ar* piercing my skull.

I picked up a rock and threw it at the demon runner, but I missed by a mile. The demon finally succeeded in tearing Rosie from its chest and it tossed her into the wall. She yelped as she smacked against the rocks, then landed with a terrible *thud* on the floor below.

"NO!" An uncontrollable rage flooded my heart. I launched myself at the beast and it grabbed me by the arms, sinking its long claws into my flesh. I screamed in pain and fell to the ground, dropping my cane.

Brooks circled above and the demon swatted at her like she was a mosquito.

A burning sensation radiated through my body. In agony, I rolled to my knees and inched toward Rosie. Slime sizzled through my shirt sleeve, burning my skin like acid.

The demon grabbed hold of my short leg. Its claws ripped through my jeans and into my calf muscle.

"Get off of me, you slime-bag!" I shouted, twisting onto my back as the demon dragged me across the ground.

"You. Free Ah-Puch," it hissed.

It headed toward the dead-end tunnel we'd come from, not caring that my head was bouncing against rocks along the way. Brooks flew overhead with my warrior cane in her mouth. She dropped it next to me, but my arms felt like noodles as I reached for it. *An effect of the slime?* I wondered dizzily. I managed to snag the cane and I clutched it tightly to my chest.

We reached the wall the demon runner had been dismantling before. With its free hand, the demon began clawing at it again. I knew what I had to do, and I'd only get one chance.

"Hey!" I screamed. "I'll help you. Just let . . . let go of my leg, so I can stand."

The demon looked over its shoulder at me. Long nasty fangs curled over its bruise-colored lip. Slime oozed from the holes where a nose should've been. Lumpy ears drooped with the weight of round wooden earrings that stretched its lobes like tortilla dough. I couldn't tell what it was thinking, but fortunately, it complied.

As soon as the demon runner released me, I wriggled away on my back, repositioning myself. With my good leg, I swept the demon's ankles (Hondo's favorite double-leg takedown) and sent it sprawling. I scrambled to my feet and raised my cane as the demon awkwardly got back to a standing position.

When it turned to face me, I used the last of my strength to thrust the end of my cane into its belly. It sank right into the creature's gel-like body, and there was a disgusting sucking sound as the cane disappeared inside.

The creature howled.

I jumped back, expecting a strike.

But instead it collapsed, clutching its gut with an ear-piercing cry. I blinked as the monster dissolved into a dark pool of thick mucus, cane and all.

# 8

•••

**In that millisecond, everything I knew or** thought I knew was reduced to one word: *poison*. I fell to my knees and cradled Rosie to my chest. I didn't care if the slime on her fur burned off every ounce of my flesh. "Rosie!" I ran my hands along her body, wiping off as much of the slime as I could. Her breathing was shallow and she whimpered quietly. "I'm sorry, girl. So sorry."

Brooks was back in human form. She knelt next to me, shaking her head and apologizing over and over. It was like her voice was lost in a dark tunnel somewhere. Muffled and distant.

"How do I heal her?" I asked. It didn't matter that I sounded like a baby or my eyes burned with hot tears. Rosie trembled in my arms. "BROOKS!"

The nawal seemed lost, scanning the ground as if the miracle answer were there to be plucked from the cave. Rosie looked at me with those big brown eyes like she was pleading with me to make it all better. I hated myself for breaking my promise, for letting her get hurt.

"Hang on, girl," I said, standing up. I started to carry her out. All the muscles in my legs screamed. I could do this. One careful foot in front of the other, like walking the volcano's rim.

Rosie's breathing grew heavy. A deep, awful kind of heavy that made me want to punch a hole through this stupid world. And then she shuddered for the last time. Her body lay there in my arms, still. I fell to my knees. I couldn't even inhale.

Then... in a single instant, Rosie vanished into a shimmering stream of blue dust.

I stared blankly at my now-empty hands. "Rosie? Where's Rosie? What just happened?"

Brooks looked as stunned as I felt.

"Brooks! Where did my dog go?" I was angry now. A freaking-out kind of angry.

She shut her eyes and shook her head slowly. "Xib'alb'a. The underworld."

"No! How?"

"She was... killed by a demon runner, and that means—"

"It's a real place? Where is it? I need to go find her!" I was shouting now.

"You... you can't go there."

"Why not?"

"Because you'd have to be dead."

My anger turned into a terrible heat that raced through my blood like lava.

"We have to get out of here!" Brooks cried. "More demon runners will come and try to—"

"Not without Rosie."

"She isn't here, Zane! It was hard enough getting rid of one demon runner. Imagine fighting half a dozen of them." Brooks grabbed me by the arm, making me look her in the eyes. "Please."

"What about your big quest?" I said, shrugging her off.

Brooks's bottom lip trembled. "The prophecy is supposed to come to pass during the eclipse." Her voice was quiet and small. "We still have a day left to . . . find the artifact. But right now I have to get you out of here. This isn't the right time. . . ."

I heard thunder boom outside. My heart didn't want me to leave, but my brain knew I had to. If I was going to help Rosie, I needed answers, and they weren't in the cave. Puke, his stupid artifact, and all his demons could rot for all I cared.

"I won't forget you, Rosie," I said into the darkness. "I'll come for you."

Back outside, a sudden rain slashed the desert, soaking us in an instant, washing away the slime and soothing my skin. My bum leg was bleeding from the puncture wounds in my calf. My head throbbed, and every inch of me ached.

Brooks could've left me behind, but she didn't. She followed as I stumbled to the bottom of the muddied trail.

I turned my hands over, assessing the poison's damage. My palms looked and felt like someone had scalded them with hot water.

Brooks rubbed her own hands together in the rain. "When a demon runner is . . . threatened, they . . . their skin oozes venom. It's a defense mechanism."

"How come it . . . killed Rosie but not us?"

Brooks didn't look at me. "Rosie is just a dog."

"She's *not* just a dog!"

"That's not what I meant," Brooks said hastily. "I meant . . .

I'm a nawal, a supernatural, so the poison couldn't kill me. And you're—" Her voice cut off.

"What?!"

"You're a supernatural, too."

"Supernatural?" I echoed in disbelief.

Headlights shone from across the desert. Someone was driving toward us.

"I've got to go," Brooks shouted as the rain subsided.

"First tell me how to get Rosie back!"

Brooks pushed her sopping-wet hair off her face. "I don't know." Her voice was wobbly and I thought she might start crying, but no tears came—or maybe the rain hid them. "It's my fault," she said. "I thought I could do this. I thought I could make everything better."

"Better? Make what better?"

The headlights were only twenty yards away. Whoever was coming already had us in their sights. I dragged myself forward, determined to find my dog as well as some answers. If Brooks didn't have them, maybe my Maya book would. I'd read about the underworld before, and I sort of remembered a story about someone who'd gone there. Or come back from there—I wasn't sure which.

When I turned back to ask Brooks if she knew that myth, she was gone. She must have flown off.

A scratching sound nearby caught my attention. I lifted my gaze to see an owl blacker than ink perched on a boulder above me. It was the same one from the other night. That couldn't be Brooks, could it? The owl's yellow eyes glowed like two flickering flames as they peered at me. No, Brooks only knew how to turn into a hawk. And she wouldn't choose the form of an owl even if she could. Mom said they were omens of death and to stay far away from them.

The headlights shone across the space and the owl spread its wings. Its penetrating gaze held me frozen as it said in a woman's raspy voice, "The prophecy has begun."

A talking owl? After the day I'd had, why not? I picked up a rock and launched it at the bird, missing its glistening body by a long shot. "I'm not part of any stupid prophecy. I only want my dog back!"

The owl let out a single cry (it was more of a screech than a hoot) and took off into the sky.

I recognized the little red truck as soon as Ms. Cab stepped out. It was a hunk of junk that had sat in her driveway ever since I could remember. It took a second for my brain to click. Blind people don't drive. How was she here? I wondered. How had she known where to find me?

"Zane, you need to come with me," she said.

My stomach suddenly felt queasy. My knees buckled, and then I passed out.

When I woke up, I was in Ms. Cab's house. The ceiling fan turned in lopsided circles above me.

"Oh good, you're awake," she said as she sidestepped the piles of paper and books strewn across her cluttered living room. I'd never understood why she had so many books, her being blind and all. I sat up on the yellow velvet sofa. It was where I always sat when I answered her psychic hotline. Her place smelled like wet desert and pencil shavings. Probably because the walls were made of little mud bricks with straw poking out.

She sat in her usual red leather chair with the nailhead trim. "I've applied some healing ointment to those burns."

I looked at my hands, thinly layered in a goop like aloe vera. Already I could see the red burns diminishing.

The phone rang and Ms. Cab picked it up with a sigh. "On vacation until further notice," she said, then set the receiver back down. "Tell me what happened, Zane."

Ms. Cab's voice sounded like a slo-mo recording. I stared up at the ceiling fan for I don't know how long, and then reality came crashing down on me. According to some stupid prophecy, I was going to release the god of death, darkness, and destruction into the world. I'd cleared a path to the cave, setting everything in motion. That demon runner—it had said my name . . . and killed Rosie. She was really gone. Tears stung my eyes.

Ms. Cab folded her wrinkled hands in her lap. "Zane?"

I sat up, studying Ms. Cab. "How'd you know I was out there? And how did you drive blind?"

"All will be revealed in time," she said. "First, though—"

The teapot screamed, making me jump.

"Hold on," Ms. Cab said. She went into the kitchen and brought back two cups of brew. I wasn't in the mood for tea. Actually, I was never in the mood for the stuff, but I knew better than to argue with Ms. Cab, so I took a sip. It was worse than licking a dirty ashtray. I scrunched up my nose and stuck out my tongue.

"It'll heal your insides and help you relax," she said. "You took quite a beating. I told you to stay away from that dreadful place."

If only I'd listened. Rosie would still be alive.

Ms. Cab took off her glasses. Her eyes were milky white with no irises. "What happened at the volcano, Zane? Why were you with that nawal? What did she tell you?"

A bitter anger pulsed beneath my skin and I wanted to say, *You're a psychic, figure it out.* But instead, I said, "Rosie's gone."

Ms. Cab shook her head. "I'm sorry about that. Hand me that box next to you, would you?"

My hands trembled as I gave her the black shoe-size box. I'd never seen it around the house before. It was light and made of rough balsa wood. On its lid were Maya hieroglyphs painted in red: a bug-eyed skull, a large-beaked bird, and a pointy-tongued snake.

Ms. Cab opened the box slowly. When I saw what was inside, my stomach lurched and I thought I might throw up.

There were two rows of eyeballs. Yeah, that's right. Real live *eyeballs*! She leaned over the box, plucked out her existing eyes like they were contact lenses, and replaced them with a new pair. She shut and opened her eyelids, revealing new gray irises. She placed the plain white ones in the box.

I was definitely going to be sick.

"Ms. Cab! You—"

"Calm down, Zane. Drink your tea."

So this was what shock felt like. Pure, buzzing, sucking-wind shock. I could only nod and blink. I blinked a lot, as if I were one blink away from all this being some bad nightmare

I was going to wake from safe in my bed with Rosie next to me. I sipped mindlessly at the nasty tea.

Ms. Cab's new gray eyes followed me.

Even though the tea tasted awful, it was making me feel calmer. "Your eyes still look creepy," I said, and as soon as the words were out I could hardly believe I'd said something so rude. "Sorry. I—"

Ms. Cab adjusted the belt on her flowery dress and chuckled. "It's a side effect of the healing tea. Makes you speak the truth. Now tell me every detail."

My brain was all fuzzy, but I couldn't stop the words from spilling from my mouth. I might've even told Ms. Cab that I thought Brooks was beautiful.

After I spat out the dreadful facts, she nodded and stood. "So it really has begun."

I had a million and one questions, but the only ones that mattered right now were focused on my dog. "I need to find Rosie. Why'd she disappear like that?"

Ms. Cab gave me a sad, kind smile, like she really did feel bad about Rosie. "Magic is so mercurial," she said. "One can never fully gauge its temperament or understand its logic. But if a demon runner killed her, well, she belongs to the underworld now. Oh dear, you look green."

The world tilted. "I don't feel so good." Then I tossed my cookies all over her tile floor.

She didn't even seem to mind, simply patted me on the back. As she cleaned up the mess, she told me that the healing/truth tea makes everyone throw up.

When I was done I felt physically better but emotionally

worse and more confused than ever. I sat down on the sofa and rubbed the back of my neck. "I don't get it. What do *you* have to do with all of this? Did you see that demon coming?" I swallowed the words I really wanted to say: *And if you did, why didn't you help me* before *my dog got killed?*

Ms. Cab walked over to the bookcase and brought out a long scroll of yellowed paper from the shelf. "I'm a nik' wachinel," she said. "A Maya seer."

Brooks had called the Great Soothsayer a seer, too. . . . No wonder Ms. Cab worked as a psychic.

But why was I suddenly meeting all these Maya?

I thought about the prophecy: *A powerful innocent with ancient blood* . . . I'd been so focused on the word *powerful,* I hadn't considered my having ancient blood. Was my dad Maya? Then I remembered the last thing Brooks said to me: *You're a supernatural, too.* I didn't even know what that meant.

My head spun as Ms. Cab continued. "It's my job to watch over you, and . . . Don't look at me like that."

I was about to ask *Like what?* when she added, "So what if I don't always see the future clearly? It's these blasted eyes! I'm going to have to have a serious talk with my supplier." She shook her head and her left eye drifted a little. "The point is, I came as soon as I got the vision of you fighting a demon runner. And as for how I could drive, my foresight might be compromised sometimes, but my regular eyesight is just fine, thank you very much."

"You mean those white eyes are fake?" I couldn't believe she'd fooled me all this time.

"I wear them in public, as a cover. Don't want it getting around that I'm a nik' wachinel—that could be dangerous." She put the scroll down on the coffee table. "And they haven't hurt me professionally. People seem to have more respect for blind psychics, for whatever reason."

"Wait. Did you say you're supposed to watch over me? No offense, Ms. Cab, but, um . . . you don't seem like someone who could protect me." I mean, she was almost as short as my mom, and older than her by like thirty years!

"You're safe, aren't you? At least for now."

"Safe? That demon took Rosie. . . . And it dragged me across the cave to make me set Pukeface free."

"Yes, well, sometimes I can't be sure if my visions are happening in real time or the distant future. It's called a delayed response. But at least I found you when I did, or that girl would've had you releasing Ah-Puch into this world."

"No." I frowned. "Brooks was here to warn me, and to take the artifact far away. To stop the prophecy."

"Nawals can be tricksters, Zane. They can't be trusted."

I thought about that. Brooks had said loyalty was in her DNA. She had helped me fight the demon runner . . . hadn't she? But I still didn't know much about her or her so-called quest. And if her quest was so important, why did she insist that we leave the cave? Had she felt so rotten about Rosie she couldn't go on? Or was she really scared of more demon runners showing up?

Ms. Cab stuck her finger on her left eye and rolled it slightly until the iris was back in the center. "You might get sick again later, depending on how many lies are inside you," she said matter-of-factly, as if she were describing flu symptoms.

"How many lies are in *me*? I haven't lied!"

Ms. Cab ignored my outburst and went on. "Also, you're going to have to keep a low profile. Where there's one demon runner there are bound to be more, and when they find out you've killed one of their own . . . ay, Dios." She shook her head casually, like I'd broken a teacup instead of stabbed a monster.

Oh God, just thinking about the demon runner made me feel sick all over again. "We need to run!" My voice quivered. "Get my mom and Hondo and go far away, like Alaska or Tibet or something." Definitely somewhere with no volcanoes.

Ms. Cab walked to the window nonchalantly, pulled the lace curtain back, and peered into the night. "I'm afraid that won't do us any good, Zane. You see, the Prophecy of Fire is powerful—more powerful than your will." She must've seen the confusion on my face, because she came over and sat next to me. "It's like sleep. No amount of running or hiding is going to keep it from finding you. It will always come, no matter what."

I didn't even try to understand her words with the logic part of my brain. Clearly, facing this new reality was going to take something more, something I wasn't sure I had in me. A belief in the impossible.

I threw my head back against the sofa and rubbed my eyes. "Why me? I'm just some kid who doesn't even matter."

"Actually, you're not just *some* kid. You're . . ." She hesitated.

"A supernatural? Yeah, Brooks told me. What does that even mean? Am I a nawal too?"

If Ms. Cab was surprised, she didn't show it. She patted my short leg and said slowly, "It means you're only part human."

The words reached my ears, but it took a few more seconds for them to penetrate my mind.

"I know it's shocking for your human side to take in," she said. "So I'll give you a few minutes to absorb it."

A few minutes was really five seconds, because she launched right into the next part, and what she told me turned my world upside down and inside out.

# 9

····

**"Part human?"**

"Yes," Ms. Cab said. "Your father is a supernatural. And your leg? It's defective for one reason only. Supernaturals and humans don't mix—it so often ends badly. Bum legs, terrible eyesight, missing fingers or toes, anger-management issues."

I realized in that moment that the human brain is built for only so much shock. It's like trying to cram into a bathroom stall with ten other guys—pretty soon the walls are going to come down.

"On the plus side," Ms. Cab said, "your supernatural heritage is the reason the poison didn't kill you."

I perked up at that. Maybe being a supernatural would give me other awesome powers—powers I could use to get Rosie back. I needed to know what I was dealing with here. "What exactly *is* a supernatural? And who is my dad?"

"I have no idea who your father is, so don't ask. But he could be any number of supernatural beings," she added. "A nawal, a demon, a spirit guide, a dwarf."

A dwarf. Perfect. My dad could be a Maya supernatural dwarf.

"Does my mom know?" My voice rose a few notches. "I mean that she fell in love with some kind of . . ." I didn't have the right word. *Creature? Thing? Monster?* No way would Mom fall for a knuckle-dragging, hairy Brillo pad....

"She knows your father was a supernatural but not about the Prophecy of Fire. If she were to have that knowledge, it could be very dangerous for her. A mother's love is the most illogical of all types of love. If she knew, she'd do *anything* to protect you, and that could end up backfiring—on her, you, and the world. Which is why I'm here. But if you want details about your father, you'll have to ask her. I'm certainly not privy to the contents of her heart."

"And Hondo?"

"Clueless."

That figured. Then I thought about Mr. Ortiz. Was he some kind of Maya protector, too? When I asked Ms. Cab, she laughed. "Heavens, no. That man is all human."

I didn't know if that made me feel better or worse. My neck started to sweat. "Why is all this happening to me now?"

Ms. Cab threaded her fingers on her lap. "It was meant to be. Why do you think you happen to live next to the place where Ah-Puch is imprisoned?"

"Er...bad luck?"

"You chose this place. Or, I should say, the prophecy's magic did."

"But I wasn't even born when we moved here."

"Your mother was pregnant with you. Even then, the magic drew you here by influencing your mother's choices. Stay with me, Zane." She fanned my face with her hand. "This isn't exactly where I wanted to be, out here in the middle of the

desert with old Ortiz fawning all over me, but a seer under-
stands duty above all else."

"What, you're like secret service for hire?"

"I am a descendant of the Great Soothsayer's secret keep-
ers. It's my ancestral legacy," she said, sitting taller. "I'm protecting a secret that I and those who went before me are bound
to keep."

Heat flashed through me. "And you never thought to tell
me any of this?"

"It wasn't time."

"Why's it time now?"

"When the demon runner escalated things so close to the
eclipse, I knew the prophecy was beginning to unfold."

I didn't tell her *I* was the one who escalated things when
I cleared the path to the cave so old Pukeface could send his
stupid distress signals to his lame-brain demon runners.

I scratched my head. "So let me get this straight. All these
Maya—you, Brooks, the demon runner—are here because the
god of death has been living in a magical artifact in my volcano for hundreds of years, waiting for me to let him out?"

"Yes. Haven't you ever wondered why you can see so
clearly in the dark?" Ms. Cab asked.

"How did you...?"

She let out a long breath. "I know everything about you,
Zane Obispo. I was there when you were born."

I wanted to run home and confront my mom about my
supernatural dad to see if she could give me any more details,
but right now, I had a more important goal. Okay, maybe two
goals: find Rosie, and stay alive.

I sat up straighter. "I need to go to Xib'alb'a. Can you help me?"

Ms. Cab shook her head vigorously. "You can't go to the land of the dead, Zane."

"Because I'm not dead?"

"Because it's too big a risk. They don't exactly throw out the welcome mat for the living, and if you did show up, well, the underworld would suck you in and never let you go. The inhabitants simply adore flesh.... It's quite a delicacy, you know."

I held my hand up in sickened protest. "I get it, I get it."

"I'm afraid you're going to have to accept the fact that Rosie's gone."

Ms. Cab looked genuinely sorry, but her words made me want to scream. Rosie was *not* gone! She couldn't be.

I swallowed the lump in my throat. "Fine," I managed. "Then *you* could bring her back. I mean, you're a powerful seer." (Yeah, I know it was a stretch.) "I mean, they might need someone with your skill set, right? You could use that to maybe negotiate or something."

"Zane, we have to focus on what's most pressing—keeping you safe."

I sprang off the couch and started to pace like a maniac. "Rosie needs me! I don't care about staying safe."

This wasn't happening. I know it was selfish, maybe even stupid, but I couldn't get Rosie off my mind. I remembered the day I found her and how I'd pulled stickers out of her paws and given her a bath. She'd been trembling all over, so I'd rolled her in a towel and held her close and promised I'd never let anyone hurt her again.

I was a liar.

Ms. Cab unrolled the scroll she had placed on the coffee table. Pointing to a series of odd symbols, she said, "Tomorrow is the solar eclipse. The day of reckoning. The day of numbers. It's when the Prophecy of Fire will finally unfold. We may need a good escape route."

I wiped my sweaty, sticky palms across my jeans. "But we still have a few hours left! There must be something we can do to get Rosie back."

"I don't want to give you false hope, Zane. Even if I could get her back, she wouldn't be the same dog. She'd be..." She hesitated. "Changed."

"Changed how?"

"I don't know. But I've seen a few souls brought back, and they were never the same."

"So it *can* happen!" I didn't care if Rosie was a little different. I was different, too. I couldn't stand the idea of my dog being stuck in such a terrible place. "Please, can't you *try*?"

"Zane." Ms. Cab raised a single brow and shook her head. "I'd have to travel to another realm and leave you unprotected. It would go against my purpose and my nature. I'm sorry. Rosie is not my concern. *You* are, and tomorrow, when your destiny is fulfilled, I must be here."

I was getting pretty sick of people telling me I was going to set this Puke monster free. I didn't care about him or the stupid Prophecy of Fire. "Why would I release Ah-Puch, knowing he wants to destroy the world? And what's his deal, anyway? How come he hates humans enough to want to kill them all?"

"It started eons ago. The creator gods, namely Hurakan

and Kukuulkaan, were very powerful and wanted to make creatures to worship them."

"Right," I said. I'd read this creation story before. "They made the first humans out of mud."

"And the humans were weak and useless," she added. "Couldn't even think, so the gods destroyed them. Then they made a different batch of humans out of wood, but they were dumb as ... well, wood, so ..." She ran her finger across her throat like a blade.

"The gods sure liked destroying things, didn't they?"

"They wanted to get it right. To create a human that could think and mark time and keep records."

Remembering the next part of the story, I smirked. "So they made them out of corn?" Made perfect sense.

Ms. Cab nodded. "Those humans were smart and could understand *too* much, so the gods sent a great fog to obscure some of their knowledge."

"First they want smart humans, then the humans are too smart," I grumbled. "Geez, these gods have serious issues." (You gods could *really* use some psychoanalysis.)

"They hate competition."

"How could humans ever compete against the gods?"

"Have you heard of the hero twins?"

"The brothers who tricked and killed some lords of the underworld?" They had gotten four whole pages and three illustrations in my book.

"Those lords"—she flapped a hand dismissively—"were weak-minded monsters ruled by Ah-Puch."

Yeah, the "hero" part of the twins' story had seemed a little overblown. Basically they wanted revenge because a few stupid Xib'alb'a lords had killed their father and uncle.

Ms. Cab went on. "After the twins tricked and killed the lords, legend has it that the twins then defeated Ah-Puch himself. Humans loved them for it and then saw the underworld as weak. Then humans stopped fearing the god of death, and there's never a good outcome when people ignore the gods."

"So Ah-Puch wants to destroy the world for the fourth time and make new humans that will pay attention to him?"

"Something like that." Ms. Cab studied the paper spread across the table. "When you release Ah-Puch at the moment of the eclipse, he's going to be good and mad, and out for vengeance. In his rage, he is likely to thirst for your blood."

"Hang on! Why would he want to kill the one guy who finally let him out?"

"I didn't say he was logical. Imagine being cooped up for over four hundred years."

It would suck, sure, but I was pretty certain it wouldn't make me thirsty for blood. More like an extra-grande chocolate milk shake. "So do you have some sort of magical dagger that kills gods or something?"

Ms. Cab's eyes went wide. "Heavens no. My job isn't to *kill* him, Zane. I'm not an assassin!"

"But we can't let him destroy the whole world. I mean, everyone would die." Mom. Hondo. Mr. O. Brooks. I felt sick.

Ms. Cab inhaled sharply through her nose. "It's not my job to stop his reign of terror, Zane. My ancestral legacy is very clear. Keep the prophecy's secret and make sure you're safe."

"Don't . . . don't you care about the world?"

"My ancestral legacy is very clear," she repeated in an annoying tone, like a robot. "And besides, I don't have the power to kill Ah-Puch. Only the gods do."

"Then let's call them right now! You have a direct line, right?"

"No, Zane. I do *not* have a direct line." Ms. Cab rolled her eyes. "And even if I did, I wouldn't call them. That's not my job. I am not to interfere with or do *anything* other than fulfill my ancestral legacy."

"I don't know, Ms. Cab," I said, trying to sound calm. "Seems like they'd want to know the dude they locked up forever ago is getting ready for parole."

"It is not my duty—"

I held up my hand to stop her. "Right. I get it. Ancestral legacy."

Fine, if she wasn't going to alert the gods and she wasn't going to off the guy, then how was she going to make sure I kept all eight pints of blood in my body?

Ms. Cab's face was tight and pale. "Soon after Ah-Puch is free, the gods will know it. Believe me. Then *they* can worry about how to deal with him."

"So how are you going to stop him from . . . you know, killing me? He's a god, Ms. Cab!" I said, as if she needed a reminder.

"I will bring him an offering."

"Offering?" The word practically got stuck in my throat. "Like . . . a present?"

"Like fresh blood."

I was starting to see white spots. "You don't mean like a live animal or . . . a person, right?"

She stroked her chin, thinking. "He prefers snakes."

"Seriously? The dude drinks snake blood?" *Maybe someone should make him a carne burrito smothered with green chile*, I thought. *He'd never go back to blood again.*

Ms. Cab stood. "We need to focus. You must be strong now, understand?"

Strong? I'd just killed a demon runner! Which only reminded me of Rosie. I'd failed her, and I vowed to myself that I would make things right again.

I stood, locking eyes with Ms. Cab. "I . . . I'll help with the prophecy, and the . . . offering or whatever, but *after* I get Rosie back. You're her only chance, and if I lose her, then *I* won't be the same. . . ." My voice cracked. "Please, Ms. Cab, I'm begging you."

"You would risk everything for a . . . a dog?"

I didn't bother to explain that Rosie was more than a dog to me. We were one unit. I simply nodded.

Ms. Cab pinched the bridge of her nose and gave a deep sigh. "I'll investigate, reach out to some old friends who help souls cross over, see if they've seen Rosie. Perhaps they can watch out for her. But I won't go far, and I'll be back before the eclipse tomorrow."

It was better than nothing. At least I could get a report and then figure out what to do next.

"But you must promise me not to go near that volcano or that girl in the meantime," Ms. Cab said. "Brooks had no business coming here. You are not to trust her, do you hear me? Stay inside your house until tomorrow. If you can do that, then I will do my part."

"Deal!" But then I wondered why I was in danger if the demon runners *wanted* me to release the Stinking One. What had Brooks said about trying to make things right? And how could I turn my back on her? She'd risked her life in that cave to attack the demon runner.

Ms. Cab mumbled something under her breath as she studied the paper.

I looked down at the sheet. At first it reminded me of a crinkled bus map with crisscrossing lines in all different colors. Then I saw a dozen or so blue squares that started flashing as if they were on a computer screen. I'd never seen anything like it.

"This is a rare item, Zane. Most gateway maps have been destroyed. Like a near-extinct species, there are only a few left." She adjusted a bobby pin in her hair. "Those who possess one keep it secret. Do you understand?"

"Yes . . . I understand."

"These flashing squares mark the gateways to the different layers of the world," Ms. Cab said. "They change every day. See how this one is flashing faster than the others? It means it's going to close here and open somewhere else very soon. Look for one that's blinking more slowly."

"So how do you know where these places are?" There weren't any names on the map, only strange unrecognizable symbols, hieroglyphs of some sort.

"That's easy. The map corresponds with the cosmos, and

it shows the four directions—east, west, north, south—in four different colors. But you have to be trained in reading the lines and the various glyphs. Right now, the closest"—her finger traced one of the black lines to a bright blue square that was barely flashing—"is in Lola's Taco Shop in Tularosa."

"There's a gateway to another world in a taco shop?"

Ms. Cab blinked as if that was the stupidest question she'd ever heard. "Yes, and it will deliver me to the sixth layer of the Ceiba Tree, also known as the World Tree. From there I'll reach out to some contacts. It's been a long time since I've traveled in this way. So I'm a bit rusty."

I'd read about the Ceiba Tree. It starts in the underworld, grows through the middle of the world (that would be Earth), and reaches all the way up to paradise. But I'd never imagined it was a real thing.

I started to say something else when she held up her hand. "No more questions tonight. Your head is likely to explode. Now, you must repeat your promise to me."

I never liked the sound of promises I might not be able to keep.

"Repeat after me. I, Zane Obispo," she began, "promise not to leave my house for any reason until Ms. Cab returns tomorrow."

Good thing tomorrow was Saturday and I didn't have to go to school. "What if a demon runner comes to my house? Can I leave then?"

She tapped her foot impatiently. "Those dim-witted monsters are too busy duplicating like cockroaches, probably crawling all over Ah-Puch's resting place. Trust me, they're waiting for *you* to come to *them*."

So that was a totally gross image. They could wait until the end of time. No way was I going near that volcano before Rosie was back, prophecy or no prophecy.

"Speaking of those monsters," I said, "how come my mom couldn't see the demon runner the other night and I could?"

"It's a demon thing. No human can see them unless those monsters *want* to be seen. It's the same way with gods—they too are camouflage kings. *You* were able to see the demon runner because you're a—"

"Supernatural. Right." No way was I ever going to get used to *that* idea.

"Now"—Ms. Cab clapped once—"I've put a bit of magical protection around your house so no other supernaturals can get in, which is why it's the only place you'll be safe. Do you hear me?"

I said the words she wanted to me to say.

Ms. Cab walked me to my doorstep and made sure I went inside. As I started to close the door, I jerked it back open and said, "Hey, Ms. Cab?"

"Yes?"

"Buena suerte."

With a huff, she said, "Seers don't need luck. Just remember your promise."

# 10

## The house was quiet.

It took me a few seconds to remember it was Friday night, and that meant Mom was helping Hondo at the bank. Eight o'clock. They wouldn't be home for another hour or so.

I had a million questions for her, starting with: *Who the heck is my dad?* I was hoping he wasn't a demon, because that would mean my life was officially over. Ms. Cab had told me that supernaturals come in many different forms. Some could be normal-looking, even handsome like Hollywood actors or NFL quarterbacks.

Question number two: *How come you never told me I'm only part human?* Just thinking those words made me want to jump out of my own skin. And the third question: *Were you ever going to tell me?*

I went to my bedroom and stood in front of my closet, trying to get up the nerve to open the door and retrieve my Maya book. What if one of those demon illustrations came to life and jumped off the page? "Get ahold of yourself," I muttered. "It's only a book."

After I fished it out of the dirty clothes pile, I sat on the edge of my bed and opened the book slowly. I started reading from the beginning. Some pretty treacherous stuff was described in there, but nothing as bad as Xib'alb'a, the under-world, aka the Place of Fear, aka Where Rosie Was. My stomach turned.

The book confirmed everything Ms. Cab had told me, including that Ah-Puch was the jefe of all of hell's lords. I took some notes to help me keep them all straight, though I hated to write their creepy names down. Let's see what I can remember....

Flying Scab and Blood Gatherer—sicken people's blood. (Gross!)

Pus Demon and Jaundice Demon—make people's bodies swell up. (Seriously, who named these guys?)

Bone Staff and Skull Staff—turn humans into skeletons.

Sweeping Demon and Stabbing Demon—stab you to death.

Wing and Packstrap—make people die by coughing up blood until they drown in it. (Definitely a worse way to die than Hondo's suggestion of being thrown into a vat of acid!)

If those names weren't nasty enough, the pictures were even worse, and I'm not talking about a bad hair day. I'm talking rotting teeth, bloated guts, bleeding ribs, and bulging eyes. The demon runners were basically these guys' hit men.

I kept turning the pages, and as I read about all the horrors of Xib'alb'a, my insides collapsed slowly. *I* should've been the one to have to cross Blood or Pus River. Not Rosie.

The house felt empty and awful without her. It was hard to even remember a time she wasn't here, bouncing, wagging her tail, and dropping a ball at my feet so we could play fetch.

Did I tell you how easy she was to train? Never jumped on the furniture or begged for food at the table. And when I was sick, she lay in my bed like she was sick, too.

Rosie was the truest friend I ever had, better than any human, and I couldn't protect her. I couldn't run fast enough, kill the demon runner fast enough, do anything fast enough. All because of my stupid leg. Which—let's get real—doctors couldn't fix, because I was the son of some monster!

I took a deep breath as I turned the page to Ah-Puch: Maya God of Death, Disaster, and Darkness. According to the book, ancient Maya were terrified of death, and I didn't blame them if they had to spend eternity with this guy.

His picture took up a whole page. He looked like a bloated zombie with decomposing gray skin with nasty black spots, and he had a dark, twisted smile. That wasn't even the grossest part. He wore this weird helmet that had eyes hanging off it, the eyes of the people he'd recently killed. Around his fat neck was a red cape made of human skin, and stitched to the hood was an owl's head. My eyes froze on that image. It looked exactly like the black yellow-eyed owl that had whispered to me and shook me up earlier.

*The prophecy has begun....*

My pulse pounded in my ears, but I couldn't look away. It was like driving by an accident you know is going to be awful and you don't *want* to look but you do anyway. Apparently, the mangy black owl was Puke's evil pet, Muwan, which acted as his messenger and spy. Could she have helped the demon runners find him at the volcano?

In the days when Ah-Puch roamed free, he used to go to the houses of the sick and dying and wait outside, his rusty laugh echoing in the wind. The guy was about as evil as you could get.

I slammed the book closed. No way would I *ever* let him out! I didn't care what the Great Soothsayer thought she saw. Or how strong the magic was. It could call me all it wanted, but I wasn't going to answer.

That was it. No more wasting time. I hated to break my promise to Ms. Cab about staying put, but I couldn't wait another second to get the truth out of my mom.

A minute later I crossed the street toward Mr. O's house. It was the biggest one on the road—two stories with a red-tile roof, huge windows, and a giant stone wall that surrounded the place. But the best part was the spiral staircase that led to the roof, where he let me keep my telescope. In the summer, we'd hang out up there, eat tacos, drink virgin strawberry margaritas, and stare at the constellations. I tried to teach him their names, but he never cared about the details. He simply wanted to *see the stars*.

A pack of coyotes cackled in the distance—they sounded like a group of witches. I kept my eyes open for demon runners, but even more open for Brooks. I was hoping she would slip out of a shadow—okay, maybe not in a surprise-attack kind of way, but in a *hi-sorry-I-bailed* kind of way. I admit it. I really wanted to see her again. I had so many questions for her, but mostly, how did she know about the prophecy? And where had she gone?

When Mr. O opened the door, he stepped aside, gesturing for me to come in. The smell of fresh-roasted green chile wafted from inside. My stomach growled.

"Dinner's ready," he said.

Then I remembered. He was supposed to show me his discovery tonight. I'd forgotten all about it. I tugged up the zipper of my jacket. "Sorry, Mr. O, but can you drive me into town?"

"Now? The caldillo is ready. And my secreto. I'm so excited to show you."

"Can we do it tomorrow? I . . . I need to talk to my mom."

We were in the car two minutes later.

"Are you in trouble?" he asked as we drove down off the mesa's dirt roads and into the valley.

I almost laughed. Yeah, I was knee deep in the stuff without a shovel. All of a sudden I wondered if going to the bank was such a good idea. Maybe I should've waited for Mom to get home.

We parked next to Mom's little Honda at the Land of Enchantment Bank. The lot was dark and eerily quiet.

"You can leave me here," I told Mr. O. "I'll go home with Mom."

"It must be muy importante for you to come here," he said. "Maybe I should wait."

"Nah, that's okay."

"Just until you get inside," Mr. O insisted.

I got out of the car slowly, suddenly unsure of myself. Heaps of worry filled my head. What if she didn't want to talk about it? What if she lied? What if she told me the truth, and it was that I was part demon? What if I didn't really want to know? Did that make me a wuss?

I lumbered to the glass doors and peered inside. Mom was vacuuming the lobby in a dancing kind of way. She had on earbuds and was singing to some song I couldn't hear.

I banged my old cruddy cane on the locked door.

She kept vacuuming. I pressed my face to the glass. Where was Hondo? Wasn't he supposed to be here? He'd probably gotten sidetracked by some girl, or maybe he'd signed up for a wrestling match down at Chachi's bar. It wouldn't be the first time he'd bailed on Mom for a "better deal" only to end up with a black eye.

I looked over my shoulder at Mr. Ortiz. He smiled and waved. The bank was tucked away from the road beneath a canopy of huge oaks. If it weren't for the neon sign, it would be easy to miss the place. When I turned back, Mom was opening the door and tugging her earbuds loose. "Zane? Is everything okay?"

*Okay?* No, everything was *not* okay. Rosie was gone. I'd killed a demon runner and spit up a million lies all over my magical neighbor's floor. Definitely not okay! But all I said was, "We need to talk."

Mom waved at Mr. Ortiz, then looked back at me. "Is there an emergency?"

"You could say that. Where's Hondo?"

"We needed some bleach wipes. What's wrong?"

I stepped inside. "Why didn't you tell me I was only part human?"

Mom's face fell. But to her credit, she didn't walk away or try to lie. "How did you—?"

"Find out?" I finished her sentence, feeling a little bolder.

"Ms. Cab..." she said softly. "I was supposed to be the one...She promised me."

"When, Mom? When were you going to tell me?" I gripped my cane and took a deep breath. "Please tell me I'm not part demon."

A hideous cry sounded outside. Mom and I looked out the window, and on top of Mr. O's car stood a strange figure. It was two feet tall and looked like some kind of goblin with patches of dark hair poking out of its abnormally large head. It peered at me with yellowish eyes and a sinister smile, and between its pointy teeth it clutched a dagger.

Mom grabbed hold of me, pushing me behind her as she locked the front door.

"Mom! We can't leave Mr. Ortiz out there!"

"Something tells me it's not here for him."

I looked back and the thing was gone. Mr. O was nodding off, oblivious. Mom grabbed me by the shoulders. "Zane, do you trust me?" That was not the right question. But I guess even after everything she was still my mom, so yeah, I trusted her.

"We need to get to the car and get out of here," she said. "So I need you to be faster than you've ever been."

My mom was freaking me out. I'd never seen her like this—so stern, so commanding, so afraid. As she reached for the front door, the lights went out in the bank and we stood in total darkness.

Mom jumped.

I looked around. Past the lobby there was nothing but desks, chairs, teller windows, and eerie shadows cast from the moonlight on the trees outside.

"What is that thing?" I whispered.

"An *alux*," she whispered. She pronounced it *ah-loosh*. "And it's very dangerous."

Yeah, I got that just by seeing its nasty face and sharp teeth. Mom's breathing filled the darkness. Then came the sound of small but heavy footsteps approaching, and I suddenly felt like I was in a horror movie, about to get chopped into bits.

"It's inside," Mom whispered.

I tried to open the front door, but for some reason it wouldn't budge. "What do we do?"

"Run!" And with that Mom was dragging me through the main part of the bank. "Get to the cage!" she cried. We raced toward the back wall. I knew what she was thinking. If we could lock ourselves inside the safety-deposit-box cage, then maybe we stood a chance against the little monster.

In the same instant, I heard Hondo's voice behind us. He had just come in from the parking lot. "What's going on in here?"

"Hondo!" Mom cried. "Get out!"

A terrible wind whipped up outside, hard and fast, and a tree branch crashed into a window, breaking the glass. Lamps flew off desks. Paintings fell from the walls. I grabbed the edge of a table for balance.

The creature stepped into our path right before we reached

the cage door. "You cannot run," it said in a high, screechy voice.

Up close, I could see the bulbous nose and the gray sharp teeth. Its skin was pitted and puffy and it had a lazy eye that roamed too far to the left. The wind blew its dark mangy hair back.

"What do you want?" I asked, jabbing my cane in its direction.

"Please," Mom cried. "Leave him alone. He's only a boy."

"He's more than a boy," it said.

Hondo appeared from the lobby and leaped on the creature, letting out a warrior cry like I'd never heard. "Get out of here!" he screamed at us.

"Hondo!" I hurled myself on top of him, but Mom pulled me off. While my uncle tussled with the alux, she hauled me back through the bank and out the front doors then stuffed me into her car.

Mr. O waved at us as we sped away.

"Hold on tight!" Mom commanded me. She gunned down the road. Only problem was, the Honda couldn't go past sixty.

"We have to go back! We can't leave Hondo there."

Mom ignored me, shaking her head and mumbling words I couldn't hear. Then came a *thud* on the roof. The thing had caught up to us. But how? And where was Hondo?

Mom whipped the car around a median, doing a one-eighty like some kind of pro stunt driver. But the creature hung on, laughing a sick sort of cackle that was definitely going to give me nightmares.

"Leave us alone!" I shouted, banging my fist against the roof.

Barreling down the road, Mom took the first turn on two tires. "I can't shake it off!"

The creature climbed onto the windshield. Its eyes glowed, and I decided it might've been only a hair less ugly than the demon runner. They were definitely neck and neck in the contest for the nastiest-looking thing on the planet.

We were going max speed on a back valley road, whizzing past farmland and cow pastures. When the heck had she learned to drive like this?

Suddenly, the engine choked. We came to a crawling stop next to a field of sleeping cows.

"You can't escape me," the alux said through the glass. Then it hopped down to the ground.

I heard footsteps on gravel outside the car. Mom reached under her seat and pulled out a crowbar. Whoa! Did I even know this mujer?

"Wait here." She opened her door and jumped out.

"No way!"

But Mom was outside before I could stop her.

"You cannot have my son!"

She stood in the headlights, swinging that crowbar like a champ.

"Mom!" I tumbled from the car.

"Run, Zane!" she hollered.

*Run?* Was she kidding? Even if I *could* run, what was I supposed to do, hide between the cows?

I got to my feet, holding my cane in front of me like a sword. "Come out, you . . . you mangy dwarf!"

From the shadows, the thing pounced. It leaped onto Mom's back and held the knife to her throat. Her eyes were wild with fear.

"Let her go!" I shouted. "She doesn't have anything to do with this!"

The alux dangled its legs casually over Mom's shoulders like it was just some kid on a stroll through the park.

"Please," Mom begged. "Leave my son alone!"

The alux jerked Mom's head back by her hair and mimicked her desperate voice. *"'Leave my son alone!'"* Then it focused its wicked beady eyes on me. "What're you going to do?" The creature pretended to tremble. "Hit me with your cane?" It smiled. "My job is becoming way too easy. Sent to kill a half-breed nothing of a—"

Mom growled, "That 'half-breed' is the son of—"

A loud *kee-eeeee-arr* interrupted her, and Brooks the hawk swooped down, picking up the monster by the back of its neck. It kicked and screamed, clawing at her with its gnarled hands. Brooks shook it hard like it was her mouse prey and she was trying to break its neck.

The alux snarled as Brooks took it higher and higher, spinning in circles so fast that even I got dizzy.

I raced toward my mom. Her neck was bleeding, but the cut wasn't deep.

"Are you okay?" I asked.

She pressed her fingers to her wound. "I'm fine. Just a scratch."

Brooks let out a horrible screech, but I couldn't see her anywhere. Was she all right? I hobbled across the field, weaving between the cows, wishing I could fly, too.

Then came the sound of bones breaking. Monster bones, I hoped.

# 11

Brooks circled above and the moonlight caught the tips of her widespread wings. It was an awesome sight.

Mom glanced around. "What happened to the alux?"

"Brooks took care of it," I answered with a goofy sort of smile. Ms. Cab had said nawals were tricksters, but she had to be wrong, because Brooks had just saved our lives.

Mom looked utterly confused. "The girl from school?"

"She's . . . she's sort of a hawk." I pointed to the sky.

"Hawk?" Mom looked up, mouth agape.

"She's a shape-shifter."

"Shape-shifter . . . Okay . . ." Mom narrowed her eyes. "What's going on, Zane? What aren't you telling me?"

What was *I* not telling *her*? How is it moms always know how to turn the tables?

Before I could answer, Brooks landed in hawk form next to us. The air shimmered and she was human again. "You guys okay?"

I nodded. "How'd you find us?"

Brooks blushed. Actually blushed! "Hawks have exceptional hearing. And eyesight. Superior to every animal in the world," she said. "Makes tracking pretty easy."

She'd been following me and didn't want to admit it. Being

the nice guy I am, I let her off the hook. I mean, since my mom was there and everything.

"Th-thank you," Mom stuttered, looking a little stunned.

"You totally got rid of that thing!" I said.

"The little monsters hate heights," she said casually. "Best way to take care of them is to . . . are you sure you want to know?"

I rolled my eyes. I'd killed a demon runner! Or had she forgotten?

Brooks said, "I snapped its neck and dropped it into a den of coyotes."

"Okay, kids, help me out here. I'm lost," said Mom. "What's going on?"

Brooks looked at me warily, but she didn't need to worry. I wasn't going to spill. Ms. Cab was right—Mom would do anything to save me. She'd risked her own life with that psychotic dwarf-thing. The less she knew, the safer she'd be.

"I . . . I don't know." The lie tasted worse than all the ones I'd thrown up earlier. "But we should go back to the bank, make sure Hondo's okay."

Mom scowled. *"You're* going home, where you'll be safe."

I started to argue, but Brooks shook her head. "Hondo's fine. They don't want him."

"How do you know?" I asked. "That thing attacked him. It could've killed him."

"I was following it," Brooks said. "Hondo held his own. Which is super impressive, because aluxes might be small, but they can be vicious."

Relieved, I got into the car, sliding into the backseat with Brooks. Mom turned the key and the engine started right up.

"Did that thing temporarily freeze the engine or something?" I asked as Mom drove the two miles toward home.

She told us that aluxes were magical and masters at playing games with humans. Okay, so she knew a thing or two about Maya creatures. What else did she know?

Brooks crossed her arms and whispered, "They're vile little monsters, created by someone for a specific purpose. So the question is . . ."

I gazed out the window. *Who's trying to kill me?*

"Why would it come after you, Zane?" Mom's voice trembled.

Brooks offered, "Mistaken identity. Happens all the time. I actually think it was after *me.*"

I immediately saw what she was doing, and I was impressed she could think on her feet like that. She didn't want my mom to worry or get in the middle of this. That made two of us.

"Okay, then why would an alux be after *you*?" Even though the question was directed at Brooks, Mom looked at me in the rearview mirror, and I could see the doubt in her eyes.

Brooks fabricated some big story about how her dad traded antiques around the world and the alux's owner had accused him of selling her a fake Maya death mask. It all went south from there. Brooks got separated from her dad the night it all went down, and she hadn't been able to find him afterward. Now she was on the run.

She was seriously convincing.

Mom's shoulders sagged. "So you have no one?"

Brooks looked out the window. "I'm trying to find the only real family I have left."

Something told me *that* wasn't a lie.

My head was swimming in a million directions. So someone had sent the monster to kill me, to prevent me from releasing Ah-Puch. . . . But who? Hadn't Ms. Cab said that only she, some dead seers, and now Brooks knew about the ancient prophecy?

I wanted to ask Mom to finish her sentence, *That half-breed is the son of . . .* but it was too awkward with Brooks in the car. To be honest, I didn't really want to talk to Mom right then. It would only lead to her asking me loads of questions I wasn't ready to answer. Maybe we could have a serious talk *after* the eclipse. Then I'd finally find out who my father was.

Hondo was home when we got there, wearing down the carpet in the living room with his anxious pacing. He had a puffy eye and a bloodied lip. "It's about time!"

"Come on," Mom said, and we all went into the kitchen, where she pulled some wrapped burritos from the Frigidaire and nuked them. Brooks pecked at the edges of her tortilla. I must have been starving, because I wolfed down two while Hondo told us his war story.

Thankfully, it had been so dark in the bank when the lights went out that Hondo never figured out he was fighting an ancient Maya elf or whatever it was called. And the security cameras hadn't picked up anything, because they had "strangely" malfunctioned. After we left, the intruder had run off. Hondo had pulled the alarm and stuck around to answer the cops' questions about the "attempted robbery."

"What the hell *was* that little thing?" he said. "It had some serious moves. I mean, not as good as mine, but still. . . ."

"A wanted criminal," Mom blurted. "Works for an underground organization, some kind of mafia."

I couldn't believe how fast the lie came out.

"A mini mafioso?" Hondo asked. "Kind of like that wrestler, the Goblin. Remember him, Zane? Real small, but wicked fast."

By the time we finished eating, Mom looked exhausted. "We should all get some rest. We can talk more in the morning." She turned to Brooks. "You'll stay here tonight."

What? A girl spending the night? In *my* house? Then I realized I actually had no idea where Brooks went whenever she took off. When she agreed to stay over, my breath hitched in my throat. I offered my room, but Mom said Brooks could have hers.

"I'll sleep in the chair in Zane's room," Mom said when Brooks tried to argue. "To make sure . . ." She hesitated. "Just in case."

"I can take care of myself, Mom!"

She messed up my hair playfully. "Maybe I want *you* to take care of *me*," she said with a smile.

While Mom did the dishes, I went to find Brooks. She was sitting on the edge of Mom's bed, kicking her feet. I briefly thought about what Ms. Cab had said about not being able to trust her. But she'd just saved our butts, and evil people didn't do that sort of thing. "Brooks?"

She stared straight ahead with a faraway look in her eyes. "Whoever sent that alux is going to figure out it didn't succeed."

"Yeah, I know."

"Someone wants to stop you from releasing Ah-Puch, and they're willing to kill you to do it."

"The demon runners are *rooting* for me to do it, and some mysterious person wants to *prevent* me from doing it. Who do you think it could be?" I swallowed the lump in my throat, thinking about all the creatures in my Maya book, trying to decide which was the least evil.

"No idea," Brooks said. "Ah-Puch has a lot of enemies. It could be anyone."

I was sort of hoping she could help me narrow it down through the process of elimination. Then at least I'd know what I was dealing with and where I stood. But, truth be told, I didn't even know where I stood with Brooks. "How did you find out about the prophecy in the first place?"

Brooks's mouth was a thin line. "Secrets like that are hard to keep."

That's how it was in school, too. Someone would tell a secret at lunch and by the end of the day, the whole school knew about it. I picked mindlessly at a chip of paint on the doorjamb.

"Who told you?" I asked.

"I promised I wouldn't tell." She looked miserable, like she wanted to break that promise. "I . . . I would if I could."

I didn't know what to believe. On the one hand, Brooks acted like a friend most of the time, but she was so secretive and mysterious. On the other hand, Ms. Cab had warned me not to trust her. Why would she tell me nawals are tricksters if it wasn't true?

"You saved my mom. So . . . um . . . thanks." Then our eyes met. It was really hard to concentrate when she looked at me like that, all soft and understanding. I cleared my throat. "We have to stop Ah-Puch."

"We will."

The way she said it, with all that determination in her voice, made my spine tingle. I tapped my fingers on the door and said good night.

Back in my room, I sat on my bed and pulled out the Maya book again. There were so many gods, legends, and creatures, and all of them had different names and stories, depending on the Maya region of either Mexico or Central America. Mom had said my dad was from the Yucatán, but nothing in the book was categorized by geography. I fell back against my pillow in frustration. My muscles ached. My eyes burned. I closed them for a second. . . .

When I opened them again, it was already two in the afternoon. The eclipse was only three hours away. How had I slept for so long?

I stumbled into the living room, where Hondo was watching TV, as usual.

"Where's Mom?"

Hondo didn't look up. "Had to give the cops a statement. Then she had something else to take care of."

"Take care of?"

"Yeah. She said she'd be back tomorrow and you're supposed to stay home with me. Don't worry, kid. I'll make sure you don't starve."

Sudden gusts rattled the windows. Thunder crashed in the distance.

"Why didn't she wake me up?"

"She tried, but you were dead to the world."

I rubbed my head. It must've been the tea Ms. Cab gave me.

"Iron Skull's wrestling," Hondo said. "Want to watch?"

"What about Brooks? Is she still here?"

"Think I saw her out back. Why she'd want to be in this nasty wind, I have no idea." He rocketed off the couch when Iron Skull body-slammed his opponent. "Did you see that?"

Something felt off. Where would Mom go that would take more than a day? Maybe it was a good thing she wouldn't be here for the eclipse. My stomach turned when I remembered what I had to face. *Ms. Cab better get here soon with Rosie,* I thought.

I started for the back door, then realized I was in yesterday's clothes and probably smelled like Hondo's gym bag. So I took a record-breaking thirty-second shower and brushed my teeth. As I was pulling a T-shirt over my head, I heard a long howl in the tangled wind. I froze, not sure it was real.

There it was again.

"Rosie?"

I'd know that cry anywhere.

It was Rosie! Ms. Cab had brought her back!

With my cane in hand, I lumbered outside and looked around the yard. No Rosie. I was about to head to Ms. Cab's when I realized which direction the cries were coming from.

The volcano.

# 12

**A voice in my head was screaming,** *Don't do it!*
But this was Rosie. My Rosie!

I hobbled past Nana's headstone and across the desert,
zigzagging between the mesquite and ocotillo. A jackrabbit
skirted out from a bush, and I nearly stumbled over it.

Huge black clouds formed, so thick they blocked out the
sun. The wind kicked and screamed, doing its best to knock
me off my feet, but I pressed on toward the Beast, still hearing Rosie's cries, and keeping an eye out for Brooks the whole
time. When I got to the secret entrance, Rosie's cries sounded
even more desperate.

I scurried inside, crawling through the narrow passage
and then balancing carefully down the steep slope to the bottom. There was nothing but heart-stopping silence. Even the
wind had stopped howling.

"Rosie?" My voice squeaked.

The place still reeked of vomit and rot, which reminded
me of the demon runner, and just thinking about that stinking monster made me want to punch something. Suddenly,
my blood ran hot—so hot, I felt like I might burn from the
inside out. That's when I looked down at my throbbing hand.
It was covered in yellow ooze. The demon runner must have
left slimy residue on the wall I had touched.

Panic rose fast and furious. The poison! It pulsed and stung. My skin began to puff up with big purple welts. Sweat trickled down my neck, and when I wiped it away with my clean hand, I saw that my perspiration was yellow.

I closed my eyes and took a few deep breaths.

I heard the rustle of wings behind me. When I opened my eyes I saw Brooks the hawk swoop into the chamber. She changed into her human form right before my eyes. I didn't think I'd ever get tired of seeing that kind of magic—the way the air shimmered around her in blues and golds and greens.

Brooks's eyes searched my face, then landed on my neck. "The poison. We have to get it out."

"I'll be fine." My blood would protect me, Ms. Cab had said. But without her tea as a pain suppressant, how bad would it hurt? On a scale of one to ten, I was shooting for a one.

Brooks shook her head. "The poison's had time to ferment since yesterday," she said. "It's more toxic now."

I snapped. Maybe it was the poison talking, but when your blood's boiling, and venom is in your bloodstream, and you have no idea if you're half monster, you do and say things that are completely whacked. "Why'd you really come here? If this Ah-Puch is so wicked and can really destroy the whole world, then why send some random girl to find him?"

Brooks clenched her jaw. I could tell she was trying to decide if she should let me have it with words or with a punch to the gut. She did neither. "I can help you."

"I don't need your help!"

Brooks ignored me. "It's going to hurt."

Why do people always say that? As if the warning some-how makes it better. Truth is, I'd rather not have known what she was about to do. But I found myself nodding, and she changed back into a hawk before I could stop her talon from slicing my arm open from elbow to wrist.

The pain was terrible. Yellow ooze rushed out of me instead of blood, pooling on the ground, where it sizzled and smoked. And let me tell you, it smelled worse than ten-day-old fish and vomit combined. I gagged.

Brooks took her human form and said, "Squeeze it out," while she demonstrated by kneading her own arm.

My eyes were half-closed and I shook my head. Had I been more coherent I might've screamed *N to the NO!*, but my hand must've ignored my brain, because it started to squeeze.

The burning was worse than anything I'd ever felt. A million whispers bounced off the cave walls, angry and tormented. The cave began to spin, and I thought I might pass out.

Then, gradually, everything came back into focus. The whispers disappeared, and bit by bit my pulse steadied until I felt like myself again. When I looked down at my arm, the wound closed up right before my eyes. "That's freaking amaz-ing!" I felt supernatural and totally awesome. My skin had just healed itself!

"It's a nawal thing."

"Pretty sure it has to do with me being supernatural."

Brooks gave a small shrug.

I shook out my arm. "How'd you find me?"

"I knew you'd be reckless enough to come back here alone. I was waiting, up top," she said, pointing above. "But when I called to you, the wind swallowed my voice." She inched closer. "So, the magic summoned you?"

"No, but I heard Rosie."

"What do you mean?"

"Her cries. They were so loud I was sure she was here."

Brooks's face fell. "That . . . that wasn't Rosie, Zane. Don't you see? They're tricking you."

"I know what I heard!"

Taking my hand, she said, "The eclipse is coming, and we have to find the artifact before then. I can't do it without you. You're the one in the prophecy."

"And then what?"

"I have to leave."

"But you just got here!" I blurted out. I couldn't help it. I'd only known her for a few days, but the idea of life without Brooks around seemed so . . . boring.

"Do you hear Rosie now?" she asked.

I shook my head and circled the cave. Careful to avoid toxic slime, I pressed my ear to the walls like maybe my dog was inside one of them.

Brooks followed closely, speaking in hushed tones. "You're right, you know. Who am I to think I can stop the evilest god of all time? I'm doing it to . . ." Her voice trailed off. Then she added, "I'm only part nawal. It's why I can't shape-shift into anything except a hawk—no one wants to train a half-breed. But if I could accomplish something big, I wouldn't be a nothing my whole life."

I recalled what the alux had said to my mom. "Yeah, being a *half-breed nothing* would officially suck." I kicked a rock across the ground.

"Ugh! I'm so stupid! That's not what I meant. I mean—"

"It's okay. I get what you mean." I could identify with her need to be something bigger, a better version of herself. "So nobody sent you? You just, like, ran away?"

"You could say that."

"From where?"

"A place I can't go back to. But don't worry, no one's looking for me."

"What about your mom or dad?"

"My dad's off with his new family and . . . and my mom's dead."

"Oh—um, I . . . I'm sorry." I snatched a pebble from the ground and rolled it between each knuckle. "Maybe you could stay with us, then. . . ."

"That's impossible."

"Why? You can't just fly around on your own out there."

She focused on the rolling pebble. "It's not that I wouldn't want to or anything, I . . . I just can't."

I felt stupid for suggesting it.

"Hey! I bet you're part magician," Brooks said, changing the subject and considering my whole body in a way that made my face flush a million shades of red.

"Magician? Like pull a rabbit out of a hat?"

"No, like a powerful wielder of magic."

"Yeah, well, that wasn't one of the options Ms. Cab listed."

"They're smart, even devious, but also very loyal and . . ."

"And what?"

"Dangerous. I mean, if you cross them. There's a place down in Uxmal, Mexico, called the Pyramid of the Magician and—"

"Wait!" I cut in, remembering something about that in my book. "Isn't it also called the Pyramid of the Soothsayer?" I wondered if this was referencing the *Great* Soothsayer? It had to be, if she had a whole pyramid named after her.

"Yeah, it's called that, too," Brooks said. "Maybe someday you can go there and see for yourself. We could even—"

"You've been there?"

In the same instant, another one of Rosie's whimpers echoed across the chamber.

"Did you hear that?" I hurried down the tunnel and to the rock wall, the same one the demon runner had been clawing through the other day.

"Hear what?"

I began pulling the rocks free. They were loose and came out easily. My adrenaline was pumping. "Rosie!"

Suddenly, the wall began to crumble like dust. A narrow passage revealed itself and a barely there light flickered from beyond.

Rosie's cry carried through the opening. Part of my mind knew it was a trap, but the other part didn't care. I mean, what if it really *was* Rosie and I missed my only chance to save her? I wedged myself into the narrow opening.

"Wait!" Brooks cried. I thought she might try to stop me, but instead she reached into the collar of her shirt and pulled out three leather strings, each with a mini flashlight attached. "I brought backup this time."

"Did you remember the batteries?"

Brooks huffed. "Let's go."

We made our way through the cramped corridor for about twenty yards until we came out into an enormous cavity.

The flashlight's yellow beam circled the place. In the center of the floor was a green pool. Stalactites clung to the ceiling overhead, dripping water into the pond with a hollow echo that made my blood run cold.

Rosie was nowhere to be seen.

I swallowed hard.

We took a few steps past the pool. It gave off an overwhelmingly foul smell, like it was filled with rotting fish. Pale rock columns, about two or three feet tall, grew out of the sloping ground and surrounded a taller stalagmite with a flat surface. On top was a large stone bowl.

I hesitated, then drew closer and peered inside. Two cracked animal skulls were sitting on a pile of skinny white sticks. No, not sticks—they looked more like bird bones. Well, didn't that just spell *Welcome!*

"This is a sacrifice chamber," Brooks whispered. Her voice was tense in the cold air. "The demon runners did this—they prepared the place for Ah-Puch's release."

My eyes bounced over the rough ash-colored walls and across the uneven floor. I shivered. "I guess that means we're in the right spot. Or the wrong one, depending on your perspective," I said, looking over my shoulder for any demon runners who might have followed us. I just wanted to find the thing Ah-Puch was hiding in so Brooks could take him away and make sure he never got out. Then we could prove that soothsayer wrong.

I kept expecting Ms. Cab to show up any minute too, to *poof* out of thin air. She was supposed to be back before the eclipse.

Brooks stood and turned to me. "When you heard Rosie, it must've been the magic calling you. Clever."

"I guess. . . ."

She looked pale. "Come on. We need to move fast. We only have a couple hours. Do you hear anything now?"

"Aren't you the one with the super-bionic senses?"

"I tried, remember?" she said. "I can't hear this frequency. The magic will only call to you."

I tuned my ears, but all I heard was the *drip, drip, drip* of the water and a strange breathing sound like the walls themselves were inhaling and exhaling.

A dark ripple shifted across the water.

"It's in there," I said, pointing to the pool.

"That puddle? Are you sure?"

"I'm sure."

"Like eighty percent, or a hundred?" Brooks asked, frowning. "I mean, there's a big difference."

I was positive. I could feel the air pulse and buzz with a strange energy when I stepped closer to the water. Despite the stink, I felt drawn to it, and every second we stood there, I found myself wanting more desperately to jump in. "I'm a thousand percent sure. And it's not a puddle. It's deep." I'm not sure how I knew, but I did. Just like I knew it would be cold.

Brooks sucked in her lower lip. "Well, that's unfortunate."

"Why?"

"I can't swim."

Okay, so unless the animal skeletons came to life and decided to fish Ah-Puch out of the water, I was the lucky retriever. Great!

Brooks raised the flashlight beam to the ceiling. "Holy K! We're doomed."

Those are not the words anyone wants to hear when they're standing in a dark chamber of sacrifice with the lord of the dead trapped in a smelly pond a few feet away. I swore under my breath, then craned my neck.

The stalactites trembled, then split open with a bone-cracking sound that sent chills down my spine. Bits of rock fell and we ducked out of the way. When I looked back up, I stumbled and gasped.

At the base of the stalactites, dozens of glowing blue pods clung to the ceiling. A black ooze dripped from them into the water. Optimist me thought maybe we'd made some kind of cool archaeological discovery. Then I saw that the translucent husks were pulsing and stretching. Definitely not a cool archaeological discovery. Sleeping demon runners. Just like Ms. Cab had said, they'd been busy duplicating in Ah-Puch's hiding place. It was time to bolt.

But as soon as I grabbed Brooks's hand to lead her back the way we'd come, a demon runner leaped down from the ceiling, blocking our path. He swiveled his head slowly, like he was searching for us.

We froze in our tracks. Brooks squeezed my hand so hard I thought she might break my bones.

Then, one by one, the lights went out in the pods above, and if you've ever heard someone slurp the last of a shake through a straw, you'll understand the sound that filled the cave. The sacs were opening.

The demon runner squinted. This was one time I wished I *didn't* have night vision. I didn't need to see the way his evil beady eyes roamed the chamber. "Zane Obispo," he hissed, stretching his arms toward us as we slowly backed away.

"Demon runners, or pool?" I whispered. Every muscle in my body tensed, ready for flight.

"Neither?" Brooks breathed.

Above us, a newly hatched demon runner hung upside down like a bat, stretched its neck, and turned its head 180 degrees until its fiery red eyes found us.

"They don't want me here," Brooks whispered.

It opened its mouth to scream, to wake the others. The demon runner in front of us inched closer, groping through the dark. "Stranger," it said in a rusty voice.

"No matter what, Brooks, don't let go of me!"

Her eyes widened and she pulled away from my grasp.

The demon runner let out an ear-piercing cry that seemed to shake the walls.

I grabbed Brooks's hand and we jumped feetfirst into the dark pool.

# 13

●●●

**As I'd predicted, the water was arctic cold, like** a million shards of ice stabbing my skin. I held Brooks's hand tightly as I pulled her down and down. Was there a bottom? I wondered.

I was feeling pretty grateful that my mom had made me take swimming lessons at the city pool when I was little. I liked swimming. In the water I didn't have a limp. And I was glad my eyes could see through cloudy water, too. A hundred points for team supernatural. Beneath us were several other passages that branched off in all directions. I had to choose the right one or we'd end up as skeletons at the bottom of this pool. I peered through the dark until I saw a shimmering light down the corridor to the right. Swimming furiously, I led Brooks into a narrow tunnel. I floated on my back, feeling with one hand for an airhole in the razor-sharp rock ceiling. Just when my lungs were about to collapse, we came upon an opening about four feet in diameter.

I stuck my head out and sucked in air. Beneath me, Brooks was still thrashing around in the water. I hauled her up, turning her over slowly until she could take a huge gulp of oxygen.

"We're . . . going . . . to . . . die . . . in . . . here!" she cried between gasps.

"I saw a light," I choked out. "Up ahead. We need to try and reach it."

"I... I can't do it, Zane."

"Yes, you can!"

"It's coming. The demon runner," she said, panting. "It's right behind us, and it wants me. It knows why I'm here."

There wasn't time for more talking. "Take the biggest breath you can, and on three we're going to dive under. One, two..."

Suddenly, Brooks was yanked under the water and out of my grasp. The demon runner!

I dove down, groping in the murk until I found Brooks's hands and ripped her free. With adrenaline coursing through my veins, I cut through the water with amazing speed I didn't know I had. I hauled Brooks into another narrow passage, toward the trail of light.

Ten more yards. Could we hold our breath that long?

*Almost there. Hang on, Brooks.*

*Hurry!* Brooks's voice rang out. But not in my ears... I heard it in my mind! And it wasn't my imagination. She screamed, *He's coming back!*

*I thought the demon runners wanted me to free Ah-Puch!* I said in my head, hoping she heard me.

*They do,* she said. *It's me they want to stop.*

*Just hold on! Ten more seconds.*

My lungs were ready to burst.

Finally the tunnel ended, opening into a large pool where we could emerge. With one hard tug, I broke the surface, gulping in air. I pulled Brooks up behind me and rolled her onto her back so her face was out of the water. Her eyes were closed and her mouth was open.

"Brooks!" I hefted myself up onto the rocky ledge and hauled her behind me. It was difficult to keep my footing on the slippery surface, and I fell on my butt.

The demon runner surfaced. His skin had gone from blue to gray, and it was coming off in chunks like soggy bread.

I scrambled to my feet, putting myself between the monster and Brooks. "You can't have her!" I screamed.

He kept coming toward us, crawling out of the pool on his belly like a salamander. When he had fully emerged, he stopped and looked down at his body. That's when he realized he was disintegrating. I guess he hadn't known water would do that to him. He screamed and hissed as his flesh fell off in chunks. Then his bones liquefied, leaving only a pool of tar-like goop floating on the pond's surface.

I rushed to Brooks. She wasn't breathing.

"Hang on, Brooks!" In a panic, I began mouth-to-mouth resuscitation.

*Please please please.*

*Breathe.*

*Breathe!*

Her eyes didn't open. She simply lay there, her skin a terrible pale gray. Then, slowly, the air shimmered and Brooks turned into a hawk. Not her usual grande size. She was small and fragile-looking. I felt her feathery neck for a pulse. It was there, but just barely.

My own heart nearly stopped. No, this couldn't be happening. She'd just been talking to me in my head. Being her pushy self, telling me to hurry.

"Brooks!" I shook her gently. "Wake up! We made it! I'm not doing this alone," I said, like I could guilt her heart into beating stronger.

At the same moment, a strange silver light filled the little cavern. I looked around for the first time. Pale green stalactites hung from the low ceiling. The walls looked porous, like stone sponges.

Wiping water from my eyes, I followed the light to its source, a sand-colored stone column to my right. It was painted with the image of a tightly coiled serpent. In a single blink, the image came to life. The snake uncoiled and started slithering down the column.

It whispered to me. "Zane."

"Go away!"

As the reptile descended, the column became translucent, like a block of ice, and inside I could see a small black statue. It was an evil-looking owl, about six inches tall, with slits for eyes. The wings were spread out as if it were going to take off any second. It looked so lifelike that I knew what this was: Ah-Puch's prison. He was inside a replica of his own pet, Muwan.

My hand trembled as I clung to Brooks. "I'll fix this," I told her. "Just hang on." My insides were on fire, and a terrible burning sensation was pricking my legs.

Then came a voice. It wasn't the snake. It was Ah-Puch.

*I can save her.*

I stayed focused on Brooks, on her golden-brown feathers, on her heart that was still beating. What was I going to do? I couldn't drag her back through that pool, and from where I sat, I didn't see any exit in the rock wall.

Terror made me desperate enough to talk to Pukeface. "How do I get out of here?" My voice echoed across the cave.

*I can save her,* he said again.

"How?"

No response. Maybe because he'd already given me the answer.

I stood up, wobbly at first, then went over to the serpent column. With trembling fingers, I reached out to touch it. Did I mention that I hate snakes? The serpent slithered across my hand, and a vertical crack appeared in the post. The two halves opened like double doors.

My mind was on autopilot as I pulled the clay owl free. The statue vibrated in my hand and a strange energy surged through me like a speeding train.

*Yes,* Ah-Puch whispered.

With the figure clutched in my hand, I collapsed back onto the ledge near Brooks. She began to shimmer again, and I was scared she was fading, like Rosie had. "No! Not yet!" I shook the little statue. "You said you could save her!"

A ray of sunlight penetrated a crevice in the chamber's ceiling. The eclipse was happening!

Sweat trickled down my neck as a painful heat boiled my insides. I needed air desperately.

One of the cave walls was angled and pitted enough that I thought I could climb up to the opening I hadn't seen. I shoved the statue into my jean pocket and started up.

"Don't go anywhere, Brooks!" I called down.

When I got to the top and peeked out, what I saw wasn't the volcano crater or the desert. It looked like the surface of Mars, miles and miles of red rock, dust, and no life. I turned toward the sky, shielding my eyes so I couldn't look directly at the eclipse. The sky was a deep bruised blue, turning darker and darker with each passing second.

I tugged the owl figurine from my pocket.

*The time has come,* Ah-Puch whispered.

"Save her!"

*You have to free me first.*

*What do I do, Brooks?* I hoped she could hear me, like when we were under the water. *I can't let you die.*

"Your demons did this to her!" I screamed at that stupid smiling owl.

*She wanted to keep me in my prison.*

"So do I!"

Ah-Puch laughed cruelly. *Seems circumstances have changed.*

He was right. I didn't even know where I was, and Brooks was barely holding on. I dropped my head, feeling pathetic and defeated. "If I let you out, you promise to save her?"

*Or you could just wait and see.*

"And you can rot! CAN YOU SAVE HER?"

*I'm the lord of the dead. I can save her.*

I remembered what Ms. Cab had told me about Puke

waking up thirsty for my blood. But that didn't matter. Not if he could save Brooks. I know it was foolish, trying to save one life by releasing a god that could destroy the whole world. But I'd worry about that later. Right now the only thing I cared about was making sure Brooks didn't become the newest resident of Xib'alb'a.

The moon crept across the sun, slowly strangling its light.

*Set me free.*

"And I want Rosie back, too. She's my dog stuck in your underworld."

*Yes.*

As the moon's shadow blotted out the sun, I took a deep breath and did what I swore I'd never do. I slammed the clay figure on the sharp rock edge in front of me. The owl busted open, its wings flying off in opposite directions. Dust rose from the broken shell, briefly obscuring the object inside. I coughed and fanned the air, then saw that it was a long folded strip of paper, dark and soft, like wet tree bark. I picked it up to examine it more closely, and it shimmered faintly in my palm. Then it unfolded itself three times. There was no writing or picture on it—what was up with that? I traced my fingers along its blank curled edges.

Suddenly, it lifted into the air, burst into blue flame, and a tower of black smoke billowed out, followed by a sickening screech that pierced my eardrums and drove me to my knees.

# 14

A creature—Ah-Puch, I guessed—appeared on
the rim of the volcano with his back to me, crouched like a wild
animal. He didn't look like an all-powerful god of the dead.
He was skeletal, and his skin was so paper-thin I could see his
crooked spine. It writhed and twisted like a snake as he heaved
and moaned. And the guy didn't just smell bad—he filled the
air with a bitter, poisonous odor that I was sure would kill me
with one whiff.

At the same moment, the black owl, Muwan, appeared.
Her feathers were slick with oil. She turned her enormous
eyes toward me.

A trail of black smoke rose from the bird, and it shifted
into a woman with long gray hair. She was wearing some kind
of headdress made of red and yellow feathers.

She kneeled next to Ah-Puch and said with a bad lisp, "My
lord, I bring you a *thacrifice* to give you power." Her gauzy
black skirt swept across the rock.

She reached into her skirt pocket and pulled out a small
clay figurine, but I couldn't see the details from where I sat.
She smashed it against the rim. There was a terrible screech.
Then she handed Ah-Puch a creature with two goat heads and
a body like a yellow snake. It squirmed and bleated, trying to

wriggle its way free. Ah-Puch scrambled to clutch the thing. Bones snapped. Then he brought it to his mouth, bit its neck, and sucked all the blood from it before tossing the drained corpse to the cave floor below like an old orange peel.

My stomach lurched.

Ah-Puch's skin began to bubble. Gray worms emerged and crawled all over the outside of his hunched body, latching onto him and somehow thickening his skin. Ah-Puch rose to his feet slowly, groaning.

I was glad he wasn't facing me. I really didn't want to look this guy in the eyes. But I had to. He'd made me a promise.

"Zane Obispo." His voice was deep and gravelly.

I closed my eyes and took a deep breath. Then, slowly, I looked up at him.

*Whoa!* He'd somehow morphed from the gross blood-sucking worm monster into a regular guy dressed in a black suit, crisp white shirt, and dark silk tie. It was an expensive suit, too—not the shiny kind with loose threads like my old history teacher always wore.

Ah-Puch was at least six foot five, but that's not what made him so...intimidating. It was his black eyes, chiseled face, and broad shoulders that screamed *power.* (Sorry, gods who hate Ah-Puch. You said you wanted the truth.)

He waved his hand, and the ledge I was standing on shimmered. A second later, Brooks materialized, in comatose hawk form. I pulled her in to my chest and held her closely.

"We had a deal," I said, feeling her still-faint heartbeat. "You said you'd save her!"

Ah-Puch's black eyes found mine. "You risked everything for a nawal?"

"That's none of your business. Now wake her up."

He ignored my demand and glanced around. Then, with another tiny movement of his hand, the dead space beyond the volcano turned into a bustling city. "That's much better," he said. "I'm so weary of silence."

Suddenly we were standing on the roof of a skyscraper that overlooked a whole cityscape. Below us, millions of cars inched along the freeways like bugs. I stumbled as I looked around, trying to get my bearings. Where were we? New York? Chicago? Being a non-traveler, I only had movies and books to help me out. To the left was a mountain with big white letters on it: HOLLYWOOD. We were in Los Angeles?

Ah-Puch took a deep breath and closed his eyes. "Ahh . . . such chaos. I can feel its sweetness buzzing all around."

"What about Brooks?" I insisted as I scanned the dark rooftop. As a small hawk (who seemed even smaller than she was inside the cave moments ago) she wasn't heavy, but I needed a place to lay her down for when he made her human again. I spotted some lounge chairs near a lap pool. This was some kind of fancy hotel or apartment building. A small fountain spilled into the pool and there were potted palms in the corners.

Muwan smiled, except she didn't have any teeth, which explained her lisp. "The gods don't know you've awakened, my lord. They are too *buthy* getting fat and *lathy* to even notice."

"You are my most trusted ally, Muwan," Ah-Puch said, petting her head. "What's happened to you?"

"Weak without your power."

He continued petting her head and slowly a blackish mist rose, slithering up Muwan's legs, then body and head, until . . .

I blinked.

Muwan had shed the old-toothless-hag look for a magazine-photo-shoot look. She was about Hondo's age, with shoulder-length raven hair and bronze skin. She wore a long silver gown that hugged her now-healthy form. And her eyes glinted lilac and green in the light like rare gemstones. She smiled at Ah-Puch, then kissed the back of his hand. "Thank you, my lord."

Ah-Puch gave her a barely there nod, then asked, "And the seers?"

"Taken care of."

"Hold on," I butted in. "What happened to the seers?"

Ah-Puch walked to the edge of the pool and stared at his reflection in the water. "Don't worry, your pathetic protector is alive and unharmed. I thought about killing her—slowly—but realized her divination abilities and knowledge might come in handy."

No wonder Ms. Cab hadn't shown up. This monster had done something to her! I felt myself flush with anger but tamped it down. I had to keep him focused on Brooks.

"So, um . . . our deal?" I reminded him.

"Deal?" He glanced at me.

My insides collapsed. By the blank look on his fearsome face, I knew he'd already forgotten. "Please." I didn't care if I had to beg. "I know you don't have to keep your end of the bargain. I'm just a weak human . . . and you're, well, you're a super god. The most powerful."

"Power..." he mumbled, then squatted and ran his fingers across the pool's surface. Inky clouds bloomed beneath. "I'm curious," he said, keeping his gaze on the darkening liquid. "How did a mere boy wake me...?" His eyes darted across the water like there was some kind of magic in it that held all the answers.

He stood to his full height and let out a long breath. "I see now," he said, looking at me with a wry smile. "You're more than a mere human, Zane Obispo."

I didn't know if that was a good or bad thing, or if it would affect his keeping his end of the bargain, so I didn't say anything. Better to keep him off-balance and guessing. That's what Hondo always said.

Tucking a shiny stray hair behind her ear, Muwan said, "He looks like nothing, my lord."

*Nothing.* There was that word again. I struggled to keep my temper in check.

"Looks can be deceiving, can't they?" Ah-Puch walked over to me with so much confidence I thought he should run for king or president or something.

"Zane Obispo." His mouth turned up. "Such a perfect and unexpected surprise."

"Yep, that's me. One big surprise. Now, our deal."

He loosened his tie and took in the cityscape with a deep breath. "I like this city," he said to Muwan. "A very good hiding space. But they can't hide from me for long."

*They?* Who was he talking about? I wondered if all gods had this hard a time staying focused.

Cars zipped below us. Horns honked. Planes flew overhead.

The stars were shadowed by the bright lights. I'd never seen anything like it.

I hated to interrupt his little moment with Muwan and all, but...

"So, our deal?" I said again.

Ah-Puch's brows came together. "I must say, I am impressed with your bravery, and you did set me free from my dreadful prison. Imagine being imprinted onto the World Tree's paper."

"Yeah, imagine," I muttered under my breath. *World Tree's paper?*

"Being that I'm in a glorious mood," he said, "I'd say one favor deserves another. See how generous I can be?"

*Okay, so far, so good.* "So you'll heal Brooks?"

"I say we sweeten the deal. Your girlfriend's life for a small pledge."

*Er, pretty sure that wasn't the deal.* "What kind of pledge?"

"To Xib'alb'a." His black eyes glistened in the city lights. "To me."

It was like a punch in the gut. Yep, I was definitely going to throw up. The pool water began to boil. Black ribbons of steam rose into the smoggy air.

"Agree to be one of my soldiers of death," he said, "and I will give you back these worthless souls you seek."

*Soldier of death?* Was he for real? "We already made a deal," I argued.

"I've changed my mind. And since I'm the one with all the power, I make the rules."

"Yeah, well, your rules stink."

"Make your decision."

I had a feeling he wasn't going to ask twice. Always the optimist, I asked, "So, a soldier of death is what, like a couple-year gig?"

"Lifetime appointment."

*Oh.* Well, that officially stank. Gritting my teeth, trying not to think about what being a soldier of death actually meant, I said, "If I did it, I mean, became one of your . . . soldiers, it would be like, um . . . later. Like when I die as an old man, right?"

Muwan sauntered to the roof's edge, laughing lightly.

"You have until the third moon," Ah-Puch said. "When I call, you will answer. I will finish this world and start again. We will have a new order."

The third moon . . . Did he mean three nights? That might give me enough time to figure things out, rally some help. My insides twisted. I was just some thirteen-year-old kid with a bum leg. Not exactly the world-saving type.

As if he could read my mind, Ah-Puch said, "Aren't you tired of being a weakling? A boy who can't run? Can't fight? Can't do much of anything? You are no warrior, Zane Obispo. But I can make you one."

Shame dug its claws into my gut. "I was strong enough to set you free!"

His eyes glinted with some kind of knowledge I knew he wasn't about to share.

Muwan turned and glanced over her tan shoulder. Whatever Ah-Puch knew, she knew it, too.

"In Xib'alb'a," he said, eyeing my leg, "you'll be whole and strong. You'll be able to do what only gods and kings can do. You'll have power beyond your wildest dreams."

The words raced through me. *Strong. Gods. Kings.* That all sounded pretty good. And it would save Brooks and Rosie, too. . . .

Just as I was about to shake on it, another voice whispered in my ear. But it for sure wasn't Brooks. It belonged to a man. *Don't do it,* he said.

I glanced over at another skyscraper. It was even taller than where we stood, and its windows shimmered, reflecting the full moon. In an instant the building melted, to be replaced by a pyramid with steps on the sides leading to a platform on the top. The image was blurry, barely visible. On the platform stood a tall dark-haired man in a black trench coat, but he was so far away I couldn't see any details on his face.

I walked to the edge of the roof to get a better look.

Ah-Puch followed, his eyes trailing my gaze. I could tell he couldn't see what I could, because he turned to me, unfazed, and asked, "Do I have your pledge?"

The man on the pyramid shook his head. Then the image vanished.

*Who was that?* I wondered briefly, but I had more pressing things on my mind.

I swallowed the lump in my throat and looked Ah-Puch in the eyes. It was loco to make a deal with the god of death and darkness. But what choice did I have? "You promise you'll save them, Brooks *and* Rosie?"

Spears of lightning stabbed the sky.

He nodded.

"Okay."

Ah-Puch adjusted his shirt cuffs. "It's not that simple, my friend. You must say the words to bind yourself to me."

A sudden wind raced across the roof, so fast and violent it caused the pool water to splash over the sides.

"I, Zane Obispo . . ." Ah-Puch shouted.

"I, Zane Obispo . . ."

The sky split open and rain poured down on us.

"Finish it!" Ah-Puch commanded.

Wiping the rain out of my eyes, I hollered over the storm, "I pledge myself to Ah-Puch and Xib'alb'a as a soldier of death."

Ah-Puch tilted his head back and opened his arms wide. "It is done, old friend, and now he's mine!" Then he smiled, lifted me by my collar, and dangled me over the side of the building.

"Hey!" I squirmed and kicked. "We had a deal!"

"Of course," he said. Then he let go.

# 15

**I tumbled through the air in slow motion, so** slow I could see myself in the skyscraper's glass exterior. Then my reflection vanished and instead I saw an image of my mom repeated in every window.

She was walking on the shore of a forest lake with a tall dark-haired man. They held hands, laughing like a couple of kids. Then they skipped stones. It was kind of embarrassing to watch.

I'd figured it out by now—the guy was my dad. It was the same man who'd been on top of the pyramid, warning me not to give in to Ah-Puch. And he looked normal, not like a demon runner or monster or anyone I wouldn't want to be related to. At least not on the outside. They sat near a fire under the stars. I was so lost in the image, I stopped thinking about the skull-busting cement I was plummeting toward. It was as if this vision of my parents was a net that could save me.

The man put his arm around my mom and whispered in her ear, but I couldn't hear what he said. All I know is my mom's face lit up . . . and in the same instant he was gone, vanished like a puff of smoke.

"Mom!" I called out.

She was there in every window, but she couldn't see me.

The world sped up again. I was in free fall. Ah-Puch's words echoed in my ears: *It is done, old friend, and now he's mine!*

As the ground rose up to meet me, I felt someone shaking me.

"Zane! Wake up!"

Brooks!

I opened my eyes. It was night and I was back in my room, flat out on my bed. Brooks hovered over me. Did I mention her eyes change from amber to chocolate brown when she's scared?

"It's about time!" Brooks socked me in the arm. "How can you sleep at a time like this?"

I couldn't help it—I smiled. "Great to see you, too."

She blew a long piece of hair out of her face, clearly annoyed. "How'd we get here? What happened?"

I swear I could've barreled into her and hugged her to death. Okay, bad choice of words, but you wouldn't believe how happy I was to see her breathing. "You don't remember?" I sat up, patting my dry chest and legs to make sure nothing was broken.

"I . . . I remember you pulling me through the water and . . ." Her mind was turning. "The eclipse . . ." She turned back to me with terrified eyes and whispered, "You let him out."

I couldn't lie. "I didn't have a choice. I had to save you and—"

*Rosie!* I jumped up and rushed out to the living room. "Rosie? Come out, girl!" I frantically checked everywhere— under beds, in cabinets, behind the TV. Where was she? Ah-Puch had promised!

"Zane!" Brooks was right behind me. "What's wrong with you?"

"Rosie?"

I raced outside, whistling for her, but she was nowhere to be seen. "Rosie!"

Nothing but silence answered me. Heat clawed its way through my chest. "WE HAD A DEAL!" I shouted to the moonlit sky, as if Ah-Puch could hear me.

Brooks placed her hand on my shoulder. "Zane?"

I was borderline hysterical. Maybe it was like post-traumatic stress disorder, that moment when the reality of everything hit me. And I wasn't built for the impact. *How could I have been so stupid? But why would Ah-Puch give me back one and not the other?*

"Because he's a twisted, bitter god who can't be trusted," Brooks whispered. Her hands flew to her mouth. "Holy K! I heard your thoughts."

"Whoa!" I jumped back. This had happened before, when we were in the pool, but I thought that had been a fluke. I did *not* want her in my head. It was wrong on so many levels.

"Can you hear mine?" she asked.

"No."

"How about now?" She took my hand in hers. *I'm thinking you're the biggest idiot on the planet to make a deal with Ah-Puch!*

I jerked my hand free. "How'd you do that?"

Brooks blinked fast. "It must happen when we're touching." She paced nervously. Then she froze and her gaze met mine. "Holy K! I know what your dad is."

"If it's something bad, don't tell me!" I clapped my hands over my ears.

"It's not a demon."

I lowered my hands. "Yeah, I kinda figured that," I said, thinking of the man in the vision of my mom. "Is it a magician?"

"No."

"Okay." I braced myself. "Then what am I?"

She stared at me, scanning my face, my neck, my chest.

"Tell me!"

"It's not possible."

"Brooks!"

"You're part *god*."

I almost laughed. Me? Part god? The desert tilted and I felt light-headed. Maybe her brain had gotten fried when she was knocked out. There was a higher chance of that being true than of me equaling one-half *god*! "No way!"

"Only gods can do telepathy."

My knees buckled and I stumbled. She caught me by the elbow.

"Are . . . are you sure?" I asked.

"A thousand percent. You, Zane Obispo, are the son of a Maya god."

Holy smokes. That sounded kind of . . . cool.

"Which one?" I asked. "Please don't say some evil guy like Puke."

"I have no idea, but I get it now. No wonder you had the ability to release Ah-Puch. I mean, the prophecy was clear: *a powerful innocent with ancient blood*."

I wasn't following.

"Think about it," she said excitedly. I could see her mind churning as she paced. "The gods put him away, so maybe that meant only a god could let him out."

"Whoa! You never mentioned that before."

"I didn't figure it out until just now. I was so focused on the 'powerful innocent' part, I didn't go any further. Plus, a god is *never* innocent, so it wouldn't have made sense." She shook her head. "The gods probably thought their plan was foolproof, because they all hate Ah-Puch. None of them would *ever* set him free."

Okay, so Brooks's logic sort of made sense. It wasn't all that different from middle school, where the cool kids band together against someone they can't stand.

She took a deep, shaky breath. "They didn't count on *you* coming along."

(Did you hear that, gods? You got duped!)

"What's an innocent?" I asked.

"I didn't understand before, but now I get it. It's someone who has no knowledge of his lineage. As in you're not ruined by your power yet."

Power? But I didn't have any. Unless you counted seeing in the dark, and I guess now, telepathy. "So if gods can read minds," I said, "then how can *you* read my thoughts? Are nawals gods?"

"No." Brooks dropped her gaze. "It means you trust me. Or else you wouldn't let me in."

It was dangerous to have Brooks in my head, knowing my secrets. Like that I thought she was beautiful and . . . "No offense, but how do I keep you out?"

Her eyes searched my face and I could tell I'd hurt her. "Just put up a wall. Easy as that." She spun on her heels and began walking back to the house.

I followed, not knowing what to say. I mean, could she blame me? It was like reading someone's diary, but way worse!

"Brooks, hang on." I couldn't keep up. Yeah, some demigod I was.

"You think I want *you* in *my* head?" She whipped around to face me. "You think you're the only one who has problems? The only one who's in danger? Well, let me tell you..." Her face was red with anger as she poked me. "Not everything is about you, Zane Obispo!" Brooks froze in mid-thought, her finger still on my chest. "Holy K! You made a deal...to save me?"

"Um—you were sort of out cold. I don't think your memory is exactly running on all cylinders...."

Tears filled her eyes and she socked me in the arm. "You're such an idiot!"

Oh boy. I hated it when Mom cried, and this felt infinitely worse. "Don't cry," I said, patting her shoulder, as if that would stop the waterworks. "It's fine. I...I couldn't let you die. We're like...family now, right?"

She threw her arms around me, squeezing me so tight I thought she might choke me to death. Her hair was soft and smelled like lavender soap. I felt like a wooden soldier, arms stiff at my sides. Was I supposed to hug her back? I mean, I definitely wanted to, but...

When she let me go, the scowl was back. "I can't let you be that monster's soldier for me. That's so *not* happening."

"Wait a second," I said, glad to change the subject. "How come I've never been able to do telepathy with anyone before now?"

Brooks shrugged. "Maybe it's because you've been touched by our world, or by the magic...or maybe because of the eclipse. I don't know for sure." Then she grabbed my arm and turned my hand so she could see the inside of my wrist. A black symbol was inked there like a tattoo. A quarter-size skull, with sleeping eyes. "He's claimed your life," Brooks whispered in horror.

I gripped my wrist, covering the tattoo, knowing it was more than a design. It was a binding promise.

"Zane Obispo!" Brooks threw her fists onto her hips. "If you think I'm going to let you turn yourself in to that evil stinking god and spend your eternity in the land of fear, then—"

"You're not."

She blinked.

"We're going to stop him first," I said.

# 16

"It's my stupid fault," Brooks said. "If I'd done my part, we wouldn't be here right now. I've ruined everything!"

"No, you'd be in the underworld, swimming in Pus River," I mumbled. My eyes scanned the desert. I needed a walking stick, since I'd lost another cane to another lousy monster. At this rate, I was going to need a jumbo pack. I broke off a long branch from a creosote bush. It was skinny but better than nothing.

"Zane." Brooks's voice was small. "I have to tell you something."

But before she could say anything else, Hondo threw open the back door.

"We've got a problem."

"Um, what's up, Hondo?" I asked.

"There's a grande chicken that's been pecking at the front door for the last two hours and it won't go away."

Three days ago I would've considered it a prank, but after everything that had happened? I started for the door. "Let's go see this pollo loco of yours."

A minute later, the three of us stood on the front porch looking down at the three-sizes-too-big chicken that wasn't acting like a chicken at all. It didn't bob around with its head down. It hurried back and forth in a frenzy, spreading its wings, clucking and clicking up a storm.

"It's rabid," Hondo said. "Like in those scary movies when the animals kill everyone? You ever see *Cujo* or *The Birds*?"

Brooks cocked her head. "Do you think it's trying to tell us something?"

Forgetting that Hondo was standing there, I asked Brooks, "Can you use your bird brain . . . er, I mean your bird *connection* and figure out what it's saying?"

"You think all bird-speak is the same?" Brooks tilted her chin up proudly. "Pu-lease."

Hondo gave me a weird look, and right when he opened his mouth to say something, the chicken turned and bolted toward Ms. Cab's house.

"Hey, wait!" I shouted as we all hurried after the bird.

The chicken pecked at Ms. Cab's front door, then tilted its head at me. It rolled its eyes before it went back to striking the door with its beak.

"I think it wants to go inside," I said.

Brooks rang the doorbell and peered in through the front window. "No one's in there."

Hondo turned the doorknob. It was unlocked. He raised a brow and gave me a sly smile. "Let's see what the pollo wants."

Ms. Cab would string us up by our ears for going in uninvited, but before I could protest, the chicken bolted inside and over to the living room. It jumped onto the coffee table, stomping and clucking loudly.

Hondo looked around. "This place is creepy, Zane. How can you work here?" Then he picked up the box of eyes.

I hollered, "Stop!"

But it was too late. He had already opened it, and his face was turning green. "They're . . . they're moving!" He dropped the box and all the eyeballs rolled out onto the floor. And then my iron-biceps, champion-wrestler uncle passed out.

Brooks hurried over and put a pillow under his head while flapping her hand back and forth across his face. "Hondo? Hondo?"

The chicken hopped off the table and hurried around the living room, picking up the eyeballs one at a time and putting them back in the box. Except one unfortunate eye that went *splat* in its beak.

That's when I realized. "Ms. Cab?"

She stuck the last eyeball in its place and nodded slowly. How the heck had she turned into a chicken? Then I remembered what Muwan had said, that all the seers had been *taken care of.* If the seers had all been turned into animals, they couldn't warn the gods about Puke's evil plan.

Hondo stirred awake, rubbing his head. "¡Ay! Necesito un médico. O tequila. Necesito tequila."

He was like my mom—whenever he got freaked out (or mad during a wrestling match), Spanish flew from his mouth like hurricane winds. As I helped him sit up, I said, "Pretty sure Ms. Cab doesn't have any tequila. Do you really want me to call a doctor?"

Hondo shrugged me away. "Who said anything about a doctor?"

Then Mr. Ortiz walked in the open door. "¿Qué pasó? Where's Antonia?"

Brooks and I shared a glance. Ms. Cab jumped onto the sofa and ran back and forth, squawking like a bird on fire. She was trying to tell me something, but what? Hondo got to his feet groggily, rubbing his head. "Tell that thing to shut up. It's giving me a headache."

I sat on the sofa and began to pet Ms. Cab's feathery head, thinking maybe that would calm her down. She jabbered on and on, until her clucks began turning into words. *Bawk! What—Bawk!—do I have to do to—Bawk! Bawk!—get your attention, Zane Obispo?*

"You can talk?!" I shrieked.

Everyone went stone still and stared at me. Even Ms. Cab stopped fussing. *Oh, Zane,* she said. *You can hear me. Thank the gods.* Then she blinked and her beak formed a perfect O. *Oh my . . . that means . . .*

"I'm part god." The words felt like marbles in my mouth. "Telepathy."

The others rushed toward me with a flurry of questions. "It can talk?"

"You can understand chicken-speak?"

"What do you mean *part god*?" That was Hondo.

I held my hand up to silence them. "This chicken is Ms. Cab, and she's talking to me, and I can't hear her over your voices, so *stop jabbering*!" Yeah, they looked at me like I'd just fallen off the loony-bin truck—everyone but Brooks.

Ms. Cab stretched her neck, and I resumed petting her. *I was kidnapped, Zane . . . at the crossroads to Xib'alb'a. Some stupid lower demon of the underworld threw a sack over my head.* She shuddered. *Me! Secret-keeper of the Great Soothsayer!*

As she spoke, I translated for everyone. She continued, talking so fast it was hard to keep up, but every time I tried to get her to slow down she gave me the evil eye and chattered even faster. *Xib'alb'a isn't what it used to be,* she sputtered. *Ixtab has taken over, set up new rules, even redecorated the place. And let me tell you, she has no taste!*

When I translated, Hondo raised a brow and looked around Ms. Cab's cluttered living room, which was filled with different-size plastic snow globes from all over the world. "Right. No taste," he muttered.

Apparently, when good old Ah-Puch was sent away, a goddess named Ixtab, the keeper of the souls of warriors and women who died in childbirth, took his place as the ruler of the underworld.

Ms. Cab said, *She had to battle a few other gods to win the throne of the dead, which made those gods good and mad. But more importantly,* she went on, *some of the demons were like double agents, playing both sides. Someone had somehow learned of the Prophecy of Fire and told Ixtab all about you, Zane.*

"But who?" I asked after I'd translated for everyone.

Hondo rubbed his forehead. "Hang on, Zane. This is crazy talk! Who the heck are Ixtab and Ah-Puch?"

Mr. O stuffed his hands in his pockets. "¡Ay Dios! I know magic when I see it." He glanced at Ms. Cab and said, "I still think you're hermosa."

To which she squawked, *Oh, lords of fright. This man is a senseless fool.*

I didn't translate that part.

Ms. Cab lowered her voice, as if anyone could understand her, and said, *Why is that nawal here? I told you not to trust her.*

"She saved my life," I said.

Ms. Cab tried to harrumph but clucked instead.

By this point there was no use trying to keep everything else secret, so I told Mr. O and Hondo about the prophecy, making Hondo promise he wouldn't tell Mom. I even told them the part about Los Angeles, leaving out the deal I'd made with Ah-Puch, because Hondo would punch my lights out.

"Maybe I do need some tequila," Hondo said, looking a little pale.

My mind went into overdrive. "So *Ixtab* was the one who sent that little assassin alux. She wanted to prevent me from fulfilling the prophecy so she wouldn't have to fight Ah-Puch for the throne!"

Brooks chewed on her bottom lip, pacing the room. What was her deal? How come she was so quiet? It was seriously starting to make me nervous.

Ms. Cab's wing trembled and she blinked up at me. *Tell me every detail of when you let Ah-Puch out. Even how the monster looked. Probably more hideous than before! He always was the ugliest god . . . or at least in the top ten.*

I didn't want to talk about it in front of everyone else, especially Brooks, so I let down my guard and allowed Ms. Cab in, hoping it would work like it did with Brooks. *Can you hear me?*

Ms. Cab cocked her head and hopped into the air. *Yes!*

I brought her into my lap and told her everything, leaving

out the soldier-of-death part. *I had to let him out. Otherwise Brooks would've died.*

*I felt something the moment he was released.* Ms. Cab shook her skinny chicken head. *The earth stood still for a split second. Of course, none of the gods would notice, being such dense, self-obsessed beings. But we seers—we knew. Problem is, there was nothing we could do about it, because we couldn't pinpoint his location. It was like he went off the grid. I lost all contact with the other seers, which tells me they're all in nonhuman form, too.*

"What's she saying?" Hondo asked restlessly.

"The gods are dense and the other seers are probably chickens, too," I said.

Brooks folded her arms and nodded. "They *are* kind of dense. Except for Kukuulkaan, of course."

Gee, that made me feel really good about being a halfer. Unless, of course, I was Holy K's son. What had Brooks said—he was the god of coolness? Yep, could definitely see the resemblance there. "How would you know?" I asked. "Do you hang out with the gods?"

There were still so many secrets swirling around Brooks, I couldn't help but wonder what she wasn't telling me.

"No," Brooks said. "Um...I mean, I read all about them. And"—she rolled her eyes—"everyone knows they changed when they came to America."

"Changed how?" Hondo asked.

Brooks fidgeted with the hem of her jacket. "Like they forgot the old ways—they lost their edge, you know?"

"Huh," I grunted. "They seem pretty edgy to me, or at least

old Puke does." Looking back to Ms. Cab I asked, "Why would he take me to LA?"

*He could've picked anywhere. Interesting that he picked a busy city. You said he liked the chaos?* Her eyes went wide. *Of course! Chaos will hide him from the other gods. And vice versa.* She flapped her wings. *He said someone is hiding from him?*

I repeated everything Ms. Cab was saying, while pondering who Ah-Puch could have been referring to.

Hondo slugged me in the arm. He hadn't stopped looking at me with a goofy smile since the big demigod reveal. "I knew there was something different about you!" he said.

"You did?"

Mr. O took off his hat and rubbed his bald head.

"When you were a baby," Hondo said, "you used to do loco things like talk in full sentences before you were even a year old. And one time you touched your mom's hot curling iron but didn't get burned. Another time we found you crawling in the desert toward the volcano." He ran his hand through his hair excitedly. "It makes sense now. You really *are* a freak." His face got serious. "I mean, in a good way. So do you have any superpowers? I mean, beyond creeping on people's minds?"

"Seeing in the dark, I guess. . . ." I thought about the recent storms. They always came when I was scared or angry. Had *I* caused those? And what about that freak storm in LA? What had *that* been about? Did it have something to do with my dad making an appearance?

I hadn't seen Hondo this excited since the last world wrestling championship three years ago, when he won a thousand bucks betting on Bone Crusher. It felt good to let it all out, to share all the weirdness of the last few days with him and Mr. Ortiz. If only Mom were here, maybe she could fill in the gaps. But I couldn't let her get mixed up in this. Where *was* she, anyway? I hoped she was okay....

Hondo slung his arm over my shoulders. "So how do we take down this sonofa . . . er, I mean, this Stinking One?"

Ms. Cab set a wing in my hand. *I'm sorry I failed you.*

I let out a big breath. *You tried, at least. Did . . . did you find out anything about Rosie?*

She blinked her little chicken eyes and I could see the sadness there. *I sent messages everywhere. If any of my friends see her, Zane, they'll try and protect her.*

My heart wedged itself into the big hole in my chest. *Thanks, Ms. C. By the way, where did you put that gateway map?* I asked, hoping she wouldn't catch on to my plan.

*In the bookcase, like always. Why?*

I walked over and pulled out the scroll. I unrolled it in front of her, then took hold of her wing again. *Show me how to use it.*

*Absolutely not!* Ms. Cab said. *Do you know what others would do to get their grubby hands on this map?*

I knew we were running out of time. Ah-Puch had given me three moons, and if this map could get us to where I wanted to go, I needed to know how to read it.

"Mr. Ortiz?" I looked up at him.

"Yes?"

"Can you watch over Ms. Cab?"

A broad smile formed and his eyes danced. "¡Claro que sí!"

Ms. Cab shook her head vigorously. *Zane Obispo! I don't need a babysitter. I am a great Maya seer! And he's just . . . just a pathetic human!*

My mouth turned up. *No offense, Ms. Cab, but um, you're a chicken right now.*

That silenced her for a few seconds.

*At least take an eyeball!*

*For what?*

*So I can visit you in your dreams, and so I can keep an eye on that girl.*

I seriously didn't want Ms. Cab in my dreams. And I for sure didn't want to carry around one of her eyeballs.

*You'll need my guidance!* she screamed. I let go of her wing and put up a wall in my head so her words just spun into clucking.

"Where are you going?" Mr. O asked.

Brooks and I shared a glance. "Can you read this map?" I asked her.

"It's a gateway map," she said, her voice trembling. "I can read some of the glyphs . . . not all." She ran her long fingers along the distressed edges. "I think I can figure it out."

Ms. Cab was squawking at the top of her chicken lungs.

Hondo popped his knuckles. "I'm coming, too."

"No way," I said.

"You want your mom to lose her mind, call the police?" he said. "It's the only way. I'll leave her a note, telling her we went fishing for the weekend. That'll buy us time. Besides," he said, flexing his biceps, "you're going to need my luchador moves."

He was right. I couldn't involve Mom, and I couldn't just

up and leave. She'd lose it for sure. Plus, I didn't need the attention of being a missing kid. "Fine," I said reluctantly.

Mr. O took my arm gently. "Before you go, I have something that might help your journey. Come."

So I followed him out, but not before I grabbed the smallest and least creepy eyeball I could find.

# 17

**Mr. O asked the others to wait at Ms. Cab's,** because what he had to show me was a secret. We made our way across the road and through the side gate to his greenhouse.

"You cannot believe my discovery," he said as we stepped inside his little oasis. There were rows and rows of pepper plants: red, green, purple, and yellow. And they came in all sizes. Some of the peppers were as small as walnuts and others were as long as bananas.

The place was warm and smelled fresh, like the desert after a summer rain. I didn't want to offend the guy, but I didn't see why I had to drop Mission Puke to see his garden. Especially when the future of the world was at stake.

Mr. O paced, rubbing his chin. "I've done it, Zane." He pointed to a single red pepper shaped like a bulging tomato. It clung to a tiny green plant, its weight bending the stem. "Meet *La Muerte*."

"You named a pepper after the Grim Reaper?"

"The Guinness Book will put my name in writing now." He pushed back his straw hat and smiled.

"For a pepper?" I didn't mean to sound unimpressed, but I didn't get what was so special about La Muerte.

He tugged on his pant leg and smiled, still pacing. "If I get in the book, Antonia . . . she will find me famous. She will go to dinner with me."

My face must've been blank, because he clapped me on the shoulder and laughed. "I asked her, 'When will you go out with me?' and she said, 'When you are famous.' Do you see now? If I'm famous, she will love me."

*Oh. OH.*

I had to give the guy credit. I mean, he had a goal to marry Ms. Cab, and no matter how many times she told him no, he never quit. I didn't have the heart to tell him I didn't think his being in a book could make someone love him. "So how's the pepper going to get you in the world record book?"

"The one in the book now—it's the hottest in the world. It—how do you say?—it paralyzes only the brain."

*Only?*

"Like, forever?" I asked.

His eyes glittered with excitement. "For maybe dos horas. But *my* pepper, it lasts many hours longer. One bite and she will freeze your legs, then your arms and hands." He stood stiff to illustrate. "Then the brain. So La Muerte is now the hottest. I break the record."

Definitely respected the guy.

Mr. Ortiz had taught me about how, long ago, the Spanish used to grow peppers in monasteries and thought they had magical properties. I knew he grew weird varieties, but all this time his top secret mission was *this*?

What he said next was an even bigger surprise.

"But that isn't important anymore." He grabbed my arm and shook it excitedly. "I have spent years to make this, Zane.

All the other fails were good steps to this moment." He swept his arm in front of him. "All these plants, they grew only to give me *this*. It was their destiny. Don't you see?" he said, still grinning like a kid on his birthday. "I thought all this time I was trying for the world record, but it was for you. Destiny had a different plan. Yes?"

The thought grew slowly, and . . . I finally caught on. Mr. Ortiz wanted to give me his pepper to stop Ah-Puch! Could it work? It was one thing to paralyze a human, it was something else to try and paralyze a god. He tugged the pepper off the vine and very carefully set it in a small burlap bag. "For you," he said, placing the sack in my hands. "To stop the Stinking One."

"What about the Guinness Book and Ms. Cab?"

"No good to have a world record if the world is gone."

He had a point.

I didn't know what to say. "What . . . what if it doesn't work? What if I can't do it?"

He clapped my shoulder. "I always knew you were very special, Zane. I believe you can stop this monster."

It felt really good that Mr. Ortiz had so much faith in me, but it also felt like a heavy burden, because I didn't know if I deserved it.

"Destiny smiles on me, Zane. She was asleep for many years, and now she has come to my door so I could give you this chance. All I had to do was open it."

I gripped the sack. "But if your destiny had been something else, something dangerous . . . would you still have opened the door?"

Mr. Ortiz thought for a second, rubbed his chin, then looked at me. "If you don't open the door, she will come in through the window."

Before I left, I turned to face Mr. Ortiz. "Could you not say anything about all this to my mom? I—"

"I will honor your wishes to keep her safe." He placed his weathered hands on my shoulders, tightening his hold. "No te preocupes. I will protect both of them."

Hondo wrote six versions of the note for Mom before I finally approved this one:

*Hey Sis,*

*Me and Zane went fishing. Wanted some fresh air, some bro time, after the bank heist. Back in a few days.*

I picked up the pen and added:

*We can talk about my dad*

My hand hovered. I didn't know if I should write *when I come home? If I come home? Later?* I finally wrote *later* then signed my name and stuck the note on the fridge. Where could she have gone after she talked to the cops? At least I felt a little better knowing Mr. O would keep an eye on her and Ms. Cab.

Hondo left to get money from the ATM, and when he came back, he tossed a stack of hundred-dollar bills onto the kitchen table, where Brooks had the gateway map spread out.

"That's a lot of money," Brooks said, leaning across the table for a better look.

Hondo smiled. "Been saving for a speaker-system upgrade for the truck, but...I figured we'd need some coin for food and stuff."

"I can't let you waste all your cash," I said.

"On saving the world?" Hondo laughed. "What good does it do me if we get blown to smithereens?"

"Can't argue with that," Brooks said.

Hondo grabbed a big sack off the counter, reached inside, and pulled out a leather tool belt. Then, one by one, he began stuffing tools from the sack into the loops: a hammer, a screwdriver, a small ax.

"What's all that for?" Brooks asked.

"Some war stash," Hondo said. "Gotta be prepared."

I highly doubted his tools were going to save us. But how *do* you prepare to save the world when you're a featherweight up against an immortal heavyweight?

Hondo swung his arm around my neck. "So what's the plan? Go find a few gods to help us take this guy down?"

I'd thought the same thing until Brooks saw the flaw in that plan. "Tell him, Brooks."

"Wouldn't do any good," she said. "The gods are pretty much equal in strength and power. It would only start a war that would bring about the same result: everyone dead."

Hondo didn't even flinch. "Okay, then we find a magical gateway to the underworld and pummel this guy ourselves?"

I wished it were that easy. But I knew Ah-Puch wouldn't be in Xib'alb'a. He'd had hundreds of years to plan his revenge, and I figured he wasn't about to just waltz into hell and ask for the keys back. Besides, battling Ah-Puch ourselves would only end in disaster. He'd head-drop us in less than a second.

I had something different in mind. A backup plan, because I couldn't balance the whole world's survival on a single chile pepper. Despite my promise to Mr. O to keep it a secret, I'd already shown the pepper to Brooks and Hondo. I had no choice—too much was at stake. And they'd agreed: We definitely needed a plan B.

"You ever heard of the hero twins?" I asked Brooks. Her face went blank. I waved my hand in front of her eyes. "Earth to Brooks."

"What?"

"Have you heard the story of the hero twins?"

She rolled her eyes. "Jun'ajpu' and Xb'alamkej?"

"Yeah. Whatever you just said."

"What about them?"

"They defeated the gods of the underworld."

"And they never let anyone forget it, either," she argued. "Big braggers, if you ask me."

"You actually *know* them?"

Brooks looked back at the map and twisted her mouth like she was trying to keep it closed.

"You *do* know them, don't you?"

"Might've met the dirtbags once or twice."

A vein in my forehead throbbed. "And you didn't think you should tell me?"

"Why would I ever want to tell you about those losers? What do they have to do with *anything*?"

Hondo rubbed the back of his neck and his eyes bugged out like he knew a storm might be brewing.

I threw my hands up. "Oh, I don't know. Maybe the fact that they're the only mortals to have defeated Ah-Puch. They have to have his playbook, right?" I knew Brooks was too smart to have overlooked this connection.

Her nostrils flared. "Those guys are nothing but trouble. And they're not exactly mortals," she added. "Their mom was the daughter of some lord in the underworld, and their dad was the god Jun Jun'ajpu'. Except he wasn't actually alive...I mean, when the mom met him, he was just a head, a skull."

Hondo grimaced. "She fell for a skull? Was she desperate or something?"

"I don't even want to know," I said.

Brooks shrugged. "Not worth knowing."

"The twins might be our only shot," I said.

Hondo popped open a bag of Cheetos and stuffed a few in his mouth. "I get where you're going with this. Maybe they'll share their war strategy with you."

"Exactly."

"Okay, first of all," Brooks said with a huff, "they're arrogant, selfish, obnoxious, weaselly...." She crossed her arms. "They've never told anyone the *real* truth of how they defeated Puke. Mostly they've let the story build them into some stupid legend status so they can keep the magical powers the gods gave them for being such"—she made air quotes—"'heroes.' I mean, who cares that they took down stupid Seven Macaw? As if that's hard or something."

"Seven who?" Hondo said.

"Some guy who wanted to be the supreme god," Brooks offered.

(Was there ever a time you arrogant gods *weren't* trying to knock each other off to gain more power?)

"Okay," I said. "So aside from their being jerks, do you know where to find them?"

Brooks reached into the bag of Cheetos, grabbed a handful, and tossed them into her mouth.

"Brooks!"

She groaned. "Venice."

"Italy?" Hondo rubbed his chin. "We don't have enough cash for *that* kind of mileage."

Brooks shook her head, looking suddenly sour. "Venice Beach, California."

That was in Los Angeles. *Los Angeles.* It started to make sense. "Crap!"

"Crap?" Brooks wiped some orange powder off her mouth. "Crap what?"

I told her what Ah-Puch had said: *But they can't hide from me for long.* "I bet Old Puke is there for the twins."

"Why would he care about *them*?" Brooks asked.

"Hondo, why would old Puke want the twins?" I said, knowing he was following my logic.

Hondo smashed his fist into his palm and a slow grin spread over his face. "Revenge . . . of course."

"I mean, he didn't just pick that city out of the blue, right?" I said. "But if I can get there in time to warn them he's coming for them, they'll owe me. A favor for a favor."

"Zane," Brooks said, "they won't help you. They don't care

about anything but themselves. Even if we made the trip, they wouldn't agree to see you."

"Why not?"

"You have to *earn* their attention . . . it's a Maya thing."

"What's that supposed to mean?"

"I should say it's a Maya *supernatural* thing. Those with power want to keep it, which means they only hang with those who have the gold. They don't wallow with common humans. No offense, Hondo."

Hondo shrugged.

"But I'm *not* common," I said. "My dad's a Maya god!"

"Right," Brooks sighed. "But we can't *tell* them that, now can we?" She leaned across the table. "Please forget about it." Her voice quivered. "It's too risky."

"Riskier than facing demon runners? The god of the dead?" I looked from Hondo to Brooks. "Does anyone have a better idea?"

"You're right, Zane," Hondo said. "Can't rush into a match without a game plan." He rubbed his chin, turning to Brooks. "Risky how, Brooks?"

She looked glum, like what I was asking her to do was worse than jumping into a fire pit. "They're tricksters," she said. "People wait years to get in to see them, to ask for favors. Like once, this guy needed some protection for his family— they lived in a really bad neighborhood—and you know what those idiots told him?" Brooks scowled. "They laughed and told him to learn how to fight."

"What are they, like in the Mafia or something?" Hondo asked.

"Not *in* the Mafia," Brooks said. "They're the kings of it."

I shook my head. "Hang on—the hero twins? The ones who defeated the underworld? They run organized crime now?"

"Not crime," Brooks said. "Organized magic."

"Oh," Hondo said, smashing the now-empty Cheetos bag. "That sounds better."

I leaned closer to Brooks. "If you don't want to go, I get it."

Brooks twisted her hair around her pinkie. "You'll need to bring them a gift."

"Why?" Hondo asked. "Is that like some kind of honoring-the-king thing?"

"Not a king thing—a birthday thing. Tomorrow's their birthday," Brooks said. Then she mumbled, "Trust me, they don't even deserve a birthday."

*Trust?* Ms. Cab had said not to trust Brooks. I'd ignored the advice, because I didn't want it to be true. But I suspected Brooks wasn't telling me everything. She'd been weirdly quiet at Ms. Cab's, and I could tell wheels were turning in her mind.

But what choice did I have? Brooks knew important stuff I didn't. And we didn't have time to argue. I had to trust her. I rolled up the map and headed for the door.

Brooks caught me, grabbed my arm, and twisted me around. "Zane, are you one hundred percent sure you want to do this? No one ever leaves without owing them something."

She released her hand quickly, probably thinking I would jump into her mind.

"I already owe a debt to Ah-Puch, and after tonight we only have two moons to change that," I said more boldly than I felt. "We have to try."

She twisted her mouth to the side and let out a long breath. "You risked your life for me, made a d—" She stopped herself before spilling any more to Hondo. "Okay . . . I'll take you there. It's the least I can do."

"You don't have to," I said, feeling suddenly guilty. "I mean, I want you to come, but if—"

"You'll never get in without me. Let's just hope we don't run into any more demons."

"I know you're scared. . . ."

"I'm *not* scared, Obispo. I've lost all my demon-tormenting flashlights and I'm not about to go back to that cave to retrieve them." She tucked a piece of hair behind her ear. "Now about this map. . . ."

"Are we using a magical gateway?" Hondo's eyebrows shot up.

Brooks said, "There aren't any close enough."

"How do you know?" I asked. "Did you . . . You learned how to read the map?"

"No, I . . . I mean, I told you I could probably figure it out and . . ." She sighed and unfolded the map. "See how it's in panels?" she said. "Well, when folded the right way, the hieroglyphs connect and their meanings change, so it's always fluctuating. But if you follow this blue line . . ."

Hondo and I leaned closer, trying to follow.

"It travels to California, right?" she said. "But there aren't any flashing gateways between here and there. The closest one is in Texas, which would lead us to the North Pole, and . . ." She folded the panels a different way, giving us a new view. "Once there, we'd have to go to Iceland. . . ."

"What? No direct flights?" Hondo said. "What a rip-off."

"Okay, okay," I said, my head spinning. "I get it. We'll have to drive."

Brooks nodded. "But we need to be there by nine p.m. if you want to see the twins. Or else you'll have to wait another day, and we don't have that kind of time."

"What's so special about nine?"

"Doors close after that."

"How do you know?"

Brooks rolled her eyes. "Their birthday is, like, a universal event, and invitations went out. I . . . I sort of got one."

Hondo nodded slowly, and grinned. "So you're an *it* girl. Niiiice."

Brooks slugged Hondo in the arm. "Call me that again, and I'll drop you from the top of a mountain."

Brooks? An *it* girl? I wasn't even sure what that was, but I guessed it meant she was part of the cool crowd. But that made no sense. I mean, cool girls don't usually wear beat-up combat boots, basic black hoodies, and zero makeup. And they for sure didn't talk to *me*.

# 18

**We piled into Hondo's black F150 truck. The**
thing was a beast on huge wheels. Hondo spent much of his
free time waxing her to a shine, and most of his money tricking her out.

We were on the open highway a few minutes later. I let
the window down and leaned out. The cool night air whipped
through my hair. I'd put Ms. Cab's pinkish eyeball (it looked
like it once belonged to a giant rat) in a plastic sandwich bag
and carefully stashed it in my backpack on account of not
wanting it to pop like a grape in my pocket.

"Looks like we should take I-10 straight through Tucson
and Phoenix," Brooks said, studying a road map Hondo had
picked up.

Hondo grinned and turned on some really bad punk rock
that rattled my bones.

I'd never been out of New Mexico, so crossing the state
line into Arizona felt like a *get out of jail free* card. The whole
landscape changed from familiar yucca and mesquite to
funny-shaped cactus with arms—Hondo called them *saguaro*.
In the dark, the tall cactus looked like living things that could
uproot themselves and chase after us. Okay, so I was paranoid. But who wouldn't be after the day I'd had? Fighting off
demon runners, swimming through darkness, cutting deals

with the lord of the dead, talking to a very angry chicken, and saving a life. Bet that's even more than you gods typically do in just a few hours.

It was already close to midnight and the exhaustion was settling in. My whole body felt like it had been battered with stones. Hondo must've seen me fighting sleep. "Go on," he said. "Take a snooze."

"I can stay awake," I said. "Talk to you..."

"Nah, I'm used to being up all night. Go on," he insisted, "catch some z's."

I looked over my shoulder at Brooks in the back cab. She was slumped against the door, fast asleep. *Even though I'm terrified of becoming a soldier of death,* I thought, *I would still make the same deal to save her.* A few minutes later I closed my eyes and fell into a foggy dream world.

I was in some kind of night jungle. The trees were made of aluminum and had sharp clawlike branches. A distant howl drew my attention toward a narrow dark path. Strange whispers bounced off the trees. A single bar of moonlight crept through the silvery branches, and that's when I saw her. Standing on the path right in front of me.

"Rosie!"

I took off running. My legs were long and lean and fast. It was incredible, even better than flying in a dream. I could run like this forever. As soon as I reached her, I fell to my knees to wrap my arms around the old goof... but she turned to mist and disappeared.

The trees shimmered with a strange image.

There were dozens of her reflected in the shiny trees. I felt like I was in a house of mirrors trying to find the real Rosie.

I went over to one to get a closer look. The metal was cold and the dog in the reflection was black. I glanced at the next tree. This Rosie had yellow eyes, and the next one had long fur. I realized they were all bad imitations of my dog.

A wicked burst of wind blasted through the trees and the metal branches scraped against each other, making a screeching sound that sent chills down the backs of my legs. The full moon shifted color from bone white to blood-red. Rain pummeled the earth, instantly flooding the jungle. I found myself riding a giant wave toward a million lightning bolts violently striking the earth, setting fire to a vast desert landscape. A terrible burning started in my hands, and yellow and red sparks jumped from my fingertips. Just as I was about to be thrown into the flames, I heard Ms. Cab's voice: "You left me as a chicken!"

I woke with a start, yelling, "FIRE!"

Hondo jumped in his seat, and the truck swerved. "What the heck, Zane? You scared the bejesus out of me!"

Brooks groaned and sat up sleepily. "Way to ruin a perfectly good dream."

"Sorry, guys." I rubbed my eyes, trying to shake off the vision that had felt so real. I swear I could still feel the heat of that fire in my fingertips. And if Ms. Cab was going to yell at me about being a chicken, I was going to toss that eyeball onto the highway. "Where are we?" I looked out at the darkness whizzing by.

"The desert," Hondo said with a chuckle.

Brooks glanced out the window. She opened the road atlas, studied it, then looked out again. "Um . . . Hondo?"

"Yeah?"

"I think you missed the fork to I-10."

Hondo craned his neck to see her in the rearview mirror. "You said to head straight."

"On I-10."

Hondo threw his head back and groaned. "I'll turn around."

"We've gone too far to turn back," Brooks said. "We'll have to head north from San Diego."

Hondo hit the gas. "I'm on it, Capitán."

"Maybe it's a sign we shouldn't go," Brooks said, twisting her mouth.

I turned to face her. "You really hate these guys that much, Brooks? What did they ever do to you?"

Brooks glared back out the window. "Just get me to Venice. I'll do the rest."

A restlessness crept over me as I once again wondered how much Brooks hadn't told me. What was her deal with these guys? I'd stashed my Maya book in my backpack in case we needed it. I consulted it, but there was nothing new about the twins in the pages. Anything else I wanted to know about them was going to have to be learned firsthand.

It was three in the morning when we got to Yuma, a tiny desert town bordered by flat green farmland. We saw a sign for food, lodging, and gas.

Hondo exited the highway and dropped Brooks and me at

a Jack in the Box while he went to fill up the truck at the gas station next door.

Inside, the cashier was sitting on the counter, playing on his phone. When the door pinged, he didn't even look up.

"Uh, you open?" I asked.

"Hang on," he said. "A few more zombies to get to the next level."

Gunshots, screams, and gurgling sounds filled the empty place.

Brooks tapped her foot. "We want three Jumbo Jack meals with cheese, and you'll get a good tip if you hurry it up."

The guy looked up. "Tip?" He had acne on his cheeks and his mousy brown hair fell over one eye. "Coming right up," he said with a friendly smile.

A few minutes later the three of us were sitting by the window devouring our burgers and fries. The zombie-fighting cashier was in the next booth, back to playing his game.

"This place gives me the creeps," I admitted before taking a gargantuan bite of my cheeseburger. Man, it tasted so salty-good, I wished I'd ordered two.

Hondo took a gulp of his Coke. "Just a case of the night-creepers. World's different after midnight. I used to feel it, but now I like working at night. It's quiet, and no one expects anything from you."

Brooks ate all her fries, but only partway, leaving a pile of unwanted ends on her tray.

"You don't like your fries?" I asked, scooping up the left-overs.

"I never eat the ends I touch."

"How come?"

"What's it to you?" she asked, frowning as I scoured her tray for any remaining scraps.

"Sue me for being hungry."

A rumbling noise in the parking lot caught my attention. A trio of Harley riders pulled up to the joint. They wore leather vests, knotted headscarves, and narrow black sunglasses shaped like alien eyes. I felt suddenly claustrophobic, like the walls were closing in and the ceiling was about to fall on our heads. The fluorescent lights buzzed overhead. The violent screams coming from the guy's cell phone didn't help.

The door flung open and the buff riders stepped into our space.

"You smell that?" Brooks whispered, never taking her eyes off her tray.

"Smell what?" Hondo asked. His back was to the door, so he hadn't seen the dudes yet.

I wanted to pretend I couldn't detect the vomit and motor oil that permeated the greasy air, but it was too powerful to ignore. These riders weren't human and had the after-smell of the underworld. My stomach plummeted.

The cashier clicked off his video game and headed to the register to take the guys' orders. But they weren't interested in burgers and fries. The tallest of the bikers turned his head in our direction. His skin was waxy-looking and pulled tight over his skull. Okay, so maybe it was too late for a smooth exit.

"How'd they find us?" I asked.

Brooks bent across the table and spoke in a low voice. "Sure wish someone had thought to pick up my flashlights."

"I was busy saving your life!"

Brooks rolled her eyes. "There's another exit over there. Let's get up slowly and carefully."

"What's with you two?" Hondo glanced over his shoulder. "You're scared of a few flabby Harley dudes?"

My neck was sweating. "Er...what if I told you they were...more like demons?"

Hondo stuffed a few fries into his mouth and tossed his napkin onto the tray. "I'd say let's blow this joint."

The cashier leaned over the counter and asked the demon bikers, "You guys going to order or what? No bathroom if you don't pay for something."

The three ignored him, keeping their glares on us.

Brooks inched toward the edge of her seat. The bikers headed our way. Their belt and boot chains jingled as they stomped across the linoleum.

"NOW!" I hollered, and the three of us raced toward the opposite door and out into the parking lot. But when we got to the truck, the trio was blocking our way. I did a double take, not believing my eyes—the bikers were *us*!

"Are you seeing what I'm seeing?" I asked, frozen in my tracks.

"Dude," Hondo groaned. "Am I really that short?"

Brooks grabbed my hand. Her thoughts came at me full force.

*It's shadow magic. A war tactic to confuse your opponent.
No one wants to pummel their own face.*

*What do we do?*

*I don't know. I've only read about it, never actually seen it.
But there's always a weakness, if you know where to look.*

Hondo growled, "We can take these guys."

"They're not guys," I mumbled. "They're demons."

"WIIICKED!" Hondo let out a low whistle. "Demons that
ride motorcycles?"

"It's an illusion," I told him. Then to the monsters, I said,
"I had a deal with your boss. And I've still got two nights!"

The one that looked like me, down to the chin freckle and
messy hair, popped his knuckles. "Not *our* boss. The master
of the underworld sent us."

The fake Hondo and Brooks grunted in agreement.

Okay, these weren't your average demon runners. They
could string together whole sentences. And what did they
mean, *master of the underworld?*

"You mean Ixtab?" I ventured.

My head went into overdrive. If they were working for
her, she must want to rip me a new one for releasing her mortal enemy. Maybe I could reason with them, impress them
enough that they wouldn't chop off our heads. I clenched my
fists at my sides. "Tell your boss that Ah-Puch's out to destroy
the whole world, and I'm—*we're* going to stop him."

"We're not here for you, boy," my look-alike said.

*Wait. What?* Did they say they weren't here for me? Didn't
they know who I was?

He snorted. "Ixtab doesn't care what happens to this world,

you little fool. A new world will always rise, and where there is a world, there is always death."

Hondo whispered in my ear, "I'll take the one that looks like me."

*I can scratch out their eyes*, Brooks offered, squeezing my hand tighter.

My companions were right. There was no way past these dirtbags, only through them.

"Um, no offense, guys," I said to the demons, "but I've got some travel plans. Maybe I can swing by later?"

"Give us the girl," my clone said.

*Girl? Brooks?* I held up my hand in protest. "You guys have it all wrong. It's *me* you want."

Just when I thought the demons were going to lunge, thick handfuls of coarse black hair grew out of two of the demons' mouths at an alarming rate. It cascaded down their bodies and onto the ground, where it crawled toward us. We all screamed.

I ducked, slipping between my look-alike monster's legs, but not before the hair reached me, climbed my body, and wrapped itself around my neck, covering my mouth and pinning me to the asphalt.

Clutching the band of hair to allow me to breathe, I glanced over to see Brooks in the same position, kicking and squirming while the hair nearly obscured her face. But where was Hondo? Oh God—had the hair already smothered him? Had his twin taken him down?

No—I saw him head-ramming his clone. Or was his clone head-ramming *him*?

With every ounce of strength I had, I tried to tear the

hair away from my throat and out of my mouth, but it was impossible. It was too powerful. I was going to get choked to death by demon hair!

All of a sudden Hondo was swinging a butcher knife around like a crazy man, hacking away at the black ropes. The hair hissed and writhed. Finally it let me go.

I scrambled to my feet. Hondo gave me a *these-guys-are-nothin'* smile. But before I could shout *Look out!* his twin whacked the knife out of his hand and head-butted him in the back. He collapsed to his knees.

Brooks rolled across the asphalt, grabbed the knife, and stabbed her demon in the leg. It fell to the ground, howling.

My demon spun me into a headlock. It was too weird clutching my look-alike's skinny arm. Then it came to me. I knew the demon's weakness! With a left jab to his groin, I slipped out of his grasp, circled behind him, and swept his bad leg. As he collapsed, I jumped onto his back, locking him in a choke hold.

Brooks was busy running and ducking out of the Hondo monster's reach. Where the heck was Hondo? I jerked my guy's neck back like my uncle had taught me.

*Schripp.*

*Uh-oh.*

His thin-skinned neck ripped open easily. Brooks was right; it was pretty creepy to demolish someone who looked exactly like you. He crumpled to his knees and I hopped off his back as he gripped his open neck. Black tar-like gunk oozed out, along with chunks of hair. Man, the smell actually singed my nose hairs. Then he turned into a ribbon of black mist and was gone.

One down. Two to go.

I spotted Hondo, tool belt secured around his waist, charging madman-style—wild eyes, screeching howl. A screwdriver hurtled through the air and wedged into the Hondo demon's skull.

"Bull's-eye!" Hondo hollered, pumping his fist.

The Hondo-demon stumbled, jerked the hammer free, and righted himself. His face began to crack like dried mud, crumbling to the ground to reveal . . . you guessed it, a blue-skinned monster head. Green veins throbbed and bulged.

Slime oozed from the holes in his face and his monster chest heaved.

"We want the girl alive," said the demon. "But we'll take her corpse if we have to."

The air twisted and shimmered. A silvery smoke rose from the ground and now, instead of two Brookses, there were six. Three of them had the other three in a choke hold.

Hondo crouched like a tiger ready to pounce.

My eyes searched each Brooks frantically, looking for any clue to tell me which was the real one. "You'll have to take us down if you want her," I said.

"Zane," all the Brooks captives said in unison, "it's a trick." They were exact replicas—the voice, the freckles, the desperate eyes. How was I supposed to know which one to save?

It was like my dream where Rosie had appeared in all the trees. I remembered the flood, the fire . . .

My fingertips tingled. I felt an energy pulse beneath my skin and a power twisting from . . . the vat of frying oil inside the restaurant. Or was it coming from deep in the earth? Whatever it was, it was blazing hot. Something expanded inside of me, too big for my body to contain. . . . I took a deep breath and—

Then it was gone.

"What do we do?" Hondo ground out.

Immediately, the answer hit me. "Change, Brooks!" *Change into a hawk!* It was one thing to *look* like Brooks. It was another thing to *be* Brooks.

The Hondo demon said, "No need for anyone else to die tonight."

"You're not taking her," I growled.

"Seems we're at an impasse," he said.

"I'll go with them," one Brooks said. Then another said, "Please, Zane. Let me go."

Why wasn't she changing?! It would be so easy, if she would only shift into hawk form, because I was sure that was a Brooks thing no clone could pull off.

"Take me instead of her," I said.

"Zane, NO!" one Brooks hollered only to be echoed by the others.

The Hondo demon laughed. "Why would Ixtab want *you*?" His eyes roamed my short leg.

"Because I'm the one who set Ah-Puch free." I inched closer, heart racing, panic rising. But there wasn't time to be afraid. "And he's coming for his throne," I said. "It's too bad you guys are here fighting us instead of protecting your precious underworld. I bet Ah-Puch's already beaten down the door and stormed the place."

A low growl came from the demon. His face tensed, and he looked like he was about to lunge. "We don't have a door," he hissed.

Hondo clenched his fists at his sides. "I'm going to enjoy knocking this guy's head off."

Out of nowhere, the cashier appeared and threw a pot of hot frying oil on the Hondo demon's head.

"Run!" I screamed at the kid. "This isn't a game!"

The cashier actually smiled before he took off.

The Hondo demon, on the other hand, wasn't smiling. He clawed at his melting face as chunks of his body fell to the ground, vanishing like steam.

That left the three Brooks demons, gripping their twins by the throats.

"What's it gonna be?" Hondo said fiercely.

With a thrust to a demon's gut, one of the Brookses wriggled free, but her action was soon mirrored by her twins. The first Brooks locked eyes with me. "Holy K, Obispo," she gasped. "You going to stand there all night?"

"It's her!" I shouted to Hondo, and we charged.

The demons howled, then vanished into a thin trail of black smoke.

Brooks fell to her knees, grabbing her throat.

"Brooks!" I hurried over.

"We better get out of here before anything else goes down," Hondo said, glancing around nervously.

I helped Brooks to her feet. "Why'd they give up so easily?"

I asked Hondo. It didn't make sense. They'd had the numerical advantage.

"Probably to bring back an army?"

"I'm fine," Brooks said, shaking her head. But she was trembling. "I'm fine!" she repeated, then crawled into the bed of the truck.

I followed her even though she said she wanted to be alone. We both lay there, not talking, just looking up at the dark sky.

Hondo had us back on the highway a minute later. The world hummed by with the steady drone of the engine. I turned to face Brooks. She kept staring blankly at the stars. I didn't know what to say. But I felt like I needed to say something, to bring her back from wherever she was.

I picked a few nasty demon hairs out of my mouth and cleared my throat. "I think . . . maybe," I began, "I felt some kind of connection to . . . to something that felt like heat or the center of the earth . . . I can't be sure." I tried to find the right words. "Is that crazy?" My mind went through all the gods in my book—was there a god of the earth?

"It was probably just a coincidence," Brooks said sharply without looking at me.

"But I could feel it . . . in my fingertips, like I was holding on to some rope made up of heat and energy. And it felt dangerous, like I had to control it or *it* was going to control me."

"You should've let them take me," she mumbled.

"But . . . why would they want *you*?"

Brooks kept her eyes fixed on the sky.

I sat up. "Are you listening?"

"I heard you, Zane! You've got some godly power. . . . Good for you!"

"Hey. You okay?"

"You've ruined everything!" She sat up and huddled against the cab.

"Whoa! What're you talking about? I saved you!"

"*Saved?*" She let out an exasperated laugh, like she was offended or something.

I wanted to argue, to let her know she wasn't the only one freaked-out or scared or . . .

She fidgeted with the string on her hoodie. I was too afraid to say the wrong thing, so I bit back the words. And waited for the gears in her mind to stop turning.

It was like she was getting up the courage to tell me something I might not want to hear. I knew if I pushed too hard she'd never tell me anything.

A few minutes later she said, "Whenever I changed into a hawk, I could feel the sky. It was like a part of me. Even after I changed back, I could still feel it." She looked up at the stars. "I tried to . . . I wanted to claw out their eyes, but . . . nothing worked."

"What do you mean?"

"It's . . . it's gone, Zane."

I got an empty feeling in the pit of my stomach. "What's gone?"

"I'm . . . I'm not a hawk anymore."

## 19

"**What? How? You're a shape-shifter. How can**
your power just disappear?" My pulse raced.

"How should I know? But it's gone and—"

"Try again. Maybe you were nervous or something."

Brooks looked at me, her face like stone. "I *told* you. It's
gone!"

"Brooks . . . what's going on with you? Why aren't you telling me?"

"Forget I said anything!"

She knocked on the back window to ask Hondo to stop.
When he did, we climbed into the truck's cab. Without saying anything, Brooks made it clear that I wasn't to join her
in the backseat.

When I first met Brooks, I thought her eyes could hide
mountains. I always knew they held secrets she would never
tell me. But tonight, her eyes were cold and unblinking, and
they made me feel like I was walking on a crumbling stone
wall. She wasn't just hiding something big.

She was hiding something dark.

I rested my head against the window, trying to make
sense of everything. But Hondo wanted to relive his hammer slam over and over. "And did you see how the claw of the
hammer drove right into that monster's skull? It was a thing

of beauty, Zane. A real thing of beauty. Actually, it was kind of creepy, to see a hammer going into my face, or a face that looked like mine, but still..."

"Yeah, true beauty." I thought about the shadow magic Brooks said they used to make the imitations of us. What else could shadow magic do?

"Hondo?" I kept my eyes on the headlight beams shining across the highway.

"Yeah?"

"Thanks for coming and, er...for spending your money and..."

"Being a demon-fighting tank?" He chuckled. "You kidding? This is a rush, kid. Better than watching any wrestling match—even better than that time Meat-Grinder stole the title from reigning Dead Thief. Remember? Poor Dead Thief went to work at Home Depot after that." He shook his head like he really felt for the guy. "Who wants to be a ring-rat when they can actually be *in* the ring? No one, that's who." He slugged me in the arm. "You got guts, kid. Real guts."

Did I? I didn't feel so gutsy.

"But wrestling's a sport," I said. "This is...it's real life, and we could actually die." I'd hate myself if anything ever happened to Hondo.

"Better to die a freaking warrior," he said, "than a night-crawling janitor."

I don't think I'd ever loved the guy more.

As soon as I was asleep I fell into a dream. I was back home, walking through the desert toward the volcano. The sky was blood-red and a hot dry wind blew from the east. I looked down and saw that I was pushing a grocery cart, and inside was Ms. Cab in her chicken form, hopping from one foot to another.

"What're you doing in my dream?" I asked her as I pushed the cart over the bumpy earth.

"This is a futile effort."

"Are you going to yell at me again?"

She opened her beak, then closed it like whatever she was going to say, she'd changed her mind.

I asked, "How's Mr. Ortiz?"

She clucked, then said, "These dumb chicken eyes are worthless!"

"When I kill Ah-Puch you'll go back to your regular self."

"You must attack his blind side."

The earth began to shake and sparks flew from the volcano, launching themselves across the desert like mini fire-missiles aimed at my head. A terrible rumbling sound echoed across the land and a stream of lava burst out of the Beast, racing down the mountain right toward us.

Ms. Cab shook her head. "Time to wake up, Zane."

I spun the cart and raced away from the lava. "You can't outrun it," Ms. Cab said. The earth turned to quicksand and I began to sink along with the cart. Her beady chicken eyes narrowed. "I said to wake up, Zane. I'm in no mood to be swallowed by the earth."

"I'm trying!"

"And when you do, make sure to remember *I'm a chicken!*" She leaped onto the cart's handle and rammed her beak into my hand as the lava licked at my heels. I started to scream, but then I woke up, gripping my hand and kicking my legs.

The car was parked in a lot off a two-lane highway, and Hondo was gone. Brooks was still asleep in the backseat, thank God. Catching my breath, I looked at the back of my hand. There was a small red spot in the middle of it. First she'd screamed at me, and now she'd pecked me? Definitely needed to smash that eyeball.

It was barely dawn. The world was foggy and covered in gray.

I yawned, stretched my arms over my head, and rubbed my eyes.

Then I saw it. The beach. Right in front of me!

I sat there staring at it with wide eyes, because I didn't want to forget what it was like to see the ocean for the first time—the way the white waves rushed out of the fog like they were in a hurry. Or how the jagged cliffs loomed over the water like some kind of guardian.

"Brooks!" I shook her. "Check it out!"

She blinked awake, nodded, then closed her eyes again like the ocean was an inconvenience. Whatever.

Where were we? Out the window, a wooden sign read SOLANA BEACH. I reached for the road atlas, and my eyes roved over it until I saw we were in San Diego. Just a couple hours south of LA.

I got down from the truck. The air was cool and wet and salty.

I spotted Hondo over at a food truck on the other end of the parking lot. He waved at me and I motioned that I was going to check out the beach. A couple surfer guys were sitting on the back bumper of their van, pulling on their wetsuits. A golden Lab danced in place, whining.

It made me miss Rosie even worse.

I stepped onto the sand, trying to balance on my walking stick. But it was mushy and uneven, impossible to get a foothold on. The waves were only thirty or so yards away. Seeing the sea wasn't enough. I had to touch it.

I kicked off my sneakers and socks. The coarse sand was chilly and damp. Sharp bits of white shell poked out. After a few steps, I realized the stick was worthless. *This is no different from balancing on the edge of the volcano,* I told myself. One foot in front of the other, placing just the right amount of weight on each foot. I'd come face-to-face with the god of death and killed a demon runner. Surely I could walk across the sand.

I was worried Hondo would call me back any second, because once he'd had his breakfast and coffee, he'd want to get on the road. But no way was I going to waste this moment.

A seagull circled overhead as I took the last few steps between piles of brownish-green seaweed. *Ha-ha-ha,* it cried.

The cold waves touched my toes and I couldn't help but smile a huge goofy smile. Wow! The ocean was seriously a lot bigger close-up. I tossed my stick onto the beach and inched farther into the water. It was like ice, but I didn't care. I went in up to my ankles, then to my knees. My jeans were soaked and felt like they weighed a hundred pounds. A small white wave rushed toward me, knocking me over. I came up laughing, shaking the water out of my hair.

"You're not what I expected," a female voice said.

(I guess I should stop here and warn you gods that you are seriously not going to like this part of the story. So prepare yourselves.)

I turned, peering through the morning fog, but there was no one on the shore, and I couldn't see past the waves because the mist was too thick.

"Hello?" I called out.

No answer.

"Anyone there?" I shuffled backward toward the shore, shivering.

I suddenly felt like I was being watched. A tingle ran through me, and I didn't know if it was because I was freezing or something else. Maybe I'd imagined the voice. Yeah, I know, but a guy can hope, can't he?

Grabbing my stick, I dragged it through the thick wet sand. ZANE WAS HERE.

Then came the weird thing—in the empty space next to my name, new letters materialized slowly, as if invisible fingers were writing in the sand.

LOOK

What the . . . ? I scanned the empty beach, did a one-eighty to search the water, but I was alone. I dropped to my knees and wrote furiously with my finger: WHO ARE YOU?

Holding my breath, I waited. Then . . .

LOOK

I stared hard at the letters until a wave washed them away. Then the wall of mist vanished, and beyond the waves a woman sat on a surfboard, bobbing gently. She had shockingly white blond hair but was too far away for me to see any other details.

"Come out," she said, and strangely, I could hear her as if she were standing right next to me.

Was she delusional? No way was I going to dive under those waves and swim up to some stranger who could write in the sand like a ghost.

"You must hurry. . . . We only have minutes," she said.

"Why don't you come to the shore?"

"The time rope won't reach that far."

*Time rope?*

"I've had enough demons after my head." I plopped onto the sand. "So whatever you want to tell me, you can do it from there."

She waded closer. Then something jerked her back. She took a frustrated breath. "Your father sent me."

Okay, she had my attention now. I jumped to my feet. "You know my father?"

"Shhh. . . . You want them to hear you?"

I looked around. There was no one else here, unless you counted the seagull and the surfer guys still in the parking lot. "Them?"

"Time is of the essence, and the longer you stand on that shore, the less time I have to help you in your quest."

I inched toward the water suspiciously. "How do I know you won't drown me?"

"Because your father would demolish me if I touched a hair on your head."

I probably should've walked away, but I was curious.

Maybe she could tell me who my father was once and for all. Maybe he really had sent her. I hadn't forgotten the distant image of the guy on the pyramid and how he'd tried to stop me from making a deal with Ah-Puch. But since then? MIA.

Carefully, I waded in. The first wave knocked me over.

"Dive under," she instructed. "Or you'll never get past the breakers."

As the next wave rolled toward me, I dove beneath. The water was icy and dark. The salt burned my eyes and made my skin itch, and my heart raced unevenly, like a skipping stone. I came up for air just as another wave was forming. I dove again.

Finally, I was past the waves and I swam through the rippling water to where the woman waited, bobbing on her shiny black surfboard. I treaded water, keeping enough distance to vamoose if I had to.

"Hello, Zane," she said. Okay, so not only did she have white blond hair with caramel-brown streaks, it was knotted into dreadlocks and looked like she hadn't washed it in a century. She wore a tattered leopard-skin cape. It had a hood that hung to the side. Her mouth was turned up like she was on the verge of a smile, and her ears were pointed, but instead of being where they were supposed to be, they stuck out the top of her head like a cat's. And her eyes? They burned green *and* aqua-blue, constantly changing like a turning kaleidoscope.

I told myself to take a deep breath as I floated in the water. To be calm. So what if a surfer cat lady wanted to talk to me? Oh God! What if she worked for Ixtab? What if she *was* Ixtab? I remembered the image of Ixtab in my book—always with a rope around her neck. This woman was clutching a gold rope, its end trailing into the dark waters as if it was connected to an anchor.

I swept my arms forward, trying to distance myself, but the tide was like a magnet pulling me closer and closer. Okay, so this was a *really* bad idea. And just like that, the tide stopped and the waves froze in mid-crash. The air went still. It was as if the whole world had stopped spinning.

The cat-surfer ran her hands through the sea and a silver bodyboard appeared. "Join me before you drown. Quickly." So she didn't want to plunge me into the depths of the Pacific. I needed the rest, so I cradled the board and brought myself to a straddled sitting position.

"You g-g-got a w-w-wet s-suit I c-c-could b-b-borrow?" I shivered.

She looked around nervously.

Fine, no magic wet suit was going to appear. I supposed I should've been grateful for the bodyboard.

"Who ar-are y-y-you?" I asked, my teeth chattering. *Please, please, please, don't say Ixtab*, I prayed.

"I am the goddess of time. For now, you may call me Pacific," she said, arching a perfect brow.

I didn't remember ever reading about any such goddess. "How c-c-come I've never heard of y-y-you?"

Pacific's gaze intensified. "I was erased. From the glyphs, my people's stories, as if I never existed. I was one of the most powerful of the gods," she said with a huff. "The great sky-watcher. I taught the people to read the stars, to plant their harvest at the appointed time, to prepare for the seasons. But then I made a grave mistake." She narrowed her eyes. "I told of a prophecy the gods didn't want to hear."

"P-p-p-rophecy?" My voice hitched in my throat.

"I have many names, Zane. I am the Great Fate, the soothsayer who foretold of a boy who would be born unlike any we'd ever seen."

I gave her a blank stare. Holy crap! *She* was *the* soothsayer? My blood started to warm up. "You're Ms. Cab's—"

"Great ancestor. Not by blood, of course, but by secret. But that doesn't matter now. What matters is that you're a—"

"Halfer, I know."

"Half...?" She blinked slowly like she was trying to understand what the word meant.

I tried again. "You know, like a hybrid, a mix? Crossbreed?"

Pacific scooped a handful of the sea into her hand. "The gods do not measure in human terms. You may be half, or more than half."

"Half is plenty, thanks."

She sighed. "My prophecy frightened the gods because it brought to mind the hero twins, the very first godborns. Their mother was *Sh-keek*." (Spelled Ixkik'—I had to look it up.) "She was from the underworld," Pacific said. "And some say she was part human."

Right. The one who fell for the skull. Wait, did she say *godborns*? I hadn't heard that term before.

Pacific swept a piece of knotted blond hair from her pale face. "The twins inspired jealousy in the gods," she continued, "so the gods established a law that never again would such creatures be born. And the punishment for any god who disobeyed?"

"Vat of boiling acid?" I guessed.

"A long and torturous death," she said with a scowl. "Seeing their fear, I knew I could never reveal that not only would you be descended from a god, but you were also the one destined to release Ah-Puch, the very god they had imprisoned. Their rage would have shaken the stars from the sky."

Okay, so my dad was a criminal . . . sort of. He must have heard about the prophecy, and yet it hadn't stopped him from falling in love with my mom. Talk about hardheaded.

Then I had another thought. "Hang on. So how does Ms. Cab know?"

"I shared the prophecy with another seer from the bravest lineage, a lineage I could trust. I asked that she preserve its truth for generations so when the time came for the prophecy to be fulfilled, Ah-Puch could be stopped and your true identity kept a secret. But even she didn't know that you were to be a godborn."

So that's how Ms. Cab had gotten the gig. I put the events in order: godborn twins, imprisoned god of death, jealous other gods, dangerous secret. That's where I came in. *Ugh!*

She blinked her cat eyes, shifting her gaze to the dark waters. "I only told the gods an 'innocent' would be the one to release Ah-Puch," she went on. "I left out the part that he would be godborn. And you know what the gods did then? They used a powerful magic to ensure that only a god could release Ah-Puch."

So Brooks's guess was right. "They thought they made the Stinking One's prison foolproof," I said. "But then I came along—the innocent fool."

Pacific laughed lightly. "The gods were the fools. They thought they could bypass *my* sight?" She shook her head. "They never put the pieces together."

"Okay, and what about my dad? Why would he risk torture by getting together with my mom?" I didn't want to think any more about that. "And . . . you said you know him?"

"We have been friends since the beginning. He was the only one who helped me when the gods erased me from memory." She spoke quickly. "I was to be executed, but your father volunteered to do it himself. Instead, he brought me here, to live beneath the ocean, where K'ukumatz hides me. I owe him."

"K'ukumatz? Isn't he the feathered serpent? God of the sea?"

"Also known as Kukuulkaan."

*Great!* So my dad, and K'ukumatz (aka, god of coolness), and Pacific were keeping the biggest secret of all time from the other gods. My side cramped. "Why didn't my dad come to tell me all this himself? Why'd he send you?"

Pacific frowned. "And bring the gods to you? That wouldn't be very strategic, would it?"

My head was about to explode. "So who is he?"

"Only he can reveal himself to you."

*Naturally.* My heart banged against my chest like a wild beast trying to break free. "Then why hasn't he?!"

Pacific pulled her hood over her head, tucking her hair

beneath. "The gods would kill him if he were to claim you. They would know he was the one who had broken the Sacred Oath. Don't you see?"

I felt sick. My heart, my stomach, my head—they pulsed with an anger that shook me to my core. So my dad didn't want to claim me because he was worried about saving his own butt?

As if she could read my mind, Pacific leaned forward and whispered, "If the gods were to find out who you are, they would kill *you*, too. Your father is trying to protect you."

Or protect *himself*! I didn't know what was worse: being marked by the gods or having my dad abandon me on purpose. "So what am I supposed to do? Hide out for the rest of my life?"

"Yes."

She was definitely delusional. "Thanks, but no thanks! I don't care about the gods. I'm not hiding!"

Pacific sighed. "Stubborn, like your father."

I realized Pacific had a lot of information that could help me, and I wasn't about to let my dad (did I even have to call him that anymore?) get in the way of my quest. "You said you control time?" I asked. Because *that* would be awesome and totally help me crush Ah-Puch.

"I am the *keeper* of time, but no longer the controller of it. Just as I keep but cannot control fate. And now my powers have been reduced. . . . Using them too much will draw attention to me and the gods would know I live."

"What do you mean *reduced*?" I kicked my legs under the

water to try to stay warm. "You said you were one of the most powerful."

Gripping the rope tighter, Pacific said, "When the gods stole the life from the stories that made me real, they took much of my power."

Geez. These gods seemed like the biggest jerks on the planet. (Yeah, you read that right. Jerks with a capital *J*.) Pacific's eyes burned with a fierceness that made me hope I was never on her bad side.

"Wait a second," I said as an idea formed. "You said the gods don't know about me being a hybrid, I mean godborn, whatever. But *you* do...and my dad does...and two of the worst ones ever know about me, too: Ixtab and Ah-Puch." I knew that, when it comes to a secret, the more people who know about it, the more likely the secret isn't a secret anymore. "What if they tell the others?"

Pacific let out a light laugh that almost sounded like a purr. "Your father and I have protected this information for ages. We are not about to reveal it. As for Ixtab and Ah-Puch, yes, they do pose a problem, but let's hope they are too busy waging their own wars."

Was she kidding? That was a pretty big hope!

"Zane, your father," Pacific said, "he asked me to give you something."

"Why would I want anything from him? He won't even tell me who he is."

Pacific drew closer, and as she did, a huge spotted cat at least four times the normal size stepped out of her body like some kind of feline ghost. I nearly flipped off my board as the fierce cat—a leopard?—stalked across the water like it was a solid surface and stopped right in front of me, blinking its golden eyes.

"Zane," Pacific said sternly, "you must focus before they find us. Now listen, I know about your quest to defeat the great Ah-Puch. So does your father, and he isn't happy about it."

"Yeah, well, he gave up his right to an opinion when he decided to leave me in the dark!" Wait a sec...how'd she know?

She must've seen the question forming, because she said, "I'm time—I can see past, present, and future. The continuum runs through me still. They couldn't take *that* away."

"Does that mean you can see my future?" A tight lump formed in my throat. Did she know whether I was going to defeat Ah-Puch or end up a miserable soldier of death shoveling souls for the rest of my existence?

"Once, I might have been able to, but now..." Her voice trailed off, then she sat straighter and said, "There are choices that affect circumstances. One choice can lead to victory... the other to defeat. Today I fulfill my debt to your father."

I suddenly felt like I was standing at the bottom of the volcano waiting for an avalanche of rocks to bury me.

"Time is unraveling, Zane." Pacific's eyes searched the skies then found mine again. "You will need great courage to defeat Ah-Puch. More courage than you can imagine."

"I...I took down demon runners. I..." Didn't that count for something?

"Not that kind of courage. Something more."

I scanned the shore, trying to find Hondo's truck. When I was little and he was first teaching me about wrestling, he used to say that the real heroes didn't always win the match, but they always had courage. Even when defeat was staring them in the face.

Something growled beneath the ocean. Foamy bubbles floated to the surface. I gripped my board. "What was that?"

"I can't hold the time rope much longer," Pacific said with a note of panic that made me wish I was on solid ground. "It's time, Zane."

The ocean began to churn again.

Pacific narrowed her eyes. Then the leopard drew so close to her I thought it would vanish back into her body. Gently, Pacific reached into its mouth while petting its head softly, like I used to do with Rosie. She carefully removed a sharp incisor as if only thread connected it to the jungle cat's mouth.

"This is jaguar jade . . . the oldest magic in the universe. It will help you," she said, handing it to me. The tooth was about four inches long, bigger than what I expected, and it had a razor-sharp tip. As I turned it over in my hand, the tooth turned a deep green and pulsed with a strange warmth. I didn't get it. What good was a jade tooth when I was up against the god of death? Was I supposed to stab him in the eye with it?

"*This* is what he wanted you to give me?" My throat closed up as I turned the tooth, examining it. It didn't look very magical.

Pacific's gaze fell to my wrist, to Ah-Puch's mark. She let out a small gasp. "I see."

I looked down at the stupid symbol, rubbing it in the water like I could wash it off.

"Things are graver than . . ." Pacific began. She took a deep breath, straightened her hood, and said, "You must promise not to tell a soul about me." Her powerful gaze made me think she could see right into my mind. Then her eyes went wide. The rope she was holding jerked her beneath the water. The jaguar vanished and the sea tumbled violently.

Waves crashed. It was like someone had started the earth spinning again but gave it one too many whirls. As I began to paddle toward the shore, an enormous wave formed behind me, swelling bigger and bigger until it looked ten stories tall.

Pacific's voice echoed across the ocean. *When I tell you to kick, you must do so with all your strength.* I watched with fear as that wave grew. At the crest, it bulged, and I knew it was going to break any second and take me with it.

*Now, Storm Runner. Now!*

I paddled and kicked like a madman, trying to keep up with the monster wave. As it broke, I rocketed forward, then plunged underneath. I was pitched and thrown from side to side, top to bottom, spinning so violently I didn't know which way was up.

Something pressed into my back and, with great force, thrust me through the water at unimaginable speed. My lungs felt like they might collapse any second. Just as I was about to break the surface, I turned and saw the jaguar's face looming in the dark sea.

The next thing I knew, I was on the beach, choking and

spitting up salt water. My body shook uncontrollably as I rolled over into a pile of slimy seaweed.

I sat up, chest heaving, and looked all around me, but the jade tooth was gone. I must've dropped it! I scrambled to my knees and started digging, like it might be buried in the sand. But it was nowhere to be found. Panic clutched my throat and I couldn't breathe.

At the same moment, a gentle wave came in and touched my feet. I turned to see something pale green wash onto the sand. I snatched it up, and my heart pounded with relief as I stared down at the thing.

"What are you?" I whispered.

Wait a second. Had she called me *Storm Runner*?

I traced the jade's smooth edges and something stirred in me. The tooth might've looked like a cold hunk of nothing, but it was something.

Something that mattered.

# 20

**I hauled myself into the passenger seat of the**
truck.

Hondo gave me a once-over and shook his head. "You've
got a piece of seaweed in your hair." I picked it out and glanced
at Brooks. She was in the backseat studying the gateway map
and pretty much avoiding eye contact with me. What was up
with her? I couldn't wait to get her alone so we could talk, *if*
she'd talk to me.

"I need to change my clothes." I reached behind the seat for
my backpack. "Uh—can you . . . turn around?" I asked Brooks.

She rolled her eyes, then lifted the map so it covered
her face completely. I peeled off my sea-drenched jeans and
T-shirt, yanked on fresh clothes, and transferred the jade
tooth to my dry pants' pocket. I tossed the wet stuff through
the cab's back window so it could air out in the bed. I still felt
chilled to the bone, so I pulled on my gray sweatshirt.

I figured I had the worst luck in the universe. It was one
thing to have a bum leg; it was another to be the unfortunate
chump who had freed the god of death. And to have to hide
to avoid being on the gods' most wanted list? Yeah, that was
pretty awful, too. But there was something even more terrible than any of that: being the living proof that someone had

broken the Sacred Oath. It was too many shades of depressing and made me feel more different and alone than I ever had.

"So, Capitán..." Hondo slipped on a pair of Ray-Bans as the morning sun began to peek out of the clouds. "Where do we go once we're in Venice?"

Brooks didn't lower the map. "It's on the beach."

"They live *on* the beach?" I asked.

"Sort of," she said. "You'll see when we get there." Her voice was tired, and she looked pale and drained. I wanted to talk to her to find out if I could help. Maybe, if we put our heads together, we could figure out why she couldn't shape-shift anymore. I also wanted to fill her in about Pacific and the jaguar jade ... except Pacific had made me promise not to tell anyone about her.

I leaned back, folding my arms tightly over my chest.

Why wouldn't Brooks open up to me? What was her deal with Ixtab, anyway? Why the heck would the new landlord of Xib'alb'a send demons after Brooks? She must've been in some pretty big trouble, but what kind?

Then another possibility struck me, making me feel sick. Was Brooks a double agent of some sort, playing both sides? Could I trust her not to blab the truth about me being a god-born? Too many people knew about it already. Stupid secrets! They're life-ruiners.

Hondo turned up some punk rock music so loud my teeth rattled in my head.

Out of the corner of my eye I could see Brooks gazing out the window with a faraway look that worried me. Whatever Brooks was wanted for, it couldn't be half as bad as being wanted for breaking the god of death, darkness, and destruction out of prison.

We cruised up the coast on Highway 101 while Hondo jammed to his tunes. He sang along to some song about *final chances* and *all or nothing*. If there were a god of punk rock, he'd *definitely* listen to this station.

Venice Beach felt like a tightly packed box. Cars were bumper-to-bumper on Venice Boulevard, and drivers honked like somehow that would make the traffic move faster. The place was buzzing. Apartments, houses, and stores were crammed together with only narrow alleys to separate them. Telephone poles and palm trees lined the street. We passed a dilapidated building with a mural on it of a blond girl in roller skates with a thought cloud that read: HISTORY IS MYTH.

*It will be soon, if the twins don't help me*, I thought.

Crowds strolled casually down the road—people in flip-flops, cutoff shorts, and bikini tops. Some of the guys were shirtless, even. Maybe that was a thing in California, but where I was from? No chance!

As we passed narrow streets, I caught glimpses of bridges arching over water canals. I'd seen pictures of the real Venice. This place was simply a newer, smaller version. The canals disappeared into a tangle of shadowed alleys and it felt like even this *place* had secrets.

"Take a right on Pacific," Brooks said. My muscles tensed just hearing the name come out of her mouth. She went back to studying the gateway map. What was she looking for?

"Any gateways nearby?" I asked.

She folded up the map and put it in her backpack. "None."

Hondo let out a low whistle. "Before this is all done, I better get to travel through one of those gateways."

Before this was all over I just wanted to make sure the world wasn't destroyed. I didn't have a plan for after the twins. I was hoping that whatever they told us would help us figure out our next steps. I didn't care what Brooks said about them being selfish, obnoxious jerks, or kings of their own magic mafia—I wasn't leaving here without their secret to defeating Ah-Puch. With only a couple of days left, we were running out of time.

Then a terrible thought grabbed hold of me. "What if Ah-Puch's already found them?"

"He hasn't," Brooks said.

"How do you know?"

"You'll never find parking close enough," Brooks said to Hondo. "So park over there." She pointed to a public lot. Then she said to me, "Because they're really good hiders. They have the best magic guarding them. No one gets in or out unless they want them to."

That reminded me of the jaguar jade—*the oldest magic in the universe*, Pacific had said. What did that mean, and how was it supposed to help me if I didn't even know how to use it?

Maybe it was a conjuring stone. I tested it by clutching it in my fist while wishing for a stuffed sopaipilla for breakfast. I shut my eyes and held out my other hand expectantly, but nothing happened. No warm doughy yumminess for me.

A minute later we crossed the congested boulevard, then weaved down an alley lined with trash cans before emerging onto the boardwalk.

I had to stop and really take it all in. The breeze smelled like salt and old books. And there were maniac skateboarders (shirtless) zooming by, people on bikes and skates pulling their dogs along on leashes, and a row of vendors selling things: wooden flutes, T-shirts, throwback movie posters (Hondo wanted a *Scarface* poster but didn't want to pony up the twenty bucks for it). A rainbow-wigged juggler entertained onlookers while an acrobatic break-dancer competed for his own crowd. A few paces ahead there was a tarot-card reader with dreadlocks, strumming a sad blues song on his guitar.

He sang in a deep low voice: *"The prophesied days are a-comin'.... Oh, they are a- comin'. Find the shadows and hide, for the days are a comin'...."*

I tried not to look at him, because I knew the second I did, he'd wave me over and try to get me to buy a glimpse of my future. No thanks!

Brooks planted her palm on her forehead. "Ugh—I forgot our backpacks in the truck. Wait here." She grabbed the keys from Hondo and took off.

Hondo saw it as a sign that he needed to go back to try and renegotiate for that *Scarface* poster. So there I was, only a few feet away from the blues-singing, dreadlock-sporting tarot-card reader. I told myself to stay put and look busy. I stuffed my hands in my pockets, whistled a few notes of "Frosty the Snowman" (I had Christmas on my mind, because maybe I was never going to have another one, okay?), and craned my neck to the sky, but it was as if the guy's song had long arms to grab me. My feet wandered over and stopped right in front of his chalkboard that read: FIVE MINUTES FOR FIVE DOLLARS.

He wore silver-rimmed shades, and when I stopped, he smiled, showing off twinkling gold front teeth. "I have your future in my pocket," he said. His accent was thick and strange.

"Uh—that's okay." I didn't have any money, and even if I did, I was pretty sick of prophecies and doomed futures.

The man's bronze skin shone in the sunlight. "You are a boy of many troubles. I know where you're headed."

As I started to walk away, he said, "The prophecy is coming."

*Yeah?* I thought. "It already came."

He smiled again and pulled up his sunglasses so I could see his dark eyes. His eyebrows looked like they'd been burned off, leaving behind small scars. "That was only the beginning," he said. "The Prophecy of Fire. But fire spreads. Until it burns everything in its path."

It had to be a coincidence. How could he possibly know?

A faraway drum sounded. The waves crashed. Or was that my stomach acid?

Brooks came up, handed me my backpack, and grabbed me by the arm. "What're you doing?" She threw a quick glance in the guy's direction, then said to me, "Come on."

The man pulled his sunglasses over his eyes and began strumming his guitar, singing, *"There are liars in our midst and the storm is a-comin'."*

"What was that about?" Brooks asked.

"What do you mean?"

Brooks stopped and turned to me, clutching her backpack. The amber flecks in her eyes burned bright even in the shade. I decided they were definitely the eyes of a hawk, and that

gave me a strange kind of hope that her shape-shifting ability wasn't gone forever. She tilted her head and studied me.
"What did he tell you?"

"He knew about the Prophecy of Fire, Brooks! How?"

Brooks looked shaken. She opened her mouth to speak,
but nothing came out.

I looked over my shoulder. "He said a storm was coming!
Maybe I should pay him to read my future. . . ."

"NO!" Brooks shouted. Then she took me by the shoulders
and made me look into her eyes. "*You* make your future, Zane.
Got it? All these other things? Distractions. Now come on.
You have to stay focused."

"But what if he can help us?"

Hondo ran to catch up. He was holding a rolled poster.
"What's all the arguing about?"

"We weren't arguing," I said, clenching my jaw.

"Yes, we were," Brooks said as we continued walking.

Hondo gave me a *sorry-dude-but-you-were-totally-arguing*
look.

It was pretty awful when you saw and heard things other
people didn't. Maybe being part god had fried my brain and
I was officially deranged. Or it could have been some more
shadow magic to distract me. Or that guy was just my imagination at work. Oh God, maybe Pacific hadn't been real,
either. . . .

I reached into my pocket. Relief spread through me as my
fingers found the jade still there.

As we hurried down the boardwalk, I kept wondering why
my dad would want to give me a jaguar tooth, of all things. . . .

Why not something useful, like a sword, or poison-tipped daggers? Heck, why not help me bring down Ah-Puch himself? If my mom had his kind of powers, she'd take on the whole world to save me.

I wondered if she was worried about us. *Maybe I should try to call her....* Bad idea. She might wig out and force us to come home. Then a brilliant idea struck me. I could ask Ms. Cab about her the next time the chicken appeared in one of my dreams.

We made our way past more booths, vendors, and street artists. Hondo nearly collapsed when he saw Muscle Beach—a whole gym right there on the boardwalk with huge dudes pumping iron in the sun. He stopped in front of the bright blue railing and smiled like a little kid. "This is awesome!" But Brooks urged us on, saying she just wanted to get this over with.

Halfway down the boardwalk, Brooks led us into a store called Jazz-E.

There were rows of colorful bikes, with a few scooters and longboards mixed in. Dozens of surfboards lined the walls. Toward the back of the shop was a little corner filled with postcards, shells, and other trinkets. The walls were painted gold and pink, and the place smelled like the cotton-candy booth at the state fair.

"Are we renting a bike?" Hondo asked.

Brooks shook her head and went up to the cashier at the back of the store. His face was planted in one of those tabloid magazines, but I could see he was huge. Even sitting, I guessed he was at least eight feet tall. He wore an eye patch, a silver hoop in one ear, and a plaid vest with gold buttons. He looked more like a pro-wrestling fashion pirate than a store clerk.

"It's a fine day for blood," Brooks said.

"Blood for the gods," the giant said without looking up.

"Blood for the gods," Brooks repeated.

Finally he raised his eyes. A huge smile spread across his clean-shaven face. "Little Hawk!" His voice boomed. He rounded the counter and scooped Brooks into his arms. "I thought I might never see you again."

Standing up, the guy looked even weirder! He wore torn jeans and flip-flops the size of doormats. At least he had a shirt on under his vest.

"Hey, Jazz." Brooks relaxed into his hug and smiled.

When he set her down, her cheeks were flushed.

"Don't tell me you're back," he said, lifting one brow. "Surprised you got by the gatekeeper without me getting a phone call," Jazz said. "The guy's slacking."

"Gatekeeper?" I asked.

That was the first time Jazz noticed me. Yeah, he was big and burly and sported more than a few tattoos on his arms, but the guy was like a jolly giant. He couldn't stop smiling. Except when he looked at me. Then the smile disappeared like mist. "Who's *this*?" he asked.

"I'm Zane," I said, trying to sound cool, or at least not like a big chicken. But seriously, this guy could've smashed me under one flip-flop if he'd wanted to.

"We're friends," Brooks said. "And this is Hondo. He's a wrestling champ," she added, like he had just won a trophy yesterday.

Hondo tried to make himself a few inches taller by standing on tiptoe when he shook the big cashier's hand. And his voice went a few notches deeper. "Good to meet you, man."

"This is Jazz, descendant of the great Maya giants," Brooks said.

"Jazz-*E*," the giant corrected. "And no, I didn't steal my name from Jay-Z. More like the other way around. But you can call me Jazz. Just *don't* confuse me with Sipakna," he insisted. "That hombre was an arrogant, wicked giant, giving us all a bad name. I come from much better stock."

*Whoa!* I was in the presence of a real live giant! But how did Brooks know him? Was he some long-lost relative? A friend of the family's?

Jazz's gray eye crinkled around the edges when he looked at Brooks. "Any amigos of Little Hawk's are . . ." He hesitated, then laughed. "Ha! Kidding. I don't keep amigos." Then to Brooks, "What brings you back here? I know you don't need a surfboard."

Brooks glanced around the shop. "I need . . . to see them. Jordan and Bird."

Who were *they*? I wondered.

Jazz crossed his boulder-size arms over his chest. "After what they did—?"

"Jazz . . ." Brooks's voice trembled. "My friends . . . they need to talk to the twins, and you know the only way they might help . . ."

"Is to trade magic or play their game." Jazz nodded gravely like we were asking him to supply us with daggers for hand-to-hand combat.

"We don't have any magic to trade, and what do you mean *game*?" I asked. Brooks hadn't said anything about a game before this. "Like Monopoly?" I guessed. Or maybe Scrabble. I was a champ at Scrabble. Or maybe he meant mind games. I got a terrible sinking feeling in the pit of my stomach. Hondo, on the other hand, was beaming, practically salivating at the idea of competition.

Jazz rubbed his chin as he went back behind the counter, mumbling something under his breath. He tapped some buttons on the cash register, then pulled out two quarter-size black stones. They were round, flat, and shiny.

"What's this?" Hondo said, taking one from the giant.

"Our key to see the twins," Brooks said.

"Made from ancient obsidian," Jazz added. "Magician stone."

"Looks like volcanic glass," I muttered, taking the other. I'd seen it once in a museum, and I used to search the Beast for any traces of it, but I'd never found any.

Jazz closed the register and eyed me. "This kid's smart. Where'd you find him?"

Brooks said, "It's kind of a long story."

"Wouldn't have to do with—?"

Brooks cut Jazz off with an icy glare, and I wondered what she was afraid of him saying. She adjusted her pack. "So, Jazz . . . any trouble around here?"

He leaned forward, raising a brow. "What kind of trouble?"

"You know—creepy demons, angry gods, that sort of thing," I said.

"The kind that ride motorcycles," Hondo added.

I watched Jazz carefully. There was something about him ... the way his face twitched and his eyes shifted. It looked like he was uncomfortable in his own skin—like he was wearing a mask.

"Well," Jazz said, "if you're talking about Loser of the Underworld, no. We haven't seen him. Word on the street is he's out for revenge. All sorts of theories are flying around: he's aligning with his brothers, searching for his underlords, looking to free every enemy of the gods. No one knows for sure. But we've got eyes everywhere. The whole boardwalk is filled with our guys: jugglers, acrobats—"

"They work for you?" Hondo asked.

"Every vendor out there works for the twins," Jazz said.

"But—" Hondo began.

"I know," Jazz said. "They're meant to look like regular humans. Can't wear a sign around our necks, now, can we?"

So the tarot reader was a gatekeeper. I wondered how many other people I'd met were part of this Maya mayhem, hiding in plain sight.

"You need to protect more than the boardwalk," Brooks said to Jazz.

He nodded. "We've got them posted at each of the cosmic roads, too."

I was about to ask what the heck a cosmic road was when Brooks explained. "Magic roads the gods travel."

*That* wasn't in my book.

"Don't worry, Little Hawk," Jazz said. "We used extra magic to guard the place. The twins even shut down their lair, moved uptown."

"What do you mean *moved?*" Brooks said. "They've been *here* . . . for, like, ever."

"Security's orders. But their new crib? Man, it's incredible. The view . . ." He sighed.

"How far is it?" I asked. I mean, what if they'd relocated to Nebraska?

But Jazz didn't answer. He merely shook his head, then pounded his fist into his palm. "Believe me, when I catch the idiot bonehead who let Ah-Puch out, I'm going to send him spinning into the center of the Milky Way."

My heart skipped a beat. "Yeah," I muttered, "bonehead." Great! Not only would the gods be after me when they found out I was a godborn, but pretty much *everyone* would want me dead once they found out I was the bonehead who had freed Ah-Puch.

Hondo cleared his throat. "Maybe the bonehead had a good reason."

"Like what?" Jazz's face went stone still.

"Like maybe it was an accident," Hondo said. "Or maybe one of his demon runner things let him out."

"That's a lot of maybes. . . . What did you say your name was? Hondo?" Jazz opened his mouth and tilted a can of Red Bull over it. Once the can was empty, he collapsed it with one hand. "Only problem is, the gods put him away, so a god had to let him out. And no god would break the Sacred Oath, so that tells me there are some dark secrets swirling around, and wherever there are secrets, there's a teller. Give it time— someone's going to squeal."

My knees felt weak, and for the first time I had a terrible

sense I was leading Hondo and Brooks off the edge of a high cliff.

"So all the gods know?" Brooks said, twisting her mouth.

*Man, news sure traveled fast!* I thought.

"Yep," Jazz said. "But now they're pointing fingers, fighting among themselves." He tossed his crushed can into a trash can. "All the seers went dark." He spoke to Brooks as if Hondo and I weren't even there. "This is serious, Little Hawk. Very serious."

I stuffed my hands in my pockets and gripped the jade. "So then . . . why don't the gods come up with a way to recapture Ah-Puch?"

"Can't find him, kid. Even if they could, it would start a huge war. Alliances would crack, deals would be struck, and we'd all end up dead anyway." Then, with a shrug, he added, "I guess we've had peace for too long."

Brooks turned to me and Hondo. "The Sacred Oath was meant to keep the peace."

"Like a treaty?" I said. "Did they sign it?"

"Blood is thicker than ink," Jazz said.

Brooks shuffled her feet uneasily, then said to Jazz, "We need one more thing. . . ."

Jazz straightened his eye patch. "What's that?"

"Encantamiento."

I wondered what Brooks meant by *enchantment.*

Jazz nodded. "Harder to come by these days. But for you? Anything." Then he started humming the same song the tarot-card reader had been singing.

"That song . . ."

Jazz leaned his beefy arms on the counter and glared at me. "What about it?"

"It's the same..."

"Kid, you've never heard that song."

I don't know why I didn't just walk away, or agree with the giant who was likely to send me spinning into the Milky Way. But the words forced themselves out. "The tarot reader. That's his song. *The prophesied days are a-comin'.*"

The giant's forehead started to sweat. He wiped it with the back of his hand and rose slowly, swaying.

"Jazz?" That was Brooks. "Hurry! Zane, Hondo—find some sugar."

Jazz kept rising, or maybe his legs were growing. And before I knew it, his head had reached the ceiling, which was about fifteen feet high. One of his vest buttons popped off, and his jeans ripped along the seams. It was like watching the Hulk transform before my eyes. Except thankfully, Jazz wasn't turning green.

"It's his diabetes," Brooks spat. She stepped between me and the giant and held her arms out in front of her. "Jazz, it's okay. I'll get you some more Red Bull. Or some chocolate." She glanced around quickly. "Any candy around here?"

Hondo hurried across the store but came back empty-handed.

"So you met Santiago." Jazz spoke slowly, but his voice had raised a few decibels, shaking the walls and hammering my eardrums. "That's *very* interesting."

Brooks found a small chocolate and handed it to her giant

friend. "Come on, you know what happens when your sugar level drops. Eat this."

Jazz's eye grew bloodshot and his face became ashen. Reluctantly, he took the chocolate and didn't even bother to unwrap it before he popped it in his mouth. I quickly slipped behind the counter before he could stomp me like a bug, and there I found a stash of Red Bulls. Up close, his huge toes were nasty and very hairy. He seriously needed to clip those nails.

I tossed a six-pack to Brooks, who opened each can and handed them over before the giant's head rammed through the roof.

Jazz guzzled two cans, then staggered. His eye ballooned, he hiccupped, and then came a burp with the force of an arctic blast, except this was warm and wet and blew my hair back. And the stench? If you can imagine Coke mixed with beans and rotting cabbage, you've got a good idea of the smell.

Hondo fell back, covering his nose and mouth. "Dude, gross!"

Slowly, Jazz began to shrink back to his normal eight-foot status. "Ohhhh..." He mopped his brow with a towel. "That was a relief."

Brooks tapped her foot impatiently. "You *know* you need to keep your sugar level up. Your diabetes is serious. How many times have I told you?"

Jazz threw his hands in the air. "I'm trying, okay?" Then his gray eye met mine and held my gaze for a long three-count. "You're sure you met Santiago?"

"Uh..." Was that a trick question?

"You couldn't have seen him," he said, like he was answering his own question.

"Why not?" I asked, insulted. I know what I saw.

"He's invisible."

"Oh," I said sarcastically. "I mean, if you put it that way." I hesitated, then let the truth rip. *"I still saw him!"*

Jazz narrowed his eye. "So tell me, *Zane"*—he stretched my name long and thin—"who *are* you, really? And what are you doing here?"

I wasn't about to admit I was the bonehead he wanted to crush, or a godborn. Geez, how many wanted lists could I be on? I tugged my sweatshirt sleeve lower to cover the god of death's stupid mark and stuffed my hand in my pants pocket.

Brooks shifted uneasily. I could tell she wanted to say something but didn't know what. *That* was a first.

"I'm searching for my dad," I blurted.

Jazz grunted like he knew it was a half-truth. I didn't like the way he was ogling me. It was like he was thinking *liar, liar, liar,* and the more he thought it, the hotter I felt. The jade turned over in my hand and pulsated.

Had someone turned on a heater? The room started to spin. Slowly at first, then so hard and fast I felt myself being ripped away from my body, one ragged thread at a time.

A terrible pain gripped me in my leg, like a million white-hot pokers were stabbing every nerve. I wanted to scream in agony, but nothing came out.

The last voice I heard was Hondo's.

*"Stop the bleeding!"*

# 21

.
.

**There was a sudden mind-numbing rush. Then** everything was a spinning blur—swirls of color, mist, and words.

*Now, now, now.*

Had the whole world turned upside down or . . . was I dead? I wondered. I was just in Jazz's store when . . . when I collapsed? No, I disappeared. No, that wasn't right, either.

Ms. Cab's voice found me in the oblivion: "Hold on tight, Zane."

The spinning stopped, and I blinked. My eyes cut through the darkness. But my vision had changed. Things seemed bigger, and their edges were fuzzier. It was like I was looking through eyes that weren't mine.

The night smelled of salt and ruin. To my left was the glimmering sea, as black as the Beast's walls. To my right were massive stone structures—pyramids with narrow dirt paths that gave way to a green jungle. And I was on top of another pyramid, high above it all.

My heart pounded. How the heck had I gotten here?

*This is only a dream*, I thought. *Any second now, Ms. Cab's going to march her chicken self out and start screaming at me.*

I willed myself back to Jazz's, but nothing happened. Fine,

I'd climb the hundreds of crumbling steps that led down from the pyramid to some sort of plaza below. I'd hack my way through the jungle if I had to!

I was about to get to my feet when I saw two huge spotted paws stretched out in front of me. I swallowed hard, hoping that the beast those paws were connected to was sleeping. Okay, so maybe I wasn't going to just cruise out of here.

Carefully, I inched my arm back.

A paw followed.

My breath stuck in my throat. I waited a few seconds, then flexed my fingers softly.

Claws emerged from the outstretched paw. *What the ... ?* That paw was *mine*! I screamed, but it came out a roar. And not even a good one. More like a raspy little cough. I looked down at my legs, my chest. I swiveled my head to see my muscular spotted back. Yep! I was a jaguar, all right.

My body stiffened. My ears pricked, nostrils flared. Even the fur on my spine stood straight up. I wasn't alone.

A shadow shifted. As if by instinct, I crouched lightly on the pads of my paws. From a darkened doorway, another jungle cat emerged. He stalked toward me. His fur was obsidian black and shone almost silver in the moonlight.

"Hello, Zane."

*Did that massive beast just talk to me?* Okay, I was definitely dreaming. His voice was dark and deep.

"How do you know my name?" Oh good—at least my brain was still human!

He fixed his piercing green eyes on me and lowered his

head gracefully. "I'm Hurakan. Some call me Heart of the Sky...."

Heart of the Sky seemed like the name of a nice old man. Or a seventies rock band. Not this panther that looked like it would rip open your throat for gazing at him the wrong way. I took a step back. *Whoa!* My legs felt powerful, as if they were loaded with tightly coiled springs.

"Did you say Hurakan? You're...you're one of the creator gods!"

"You called...?" he said slowly.

"Me? Call you? Uh—I don't think so."

"You said the words *I'm searching for my dad.* That's what brought you here."

My mind came to a screeching halt. "Did you say *dad?*"

"Yes. The jade never mistakes a call."

"Do you...do you know him?"

"Yes."

I froze. Okay, I wasn't expecting *that.* Though I guessed it made sense that Hurakan—one of the two original Maya gods—would know a lot of stuff.

He could reveal the answer I'd been craving for so long. But now I wasn't sure I wanted to hear it. I mean, what if he said something like *Your old man is a pus-sucking god of demons?*

My heart felt like it was being squeezed. I took a deep breath. "So...who is he?"

Waves rushed to the shore far below. A single bar of moonlight danced on the water's edge. Hurakan blinked his

green eyes, lifted his chin, and held it there like he was waiting to be crowned or something.

I stood taller. "Well?"

"He's me."

In that moment, all the breath seemed to leave my body
in a rush. It was like a meteor had slammed into my chest and
made a crater the size of New Mexico. I'd waited my whole
life to meet my dad, find out who he was. I always thought
our first meeting would be like a lunch date or a ball game or,
I don't know, a movie?

I shook my head and stepped back. The broken stone was
cool beneath my pads. "Prove it," I said. *Yeah, that's right, Mr.
Powerful Beast,* I thought. *I'm not some gullible human that
believes everything supernatural creatures tell him. Not anymore!* Even if I was on top of a pyramid in the middle of the
jungle, standing on four legs.

Hurakan stood taller and paced the edge of the roof.
"Humans," he muttered, shaking his head. Then, with a deep
breath, he said, "It was me on the building, trying to stop
you from making that outrageous deal with Ah-Puch. You're
stubborn. Strong-willed."

"That doesn't prove anything," I said.

A cool breeze parted the trees.

He inched closer, but I stood my ground.

"Your mom," he said. "We used to skip stones at the lake."

"So?"

"She came to the lake yesterday . . . to find me. She's the
reason I'm here now."

Okay, so this time I really did stop breathing. So *that's* where Mom had disappeared to. But if she knew how to reach him all this time, why had she kept him from me?

*Act cool, Zane,* I told myself. *Act cool.* Fine, so Hurakan was my dad. And he was the god of . . . what was it? I stretched my memory to the pages of my Maya book. Hurricanes? Earthquakes? Or was it bees? *Oh please don't let it be the god of stinking bees.*

I thought I heard him laugh under his breath. But when I looked at him, he was in this stupid tightly wound stance that told me he probably never laughed. But that couldn't be right, because no way would my mom fall in love with some god with zero sense of humor.

"You're the god of . . ." I thought I could let him fill in the blank.

"Storms," he said.

"Is that why Pacific called me *Storm Runner?*" We had runners at school, kids who ran errands for the adults. "'Cause I'm not about to be your errand boy."

This time there was no mistaking a light grunt/laugh. He lifted his head toward the sea. A fierce wind ripped across the waters, creating gigantic waves. Palms bent their heads to the ground like loyal servants. But on top of the pyramid, there wasn't even a hint of a breeze. It was like he could control what the wind touched, and what it destroyed. I guessed that made sense, since, after all, he was a god.

So I was the son of the god of storms. Was that why I sometimes felt heat in my fingertips? Why storms came out of nowhere when I was freaked-out? Thank the saints he wasn't the god of bees, because being able to create storms is so much cooler!

He kept his eyes on the sea. Was I supposed to say something next? Or was he going to launch into some big speech about how sorry he was that he hadn't been around? That he'd left me and Mom and never even sent a lousy birthday card?

"The jade I gave you," he finally said, "is infused with ancient magic. The oldest magic, from before the very first creation."

Okay, so I wasn't going to get an *I'm-a-dirtbag* apology speech.

He continued, "It allows you to travel here...to the Empty."

"The Empty?"

"This in-between place I created, away from wandering eyes and wicked ears. A replica of the great pyramids of Tulum, Mexico." he said. "It's the only safe place we can talk. And because I created it, no other gods have power here."

I looked around at the sky, the ocean, the jungle, the abandoned pyramids. It was...it was beautiful. About the furthest thing from empty I'd ever seen. Except...at the far edge of the jungle there was a blank space, like the uncolored part of a page in a coloring book. "What's that?"

"An abyss...until I finish it."

"Abyss?"

"An empty hole that goes on forever."

Oh. Well, that settled it. No abyss for me.

I gazed down at my spotted body. "Is there a reason I'm a...a cat?"

He tilted his head to the right and blinked. "You spirit-jumped, and you needed a body to inhabit. And as you can see, there aren't a lot of those around here. Would you rather be a monkey or a Yucatán jaybird?"

*Spirit-jumped.* Okay. I'd worry about that later. "Is that why you're a cat, too?"

"It's easier to talk to you if we're in the same form. Since we don't..."

"Don't what?"

"We have no familiarity, no real emotional connection. If we did, it wouldn't matter what form we took."

Yeah, well, that sounded touchy-feely, and I wasn't about to have *that* conversation right now.

He must have sensed my discomfort, because he kept talking. "You can travel here when you need to speak to me. Simply say the words or imagine this location," he said. "But be careful, Zane. Never travel to the Empty unless you're in a safe place with those you trust. Do you understand?"

"Why?"

"Your body is left behind. You will be vulnerable."

There was something very unnerving about the idea of being separated from your own body. What was happening to me back at Jazz's? I wondered. Hadn't Hondo said something about blood?

In the meantime, I itched to try out my new body. I took a few steps as a jungle cat—I was light on my feet, stealthy, powerful. *Amazing* didn't even begin to cover it!

Hurakan treaded so close I could see the golden flecks in the center of his green eyes. "You're in trouble. You will need help to defeat Ah-Puch," he said.

Resentment pulsed up my legs and into my heart. Was he for real? *Now* he wanted to help me? I took a few paces back. A low growl sounded from my throat. "Maybe you should've shown up *before* I let the god of death, darkness, and *disaster* into the world!"

I had an urge to launch myself down the steps and race through the jungle. I wanted to test these powerful legs and blow off steam, steam that had been building with the discovery of every stupid secret that had kept me in the dark for so long.

"Even *I* couldn't interrupt your destiny." He blinked and stalked past me coolly. "Let me help you now."

"I already have a plan."

"And what's that?"

"I'm going to use a deadly pepper." Okay, that sounded even lamer out loud. "And I . . . I'm going to ask the twins how they defeated Ah-Puch."

He turned to face me. "They were smart. . . ."

"Yeah, well, so am I." Why did I feel like I had to prove myself to him? He didn't even care about me!

Hurakan swiped a paw through the air and snarled. "If you would let me finish," he said. "Yes, they used their minds and their cunning. But, Zane, they are unlikely to help you."

"How would you know? Can you see the future?" It was a good plan. They were totally going to be grateful when I told them Ah-Puch was coming for them in LA. And if Hurakan thought he could just waltz into my life and tell me my ideas were stupid, he had another thing coming. I'd show him!

"Ah-Puch lacks your intelligence. I've known him for centuries. But he's learned. He's adapted. I fear . . ."

"What?"

"That he's reached out to the Yant'o Triad."

"The Yant'o what?"

"A trio of evil—Good, Bad, and Indifferent. But don't let their names fool you. There isn't time to talk about that now."

*Trio? As in three? As in one evil god wasn't enough to take down?* "Hang on. How do you know all this?"

"The Bakabs—they're the four giants that hold up the sky—North, South, East, and West. They once worked for me." I picked up regret in his voice, and something told me there was a whole story about these giants I wasn't going to hear that night.

He blinked slowly. "What lies ahead is inconceivable. . . ." His voice trailed off and I knew more words were going unspoken. What was he holding back? I wondered. "You must be prepared. There will be no time for fear. Do you understand me? Time is running out."

"Why can't you gods just fight him?" I thought it was a logical question. "I mean, shouldn't all of you care that he's loose and ready to destroy the whole world?"

"They've seen the world destroyed before, seen it recreated. They have no qualms about starting over." He let loose a low growl. "And the gods are hungry for a war—the peace has lasted too long."

"So . . . will the war take him down?"

"That depends."

"On what?"

"Some of the gods like what Ixtab has done with the underworld. Others are calling for the old ways, and the old ways include Ah-Puch."

I paced quickly along the edge of the pyramid. "How the heck am I supposed to beat him when he's got . . . what did you call it? The Yant'o Triad? I'm . . ." I was about to say *just some human, some kid from New Mexico* when Hurakan hardened his gaze.

His voice was commanding. "*You* have the blood of a creator."

I took a moment to let the words sink in. *The blood of a creator.*

He padded closer. "You are the Storm Runner."

There was that name again. "That's what Pacific called me."

Hurakan nodded slowly. "It's the name she gave the god-born, the one who would stand at the center of the Prophecy of Fire."

I liked it. It had a nice ring to it, better than Sir Limps-a-Lot or McGimpster. *Man, if only the kids at school could see me now. A jaguar, a godborn. The Storm Runner!*

"So does that mean I can control storms, too?" I asked, holding my breath, hoping he'd say yes.

But he didn't. He blinked, hesitated, then said in a low voice, "It's more complicated than that."

"I've brought wind before," I growled, thinking about times when I was scared or angry or . . .

"No, Zane. You didn't."

I was about to argue when he added, "Each of those times, that was me trying to help you without drawing the other gods' attention. The night you killed the demon runner, I brought the rain to help you get away before reinforcements arrived. They hate water. In LA I was trying to stop you from making the deal with Ah-Puch. And on the day of the eclipse, I whipped up the wind to drown out the sounds of the magic, hoping you wouldn't hear it calling." He let out a low growl. "All in vain, I admit."

First I felt deflated. Then hot anger pulsed in my chest. "Well, sorry I don't speak storm!"

Hurakan stalked closer and looked down at my right front leg. I followed his gaze. Even in my jaguar form, the mark of death was visible. "You belong to him now," he said. "Do you see? Your life is tied to his unless you can defeat him yourself first."

I felt dizzy. "Well, maybe you could show me how to use some storm powers!"

A cool wind swept across the pyramid. Hurakan paced. "The storm is a living force, made up of potent elements. As in lightning, thunder, wind. Fire." His voice grew deeper, shaking with a power I couldn't even imagine. "You must become one with it."

"Why would Pacific call me the Storm Runner if . . ." My heart plummeted all the way to Xib'alb'a. I felt the words form in my mind and heart, but they didn't make it to my mouth. It was a terrible irony. Cruel. Twisted. A deep and angry snarl came up. "I *can't* run!" There. I'd said the stupid words. Heat coursed through every muscle and I wanted to bolt.

"No, you can't," Hurakan said matter-of-factly. "Not in the physical sense."

*Gee, thanks for stating the obvious,* I thought. I felt a million kinds of terrible. "Which is officially your fault."

Hurakan's tail swished through the air. "We Maya gods have many names. One of mine is Serpent Leg."

"Are you going to tell me I have a snake for a leg, too?"

The muscles in his broad shoulders twitched. "It does indeed appear that you have inherited my serpent leg."

"Whoa! I am *not* part snake." Crap! Was I going to grow scales?

"It's not what you think, Zane," he said, and I could hear the impatience in his voice. I guess he wasn't used to having to explain himself to humans. "It is a sign of strength, not weakness."

"But how—?"

"You will learn. For now, you must focus on Ah-Puch. He made the deal with you because you're a great prize to him," Hurakan said. "He knows you're my son, and he'll use it against you."

"What did you do to the guy to make him hate you so much?"

"I put him in that prison," he said. "I created the volcano. It's likely the reason you felt drawn to it."

Ah-Puch, my mom, the Sacred Oath, the Beast . . . He had messed up everything! And now I was the one paying for it.

I backed up slowly, filled with a raw energy that needed to be spent. Without warning, my legs sprang me over the edge of the pyramid, down to the staircase. I took three steps at a time in powerful leaps and sprinted toward the cliff that overlooked the sea. I was fast. Wicked fast. The wind clung to me like we were one, and for a second I imagined remaining a jaguar forever.

Hurakan was right behind me. I came to a screeching halt before flying over the edge. Man, it was such a rush to run like that!

*Storm Runner.* Why did Pacific give me that name if I couldn't run? It didn't make sense!

"Ah-Puch tricked me," I growled.

"You shouldn't have made the deal."

I kept my eyes on the ocean below. "I wasn't about to let people I love get hurt," I said with a venom I hoped he felt like a barb.

Hurakan turned his gaze back to the jungle. "You need to get back. And it will be an unpleasant journey. I'm sorry about that."

"Define 'unpleasant.'"

"When the spirit has jumped, it's vulnerable to other forces, dark forces."

"But I was fine coming here...."

"The journey forward is always easier than the journey back."

"But..." Even though I was angry at Hurakan, I wasn't ready to leave. Not the jaguar's power, not this place. Not yet. "I have more questions. I just got here!"

"You aren't meant to stay in this state, Zane. It's dangerous."

*Dangerous?* Was he kidding? Like my whole life wasn't dangerous now?

His eyes narrowed and he lowered his head, drawing closer. "You want answers? You want to defeat Ah-Puch? Then you must go to the Old World."

"What's the Old World?" Heat bloomed in me. I could feel the threads holding me here breaking, separating me from the jaguar's form.

"A place not marked by time. When you get there, look for Saqik'oxol . . . the White Sparkstriker. Do you understand?" There was a sudden urgency to Hurakan's voice.

"Old World, Sparkstriker. Got it." What the heck was a sparkstriker? I wondered.

"Forget about the twins," he said.

"How am I supposed to get to this Old World?" I asked, ignoring his advice about the twins. I'd already come all this way to see them. Besides, I wasn't his puppet. I had my own ideas.

"Let me work on that. . . . And, Zane?"

"Yeah?"

"I'm sorry about the blood."

# 22

. 

..

**Hurakan was right. The journey back to Venice**
Beach was the opposite of the journey *to* the Empty. It was
dark and cold, and filled with sharp, invisible whispers:

*Weak.*

*Pathetic.*

I tumbled across the red-streaked sky.

*Doomed.*

*Fool.*

Through the whispers, I heard Rosie's soft cry and my
heart split in two. Then Ms. Cab: "You're wasting time."

There was no net to catch me. I slammed back into my
body. It was like belly-flopping into a pool. I couldn't open
my eyes. I couldn't move or talk or do anything but listen
and try to suck air into my lungs.

"Has he stopped bleeding?" That was Brooks.

"Stuff more tissue into his nose," Hondo said.

"Don't get any blood on the pillows," said Jazz. "They're all
the way from Marrakech!"

Thankfully, my body was on a soft bed or couch. As I lay
there, I could practically feel my blood coming alive, pulsing
through me as though it was only now remembering how to

do its job. I held on to the image of Hurakan and the words that were now burned into me like a hot branding iron: *blood of a creator.* I knew about the creator gods, the ones who had gotten together to make the world ... more than once. But if I remembered right, they were also the ones who had destroyed it. And if that was true, then that meant ...

I also had the *blood of a destroyer.*

A second later, my eyes flew open. Above me was a ceiling painted bright blue with a gold edge.

"Dude!" Hondo said. "You were out for, like, ever."

I sat up in a nest of pillows. I jerked the wads of tissue from my nose and balled them in my hand. Blood was splattered across my gray sweatshirt. *Note to self: Traveling from the Empty is cold and messy.*

"Where am I?" I asked, looking around.

Jazz smiled. "My place. I live above the store. Like it? Don't let those dirty tissues stain anything."

The place was decorated in soft blues and greens, like the sea was wrapped around you. There was enormous hand-carved furniture and the stone walls were rutted, as if someone very angry had taken an ax to them. Everywhere I looked there were shiny objects: bowls, goblets, and mirrors. And the rough marble floor was covered in pale-blue rugs that reminded me of Navajo rugs I'd seen back home.

"It's nice," I said, rubbing my head. "What happened?"

"You fainted, had a big nosebleed," Brooks said nonchalantly. "Just like the other times, Zane. I told Jazz not to worry." *Other times?*

Hondo grunted and shot me a *go-along-with-it* look.

"Happens whenever he gets nervous," he told Jazz. "Nose gushes, passes out cold."

Jazz gave me a concerned frown and I seriously hated the pity I saw in his eyes. It made me want to tell him it was all a lie. I wasn't a bleeding basket case—I was part god!

Brooks hopped onto the edge of the bed, which was about three feet off the ground. Then she took my hand in hers.

*You spirit-jumped, didn't you?*

*How'd you know?*

*Don't talk about where you went, or who you saw. It isn't safe.*

*But . . . I thought Jazz was your friend.*

*Which is why I don't want him to know anything. If anyone comes sniffing around, he could get hurt. It's better for him to be in the dark. Can't bleed someone for information they don't have.*

*Bleed?*

Jazz shook his head. "Sorry if I made you nervous, kid. We giants have that effect." I could tell he felt bad. Even though my pride wanted to tell the truth, Brooks was right. I didn't want Jazz to get into any trouble because of me.

Hondo paced at the foot of the bed. "Dude, it was a geyser."

"Yeah," I said, wiping the tip of my now-dry nose. "Sorry about that."

Jazz smiled and started taking his precious pillows off the bed while he launched into a speech about Marrakech being in the East and the East being lucky and the Bakab who held up that part of the sky was an old friend and . . .

"Did you say Bakab?" I asked.

"Yes," Jazz said. "Do you know them?"

"Yeah—uh, no . . . I mean, I've only read about them," I said with a shrug.

This pleased Jazz, because his chest puffed up. Then he said, "I've got just the thing for you," and he bounded out of the room.

Brooks was still holding my hand. *The blood's a side effect of spirit-jumping, especially for first-timers.*

*First-timers?* I wasn't sure the trip was worth the journey and if I'd ever do it again. I reached for the jade tooth, thinking I'd have to be careful about my choice of words from here on out. No more casually dropping the word *dad*.

*You sound like you've done it,* I said.

*Not yet. I've seen it done, but changing into a hawk is enough magic . . . for now.*

All this talk of magic and blood reminded me of our deadline. "What time is it?" There were no windows and no natural light to give me a hint.

"You were out for hours," Brooks said in an urgent tone. "It's almost eight p.m."

The second moon! I scrambled off the bed, landing with a thud on the marble floor. Pain shot up my short leg. "How . . . ? It . . . only felt like minutes."

"Time's marked differently in the in-between spaces," Brooks said.

"Here you go." Jazz came back holding a mug so big I had to grip it with both hands. "Drink up."

I looked into the cup. The dark, thick liquid spun in tight swirls like a storm was brewing inside. "Why is it turning like that?" I was worried something might be in there doing all the spinning, and whatever it was, I didn't want it in my stomach.

Jazz sniffed. "It's *chocolate*. . . ." But he said it with a Spanish accent—*cho-co-la-tay*. "It's the living drink of the gods," he said. "Haven't you ever heard of Ixkakaw?"

"Goddess of chocolate," I said.

"All the gods are crazy for this stuff," Jazz said. "Plus, it has enchanted healing properties. Hey, watch out." He stuck his giant hand under the cup. "Don't spill on the rug."

"There's a goddess of chocolate?" Hondo said, smiling. "I seriously need to meet *her*!"

"This chocolate is from a very good year." Jazz beamed. "Hints of vanilla, cherry, and a splash of burnt caramel. Go on, taste it."

Brooks nodded, letting me know it was okay to drink the stuff. I took a slow sip. The chocolate was warm and thick. Actually, it was delicious and went down like velvety pudding. I could see why the gods loved it. It was pretty much the best thing I'd ever tasted.

Jazz laughed and slapped me on the back. I nearly flew across the room. "How do you feel?"

I took a quick inventory. It was strange, but all my aches and pains, and the chills . . . they were all gone. I felt rested, strong. Clearheaded. "Good," I said, wishing I could have more of this drink of the gods now that my mug was empty.

"I knew it!" the giant boomed. "You're a sobrenatural. Don't even try to lie. That chocolate would've done some serious damage to you if you were human."

"What?!"

"You could've killed him!" Hondo shouted.

"Nah," Jazz said. "We giants have excellent senses. I knew he had magic in his blood the second he walked into my shop." His gaze turned to Brooks.

"Jazz," Brooks began, "I . . . I wanted to tell you, b-but . . ." She stumbled on her words. "I was trying to keep you out of danger."

"Giants were built for danger, Little Hawk," he said. "Now fess up."

I looked from Jazz to Brooks, knowing we could never tell him I was a godborn.

Lifting her chin, Brooks said with complete confidence, "He's a magician."

Jazz narrowed his eyes and unbuttoned his vest. "Then show me some magic," he said to me.

"Magic? Er . . . I'm still feeling pretty weak and—"

"He's still learning his powers," Hondo cut in.

Brooks climbed onto the bed and cupped Jazz's face in her hands. "You know I've never lied to you. And right now we have to go before time runs out."

Man, she was seriously convincing. It made me wonder how many lies she'd convinced me of. My stomach turned.

Jazz lowered his shoulders. "I trust you."

Brooks kissed him on the cheek, hopped off the bed, and hoisted her pack over her shoulder. "Thanks . . . for everything."

"Hang on," Jazz said. "I've got one more thing for you guys." He left and came back holding three garment bags on hangers. "While Zane was out cold, I ran that errand you asked for, Little Hawk. You can't go to the big birthday bash wearing"—he eyed each of us critically—"those . . . clothes."

I looked down at my blood-spattered sweatshirt. Stains aside, this was a cool shirt!

Hondo took a bag and unzipped it. He looked from the clothes to Jazz, to the bag again. "Dude, I'm not going to a funeral."

Jazz laughed. "You might be."

Yeah, that was comforting.

Brooks took her bag, looked inside, and rolled her eyes. "A dress, Jazz? Really? You know I *hate* dresses!" I couldn't even picture Brooks in a dress—as a matter of fact, I couldn't even imagine her at a party. She didn't seem like the kind of girl who mingled easily.

Jazz folded his huge arms over his chest. "Only beautiful creatures get the twins' real attention."

Hondo laughed. "No threads are going to make me look . . . er, isn't *beautiful* for girls?"

"The clothes are kind of enchanted," Brooks said to him.

"Enchanted?" I parroted, checking out the crisp white shirt and black suit in my bag. And a tie? Was he kidding?

Brooks took the bag from me, tossed it onto the bed, and sighed. "It means you'll look perfect, no matter what your true appearance is," she said. "All our faults will be gone. Everyone will only see us as . . ." She hesitated and looked away. "Beautiful."

Jazz stroked his chin. "Sort of like Cinderella. And by the way, that story's a total rip-off of my family's history, but that's another tale for another time. The enchantment has a few rules. First, have any of you worn enchanted clothes in the last year?"

Hondo and I looked at each other, confused, then shook our heads.

"Me neither," Brooks said.

"Good," Jazz said. "Now, remember, the magic only lasts two hours. So you'd better get their attention soon."

"We'll look perfect? No faults?" Hondo's grin spread across his whole face. "I am so down with this!"

Brooks rolled her eyes. "Ugh!"

"Hang on," I said. "Does this mean the twins will give us what we want if we're wearing these?"

"Not exactly," Brooks said. "It just means they'll talk to you. They really have a thing against unbeautiful people. Like I said, they're jerks."

Hondo's grin faded. "These guys sound like they need a good whupping."

Brooks and Hondo left to change and I stood alone in the sea-blue room, staring at the clothes and wondering, *Will they hide my limp?* Was I shallow for wishing they would? For wanting to be someone people noticed for something other than what was wrong with me?

I slipped on the clothes, and I had to hand it to Jazz. He had gotten the sizes exactly right. Even the shoes were a perfect fit. The guy was gifted! Which was weird all by itself, given Jazz's own fashion choices. Now for the tie . . . How in the heck was I supposed to knot it right?

I went over to a gold-framed full-length mirror in the

corner, and when I got there, my heart stopped. Not because of what I saw, but because I suddenly realized I had just walked five feet perfectly. I turned and paced. My short leg moved in perfect rhythm with my other leg.

"Holy crap!" I muttered. I ran to the bed, launched myself onto it, and hopped off. It was *amazing*! I raced back to the mirror. Maybe it was the encantamiento, but these clothes were seriously cool-looking. Best disguise in the universe.

*Disguise* . . . That's when a crazy idea struck me. I glanced over at the full mug of chocolate on the nightstand. *Drink of the gods* . . . Jazz had said the gods couldn't resist it. I could put Mr. O's evil chile pepper seed in this stuff and get Ah-Puch to drink it. Once La Muerte did her magic, I'd send him back to Xib'alb'a. It was genius!

I rushed into the bathroom, looking for something to put the chocolate in. But all I found were huge tubes of toothpaste and soaps shaped like shells. Finally, I discovered a cabinet near the sofa with dozens of liquor bottles in it. Behind the tall bottles were a few mini ones. I grabbed one that read JACK DANIEL'S ALUX BLEND and emptied it into the bathroom sink. Then I got La Muerte out of my pack. Carefully, I split open the pepper and dropped the seeds into the bottle before pouring the chocolate inside.

"Whoa!" That was Hondo. "Dude, you're like . . . seriously sick!"

He startled me so much, I almost dropped the bottle. I stuffed it into my chest coat pocket and spun to face him. I'd never paid any attention to whether Hondo was good-looking or not. I mean, he had plenty of girlfriends, or so he said (they never came to the house). But now he looked like one of those rugged, cool, relaxed guys in the fancy car commercials. He was wearing the same kind of black suit, white shirt, and thin black tie I had on.

I blinked. "You're taller!"

"I *know*! Jazz said it's part of the enchantment—the quality you hate most about yourself is hidden." He beamed. "And you? Dude, who knew you were so guapo? I mean, it definitely comes from my side of the family, but still."

With a deep breath, I walked toward him. His eyes bugged out. "Your limp . . ." he said quietly.

"Gone."

But I knew that wouldn't last forever. "We look like those dudes from *Men in Black*."

Hondo went to the mirror and adjusted his tie. "Yeah, well, they kicked some serious alien butt!"

The door opened and Jazz came in smiling ear to ear. Brooks was right behind him.

Let me tell you, I'd seen movies, and I'd seen magazines. But never, and I mean never, had I seen someone who looked like *her*. And I didn't care what Jazz said—it wasn't the enchantment, or the fact that she wore her white one-shouldered dress like some kind of Roman goddess, or the way her long dark hair was swept off her face and tied back with two small braids. It was what shone through all that— the Brooks who had showed up outside Father Baumgarten's office that day with the beat-up combat boots and million-watt smile. The girl who'd risk her own life to save yours.

I stopped breathing.

Hondo walked over to her. "You clean up good, Capitán."

I thought Brooks's face would get red or she'd look down shyly, but no, she owned it. She wore her beauty like she was . . . used to it. Her hawk eyes met mine and I was the one whose cheeks got hot. I was the one who had to look down, because, seriously, looking at her was like trying to gaze at the sun.

I was glad when Hondo spoke up. "Will there be any food at this fiesta?" he asked, patting his stomach. "Because I'm starving!"

"Plenty," Jazz said, looking at his massive gold watch. "But Sleeping Beauty here put you guys seriously behind schedule. The doors close in, like, thirty minutes. And you'll never make it in traffic."

"Can we walk?" I asked, because with my new leg, I felt like I could run a marathon.

Jazz stroked his chin, thinking. "I've got a better idea. Come on. I'll show you."

A minute later we were back in his surf shop. He threaded between a row of bikes and went to a closet where he rolled out what looked like an electric scooter, except this one was built for someone Jazz's size. I'm talking a *massive* platform and two wide wheels at the front.

"You want us to ride a scooter to the party?" Brooks asked.

Jazz sucked in a gulp of air like he was offended. "*This* is *not* a scooter!" He shook his head and added, "I call it the Super Turbo Jazz. This baby's a high-powered, heavy-duty package. Equipped with disc brakes and shockers."

Hondo was nodding and smiling while he traced his hands

over the thing like it was some kind of magic. I could tell he couldn't wait to get it on the road. "Dude, the tires are, like, built for off-roading. Check out the treads."

"And I've messed with the GPS," Jazz said proudly. "It practically drives itself. But whatever you do, *don't* hit the Turbo button."

"Why not?" I asked.

"Last time I tried it, the thing burst into flames." He rubbed his chin, thinking. "I'm pretty sure I've fixed the wiring, but I haven't tested it yet."

"Got it," Brooks said. "No Turbo button. How long will it take to get there?"

Jazz tapped the control panel, then said, "It's programmed all the way to Beverly Hills. Should take you five minutes, tops."

Brooks blinked and her mouth fell open. "You think we can go fifteen miles in five minutes in . . . in this?"

"Like I said"—Jazz beamed—"it's fast. You can weave right through traffic. Could even jump the curb. Just don't kill any pedestrians—I don't need any more tickets. Oh, and that reminds me—it's sort of an illegal vehicle, so don't let any cops see you."

"Guess we'll have to blaze," Hondo said a little too excitedly.

A second later we stood on the boardwalk with the Super Turbo Jazz. A silvery fog was rolling in. The pedestrian traffic was waning, vendors (if you could call them that) were packing up, music was fading. Even the sidewalk art seemed to be vanishing like the last traces of sun.

"So who's going to take the wheel?" Jazz asked.

"That would be me," Hondo said.

Brooks and I didn't argue.

"Sturdiest legs in the rear," Jazz said. "They're the anchor. We don't need anyone flying off this thing."

"Go on." Brooks nudged me. "You ride the back."

Did you catch that? *I* was the anchor!

Hondo stepped onto the wide platform and pressed a button and the thing vibrated silently. Without an engine I didn't understand how we were going to blaze, but by now I'd seen how peculiar magic could be.

"Do you want me to go with you?" Jazz said to Brooks. His gray eye softened when he looked at her.

With a sigh, she said, "I got this."

Jazz said we could leave our things at his place until we came back. And let me tell you, leaving my cane behind? That was the best part.

# 23

•

•••

**The Super Turbo Jazz went from zero to eighty** in like four seconds. The jolt was so sudden I thought I might fly off the back, but I rooted my legs onto the platform, willing them not to let us down. Feeling their strength was *incredible*. I felt bigger, the sky looked clearer, and the air smelled fresher.

Hondo laughed. "Man, this thing flies."

He was right. We had to be doing eighty, maybe ninety, barreling down Pacific Avenue, weaving between cars.

"Are you steering?" I shouted over Brooks's shoulder, hoping Hondo had control of this thing.

He took his hands of the wheel and said, "Look, Ma. No hands."

"*Not* funny!" I hollered.

The dark ocean whizzed by. Could Pacific see me? Could Hurakan? I imagined what we must've looked like: three overdressed musketeers, flying through the night on an illegal scooter. Car horns blared as we zoomed by. People screamed some choice words, but the Turbo Jazz raced along like it had a mind of its own. And the best part?

Brooks leaned against me and I kept one arm wrapped tightly around her.

A second later, she was in my head.

*Where'd you go? When you spirit-jumped?*

*I was . . .*

How could I explain the Empty? And hadn't Hurakan said he'd created it? That made it feel like a secret. Did all the gods create their own hideouts?

"I met my dad," I said out loud, because right then I was feeling powerful and I didn't care if wicked ears were listening.

The Turbo made a sharp right down a busy street lined with small shops, cafés, and yoga studios. A stoplight was coming up, but the Turbo zoomed right through it. A couple of pedestrians jumped out of the way.

"Sorry!" Hondo shouted to them.

They shook their fists at us. Someone might've thrown their coffee in our direction. Hondo hooted and howled like he was having the time of this life.

"Did you say you met your dad?" Hondo shouted over his shoulder.

"Who is he?" Brooks asked.

I tilted my head back and watched the first stars zip by. "Hurakan," I said.

Brooks tried to face me, but she couldn't turn around. "One Leg?"

Hondo let out a light laugh. "He's a one-legged god?"

"No," I argued, feeling my face flush. Why did it matter to me what they called him? "He has one serpent leg. Supposedly."

And so did I, apparently. Whatever that meant.

Hondo hollered over his shoulder, "Screen says two minutes. It's up ahead."

But those two minutes were cut short by a siren and red flashing lights.

"Don't stop!" Brooks warned.

We didn't have much time, and if we got arrested, we'd never get to the party.

"I can't shake him!" Hondo shouted.

A very big voice that I was sure belonged to an even bigger dude sounded over the cop's loudspeaker: "PULL OVER IMMEDIATELY!"

"What do you want to do, kid?" Hondo called to me.

I glanced over my shoulder. The cop was a few feet away. Crap! With a deep breath, I sent a prayer up to the saints and anyone else listening. Then I said, "Hit the Turbo button."

"Are you deranged?" Brooks said. "Jazz only *thinks* he fixed it."

"Thinks is good enough for me," Hondo said. Then, "Adiós, sucker!" And without hesitation he hit the red button marked TURBO.

It felt like the atmosphere burned up around us. There was an explosion of white, as if we were hurtling through the Milky Way. The air got cold and I could no longer feel the ground beneath us. All the breath was sucked from my lungs.

We came to a sudden stop. We were thrown off the Turbo and as I spun through the air all I could think was *Please land in a soft spot*. Luckily for us, that spot was a thicket of bushes spread out across a lush green lawn.

I lay still for a second, blinking, waiting for the terrible pressure in my head to disappear. Slowly, I sat up. "Brooks? Hondo?"

Brooks was next to me, catching her breath, plucking branches out of her messed-up hair. Hondo rolled to his feet, moaning and cursing. We were in front of a pink building with a grande sign that read: BEVERLY HILLS HOTEL.

"You guys okay?" I asked, glad I hadn't broken anything.

Hondo wasn't so lucky. He was clutching his left arm. "Might've busted a bone or two."

Brooks and I hurried over.

"Give it a minute," she said, lightly touching his arm. "The enchantment will fix it."

Hondo raised a single brow and tried to smile but grimaced instead.

"You mean . . . nothing can hurt us while we're enchanted?" I asked.

"Technically, you could die," Brooks said. "But as long as *that* doesn't happen, the enchantment fixes all imperfections."

She was right, because in the same instant, the grass stains on her white dress faded and her hair readjusted itself, weaving back into perfect braids. We all waited, held our breath. Except Hondo, who was still cursing. Then he straightened and looked down at his arm. He shook it out, threw a punch at the air, and laughed. "Someone seriously needs to market this stuff."

Brooks let out a breath. "It's the reason enchantment doesn't last for long and you can only use it once a year. Imagine what people would do to get their hands on something like this if it could be made permanent."

Yeah. Imagine.

A part of me regretted wasting it on the dumb twins. If I'd

waited, I could've used it to run with the storm and take down
Ah-Puch. But then I wouldn't have gotten an audience with
the twins, the only other godborns in existence, and I was
still convinced they had intel I needed. I simply had to learn
what they did to defeat Pukeface. Then I would bolt to the Old
World. Man, Hurakan was going to be seriously impressed.

We made our way to the front of the hotel, where exotic
cars were lined up at the valet: two Teslas, a Maserati, a
Ferrari, and a Bentley. Hondo let out a low whistle. "So this
is where the other half lives!"

The valet smiled at us as we passed, and some of the rich
people getting out of their cars waved like we were old friends.
I waved back, but it was super weird to be accepted as one of
the elite.

We made our way under the striped canopy and across a
red carpet into the lobby. Hotel guests and employees nodded
and waved, some said hello. It was like we were movie stars
or something.

Everything was made out of white marble. Shiny, perfect
marble. A massive chandelier hung from the ceiling, which
was held up by four glossy round columns. And as strange
as it sounds, the lobby smelled like pink. Pink flowers, pink
sugar, pink berries.

Hondo spun in a circle, looking up. "Whoa. This place
must cost a gazillion bucks a night."

Brooks pulled us through the lobby.

"You know where you're going?" I asked.

She paused to tighten one of the gold sandal straps that
wound all the way up her shin. "Jazz gave me directions."

We headed to a door marked STAIRS. "Third floor," Brooks said. "Hurry."

We raced up the staircase (yeah, that made me feel pretty cool) and when she came to the door for floor three, she stopped. "Hurakan, huh?" So she was still thinking about it.

I nodded. "You know him?"

Brooks let out a light laugh. "Are you kidding? He's sort of . . . royalty. I mean, you do know he's a creator *and*—"

"A destroyer," I finished.

Hondo shoulder-bumped me. "Don't even try to get me to call you king of anything. You still get dish duty."

Brooks pointed to the wall. "Here it is."

Inscribed there was a faded image, so faint you'd have to be looking for it to find it. Underneath the word KINGS' was a Maya glyph like this:

"What's it mean?" I asked.

"Sky," Brooks said. Her voice was on the edge of a tremble.

"Kings' Sky?" I muttered, thinking there were some seriously grande egos around here.

"Your obsidian," she said with her hand out. "Place it there." She pointed to the center bottom edge of the glyph.

I tugged the magician stone from my pocket. "What did Jazz mean about what the twins did to you? And what games was he talking about?"

"Remember when I told you they were tricksters?"

I nodded.

"They play head games. They play them expertly, and by the time you know what they've done, you've already lost."

"Man," Hondo moaned. "I was hoping it would be wrestling or even football. Some kind of contact, head-butting, face-pounding sport."

"Didn't they beat the gods in a ball game?" I said, remembering the legend from my book.

"Pitz," Brooks said.

"Huh?" Hondo raised his brows.

"Basketball," Brooks said. "Or their version of it. It's their favorite game, and no one's ever beat them."

After everything I'd read and heard, they didn't seem like the kind of guys who played games without stakes.

"So what do people play for?" Hondo asked.

"Most *don't* play. They know they can't win, so instead they come to trade. With whatever they're willing to lose," Brooks said.

"What do you mean, *trade*?" I asked.

"The twins pretty much only trade in magic."

*But I don't have any magic to trade,* I thought.

It was too late to turn back now. I set the obsidian where Brooks instructed. It locked into place. At first nothing happened. Then slowly, the door began to glow blue, and it creaked open.

And we stepped inside.

# 24

•

••••

**In spy movies, all bodyguards are identical,** with crisp black suits, massive shoulders, and murderous stares. They even wear their hair slicked back the same way, and their square faces look like they were carved from marble.

That's exactly what was waiting for us behind the door. A half dozen guys who could either be pro wrestlers or well-paid thugs. They stood shoulder to shoulder and didn't even blink when we walked into the dim classroom-size space.

I thought maybe the guards didn't breathe, either, it was so quiet. Except for the *bom bom bom* of a drum so far away I couldn't be sure it wasn't my heartbeat.

"Where are we?" Hondo murmured.

"Security pit stop," Brooks whispered. "*Shhh*...just follow my lead."

In front of us was a ticket booth lit with a sickly yellow glow. There was an opening in the glass but no ticket-taker behind it. Brooks stepped up to the window, set the obsidian stones on the counter, and mumbled some words that were definitely *not* English.

An instant later, a gray-bearded skeleton materialized.

Out of thin air! Eyeballs floated in his eye sockets, and he wore a long white tuxedo jacket with a dead red rose pinned to one of his silk lapels.

Hondo gasped. "What the ... ?"

The bearded skeleton was weird enough, but on his shoulder was a small brown monkey with reptilian eyes. Its long tail thrashed through the air and it clasped its hairy little paws together like it was smothering something between them.

"You have inveetation?" the skeleton said with a deep raspy voice.

Brooks pushed the obsidian stones toward him and said, "Just let us in, Flaco."

"No inveetation, no travel to top, even for you," Flaco said. "Them the rules."

Brooks wasn't going to give up so easily. "I'll be sure to tell Jordan and Bird you turned away fresh meat."

Hondo gave me a sideways glance and mouthed slowly: *Fresh meat?*

"Do you see what I see?" he whispered to me. "That esqueleto's wearing a tux!"

"Seriously?" I whispered back. "How about the fact he's a living skeleton! Or that he's got an evil little monkey that probably has fangs?"

Hondo folded his arms across his chest and leaned closer. "You think it has fangs?"

Flaco studied the stones, then handed them back to Brooks. "No entrance with no inveetation."

Brooks propped her elbows on the booth. "Listen, Flaco, I

lost it. And this is a surprise visit. So I can wish them a happy birthday . . . in person."

Stroking his silvery beard, the skeleton eyed me. "You a gimp? Is that why you here? You want favor?"

Brooks turned to me and whispered, "He can see through the enchantment. It's why he's got this job."

I wanted to whack Flaco upside his bony head, but I held my cool.

"He's a magician," Brooks said casually to Flaco. "It's part of the birthday surprise."

The monkey clapped and smiled. Its silver chompers were huge, and when it clicked them together it sent chills down the back of my neck.

Flaco eyed us, glanced at the row of guards, then looked back to Brooks and grunted. "Fresh meat. Hmmph. Magic. Hmmph." He gripped a pen. "They got names?" he asked her, like we weren't even there.

Brooks spat out some made-up nicknames. "El Rey and R-rana," she sputtered.

Hondo shoulder-bumped me, mouthing *I'm the king.* I had to admit my uncle looked good tall, but it felt super weird to peer up at him, even if it *was* only a couple of inches.

The monkey screeched, making Hondo and me jump at the same time.

Flaco scratched under the little beast's chin. "Neither looks like a king or a frog . . . Well, maybe that one there . . ." He was pointing at me with his bony finger. "He might be a frog," he said with a chuckle.

Rana? That was the best Brooks could come up with?

The skeleton jotted down the names, then reached under the counter. "It's your funeral," he muttered as the wall to our right opened with a groan.

Before we could go in, three guards stepped forward to pat us down. My stomach roiled when my thug found the jaguar jade and motioned for me to hand it over.

Brooks and Hondo peered closer.

Holding it up for the guy's inspection, I said, "Lucky tooth. Except it hasn't been very lucky." I tried to laugh casually but ended up sounding like a big phony.

The guy held up the stone, examined it, then handed it back to me with a grunt. I let out a long breath as I set it safely back in my pocket and entered the opening.

When Brooks pressed a button on the wall, I realized we were in an elevator. But it wasn't an ordinary elevator. It was a gold cage illuminated by a pale blue glow.

"What's that tooth?" Brooks asked.

How could I answer without breaking my promise to Pacific not to tell anyone about her? She'd never said how *long* I had to keep the secret, though, so I guess I *could* have told Brooks that I'd met the goddess of time, who was in hiding under the ocean.... But it might be dangerous for Brooks to have that kind of information. In the same way she had tried to protect Jazz, I needed to protect her.

"I got it from Ms. Cab," I said, thinking quickly.

"How come I've never seen it before?" Hondo asked.

Brooks's eyes bored into me with an intensity that made me dizzy.

"So," I said, wanting to change the subject, "Jordan and Bird are the twins?" Yeah, I was a little slow on the uptake. "If they're so tough, why do they use pseudonyms?"

Brooks looked up, watching the exposed cables carry us. "They changed their names to fit in when they came to the US. I guess they're named after some basketball stars from back in the day."

"Best clutch players ever," Hondo mumbled.

"What's *clutch*?" Brooks asked.

Hondo glanced at me, then away quickly. "Just ... er ... they work perfectly under pressure and, um ... they always find a way to succeed at the last possible moment."

My mouth went dry. I didn't want to think about the twins' super strengths anymore. Turning to Brooks, I said, "Frog? Really?"

"You know what a group of frogs is called?" she asked.

"A herd?" Hondo guessed.

I shook my head and adjusted my cuffs. "An army."

Brooks smiled softly but kept her gaze straight ahead. Okay, maybe being a frog wasn't so bad after all.

A terrible pressure began building in my chest as the elevator climbed. *Wait a second. I could've sworn this building wasn't tall, so how ...?* I peered at the buttons for the first time. Instead of numbers, there were dots and lines. Three dots in a row, a single dot over a straight line ...

Brooks caught my gaze. "Maya numbers," she explained.

"How far up does this thing go?" Hondo wondered aloud.

"All the way to the top," Brooks said.

"Er ... the building is, like, only a couple stories high."

With a shrug, Brooks said, "Magic."

The higher we went, the more I worried. What if Brooks was right about the twins? I mean, why would they want to help me? No one gives secrets away for free, and if I wanted their secrets for defeating Ah-Puch, I was going to have to earn them—except I didn't have anything valuable to trade.

The doors pinged open to a domed chamber. And at the center? A huge stone statue of two guys, at least ten feet tall.

"Let me guess," Hondo groaned. "Jordan and Bird?"

I drew closer to get a look at their massive muscles, chiseled faces, defiant eyes, and broad shoulders. I'd seen a photo of the statue of David once. That's what this reminded me of, except the twins had clothes on and looked a whole lot meaner. A falcon sat on the shoulder of one of the brothers, its wings spread, ready to take flight. These guys definitely didn't look anything like the illustrations in my book.

The statues' eyes were raised like they were encouraging visitors to look up at the domed ceiling. It was brightly lit, and every inch was covered with images of the twins in action: running down a ball court, standing on top of a mountain with spears raised, cutting off the head of a demon runner. This was their story, painted in vivid full color, for all their opponents to see before they walked in. Talk about psychological warfare.

Brooks stood in front of a pair of carved wooden doors. Music and chatter boomed from the other side. "Whatever you guys do," Brooks said, "don't make them mad."

Hondo bounced in place. "Yeah, well, maybe they shouldn't make *us* mad."

"What happens when they get mad?" I asked, not sure I really wanted to know.

"They usually throw you off the building," she said, like it was the most normal thing in the world.

"Oh," I said. "Is that all?"

Brooks pushed open the doors. It was party city! The enormous multitiered terrace was packed with people mingling, laughing, and dancing to some really bad techno music that blared from all directions. And they all wore these weird lifelike masks of lions, sharks, snakes, and skeletons.

There were palm trees that swayed in the night breeze. A few shirtless fire-jugglers flung torches toward the sky; they rotated back down at a frightening speed, casting strange shadows across the oblivious crowd. The sickening smell of kerosene filled the air as my eyes scanned the masked faces.

Hondo let out a low whistle. "Looks like a Halloween party, Capitán. Not a birthday party."

Brooks stepped behind a wall into the shadows. "It's all show. They believe the masks contain the spirit of the animal or whatever they're wearing."

"How come we didn't get one?" Hondo sounded disappointed.

"We got enchantment," I said, thinking that was way cooler than a mask.

"He's right." Brooks pressed against the wall like she was hiding. "I doubt anyone here has encantamiento. Too expensive and hard to come by these days. Masks are the next best thing."

"Who are all these . . . ?" I didn't know what to call them, because I didn't know if they were human.

"Some are human, some supernatural," Brooks said.

I took it all in. There was a massive stone fireplace with roaring flames, and beyond the roof's edge were dozens of skyscrapers. Maybe it was a trick of the light, but they seemed to be wobbling slightly, like they were made of Jell-O. I had a feeling this wasn't an actual view of LA but a magically created one.

"Can this be real?" Hondo whispered.

Brooks peered around the corner. "See that bear-masked guy over there by the waterfall?"

"The skinny one?" I asked.

"Yeah, he's human. Comes every year to ask for help with his music career. The twins have big connections in Hollywood, and most of the people here are looking for access to those. That butterfly girl over there? She probably wants to be a model. And that shark?" She pointed to a short, stout guy. "An actor."

Sounded like she'd spent plenty of time here. "You said the twins trade in magic," I said, staying focused. "But humans don't have magic."

"Sure they do."

I gave her a confused look.

Brooks let out a slow breath. "Dreams, talents . . . love."

"How're those things magic?" Hondo loosened his tie.

"In our world, they aren't so easy to come by," Brooks said. "Which makes them magic."

"Hang on," I said. "Are you telling me people actually give up their talents?"

She nodded, suddenly looking miserable. "Say you're

really good at wrestling." She glanced at Hondo to make her point. "You trade it for something else you want."

"But what if the thing you want is the thing you're good at?" I asked. "Like the singer."

"You get the favor as a loan." Brooks paused and glanced sideways for a moment. "Then, when the twins call it in . . ."

"Bye-bye talent?" Hondo guessed.

"Yup. Or whatever it is you've traded."

Okay, so *that* was twisted.

To our right was a huge pool with a waterfall cascading over massive boulders. Waiters in skeleton masks and black polo shirts and shorts carried colorful drinks with little umbrellas or offered finger foods and fancy cocktail napkins.

"I'm starving." Hondo grabbed a skewered shrimp off a passing tray and grinned ear to ear. "I think I'm going to like it here."

"Don't eat anything, Hondo," Brooks said. "This is not a good place to linger. Let's just get in and get out."

Then came a deep voice, "What's your rush?"

Brooks went stone still.

I turned and I knew. It was one of the twins. The guy seemed about sixteen, was at least six five, and had biceps even bigger than Hondo's. Actually, he was almost as sculpted as his statue and maybe fiercer-looking.

He winked at Brooks, hooked his arm over her shoulder, and said, "Hello, little sister."

## 25

**·**

**———**

**Brooks pushed the guy away from her.** "Back off, Jordan."

Before he could take a bite of his shrimp-on-a-stick, Hondo dropped it. "You're his *sister*?"

No way could Brooks have left that *massive* detail out of all our conversations about these guys!

Jordan smiled. "By marriage."

Brooks gave him a murderous glare. "Not yet."

"Your sister will come to her senses, Brooks," Jordan said bitterly. Then, with a shrug, he added, "She doesn't have a choice." He gave a fake sigh. "So, you like the new place? I designed it myself."

Brooks had a sister? Then I remembered what she'd told my mom, that she was looking for the only family she had left. Was that who she'd been talking about?

A glass shattered nearby, people laughed.

Jordan leaned closer to Brooks and said casually, "I thought you weren't coming back. Isn't that what you said, *little sister*?"

Brooks shrugged him off her.

My mind was hurtling like a comet, ready to burn up in three, two, one . . .

Jordan asked, "Who are your friends?"

Brooks introduced us, but Jordan didn't shake our hands or smile. He simply took us in with a sneer, like he could see past the enchantment as easily as Flaco had. I immediately decided I hated the guy.

I stood straighter, grasping the jade in my pocket. I didn't have time for this dude's small talk, but I also dreaded having to ask him for anything.

Hondo looked around. "Any more shrimp left?"

Ignoring him, I said to Jordan through clenched teeth, "We're here to ask for a favor."

"Isn't everyone?" Jordan chuckled. "But come on, join the party. It's my birthday. Business can wait."

We followed him to an enclosed cabana near the pool's edge. I whispered to Brooks, "You have a sister?"

"Later," was all she said.

Hondo scrunched up his face as we passed a group of girls singing along to the rap music now blaring across the party. "Who made these guys' playlist?"

A line of people wound around the tent, waiting to see the other twin, no doubt. I wondered what all these people wanted and what "magic" they were willing to trade.

A giant twice the size of Jazz stood at the tent's entrance, keeping his gaze on the crowd. He didn't blink, didn't even look at us. His gray suit was a size too big and looked more like an ugly bedspread, which made me feel sort of sorry for the guy. I knew how it felt to have to shop for "specials" because of some . . . irregularity. What had he been forced to trade to be allowed in with the "beautiful people"?

Inside the tent were purple velvet couches, a bar, three

crystal chandeliers, plenty of gold-framed mirrors, and Bird. He wore a dark suit and stood in the corner whispering something to a giggling girl. His eyes locked with Brooks and unlike smiling Jordan, his face was granite. He waved the girl away and walked over to us. Yeah, he was Jordan's twin, all right. But there was something darker about him, something that made him seem older.

"La mitad de halcón returns," he said slowly to Brooks, and I could tell he meant the half-hawk comment as an insult. "And you are looking very . . . enchanted," he said, eyeing her from head to toe. "You resemble her, you know."

I couldn't wait to get Brooks alone, to find out who/where her sister was. What the heck had Jordan meant by *She doesn't have a choice*? Was Brooks's sister being forced to marry him?

Brooks fidgeted with her dress and said, "Happy birthday." Then she grudgingly handed Bird her present—a gold-plated seashell Jazz had given us for the occasion.

Bird immediately set it aside on a nearby table. "Gold was last year's theme," he said dismissively.

I'd been bullied pretty much my whole life, but this guy? He took first place for jerk-hood. Maybe everyone was right: Coming here was a bad idea. I mean, I could abandon this plan and just leave things to chance, hope that the twins would be able to take Ah-Puch down again. But Hurakan had said something about Puke recruiting the Yant'o Triad. The twins wouldn't be ready for that no matter how much magic they had. And anyway, it wouldn't get me out of my promise to become a soldier of death—that would take me defeating Ah-Puch alone.

I had to try. I had to do whatever it took to increase the odds that the world would remain standing and the people I cared about would stay alive.

Bird reached toward a silver platter that held small meatballs on toothpicks. He took one of the hors d'oeuvres and popped it into his mouth. "You're not here for the party," he said to Brooks.

She glanced at me, then said to Bird, "I'm here to ask for a favor . . . for my friends."

"*Friends*," Bird echoed, never taking his dark eyes from us. "Yes, they must be *friends* for you to return." He paused and I couldn't tell if it was for effect or if he really was deciding what to say next. "What's the favor?"

Jordan threw himself onto one of the sofas and propped his feet on a matching velvet ottoman. "You can't be serious, Bird. She doesn't deserve a favor after what she—"

Bird raised a hand and immediately silenced his brother. "Tell us. What do you want?"

I stepped forward. "I'm the one who wants the favor," I said. "I need to know how you defeated Ah-Puch."

Some kind of recognition flashed across Bird's face. He adjusted his perfectly pressed cuff. Music boomed. Glasses clinked. Then he looked up at me like all his thoughts had been gathered in this single instant. "What do you know about Ah-Puch?"

I was about to make up some story, but something told me he'd smell the lie easily and we'd be tossed off the side of the building like Brooks had promised. *Don't make them mad.*

I weighed both options, trying to decide which would

make them angrier—a lie, or the fact that I was the one who had freed their nemesis. But if I told them the truth, they'd know I was part god.

Brooks's eyes found mine and I could see her telling me not to do it. To come up with anything but the truth.

Hondo got me out of my dilemma. He lifted his chin and hardened his gaze. "The death dude's bad news," he said to Bird. "He's busted out, and he's ready for revenge."

I nodded. "He's in LA. He knows you're here and he's coming for you." Surely they'd appreciate the warning and it would earn me *something* more than shrimp-on-a-stick.

"Your intel is a day late." Jordan laughed. "We've got the best of the best posted everywhere, and we've shielded the place with more magic than..." He stopped, then added, "Ah-Puch's too stupid to find our new digs. And even if he did find us, we don't need your help, human. We're godborn. Or didn't you know that?"

Crap! What was plan B? Did I even have one? My palms started to sweat and my tie was choking me, but I had to keep my cool.

"Yeah, we know all about the *myths*," Hondo said. I shot him a glare to remind him not to make them mad. But he kept going, like he didn't care if he was tossed off the roof headfirst.

"You think we made up our victories?" That was Bird.

Hondo threw his hands up and shrugged. "Just sayin'. I mean, whenever *I* won a championship, I went home with the gold. Something to prove it." He glanced around. "Don't see any trophies or medals, guys."

Was Hondo looking for a fight? I tried to get his attention, to send him the message *Pump the brakes!*

Jordan came at him, but Hondo ducked in time, pivoting like a pro. Bird grabbed hold of Jordan while I shoved Hondo back, trying to pin him in place. I was furious—he was going to blow this! What was his problem?

Brooks pushed at a braid. "Word on the street is," she began, "your story is made-up. That you had help in defeating Ah-Puch. That you stole your magic." Then she went in for the kill. "Kind of like now."

"*Stole . . . ?*" Jordan said. She'd struck a nerve. Every stupid twitch in his face said so.

"We've got raw power," Bird asserted, almost as though he were trying to convince himself, not Brooks. "And our magic is legitimate—" He stopped suddenly, like he'd realized it was beneath him to argue with a half-breed.

I finally caught on. Hondo and Brooks were playing with their egos. *Not* appealing to their logic, like I had planned. It was brilliant! Clearly the twins weren't going to give up anything for free. I hated to even think it, but Hurakan was right. Still, there had to be a way to get the answer out of them. *Everyone* has a weakness. Even the best clutch players in history.

Hondo had always told me to measure your opponent when you step into the ring—or, in my case, school. Find the soft spot and go after it with all you've got. *And weakness of the heart or mind,* he'd said, *is more perilous than any physical weakness.*

The twins were physically powerful, more than we ever could be, but they obviously needed human magic to sustain their power. And *that* was their weakness.

"Legitimate?" I said. "Then why do you have to take it from people?"

"Yeah," said Hondo. "If you're so powerful, why do you have to steal anything?"

"You're a pathetic has-been," Jordan said to Hondo. "And no amount of enchantment is going to hide *that*."

Hondo half grunted, half laughed. "Prove we're has-beens."

"And how would you propose we do that?" Bird's eyes flicked to his brother and they shared a *this-is-going-to-be-fun* smile.

The giant guard poked his head into the tent. "Crowd's getting restless. Ready for another applicant?"

Jordan motioned for him to let the next person in line come forward. "Hold that thought," he said to Bird.

A tall willowy man with a grasshopper mask entered, walking toward the twins slowly, like he was approaching some almighty throne. When he got close enough, he bowed. *Bowed!*

"My lords, I thank you for your generosity. For seeing me."

*My lords?* Was he kidding?

"Take off your mask," Bird ordered.

The man did as instructed. The right side of his face was pitted and melted, as if he'd been eaten by fire.

"Bird . . ." Brooks said through gritted teeth, but he ignored her, keeping his dark gaze on the guy.

"Let me guess," Jordan said, popping a meatball into his

mouth. He threw the toothpick at the man. "You want us to get rid of that hideous face of yours."

The man kept his head down, like he was afraid to look into the twins' eyes. "I . . . I have a daughter . . . She plays piano. Like an angel. But I do not have the money for lessons. No one will hire me, and I thought you could help me get a job. So I could pay for her to learn from the best. So she could be famous someday."

Bird spoke to the man but kept his eyes on me. "And what do you have to trade?"

I clutched the jade tooth. Something burned deep in my chest.

Brooks went to the man, kneeled next to him, and said, "Don't do it. Please."

Jordan watched Brooks as he passed the meatballs to my uncle. Hondo took one and bit it off the toothpick. Then he grimaced like he'd just sucked on a lemon. His eyes met mine and he shook his head and mouthed *Nasty!*

The man looked up for the first time. "My daughter is very beautiful. You can have her beauty."

"No way!" Hondo blurted. "What's wrong with you?"

This poor hombre had nothing to lose and everything to lose, and I knew how he felt. The only difference between him and me was that he was willing to trade someone else's future instead of his own.

"Guys," I said to the twins, "just give this man a break." *If I were king, I'd outlaw every bully on the planet!* I thought.

"Done!" Jordan said. But he was talking to the "applicant," not to me.

The man bowed again and again as he backed up. "Thank you, my lords. Thank you."

"Do you see?" Bird said to us, brandishing his arm in front of him. "Does it look like we steal? No, they give willingly." He motioned for the giant to take the man away.

So that was it? No contract? No handshake? No blood for the gods? Rage burned inside my skull. Brooks was wrong. These guys weren't selfish, obnoxious jerks. They were pure evil. Maybe even worse than Ah-Puch himself. Oh God, had I wasted a moon on them?

"So, where were we?" Bird asked.

Hondo balled his fists. "How about I smash your face in?"

I agreed with Hondo, but one of us had to stay sane. "You were going to prove we're has-beens," I said.

"What're you offering?" Bird asked me with a stupid twisted grin, like he knew I was the one who had something to trade.

"Play us in a game," I said. "Prove we're pathetic humans. If we win, you give us your secret to defeating Ah-Puch."

Jordan stretched his arms over his head and sighed. "You think we'd share our title? Is he serious?" he asked Bird.

If they only knew I was a godborn, too. And not just related to *any* god, but Hurakan, the creator and destroyer! A part of me wanted to tell them I was the Storm Runner, to wipe those smug looks off their perfectly chiseled faces, but I couldn't. I might as well put up a billboard, advertising myself to the gods. A strange emptiness filled me as I thought about the second consequence. If anyone found out who I was, they'd know it was my dad who broke the Sacred Oath. Why the heck should I care what happened to him, anyway? I didn't even know the guy.

"And if you lose?" Bird asked.

"If we lose, you can have this." I took the jaguar jade from my pocket. I could've easily traded the stone straight out, but it was worth fighting for. I had to give myself a chance at keeping the one thing that connected me to answers, to Hurakan.

"Where'd you get that?" Jordan closed the distance.

Bird eyed it greedily. "Ancient magic," he whispered. "Who gave this to you?"

"We all have our secrets," I said, avoiding Brooks's glare.

Bird didn't take his eyes off it. "This . . . this can be infused with the desire of the giver."

"Say what?" Hondo said.

"A conduit of pure magic," Bird said, and there was a tremor in his voice. "Whoever gives the jade away can give it any power. . . . I haven't seen a magic stone like this in . . . centuries."

I closed my hand over the jade, relieved it was as valuable as I thought. But why hadn't Hurakan told me how powerful it was? Maybe I could give it to Hondo or Brooks and tell it to make us indestructible, or maybe I could give Brooks back her shape-shifting ability. All of a sudden I didn't want the twins to have a chance at it.

Bird snapped his attention back to me. "You win, you get our secret. We win, we get this. Deal?"

"I'm in the game, too," Brooks said, tilting her chin proudly.

Jordan tried to hide his smile. "You, halcón-mitad?"

"That's three against two," Bird said sarcastically. "Hardly fair."

Jordan whispered something to Bird I couldn't hear. I only caught "gone soon."

"That's the deal," Brooks ground out angrily.

"And we get to pick the game," I said.

"I could take these guys down in the ring," Hondo muttered under his breath. "How about that for a game?"

"No way," Jordan said. "*We* pick or no deal."

I stuffed the jade back in my pocket, knowing they'd never give in and neither would we, and we didn't have time for a staring contest. "We'll flip for it," I said.

"Like a coin?" Jordan's eyebrows shot up.

Brooks put her hand on my shoulder. *Don't do it. They'll win. They always win.*

I'd come too far and I needed their secret if I was going to stand a chance against Ah-Puch. Hurakan had said I'd have to be smart and brave, that things were going to be *inconceivable.* I was desperate for every piece of intel I could get.

My stomach turned as Bird pulled an obsidian stone from his pocket. He held it up, showing me one side etched with this symbol:

On the other side was this symbol:

"Death or jaguar, human?" Bird asked.

At the same moment, Pacific's words found me: *One choice can lead to victory...the other to defeat.*

Hondo chuckled. "Seems like a no-brainer."

He was right. Statistically speaking, most people would've called *jaguar.* And if the twins really were the tricksters history made them out to be, I had only one choice.

Bird kept his dark gaze on me. "Call it."

He flipped the stone into the air and as it tumbled down, I whispered, "Death."

# 26

**The black stone twisted in slow motion, land-**ing with a dry little *ker-thud* on the rug.

Bird didn't even wait for the result. He unbuttoned his coat and peeled it off. "Slam it is."

I hurried over, blinked... The face of the jaguar looked up at me, smiling like he knew all along he was going to win. I picked up the obsidian stone, weighing it in my palm to be sure. I knew it!

"You tricked me!" How could I have been so stupid?

Bird narrowed his eyes. *"Tricked."*

There wasn't a question mark after the word.

"What do you mean?" Hondo asked me.

"The death side is heavier," I argued, holding the black shiny stone up to the light.

Bird held back a smile.

I took a few steps toward him, but Jordan blocked my path and grabbed me by the jacket collar. He sniffed the air and his eyes narrowed. He reached into my coat pocket.

I tried to squirm free, but the guy was strong. He pulled out the little bottle of chocolate and smiled. "Holding out on us, human? Check it out, Bird. Liqueur for the gods." His gaze cut back to me. "What are *you* doing with something like this?"

This guy was a bully. A stupid rotten bully. I clenched my jaw and leaned closer. "It's poison." I should've stopped there. Should've kept my mouth shut, but oh no, I had to keep going. "Want some?"

Brooks said, "Come on, guys. Let's play some ball."

Jordan let me go and laughed as he twisted off the cap and took a whiff. "Smells like a new blend. Hints of cherry?"

Bird came over and sniffed it, too.

"You really shouldn't drink any," I said as the panic started to settle in. "It really *is* poison." These jerks were about to drink my backup plan!

"I've got a nose for poison," Jordan said. "And this drink is clean. Besides, what part of *godborn* don't you get?" Then he tilted his head back and guzzled it down. I held my breath. I think we all did.

"Didn't save a drop for me?" Bird smirked.

With a shrug, Jordan tossed the bottle on the floor, shattering the glass. "Wasn't that good anyway."

I still wasn't breathing, expecting him to go all mannequin-stiff on me. But nothing happened. How come he wasn't freezing up? He'd just drunk La Muerte!

Jordan snatched the obsidian from my hand. "See you on the court, human." Then he looked at Hondo and said, "You probably won't make it that far."

And they walked out of the tent.

Hondo lunged, but I held him back. "Hey, save it for the court."

A minute later, a voice boomed over a loudspeaker: "Ladies, gentlemen, giants, and monsters. Come watch the

twins kill a couple of pathetic humans in a game for the ages—
Slam!"

A huge roar erupted followed by what sounded like an
elephant stampede.

"Kill the humans?" I asked Brooks.

A weird sound came from Hondo, like a growl.

"Hey, you okay?" I asked him. "You look..." I couldn't finish the sentence, because what I wanted to say is he looked
like a deranged murderer. His eyes had gone black and his
cheeks were super rojas.

"Oh God!" Brooks said. "Did you...did you eat anything
in here?" she asked Hondo, looking around frantically. "I told
you not to!"

"A meatball that tasted like slimy raw fish," he answered
in a slurred voice. "Actually, I think there were some bones
in it. Totally wanted to spit it out, but..."

Brooks hurried over to the tray. "These aren't meatballs."
Her tone told us this wasn't going to be good.

"They...um..."

"Just say it," Hondo spat.

"They're sort of like human steroids. They enhance the
twins' strength, but they're actually...They're poisonous to
humans."

"What do you mean, *poisonous*?" My voice rose.

"It's nothing— I mean it's...it's..."

"*Tell* us!" I said.

She took a deep breath. "Hondo will get super mad, like
hit rage-level, then, um...he'll sort of see things that aren't
there. Then..." She twisted her mouth to the side.

"Then what?" Hondo said.

"You'll puff up like a blowfish, then go into a deep sleep."

"Sleep's good," Hondo muttered.

Brooks spoke softly, and I could tell she didn't want to say any of this. "It's not exactly sleep. . . . You'll have nightmares, and it might feel like someone's peeling off your skin. But you've got this, Hondo. You're a tank. And we'll be with you the whole time."

Hondo's tough-guy veneer was starting to crack. "Yeah. I've been through worse." His mouth twitched . . . or was that a tremble?

I didn't care how many beatings he'd taken. This one would be the worst, and something about that split my heart into a million pieces. This was all my fault. I never should have let him come.

"How long will he be . . . asleep?" I hated the panic in my voice.

"Everyone's different."

"But the enchantment . . ." I was grasping. "You said . . ."

"Which is why he won't die. But this stuff is powerful, Zane. Even the enchantment can't stop it."

Hondo cursed under his breath. "That lousy little . . . He did this to me!"

"Knowing them," Brooks said, "it's their way of taking you out of the game. I'm . . . I'm sorry. I should've been paying attention!"

"Not your fault," Hondo said through gritted teeth. I could tell he was already fighting whatever was inside of him.

"Forget it!" I hollered. "We have to get him out of here."

"You made the deal," Brooks said. "You can't leave until you play."

"We didn't shake on it," I argued.

"You didn't have to. The second you agreed to it, it was binding."

Like my deal with Ah-Puch.

Brooks looked at Hondo and said, "Try to sweat as much as you can. It'll help."

We made our way to the "court" a couple of levels above the main terrace, weaving among a crowd that was eager to watch us get killed. We decided not to wear the jerseys and shorts the twins had given us. Even though our enchanted clothes wouldn't be as comfortable, their enhancements more than made up for it.

On the way up the ramp, Brooks filled us in about the game. It was like basketball, but with trampolines under each fifteen-foot-high net and basically zero rules. Which pretty much meant that fists and teeth were allowed.

"I . . . I don't want you to get hurt," I said to Hondo. "I mean, more than you already are."

He grunted. "Don't worry about me, guapo. Just take care of yourself."

I rolled up my sleeves, trying not to think about what was at stake, but it was impossible. If we lost the jade, my ability to talk to Hurakan would be gone. I was already leaving without my plan B for defeating Puke, and now I might leave without even a plan A. That meant I was headed to hell's basic-training camp. And worse, the whole world could be destroyed.

For a half of a second, I actually considered traveling back to the Empty, asking good old Dad what to do. But there wasn't time, and I for sure wasn't in a place where I could safely leave my body behind.

"How much longer until the you-know-what wears off?" I hated even having to ask, because that meant acknowledging the fact that my leg was going to go back to gimp status soon.

"Thirty minutes," Brooks said glumly.

A vicious horn blared, followed by that same booming voice. "Players Zero, Less than Zero, and Double Zero, report to the court for your beheading." Laughter. "Slam is a blood sport—don't hide out now." More laughter.

"I'm going to feed that dude's head to the crowd if he doesn't shut it," Hondo said.

"Hold on to that anger," Brooks said. "Maybe we can use it to our advantage."

A hot fury stirred inside of me. And with each step, I felt all the gods' lies and secrets trailing us like heavy shadows.

At the top of the ramp, I nearly stumbled as I took in the scene in front of us.

The court was a ginormous stadium built of massive stones. Its walls sloped inward, and hanging at the top were stone rings like in the illustrations in my Maya book, except these had anaconda-size red snakes dangling from them.

Hondo groaned. "I *hate* snakes. Those *are* snakes, right?"

"Yeah," I said. "Let's try to stay away from the walls."

"Good idea," Brooks added. "'Cause those snakes eat humans."

Of course they did.

Hondo stretched his neck and popped his knuckles. "If I

die, make sure you don't bury my bones in the backyard next to Nana."

"No one's going to die," I offered, but we all knew those were empty words. Heck, I'd never even played basketball. I'd tried a couple times, but my shorter leg didn't exactly make me layup material.

Other than the stone walls and creepy snakes, it looked like a standard basketball court. At each end was a basket with a backboard behind it and a mini trampoline underneath. Okay, how hard could it be? Get past the dirtbags, fly into the net, and slam-dunk the ball. And, according to Brooks, whichever team scored five baskets first won.

"Where did all these spectators come from?" I asked.

"Optical illusion," Brooks said. "Looks like tens of thousands—to intimidate you—but really there's only a hundred or so."

"Who cares about the people?" Hondo said. "Look at the size of those *snakes!*"

Bird and Jordan were suited up in black jerseys and shorts, running back and forth, dribbling, slamming the ball like it was nothing. Catching air like they had wings.

"We have to pass the ball every five steps, so no one can just run it in," Brooks said. "It's going to take all of us to win. We have to work together."

I wondered how we were going to manage a victory, especially with Hondo out of it. With each second his pallor was getting grayer, and his skin was so translucent I could see the veins underneath.

A minute later we stood at the center of the court. Jordan

spun a black rubber ball on the tip of his finger while wearing his signature stupid smile. Next to him stood the giant guard from the tent.

"Do you see those dragons flying up there?" Hondo said, looking at the sky.

I turned and whispered so no one else could hear, "You're definitely starting to hallucinate."

"Ooh," Jordan said with fake concern. "He's looking pretty . . . sick. Don't you think, Bird?"

My legs trembled, and heat clawed my throat. It took every ounce of strength I had to build a wall between me and these guys so they wouldn't know what I was thinking. Deep down, I wanted to feed their heads to the snakes. But that wouldn't save Hondo, and it wouldn't get me closer to defeating Ah-Puch. I had to stay focused.

"We'll even let you losers go first." Jordan tossed me the ball.

I caught it—barely. It was as heavy as a bowling ball. "How're we supposed to play with this?"

"We could bring out the ball of daggers if you'd prefer," Bird said slowly.

"Uh—no. This one . . . is fine," I said.

Jordan leaned closer, hovered, then whispered slowly, "The snakes haven't been fed for a few days."

I swallowed the swelling lump in my throat.

"First one's on us," Bird said.

I looked around. The spectators were on their feet. Some were pointing and laughing.

"First one?" I said.

Jordan rolled his eyes and said to Bird, "You should explain what *head start* means to the moron."

"You can start dribbling," Bird said slowly. "Or you can stand there staring at the ball."

I didn't need to be invited twice. I took off running (that's right—*running*!). I dribbled like a b-ball king, and to my surprise, the ball bounced lightly.

The crowd roared.

Hondo was within range, so I tossed him the ball. He ran like a wild man, one, two, three steps. Just when I thought he was going to pass it back to me, he threw it up into the air like it was on fire.

The crowd laughed.

Brooks was there in a flash, and as the ball came down, she knocked it to me. I took control of the ball. My legs pounded the court, closer and closer to that basket. Hondo was screaming, "It's going to kill you, Zane! Let it go!"

I blocked out his voice and with each step I thought *Storm Runner, Storm Runner, Storm Runner.* With a quick pass to Brooks, I positioned myself ahead of her. All the time I was wondering why the twins weren't coming after us.

Brooks raced with the ball, dribbling lightly before rocketing it to me. But she put a little too much spin on it and I had to dive onto my belly to catch it. I had so much adrenaline going I didn't even feel the pain. I rolled to my feet, jumped onto the trampoline, and launched myself into the air. I was flying toward the basket. Up, up, up. Then *slam!* The ball swished through the net.

I was king of the court! Maybe Bird and Jordan weren't so clutchy after all.

But as I came down, the net erupted in flames. Whoa! There was a burst of heat as the fire reached for me. It was like it grew arms and fingers. But the weirdest part? When I landed (okay, crashed and rolled), I wasn't singed, even though the flames had licked my face and hands.

The spectators went crazy. Most were on their feet, screaming or chanting "Zero, Zero, Zero."

*That was too easy. The twins let me score,* I thought. I scanned the audience, masked behind the twins' magic. Hearing *zero* chanted over and over by a gazillion people didn't exactly boost one's confidence. It was another intimidation tactic.

A voice behind me said, "That was a gimme." I spun to find Jordan smirking. "To show you what good hosts we can be. Give the crowd a little hope for the underdog. Everyone loves an underdog."

"*You* poisoned my uncle," I said, storming toward him.

"I only passed him the plate," Jordan said innocently.

Brooks stepped between us. "Not now, Zane," she whispered. "Not here."

Bird looked at me, raised a single brow, and said, "Strange."

"What . . . what's strange?" I asked.

"You aren't burned."

"It's 'cause he's fast," Hondo said. "Faster than fire."

But that wasn't it. I wasn't faster than the fire. My mind went to work quickly, remembering what Hurakan had said.

He was the god of storms . . . and something about powerful elements . . . and fire's an element. So did that mean . . . ?

"I see," Bird said flatly, like he knew my secret.

Hondo inched back. His face and neck were beginning to swell, stretching his gray skin so tight he looked like a puffer fish.

Brooks looped her arm in his and mumbled a few words to him. Then she looked back to the twins and said, "I call sudden death."

I didn't know what that was, but it sounded like a terrible idea. I grabbed her arm. "What're you doing?"

Hondo stepped between Bird and Brooks. "No *way*, Capitán!" He wobbled.

Jordan gave a knowing glance to his twin as Bird said, "You would call sudden death for these . . . these losers?"

Brooks tugged the braids out of her hair and clenched her jaw. "Whoever scores next takes it all." She narrowed her eyes, looking fiercer than when she was a hawk, and I nearly shrank back from her glare.

Bird and Jordan shuffled their feet, appearing for the first time like they were out of their comfort zone. They went courtside, to come up with their strategy no doubt, and Brooks spun to face me.

"What're you doing?" I asked.

"Old World rules. If you call for sudden death, the opposing team has to grant it to you. I needed to buy us some time."

"For what?"

"Thirty seconds!" Jordan called out.

"Never mind." Brooks's shoulders slumped as her eyes searched the sky. "It's too late."

"What?" I asked.

"I may not be able to shift, but I'm still part hawk and . . ."

"And what?"

"I picked up his scent."

"His?"

Three seconds later, the world trembled. Fireworks exploded in reds and golds, splitting the sky with every pop and crackle. At first the crowd laughed and clapped like this was all part of the show. I knew it wasn't.

Then slowly, ever so slowly, the sky began to fall bit by bit, like ash. No, not ash—broken glass. People screamed as shards stabbed them. The crowd scattered, shrieking and cowering. The skyscrapers in the distance began to tremble, threatening to collapse any second. But on the court, nothing touched us.

Hondo grabbed my arm. "Is this real?"

"It's real."

Then I saw her. Muwan, in owl form, flying straight toward us. Her legs were stretched in front of her, talons open wide.

The twins stared up at the shattering sky in shock.

I kept my eyes on Muwan. She was fearsome, but not as fearsome as who I knew had to be right behind her. The air vibrated. The arena shook with so much force my teeth rattled in my head.

Jordan watched in horror as the panicked crowd emptied the stadium. "It can't be!"

Hondo crumpled to the ground, and I lunged in time to

break his fall. Brooks knelt next to us and whispered, "He's asleep now."

"You mean he's in hell," I said through gritted teeth. A cold shiver ran through me. This wasn't how things were supposed to be happening. Something . . . *everything* was wrong.

A swirl of black smoke rose from the pieces of sky at our feet, solidifying into a dark column. It formed shoulders, a head, arms, and legs. The eyes came last—filled with shadows coiled like snakes. Finally Ah-Puch looked exactly like he had at the volcano, with his elegant dark suit and his sinister gaze. Except he seemed even stronger now.

Muwan landed on his shoulder. She smiled at the twins. "It's been too long, boys."

They didn't say anything—just stood there frozen.

Brooks whispered, "We need to get out of here."

I looked back at Hondo. His pale skin, his barely rising chest. Where was he now? And how was I supposed to move him? He weighed like 180.

Bird lifted a hand and the world stopped shaking. The sky stopped falling. "You think you can destroy *our* magic?" he said to Ah-Puch.

But Ah-Puch wasn't paying attention to Bird. He kept his dark eyes on me. With a grin he said, "Thank you, Zane."

The tattoo on my wrist burned as if a flame were searing it into my skin. I grabbed it and grimaced.

Bird's gaze fell on the mark. His whole face went pale.

And that's when I understood.

This wasn't just a mark.

It was a tracking device.

# 27

**"*You* did this?" Jordan's granite face looked like** it might crumble.

The mark continued to burn, the skull's sleeping eyes fluttering as if they might open any second. My heart thrashed against my ribs. I jerked my sleeve over the tattoo and stood.

"You were stupid enough to make a deal with the god of death?" Bird said with a smirk I wished I could wipe off his face.

Ah-Puch laughed. "Come now, Jun'ajpu'. Let's be gentlemen about this."

Jordan's eyes raked over Ah-Puch with so much hatred, I thought old Puke might melt and we could all go home.

"Did you really think your pathetic magic could keep me out?" Ah-Puch said to the twins. "Your little sand castle isn't as strong as you imagined."

Jordan's jaw tightened as he looked around at the broken pieces of their illusory world. The shattered walls, the splintered sky. The distant skyscrapers began to sway again.

"Such a poor imitation," Ah-Puch said, following his gaze.

"Did you come here for a fight, Ah-Puch?" Bird's tone told me he wanted Ah-Puch to say yes.

"Boys, please," Ah-Puch said. "I didn't come here to fight.

Simply to destroy your little . . . what shall we call it?" He took in the halfway-finished demolition. "Bubble? And to set the record straight." His voice rose a few godly notches for the next part. "You never defeated *me*, only a couple of my weak underlords."

The world tilted. Surely that was wrong. Surely I hadn't relied on a plan that was built on empty boasts.

"We beat you," Bird said through gritted teeth.

Ah-Puch stroked Muwan's head. "Your lies are such bitter little things. And to think I was locked away, unable to refute them. Hardly justice, wouldn't you agree, Zane?"

I gave a short nod. I mean, it really was a raw deal. "Why . . . why would Jordan and Bird lie?"

"To establish their fame, their notoriety," Puke said in a commanding tone. "To ensure that no other godborns would ever challenge them." He turned his hardened gaze on the twins. "I do admire your sinister plan," he said to them. "Lie about defeating me, inspire humans to ignore the gods, instill enough fear in the gods to make them create the Sacred Oath. That way you'd never have any competition."

I processed each bit of information, and it all made sense. Jordan and Bird had manipulated the gods into taking the Sacred Oath! I remembered what Pacific had said about the twins inspiring jealousy in the gods. "But . . . if the gods were so worried about godborns, why didn't they kill the twins?" I asked.

"Very on point. Bravo," Ah-Puch said, smiling. "The twins used their popularity among humans as leverage in a deal with the gods. 'Jordan and Bird' promised to go on a PR tour, encouraging humans to revere the gods again, to restore balance."

Man, that was messed up! I thought. But it didn't surprise me now that I'd seen their ugliness up close.

Jordan and Bird shared a glance. Beads of sweat formed on Jordan's forehead. Was fear getting the best of him?

No, this was something more serious. He clawed at his throat. His eyes bugged out and he collapsed.

Bird squatted next to his brother, pressing on his chest, calling his name over and over. He glared up at Ah-Puch. "I don't know how you did this, but I will make you pay!"

For an instant, surprise registered on Ah-Puch's face. That told me all I needed to know.

It wasn't him—it was La Muerte! The chile pepper really *had* worked! A little late, but she'd worked. I wanted to slip away before the truth was discovered, but how could I, with Hondo passed out cold?

Brooks gripped my wrist so hard, her nails dug into my skin. *This is going to be really, really bad!*

*You think?* Then I said, *If I don't make it—*

*I'm not listening.*

*Make sure Hondo gets out. Please.*

Muwan lifted off Ah-Puch's shoulder, flew across the stadium, and in one swoop, snatched up a snake with her talons and flipped it into her mouth.

My stomach turned.

Bird looked wounded, like he and the snakes were BFFs, and a second later the rest of the red reptiles evaporated with the snap of his finger.

"We're going to destroy you," Bird said to Ah-Puch.

"*We?* Apparently not," Ah-Puch said coolly, looking at the comatose Jordan. "But I'll let you try your best. In the meantime, I have some plans of my own."

Why did I have a feeling my name was written on those plans?

Muwan shifted into her human form—same dress, same bronze skin, same dangerous smile.

"You're too afraid to fight, old man," Bird provoked.

"I'm not the one trembling," Ah-Puch said with a calm but deadly glare. Then his gaze turned to me, and I didn't like what I saw: someone ready to collect what he was owed.

I inched back. It wasn't time yet. I still had a whole day to figure out how to stop him. But how? I gripped the jade in my pocket for security, careful not to will myself to the Empty and leave my body with monsters that wanted to see me dead.

Suddenly, three huge black winged creatures swooped down. They had human heads that were too small for their massive bodies. Like Muwan, they sported slick black feathers, razor-sharp talons, and wings with a fifteen-foot span.

The creatures were identical to one another: bald pates, sharp chins, bulging veins in their necks, and foreheads like their blood was too thick. The only difference was that each had eyes that glowed a different color: yellow, orange, and purple.

Bird tried to make a run for it, but the yellow- and purple-eyed monsters moved like lightning, snatching him then Jordan in their huge wings and cocooning them tightly so only their heads poked out.

"You remember the Yant'o Triad, surely?" Ah-Puch addressed Bird in a self-satisfied tone. "Allow me to reintroduce you to Yant'o, Usukun, and Uyitzin—otherwise known as Good, Bad, and Indifferent. Except we all know there isn't any Good, but it sure rolls off the tongue, doesn't it?"

Bird thrashed, trying to break free. But the only things that got loose were the curses he spat at Ah-Puch. As the words flew from his mouth, they turned into silver daggers aimed at his nemesis. Muwan batted them away easily. Jordan was a lifeless doll in the wings of his monster.

I thought about Hurakan. I mean, if Puke hated the twins for lying about beating him, imagine how much he hated my dad for sticking him in his prison for hundreds of years. Yeah, this was going to get ugly. What had Hurakan said? *Inconceivable?* Skinny kid versus god of death. Some match.

"The gods will unite against you," Bird said with a grunt.

"Yes, the gods," Ah-Puch said casually. "Last I checked, they were already at war within their ranks, trying to figure out who could have set me free. *Tsk-tsk-tsk.* You really can't trust anyone these days, now can you?"

Ah-Puch turned to me. "As for you, Zane..."

Bird narrowed his eyes at me like he was just remembering I was there. "This is your fault, human!"

Ah-Puch hesitated, as if deciding how much he wanted to say. "He's no human," he said slowly, like he wanted to savor the shock that registered on Bird's face. "But we can talk about that later, can't we, Zane?"

I didn't think I could get any words past the lump in my throat, but somehow I managed. "I'm, uh—I'm human, I mean...Sure, yeah. Later." But I was so hoping there wouldn't be a later. I'd rather disappear, hole up in the Caribbean somewhere....

Except that wasn't me. Not anymore. I'd holed up at home for a whole year because I was too afraid to face the kids at school. Too afraid to see the way they looked at my leg. Too afraid to try and be someone more than the names they threw at me. Well, those days were over. I'd told Pacific I'd never hide, and I meant it. Even if it meant going down, at least I'd do so fighting.

"So the gimp's not human," Bird finally muttered. I could see his mental gears clicking into place, but not before Ah-Puch started to laugh. I mean a giant, uproarious laugh that shook the stone walls and could've registered a ten on the Richter scale.

The creatures gripping the twins smiled. Their teeth were black like they'd been stained with ink, and their breath smelled worse than rotting meat in July. The ground trembled. The stone walls began to crumble. The skyscrapers in the distance fell in giant columns of smoke and dust. In only a few more minutes this place would be completely destroyed.

The creatures holding Bird and Jordan folded their wings tighter and tighter. Each of the twins' faces puckered like their heads were being sucked dry. Their skin turned gray, and purplish veins spread beneath. Their eyeballs bugged out and turned dark red.

"Don't kill them!" I shouted.

*This is going to be good.* That was Brooks still gripping my hand.

*You can't be serious.*

*You're no fun.*

Ah-Puch turned to me. "Trust me, I'm not generous enough to kill them quickly." Then, to Good, Bad, and Indifferent, he said, "Take them away. Their magic will make a lovely feast for us."

The Triad took flight, carrying the twins into the falling sky.

Ah-Puch started to fade.

"Wait!" I called to him. "You tricked me. This mark . . ."

He stopped, looked at me. "Clever, yes? You can't run, and you can't hide."

"Unless I burn off this tattoo!"

"The magic runs deep, and you aren't brave enough to withstand that kind of pain." Ah-Puch sighed. "I'll see you soon, Zane Obispo." He gazed around the collapsing world and said, "Very soon, judging from this house of cards."

# 28

**Brooks shook my arm. "We have to get out of** here!"

"Help me with Hondo!" I shouted over the falling debris.

But even with both of our efforts, he was deadweight. No way were we going to get him out before the place crashed all around us.

This was *not* how it was going to end. Not in a dollhouse of Jordan's making.

Brooks's eyes shifted, the gold and amber flecks glowing like they might ignite any second. And for an instant she looked like her hawk self—mythical and even dangerous.

"Go!" I told her. "Save yourself."

"Not without you!"

Why was she so stubborn?!

At the same moment, a very large figure emerged through a cloud of black and gray dust.

Jazz!

"I guessed you all might have some problems," he yelled. "I put some minicams in your clothes, and what a show it's been!" Jazz scooped Hondo up like a sack of chile pods and hoisted him over his shoulder. "We've got a boat to catch!"

I'd never been so happy to see anyone in my whole life.

Brooks and I hurried behind him, but he didn't head for the exit. I figured it was already demolished. Instead, he went to the roof's edge. And let me tell you, it was hard to keep up with a giant whose stride was like ten yards. Especially since my stupid limp was back. The time limit on our enchantment had run out.

Gusts of cold wind raged across the broken world. Umbrellas tumbled, trees split in two, glasses shattered.

I looked over the edge, wondering where the safety net was. Or maybe we were waiting for a helicopter? My answer came within seconds. An enormous flying machine with a giant red sail rose from the darkness. And you wouldn't believe who was driving—the skeleton, Flaco! Really? *This* was our ride out of here?

"Teeckets, please," he said, circling in what looked like a four-seater go-kart with a small engine near the back.

Jazz grunted. "Get closer!"

The roof quaked, splitting the cement.

"Next time he circles, jump and hold on tight," Jazz boomed.

Was he kidding? *Jump?* Couldn't Flaco land? Then I realized the roof was going to give way any second.

Brooks grabbed my hand. "Don't fall!"

"I'll do my best."

"On the count of three," Jazz said, gripping Hondo with one arm.

"Forget the count!" I hollered. "Let's get out of here."

The wind groaned angrily. Trees bent and writhed. Then a massive black hole opened in the sky, sucking everything into it. Even the oxygen. Flaco circled back, closer and closer to the edge. He was only three feet away.

"Let's fly!" Brooks shouted.

Easy for her to say. She was part hawk!

"Two," Jazz shouted.

*Wait—what happened to* one?

I imagined myself as the jaguar, with the power of those muscular back legs. Flaco was close enough that it wouldn't take much of a leap. I could do this.

"Three."

We launched ourselves into the air. I used my one good leg, thrusting myself with all I had. At the last second a gust of wind jerked the glider to the right. I came up short, barely latching onto the side rail. Everyone was tucked safely in the flying go-kart/whatever. And me? I was dangling off the side.

Brooks leaned over the edge. "Zane! What're you doing?"

"Oh, you know . . . just enjoying the view."

*Don't let go,* I told myself. *Don't let go.*

"Take my hand!"

I was scared to, I admit it. But I couldn't hang on to the side of this thing for long. With a deep breath, I reached up and grabbed hold of her hand. She hauled me into the glider, where I clung to the seat for dear life.

"No time to be a thrill-seeker," she said, shaking her head.

"Yeah . . ." I groaned. "Thrill."

"You okay?" Jazz called from the front seat. Hondo was still sagging over his shoulder.

I nodded, trying to get control of my breathing.

"Good driving, eh?" Flaco said. Who knew skeletons could beam with pride?

The engine whirred as we burst through a sheet of cold silver light, leaving the broken imitation world behind. It was like passing through a waterfall without the water.

We sailed high above Santa Monica. Over traffic-packed streets lit up with red taillights. A dark-haired woman was pushing a stroller below, and she walked with a small skip in her step. Like my mom. I wondered if she was back home yet. What had she said to Hurakan to get him to help me? Had she always known where to find him? I needed to sleep so I could talk to Ms. Cab and ask her to check on my mom. Then I realized . . . the eyeball was in my backpack, which was still at Jazz's.

"Where are we going?" I shouted. "To your place?"

"Not safe there," Jazz hollered back.

"I need my eyeball!" I screamed, immediately realizing how stupid that sounded.

"Woo-hoo!" Brooks leaned halfway out of the glider. "Faster!"

Flaco obliged, and I felt sick as I gripped the edge of my seat.

The salt air was my first clue we were headed back to the beach. When we got closer to the sand, I thought we'd land, but Flaco kept on going, right over the water, farther and farther toward the dark horizon. Brooks wasn't leaning out anymore.

Brooks tapped Jazz on the shoulder. "What...what are we doing *here?*"

"Coming in for a landing," Jazz said. "Might get a little wet."

"Jump when I say so," Flaco said.

"I can't swim!" Brooks shouted. I could feel her panic as she tensed up for the first time since we'd taken flight. Below was a double-level boat too small for us to land on. So, dark sea it was.

"I got you," I said, thinking of the disaster the last time we'd plunged into unknown waters.

Brooks paled and shook her head. "Don't let go," she said.

"I promise."

Flaco hovered about five feet over the water. "Jump!"

He flew away as we dropped into the water's freezing currents. I kept hold of Brooks, which wasn't too hard, because she clawed her way onto my shoulders, pushing me down in her frenzy.

Keeping my calm, I opened my mind and let her in.

*I need you to chill out or we're going to drown.*

She relaxed her death grip a little and clung to my back as I swam toward the boat. Jazz lifted us on board, where warm, dry towels were waiting, along with some snacks—a cooler filled with cherry Cokes, and a sack containing gummy worms and pizza pockets. All of our belongings were already on the vinyl bench seat. I hurried over and was relieved to find Ms. Cab's eyeball still tucked safely in my backpack. But when I saw my boring old cane, my heart sank. I wished he'd left that behind.

Jazz took Hondo belowdecks to the cabin, where he could

sleep off the poison, while Brooks and I sat huddled under a blanket at the stern. The boat looked like a fixer-upper fishing vessel with a rusted railing, pitted deck, and a covered second deck with a steering wheel, seat, and some gears.

I took a soda from the cooler but didn't drink any. My stomach was twisted in knots. I'd failed. Wasted way too much time on a stupid idea, and now I had nothing. No plan. No powers. No future. The gods were ready to start a war over something *I'd* done. And Hondo was suffering a pain worse than death while we sat around under the stars. Hurakan had been right when he'd said *what lies ahead is inconceivable.*

A cool breeze drifted over us as the boat rocked gently in the water. The night replayed in my mind so fast I wasn't sure any of it had really happened.

"Why'd Jazz bring us here?" I asked.

"Must not be safe in Venice Beach," Brooks said, shivering as she sipped her Coke.

I stared into the darkness. "Where do you think Puke took Jordan and Bird?"

"Wherever it is," Brooks said, "the jerks deserved it. I knew they were rotten, but I can't believe they lied about defeating Ah-Puch. I take it back. I can totally believe it. Man, they'd do anything for fame and power."

Okay, Bird and Jordan *were* jerks, but man, getting smothered by those oily, smelly black wings and carted off like a couple of corpses seemed tragic.

"I really want to know," I said.

Brooks rolled her eyes. "I have no idea. Where would you take your sworn enemies if you were the god of death, darkness, and destruction and someone had moved into your castle?"

"Probably a putrid pit filled with vicious rats and killer ants that would eat out your eyeballs."

Brooks let out a light laugh. "That's sick, you know that?"

"You asked."

La luna was a wedge clinging to the sky. I only had one moon left until Ah-Puch came to collect on our deal.

"Brooks?"

She turned away from me.

I twisted my hands together. "Something bad's coming, isn't it? When I met Hurakan . . . he saw the mark on my wrist. . . ." Why was this so hard to talk about?

"So?"

"So, he said I have to be the one to stop Puke. Because my life's now tied to his, because I was the one to let him out. And if I don't . . ."

Brooks swiveled to face me. Her eyes burned fiercely. "You'll end up a soldier of death even if the gods kill him."

Heat prickled up my spine and I wanted to crawl out of my own skin. "That about sums it up." I stood and took a deep breath. "I have to tell them."

"Tell who what?"

"I can't let the gods go to war over something I did."

Brooks jumped up and grabbed my arm. "No, Zane! That would be like . . . like double suicide. Are you *trying* to die?"

"Um, no . . . not exactly."

She paced with her usual look of determination, but that

wasn't going to get me out of my dilemma. "The gods want this war," she said. "They've been looking for a reason to start one. You telling them now—it wouldn't be worth it."

"How do you know?"

"You heard Jazz. We've had peace for too long," Brooks huffed. "Nakon's been waiting for this."

I remembered the name. "The god of war."

"He's always hungry for blood and he's been itching for a fight but never had a good excuse until now. So with or without you, Zane, the gods are going to battle it out. Don't you see? Telling them would be a huge mistake. It won't change anything!"

I nodded and we sat in silence after that, each of us mentally trying to unlock a door we didn't have the key for.

"All those people . . ." I finally said. "From the party? Are they . . . ?"

"Dead?"

Jazz appeared from the cabin below. "From what I saw on the minicams, I think they got out. They won't even remember where they were. They'll think it was another earthquake or that they have a killer hangover."

Brooks froze. "I can't believe you spied on us with those minicams."

"And here I thought you'd be thanking me," Jazz said.

I caught on. Brooks was worried Jazz had heard something he shouldn't have, like that I was a godborn. I thought back . . . Had we ever mentioned it? Or anything else that might get him in trouble?

"Thanks, Jazz," I said. "You were right. Those guys are jerks. Did you hear what they said to Hondo?"

Jazz narrowed his eye. "Don't make me feel bad, kid. The cams don't have audio, okay? I'm still working on that technology."

My muscles relaxed and Brooks let out a long breath.

"How is my uncle?" I asked Jazz, worried that Hondo would be in torment for hours.

"He'll survive," the giant said, shaking his head. "Won't be too happy when he wakes up, but it'll wear off. Eventually."

After what the twins had done to Hondo, I couldn't even think about them without hate bubbling up inside me. "So . . ." I didn't know where to begin. "Where are we going?"

The boat lurched and began moving through the waters. I looked up to the second level, but no one was piloting. Jazz's face split into a broad smile. "Captains herself," he said proudly.

"Let me guess," I said. "Magic?"

A deep frown formed. "No! Advanced Giant Engineering! A-G-E—it's the company I'm going to start once I have enough capital." He pulled a bottle of what looked like chocolate milk out of the cooler. "Chocolate from Ixkakaw. Want some? It's a new recipe."

I took some and guzzled it, hoping it would make me feel as good as before. It was liquid velvet and even sweeter than the last batch, if that were possible.

Jazz popped the lid off and swigged the whole bottle. After a loud burp, he said, "I've got some real bad news, Little Hawk."

"What could be worse than—?" I stopped myself, not wanting to reveal too much to him.

"Tell us," Brooks said to Jazz.

"After you went to the fiesta, I got a letter—hand-delivered—but I don't know who it was from."

"What did it say?" I asked.

He pointed at me. "To take *you* to the Old World."

My whole body tensed. The letter was probably from Hurakan. He had said that I should look for the White Sparkstriker there.

"The gods are on the verge of declaring war," Jazz went on. "No one's fessing up to breaking the Sacred Oath. And Ah-Puch is running loose, creating all sorts of trouble. The gods can't even agree on how to deal with him." He let out a frustrated breath. "Things are bad, Little Hawk, and they're about to get a whole lot worse."

Brooks balled her fists. My heart began to slam against my ribs. I couldn't let the gods get to Ah-Puch first. "Do you . . . do you know how to get to the Old World?" I asked the giant.

"The only way is through a gateway."

Brooks started searching frantically through her stuff. "Have you seen a rolled-up piece of paper?" she asked Jazz. "Something with a lot of drawings and lines on it?"

Jazz reached into a compartment and pulled out a scroll. "You mean this?"

The gateway map!

With a shrug, Jazz said sheepishly, "I snooped. Sorry, but it was an emergency."

Brooks snatched the map from him and unfurled it. Her eyes scanned it wildly. "It's . . . it's gone dark." She frowned. "Did you break it?"

"*D-D-Dark?* What...what d-d-do you mean?" I asked, now shivering.

Jazz raised his eyebrows, looking insulted. "No, I didn't break it! All gateway maps are off the grid right now. Portals are closed," he said. "The gods are limiting travel so they can try to find You-Know-Who."

Brooks continued to scan the map like it might come to life any second. Her dark hair swirled around her face as the wind whipped past. "How are we going to find the gateway, then?"

"My old friend holds up the sky, remember?" Jazz said.

"And?"

Jazz rolled his eye like his point was obvious. "I know things," he said. "Things like before there were maps, there were ancient gateways, secret and magical routes the gods used. *Those* portals aren't closed. I mean, they're a little rusty, and not as pleasant as the modern ones, but they'll do the job."

That was right. Hurakan had said the Bakabs used to work for him. It was all starting to come together. "Why aren't they closed?" I asked.

"Part of the original design," Jazz said. "The creator gods made four—one in each hemisphere—and they're as permanent as the sun and the moon. Or at least until Ah-Puch burns it all up."

*Creator gods*—that would be Hurakan and K'ukumatz.

"Okay," I said. "So is there one around here?"

"Not too far. According to my coordinates, we can be there by tomorrow night," Jazz said proudly. "This boat is a high-powered devil. Might even get us there a couple hours sooner than that."

"But we don't have that much time!" I argued. "The deadline is tomorrow when the moon rises!"

I looked at Brooks and didn't have to read her mind to know she was thinking the same thing. "Ah-Puch is going to destroy it all before then, Jazz!"

Jazz rubbed his chin, thinking. Then he stood and puffed up his chest so big a button popped off his purple vest. "Well, then it's a good thing you're in this dilemma with an engineering genius giant, isn't it? Let me get to work on the engine." He turned to leave, then hesitated and said, "Cabin's all made up for you. Don't drool on the pillows, got it?"

Then he was gone.

# 29

**I leaned over the railing, watching the dark** waters whiz by below, wondering if Pacific was down there, if she could see me. Maybe she could slow time or . . .

Brooks stood next to me with her back to the ocean. She tilted her head and stared at the sky. I folded my shivering arms across my chest and let out a breath I felt like I'd been holding for hours. The enchantment had worn off, but she was still . . . beautiful.

"Your dad . . ." Brooks said, kicking off her wet sandals. "He was the one who sent the letter."

"Hurakan," I corrected her.

"Whatever," she said. "He's still your dad, even if you don't call him that."

"It's not the same," I muttered as I loosened and took off my tie.

"Same as what?"

"Family. Like my mom, and Hondo . . ." *And Rosie*, I thought, my throat throbbing painfully. Being a member of my family wasn't automatic—it had to be earned. I remembered how, back on the twins' roof, Brooks's eyes had been on fire. They'd looked like they could burn up the whole world if she let them. "You told my mom you were looking for your only family. . . ."

Brooks dipped her head. "My sister."

"What happened to her?"

I was prepared for Brooks to shut me down with a single glare, but she didn't.

"She . . . she was promised to Bird by the matchmaker."

"Matchmaker?"

"Arranged marriages are our family custom," Brooks said. "Keeps bloodlines pure."

And Brooks *wasn't* a pureblood. "That sounds . . . barbaric."

"Just let me get this out, Zane, please!"

"Okay, okay."

She inhaled deeply. "But she didn't want to marry him. Quinn—that's her name."

Who could blame her for not wanting to marry the jerk? I was about to ask why she didn't tell the dirtbag to stuff it when Brooks filled in the gaps.

She wrapped her arms around herself. "It's not something you can get out of, so Quinn went . . . She went to Ixtab and asked for her help."

"What? Why would she think the new queen of hell could help her?"

Now I got the glare. "Are you going to let me finish or not?"

I drew my finger across my lips in a promise to stay silent until she was done.

With a slow shrug, Brooks whispered, "It was the only place she'd be safe. Even Bird couldn't get there without an invitation from Ixtab. New ruler, new rules." She was quiet for a while then added, "So I helped her. We told Bird we were going shopping for an enchanted wedding dress. He said she had to be the most gorgeous bride in history. It was pretty much the only thing he'd let her out of his sight for. I mean, he's pretty possessive. That's why the twins are so mad at me. But I didn't know she was going to..." Her voice cracked. "I didn't know she was giving herself to the underworld."

My mind was spinning, thinking what a strange world it was that Brooks lived in. And, as awful and scary and messed up as it was in that moment, her world was mine now, too.

Brooks wiped her cheek and I knew she was crying. Oh boy. Me and tears didn't mix. I didn't know if I should hug her, or pat her shoulder, or...hug her....

She pushed off the rail and walked over to the bench at the stern. "Stupid wind. Makes my eyes water."

"Yeah, me too," I said, following behind.

"Ixtab tricked her," Brooks continued. "In exchange for getting her out of the marriage, Ixtab told Quinn she could work off her debt by escorting souls to the underworld. It was only supposed to be for a few months, but then Ixtab changed her mind. Quinn's a powerful nawal, can shift into almost any animal. That's valuable to Ixtab. So she forced Quinn to stay."

"If Quinn is down there, how do you know all this?" I couldn't help it—the question just came out.

Brooks's voice sounded small. "Ixtab let me see her a few months ago."

I opened my mouth to say something but closed it again, thinking Brooks wasn't finished.

She rolled her eyes. "Go ahead."

"*You* went to Xib'alb'a?"

"No—we met at a gateway nearby," she said.

"Wait a second," I said. "Quinn's *alive* in the underworld?"

She nodded. "Ixtab needs her alive...for her powers."

It gave me hope for Rosie. Maybe she was still alive, too. Then I remembered what Ms. Cab had said: *She'll be changed.*

Brooks continued, "So I made a deal with Ixtab."

I was getting pretty sick of that word, *deal*. It was only four stupid letters strung together, but they had thorns that knew how to draw blood.

With a shaky sigh, Brooks said, "Quinn overheard a bunch of demon lords talking one day. They knew about the prophecy, but Ixtab didn't, so I thought..."

The sky slanted, or maybe it was the boat sinking into a swell, but my stomach shot up to my throat. I moved our stuff and sat down on the bench. "You thought you could use it to save your sister." I recalled what Ms. Cab had said about no one knowing who'd told Ixtab. About how I couldn't trust a nawal.

Brooks sat down next to me and pulled the blanket around her shoulders. "I told Ixtab I'd bring Ah-Puch back if she let my sister go and broke Quinn's tie to Bird. She just laughed and said I didn't have the strength, that I had never lived up to my family name. Not like Quinn."

I almost didn't want to ask, but I had to know. "And if you *didn't* bring Ah-Puch back...?"

"I'd lose access to Quinn forever." Brooks's eyes flitted in my direction and back to the sea. Her whole body trembled. "And if he got free, then I would have to join Ixtab."

I felt sick. Empty. Worthless. A strange heat ran through my veins. I would never have let Ah-Puch out if I'd known Brooks had promised herself to the underworld!

No. If I hadn't done it, Brooks might be dead.

Or was that the same thing?

"That's why Ixtab's goons came for you," I said.

"It gets worse."

"I don't think I can take more right now," I said, trying to understand what Brooks had done. She'd lied to me. Tricked me.

But she'd done it to save her only family. I would've done it, too. I was sure of it. Still, that didn't stop the burning sensation under my skin. . . .

"You don't get it," Brooks muttered. "The Prophecy of Fire . . . You had a choice . . ."

I didn't think I'd heard her right. "What? What do you mean?"

"I told you the magic would call to you. That part was true."

I definitely didn't want to hear any more. Maybe I didn't need to know the truth. Because guess what? Sometimes the truth stinks!

I stood up and looked around the boat, anywhere except at Brooks's accusing face. "Where's Jazz? You think he needs any help?"

"There was a way out."

I stepped away from Brooks. A cold gust swept across the boat.

Brooks fiddled with the blanket's loose threads. "You could

have walked away," she said, glancing up at me. "You could have ignored the call. You didn't *have* to release him."

Anger ripped through me so hard I started to shake. "*What?!* I'm lost here. You once said . . . You said I *didn't* have a choice!"

"I didn't know you were part *god*! No one did. And *that* gave you the power to choose."

My mind reeled. So if I'd known I was a godborn, I could have ignored the magic? A hot sensation started to climb up my bum leg. Would I have ignored the magic if I'd known? The salt air burned my eyes. "You're wrong. I didn't have a choice."

"I just told you—"

"You would've died!"

Brooks blinked back fresh tears. "I was going to be dead either way."

*One choice leads to victory, the other to defeat.* Well, thanks, Pacific. That piece of wisdom was just great—and absolutely worthless! I thought about my so-called choices. They'd all led to one disastrous outcome: death. Rosie, Brooks . . . And now, if I didn't beat Ah-Puch, he'd destroy everyone else I cared about and I'd become his servant, fighting on the wrong side of a bloody war. But even if I did defeat him, the gods would execute me for breaking some oath I'd never even agreed to!

(Are you gods catching on to how ridiculous this was?)

I sat back down. My head throbbed, filling with dark thoughts and confusion. Everything seemed impossible. I heard Hondo's voice in my head. *Find the soft spot and go after it with all you've got.*

The only problem was, Ah-Puch didn't seem to have any soft spots. I guess Hondo had never had to fight a god.

"I wouldn't blame you for hating me," Brooks said.

I had enough hate in me for Ah-Puch, for the twins, for . . .

"I don't hate you," I said. I gave a small shrug. "I guess I don't even blame you."

The air was tight and cold. And I really did want someone to blame, but everyone I mentally put up for the blame crown vanished, leaving me the only one left to wear it.

"So what're we going to do?" Brooks asked.

"*I'm* going to try to find a way to finish this without everyone dying."

"That's impossible," she whispered.

Maybe it was. But doing nothing wasn't an option.

Brooks pulled the blanket tighter. "The gods might give you a trial instead of a death sentence?" she said quietly, but it sounded more like a question than a fact.

"Really?"

"No."

"Then why'd you say that?"

"Because you look really awful, and I was trying to make you feel better."

"Well, don't. No more lies."

"No more lies."

I was sitting so close to Brooks our knees were touching. "I need to get Ah-Puch to come to the Old World. I don't know why, but Hurakan said to challenge him there."

Brooks tugged my sleeve up to reveal the mark on my wrist. "This is a tracking device, right?"

"So?"

"So, don't be dense. That means he'll follow you."

"You're brilliant!"

"You're only seeing that *now*?"

"By the way," I said, "I like your freckles."

"What?"

"They disappeared when you were enchanted, but now they're back."

Her face flushed. "You're annoying," she said through a giant yawn. Then she put her head on my shoulder.

My whole body tensed. As her breathing slowed, so did mine. She fell asleep and I stayed still, not wanting to disturb her. She needed her rest, this girl who couldn't swim but knew how to fly.

The world was quiet except for the purr of the engine, and for a minute I thought nothing could touch us. Not out here in the middle of the sea, where everything else was so far away.

A plan started to form in my head.

Carefully, I slipped out from under Brooks and eased her down onto the bench, covering her with the blanket. Then I went to the railing, leaned over, and whispered, "Pacific, are you there?"

No answer.

"I know you're down there," I said. "I could really use your help right now."

The black waters swelled.

"FYI, I'm on the gods' most-wanted list, and good old Puke has the twins, and the whole world is pretty much disintegrating while you hide out."

A sheet of fog wrapped around the boat, and I couldn't see more than a couple feet in front of me. And was it my imagination, or had the temperature dropped like fifty degrees? I was rubbing the chill off my arms when something began to materialize in the waters below.

I blinked and looked closer. It was a rowboat. Someone was inside.

And it wasn't Pacific.

# 30

—

**"You call *that* a boat?"** a voice said.

I peered through the dark as the fog lifted around the figure in the dinghy. The sea was now frozen solid, as smooth
as a sheet of glass. The man stood and stepped onto the slick
surface. He had on a pair of jeans and a plain gray T-shirt. I
couldn't see his face very well, because it was hidden under the
rim of a baseball cap that read CHARGERS with a lightning bolt
slicing the letters in half. His arms were covered in tattoos of
snakes slithering through piles of red and blue feathers.

With the force of thunder, it hit me. This was the Feathered
Serpent. As in Kukuulkaan. As in Brooks's *Holy K* god of coolness. AKA K'ukumatz.

"You're . . . you're . . . K'ukumatz. The guy who created the
worlds with Hurakan."

"Call me Mat. And for the record, he created the worlds
with *me.*"

"Mat," I repeated dumbly.

"Isn't that what you humans do, shorten honorable names?
Change them according to your wishes?" His voice was deep
with a faint accent I'd never heard before, like a cross between
Spanish and something that was sharper, harder.

The surface of the water rose around our boat until it

was flush with the deck and Mat and I were standing on even ground. Except he was a head taller. And his eyes? They were a shimmering violet. His chin was sharp and his skin weathered.

"Some also call me Kukuulkaan," he said. "But I hate that name. Imagine the nicknames: Kookoo, or Kook."

I thought about my own insulting nicknames. "You can call me Zane," I said quietly, trying not to wake Brooks.

He looked at his wrist like he had a watch on, but he didn't. "So, Zane, I was sent here by an old friend."

A lump formed in my throat. How much did Mat know? Had Pacific or Hurakan told him about me? Wasn't I supposed to be a secret?

"I know everything," he said, like he could read my mind.

"Okay." I figured I shouldn't say much. Find out what he knew first.

"I warned your father not to get mixed up with a human . . . but he didn't listen. He *never* listens. And now look at the fine mess we find ourselves in."

I didn't want to talk about the stupid mess. I already knew all its tangles and knots. "So he called you," I said. "Why?"

"He has always had the worst timing. I was at a Bolts football game, and they were actually winning. Well, with my help, that is."

"You rig football games?"

He shrugged casually. "Sometimes I use the elements to others' advantage. That makes me generous, don't you think?"

I guess that was one way to look at it. Unless you were on the losing end.

Mat cupped his hands as if he were holding something fragile. A flickering light formed in his palms, and he blew on the tiny flame. It zipped into the black sky like a streak of lightning. A second later, thunder sounded. And not just once. There was a series of booms, like someone was knocking down gigantic pins with a bowling ball over and over.

"That should give us some privacy," he said. "Now, where were we?"

How could I learn to do *that*?

"Uh . . . you rig football games," I said.

"Yes . . . I mean, no. Stay focused, kid. I'm here to expedite your journey to the Old World."

The air grew colder. "How?"

He shook his head and sighed with annoyance like I should've known the answer. "I control the elements," he said. "The water does what I command, so I'll kick some currents into high gear, put the wind at your back, and off you go. Then *I* can get back to my game."

Maybe things would work out after all.

"There's one little problem," he said.

Why couldn't things ever be simple?

"I can't be too obvious—don't want to draw attention to you, if you know what I mean. So I'll have to take it a little easy—as in no hurricanes or tsunamis. Get it?"

"Right," I said. "No storms."

Just then, Pacific materialized from the ocean mist. She perched on the boat's railing, wearing the same jaguar-spotted cape as before. "Is he being nice to you, Zane?"

"I'm *always* nice," Mat said to her.

"Mm-hmm . . . Tell that to the two worlds you destroyed."

"That's not the same thing," Mat said. "They totally deserved that."

Pacific narrowed her eyes and walked over to me. "So is he? Being nice?"

"Uh-huh," I said. "What're you doing here? Did you hear me call—?"

"I'm going to tug on the time rope bit by bit," she said. "Enough to buy you some time, but not so much that anyone figures out I'm not dead. But really, Zane, we can't make this a habit."

I had to admit, I felt a spark of hope in my chest. Then I remembered that in the end I'd still have to have a face-off with the god of death, destruction, and darkness, and the hope fizzled. "How much time will it give us?"

"A few hours . . . at most," she said. "Anything more and the gods will notice."

Thunder shook the sky and Brooks stirred, mumbling something in her sleep. Mat tucked Pacific's pale hair behind her ear, looking at her all goo-goo-eyed. They were an item? Maybe that's what happens when you live together for centuries.

"The gods are looking for a fight," Mat said, turning his gaze back to me. "We're choosing sides, getting ready for war."

"But I thought you said you were at a football game."

"You have a lot to learn, Zane Obispo. Gods can be in more than one place at a time. But what matters is that war is coming."

I started to pace. "What if I can defeat Ah-Puch? Will there still be a war?"

"Trust has already been shattered," Pacific said. "And no one wants to admit to breaking the Sacred Oath."

"Why doesn't Hurakan just tell them it was him?" I said. "Maybe he could ask for forgiveness."

Mat shook his head. "Gods don't forgive."

I was starting to wonder if I wanted to be related to a bunch of crazed, coldhearted killers. "When will this war start?"

"You have to move quickly," Pacific said. "Get to Ah-Puch first, because if you don't—"

"*We* will." Mat's jaw tensed.

And I'd become a soldier of death, because I hadn't gotten the job done myself. "Hey, Mat?"

"Yeah, kid?"

"If, as a godborn, I could have chosen *not* to release Ah-Puch, why didn't my dad tell me that? None of this had to happen." Anger pulsed through my veins. Rosie wouldn't have had to die. Brooks wouldn't have lost her powers. I wouldn't have had to make the deal of death with Pukeface.

Pacific stepped closer. "Yes, a godborn can ignore the magic, but only when he has come into his full power. And you haven't done that yet. So telling you wouldn't have made a difference."

*Full power?*

Mat folded his arms over his chest. "You don't become a god automatically, with the snap of a finger, or because of your bloodline. Godhood has to be earned. Fought for. Your power arrives gradually, and when . . ." His sentence trailed off.

"When what?"

Pacific shot him a glare then turned to me. "We can't say

any more. Consider this your head start." She smiled at me softly. I knew that dumb look. Teachers and school nurses and strangers at the grocery store had given it to me plenty: *Poor kid.*

"We're doing this as a favor to your dad," Mat said. "But remember, Ah-Puch has powerful allies, too."

"Yeah, like the Yant'o Triad," I said. "Those guys are creepy."

"You met them?" Mat pulled off his cap. Dark curls fell over his eyes.

I told him and Pacific how the twins had been captured. I lifted my wrist and said, "He's tracking me."

Mat's eyes zeroed in on the skull tattoo with moving eyelids. "He's so uninventive. But not to worry, Zane. He's busy trying to figure out his enemies' next moves right now. He won't come for you until it's time."

Oh, well, that made me feel better. Not!

"What's so important about the Old World anyway?" I asked.

Mat and Pacific shared a glance, then Pacific whispered, "It's the only place where you have a chance of defeating Ah-Puch."

"What? How?" My heart drummed loudly. "How do I beat a really angry god, especially without my own godly powers?"

Mat inched back and looked down at the frozen ocean. "Water takes many forms. It becomes what it needs to become. You, Zane Obispo, must become . . . what you were *meant* to become. The Old World is the only place you can do that."

Why did people always give me vague responses? Why

couldn't anyone just provide a straight answer, preferably with a step-by-step diagram? "You mean become the Storm Runner."

Pacific slipped off the railing and onto the water's still-frozen surface. "Yes."

"But I can't run! How am I supposed to become the Storm Runner if . . ." I thought about Hurakan, about the Empty he had created, and anger shook my bones. "Why can't he ever tell me anything himself? Why does Hurakan always have to send messengers? He's a coward!"

*"Shhh,"* Pacific warned, looking around.

"We've got to get a move on," said Mat, putting his cap back on. "We've done our favor."

"One more thing. . . ." I fished the jaguar jade from my pocket. "Other than letting me talk to my dad, what exactly does this oldest magic do?" I asked. "The twins said whoever gives it away can fill it with any power . . . ?"

Pacific tugged on a dreadlock and looked at me expectantly.

"So who am I supposed to give it to?"

"That's up to you," Pacific said.

"Chatting time is over, kid," Mat said. "It's too dangerous for us to linger." As he stepped into the rowboat along with Pacific, he ran his hand across the icy sea. In a blink, it turned back to liquid and dropped to its normal level. I heard him mutter, "If they knew I found you and didn't . . ."

He didn't have to finish his sentence. He was expected to kill me on sight. If he failed to do so, he'd be killed himself. I got it. Zane Obispo: the gods' Public Enemy Number One.

A curtain of fog rose from the ocean and I watched as they floated into it. The sea began to churn again, glossy ripples under the moonlight.

It was weird to live with death breathing down your neck. It changes your mind and your heart and your choices. Did Brooks feel the same way, I wondered, knowing Ixtab might come for her anytime?

"Zane?" I turned as Brooks sat up sleepily, rubbing her eyes. "I had the strangest dream. There was thunder and ..."

"I met Kukuulkaan," I cut in.

She rocketed to her feet. "Where? Here? Why didn't you wake me up?! Did you get his autograph?"

"He's going to help us," I said, feeling pretty cool, because Brooks was looking at me with something like admiration. "Speed up the currents, give us some wind."

Her look of admiration vanished. "You didn't get an autograph."

"Uh—sorry. Had more pressing things on my mind, fangirl," I teased.

"Mm-hmm ... Why would he help you?"

"He and my dad go way back."

Her eyes widened. "Of course!" She reached into her backpack and pulled out her socks and boots. "They worked together to create and destroy—"

"Right." Why couldn't I have been born to the god of leaving everything alone?

I looked down at death's mark on my wrist. The eyelids shifted like before, and I had a creepy feeling they were going to open very soon.

# 31

**Brooks and I lay on opposite ends of the bench**
with only our feet touching. I gave her most of the blanket as
the winds kicked up, speeding the currents. I closed my eyes
and fell into a deep sleep, where I dreamed of the strange
metal forest like before, but this time there was no Rosie.
Only Ms. Cab as a chicken the size of a rhinoceros hollering,
"Find his blind spot!"

"Ah-Puch doesn't *have* a blind spot!" I yelled. Then I felt
relieved to see her. She was my link to home. "How's my mom?"

"Your mom? You're worried about her, when every day I'm
becoming more of a chicken? Today I craved birdseed, Zane.
*Birdseed!* You must hurry."

"I get it! But I need to know . . . is she okay?"

With an annoyed cluck, Ms. Cab said, "If you must know,
that fool Ortiz has us under constant surveillance. And when
I'm no longer a chicken, I swear I'll . . ." She let her pending
threat die on her chicken lips.

Good. The three of them were safe and sound.

"Now back to old Puke," I said. "Unless you have some
secret up your sleeve, you badgering me in my dreams isn't
exactly helping. And it really hurt when you jammed your
beak into my hand!"

"Yes, well, you deserved that. I agree that dreams aren't the best way to communicate. Only some of my words are reaching you, and it's quite maddening. But it's all we have."

"So what do I do? Once I'm in the Old World?"

"Kill him."

"Great idea!"

"Zane, I'm a *chicken*! My legs are chicken legs. My eyes are chicken eyes. My brain? Well, you get the point. I'm not exactly... DID I MENTION I'M A CHICKEN? And You-Know-Who sings out of tune to me every day!"

I hoped I'd make it back to tell Mr. O that La Muerte was as powerful as he'd dreamed. He'd be so excited. "And Rosie?" I asked hopefully. "Any word from your friends?"

"Do I *look* like your secretary?"

The metal trees shimmered with warped images I couldn't make out. Then Ms. Cab squawked. "Time to wake up. Remember the blind spot, Zane. Find it!"

There was a terrible explosion, and a cloud of smoke filled the air. I jerked awake, hacking up my lungs. Brooks pulled the blanket over her head and jammed her foot against my leg.

"Sorry," I murmured, sitting up. Thankfully, the explosion had only been in my dream. The smoke had been replaced with fog so thick it swallowed the sea and the horizon. The sky above was a pale grayish blue. It was impossible to tell for sure, but I guessed the sun was rising.

Jazz rushed down from the second deck. "We've made incredible time! See? I told you this boat was amazing!"

"Are we close?" I asked, lowering my voice to avoid another kick from Brooks.

"We're here."

"*This* is the Old World?"

That got Brooks up. Her hair was a tangle of knots and she had dark circles under her eyes.

Jazz snorted. "No, this is the entrance."

Blinking, I looked around, trying to see through the mist. "Where?" I half expected a door or a gate.

Brooks was on her knees, peering over the railing. "I don't see anything."

The boat lurched and stopped suddenly, like a stone wall was blocking our way. Slowly the fog separated and curled into ribbons, creating an image. I held my breath, watching as it took shape . . . sleeping eyes, a nose, and a mouth. It looked like an enormous face.

"Holy K!" Brooks cried. "What is that?"

"How do we get through?" I asked.

Jazz grunted. "The mouth, of course."

"Do we need some kind of magic words or something?" Brooks said. "To get it to open?"

Jazz frowned, then looked at us with one frantic eye. "Give me something that belongs to each of you. Something with some weight to it."

There wasn't time for questions. Brooks yanked off her boot, muttering something about freezing feet, and thrust it at him.

Jazz turned it over in his hand.

"It's all I could think of," Brooks said. "Unless you want a dirty sock."

I looked around, grabbed my stupid cane off the bench,

and handed it to him. "You think it's going to open for a combat boot and a cane?"

Jazz launched Brooks's boot into the face. Nothing happened. "Just like I suspected," he mumbled. The fog began to curl again and the face started to disappear. "Blood for the gods, open!" He launched my cane, smacking the face on the nose.

Slowly, the mouth opened, a huge yawn that revealed total darkness inside.

"Er . . . you sure this is a good idea?" I asked.

"You want to get to the Old World or not?" Jazz rushed up the stairs and put the boat in gear. We sailed into the mouth silently until we were covered in total darkness.

"Jazz?" That was Brooks.

He drew in a sharp breath. "I'm here, kid."

As my eyes adjusted, I said, "*This* is the gateway?" My voice echoed like we were in a tunnel. A very cold tunnel that smelled like rotting roadkill.

Brooks wrinkled her nose and covered her mouth with her hand. The smell was sickening . . . like at the dairy farm back home, but mixed with raw chicken decaying in the sun. Then I saw why: in the dark waters below were bizarre-looking eyeless fish, as long as bull sharks and as bloated as puffer fish. Their pale flesh looked half-eaten, and chunks fell off as they slithered through the dark.

Whitish foam curdled on the water's surface.

Brooks's eyes were wide, trying to cut through the dark. "What do you see, Zane?"

"Looks like a tunnel." I leaned over the railing. We were

surrounded by rusted, corroded metal walls. "Or the hull of a wrecked ship."

The space was so narrow, I could've reached out and touched the walls if I'd wanted to. Which I didn't. Creaks and groans echoed through the cold space.

"Why is it so awful?" I asked, trying to take tiny breaths to avoid the rotten smell.

"Hasn't been kept up," Jazz said, flicking on a flashlight. It looked a lot like the burning-flesh kind Brooks had lost in the volcano. "When the new gateways were built, these were forgotten. Death has a way of infesting whatever it touches."

I looked up at Jazz. He was frowning, scanning me like I was some kind of lab rat. Like maybe he'd like to switch on the red beam and burn me up.

"What's wrong?" Brooks said. Her face was half-hidden in the shadows.

"When I got the letter," Jazz began slowly, "I thought there'd been a mistake. Then I got suspicious. Why would someone ask me to take them to the Old World? A place of the gods."

"What're you talking about, Jazz?" Brooks asked.

He began to hum that stupid song "The Days Are a-Comin'," and a terrible uneasiness rose inside of me.

"Only gods can *open* the old gateways," he said. "I'm not a god, and, Little Hawk, you're not, so that leaves the two others on board. And something tells me it isn't El Luchador downstairs."

I opened my mouth to say something. . . . What, I didn't know.

Brooks shot me a look while Jazz continued to unravel my secret. "Your cane," he said. "That's what opened the gate."

"How does a *cane* open an ancient gateway?" I asked flippantly, hoping Jazz might hear how crazy it sounded.

"By belonging here," Jazz said. "By belonging to a god."

I didn't like the way he was considering me with his one eye. This had gotten out of hand. There were too many clues and signs pointing to me as a godborn, and I knew it was only a matter of time before everyone figured it out. I had to get to Ah-Puch, and I had to get there fast.

A flash of movement in the water caught my attention.

Slowly, like it didn't want us to notice, the dark water began to rise. The foam bubbled and steamed.

"Jazz?" I looked over my shoulder at him.

"So," he said, still stuck on me having the power to open the gateway, "what do you have to say for yourself? You some kind of god in disguise? What kind of game are you playing?"

"Uh, can we talk about that later? Because right now we've got a problem."

"Problem?"

"Looks like the water's rising," I said more calmly than I felt.

Jazz's eyebrows shot up. He rushed to the boat's railing, aimed the light, and scanned the sea below. Shadows cast by the pale eyeless fish darted right under the surface. Then he mumbled a few curses and said, "It's even worse than that."

"Jazz!" Brooks shouted. "The walls are closing in—"

"Someone's trying to shut this gateway!" Jazz jerked off his vest. "We gotta get out!"

"Get out?" Brooks said. "How much farther do we have to go?"

"Is there an emergency exit?" I hoped.

"Just a few feet," Jazz barked. "A few lousy feet!"

I didn't have to guess who was closing the gateway: Pukeface. Blasted tracker—I should've carved it out of my skin. But I'd been stupid enough to believe he'd be too busy tormenting the twins to care about me.

Jazz scrambled up to the deck, shifted the gears so hard the boat groaned in protest. The engine sputtered. "Come on, move!" he yelled.

I felt helpless. The water continued to rise. I heard the sound of rusted gears grinding as the walls kept closing in. The air was so thick, it felt like a living thing trying to choke us all.

"Zane!" Brooks hollered. "Do something!"

I gave her a panicked but blank look. "Like *what*?"

"You're the son of . . ." She threw her hands into the air and shouted, "I don't know, like ANYTHING!"

I leaned over the edge, willing the water to stay in place. Mat had only traced his hands through the water to get it to do as he commanded. Instinctively, I raised my hand. "Stay!" Okay, lame choice of words. I mean, I wasn't commanding a dog. But it was all I could think of.

The water kept rising.

Rising and rising and rising.

My body stiffened. Jazz cursed up a storm as he rushed belowdecks and returned with an inflatable raft. "Boat's too big to get through. It's gonna get crushed like a sardine can!"

He was right. In only a minute or so the crushing would begin. Jazz raised the raft to his mouth and started blowing. Fortunately, a giant's lungs are big enough to inflate a four-person dinghy in fifteen seconds.

"No way I'm getting into that!" Brooks said to Jazz. "Those . . . those monsters will eat right through it."

"They only eat flesh," Jazz argued, rubbing his chin. "Don't think they like rubber."

"Oh," I said with a casual shrug. "Well, that makes it a super option!"

My wrist began to burn like hot wax was dripping onto my skin. I didn't want to look down. Somehow I knew that the second I did, everything would change.

*Drip. Drip. Drip.*

Clenching my jaw, I glanced at Ah-Puch's mark. The eyes beneath the eyelids moved back and forth wildly, impatiently. Slowly and painfully my skin began to tear, as if an invisible razor was slicing it open. I bit back a scream, watching in terror.

The eyelids opened. This wasn't just a tattoo. These were *real eyes*. Black eyes that could see. Now I *did* scream.

A line of blood snaked down my arm.

"What is it?" Brooks's voice shook.

A deep, dark laugh echoed off the walls.

"AH-PUCH!" I shouted so loud the walls vibrated. "You're a coward!"

"Where is your father now?" His voice was steady as a thin trail of black mist rose from the slit in my wrist and encircled me.

"Zane?" Brooks's wild eyes took me in. I could tell she couldn't hear the god of death.

Anger was climbing up my throat now, fast and furious. It burned like lava.

"Guys!" Jazz called from the front of the boat, where he'd already loaded Hondo. "Get in!"

I hurried over, tugging Brooks along, and made sure she got into the life raft. She looked back, reaching for my hand, but I'd already stepped away.

Her eyes glowed like fire. "Zane!"

"Let them go, Ah-Puch! It's me you want!" I gripped the railing. The corroded walls continued to press in.

"Zane!" Brooks shouted again. She was trying to scramble back aboard the boat, but Jazz had a hold of her. She kicked and squirmed. "Let me go!"

The dark laugh bounced off the walls. Ah-Puch was enjoying this.

The albino fish-monsters began to glow beneath the dark water, casting a putrid yellow light through the tunnel.

I glanced down at the eyes on my wrist. They were staring up at me. *Gods can be in more than one place at a time,* Mat had said. I finally understood. Ah-Puch could see me, knew my every move, but not because of some tracking device. These eyes . . . *his* eyes had become *a part of me.* I gagged.

"We're not going without Zane!" Brooks had managed to get free of Jazz and was climbing back onto the boat, which the walls were still crushing. Why was she so stubborn?

More screeching and grinding of metal on metal. Water splashed over the sides and foam pooled on the deck. The monsters below opened their massive jaws, ready to devour whatever flesh came their way.

Everything seemed to be happening in slow motion. Out of the corner of my eye I could see Brooks coming toward me with awkward strides as the boat tipped dangerously.

I dropped to my knees. I knew what I had to do. Brooks was gripping the railing, getting closer and closer. "Stay back!" I hollered at her. But I knew it was useless. She never listened.

"You're strong, godborn," Ah-Puch hissed. "But not strong enough."

Then an idea struck me. I reached into my pocket and pulled out the jade. *Whoever gives it away can give it any power.* With an outstretched arm, I tried passing it to Brooks. To give her some kind of control over water so they all could get away.

"Take it!" I shouted.

Her eyes fixed on it and I could tell she understood. She lunged, her free hand extended.

As our fingers met, the boat lurched forward, forcing me to lose my grip on the stone. It skittered down the deck.

Pivoting like a tornado, Brooks went for the jade, but she didn't have enough light to find it.

It was gone.

The shadowy sea crept up, higher and higher. Like sharks that could smell blood, the monsters gathered with open mouths.

I called to Brooks over my shoulder, "Pull me out when I tell you to, okay?"

"Pull . . . ? What . . . what're you talking about?"

"Just be fast!" I hollered. Then to Ah-Puch I said, "You want me? Then come and get me."

And I plunged my wrist into the hungry waters.

# 32

**It was worse than I'd imagined. Like acid burn-**ing through my skin. The screams that tore through the tunnel weren't mine. At first. They belonged to the god of death. But it wasn't long before my screams joined his as the monsters ate away at his eyes and *my flesh.*

Brooks grabbed my other arm and pulled me away from the water. I fell back, crashing against the deck. I heard heavy footfalls. Jazz had returned to the boat.

The tunnel walls had stopped closing in.

I gasped, shivered uncontrollably. I was in shock. Terrible, numbing shock. Brooks's voice was coming at me like she was underwater.

"Zane, what did you do?" Zane this. Zane that. *Zane. Zane. Zane.*

At the edge of my mind I remembered thrusting my arm into the water. I could still feel the monsters' sharp teeth.

I looked up at Brooks. Her dark hair spilled around her worried face. "Get me a rag for his arm," she said.

There was a sudden sound of rushing water, and our poor crunched boat pitched forward with a groan. Soon it felt like we were cruising down a river. The rotten smell had disappeared, which told me we weren't in the tunnel anymore. But the darkness hadn't let us go.

My breath evened out. My eyes focused. Terrified of the damage I might see, I squinted at my wound. The skin was raw and bleeding, like the time I'd fallen off the back of Hondo's truck and scraped my knees against the hot asphalt. From what I could tell, at least some of Ah-Puch's mark was gone. I hoped those eyes were history.

Jazz shone his flashlight on me while Brooks shoved a rag into my hand for me to hold against my wrist. She cursed under her breath while she prepared a bandage. Jazz had found some gauze in the boat's first aid kit, but it must've been for giants, because it was huge. She tore a strip with her teeth.

"You saved us." That was Hondo.

Hondo! I turned to see him kneeling next to me, a smirk sliding across his mouth. "You're one crazy, stupid-brave kid."

I grabbed hold of him, pulling myself into a sitting position, and hugged him with all the strength I had left. "I'm sorry," I whispered. Sure, my flesh might have been dinner for some creepy fish, but I couldn't imagine the pain he had gone through.

Other than the dark shadows under his eyes, he looked okay. But that's not what worried me most about him. Sometimes the bruising on the inside is what gets you the worst.

Brooks gently took hold of my arm and began wrapping it, first with the gauze then with a strip of silk lining she'd torn from Jazz's purple vest. It wasn't exactly a cool bandage, because the fabric had tiny pink flowers printed all over it.

"Not so tight!" I flinched. She definitely should never be a nurse.

Then I put my hand over hers and made her look at me. "It was my fault," I muttered, because I knew she was blaming herself for the lost jade.

She brushed away a tear and opened her mouth but said nothing.

"You're one helluva hero, running Ah-Puch off like that." Jazz clapped me on the back and I wondered if he'd meant to put that much muscle into it, or if maybe it was payback for lying to him. "You saved our lives!"

But there wasn't time to celebrate. The real battle hadn't even started. And without the jade, I had nothing to help me.

Jazz tried to start up with me. "So, you're a godborn, eh?"

"Can we talk about that later?" Brooks shot him a glare and helped me to my feet. "You're okay?"

"Other than the pink flowers?"

"Zane!"

"Yeah, I . . . I'm fine," I said, forcing a smile.

Satisfied I wasn't going to bleed out, she snapped, "You could've lost your arm, you idiot! What were you thinking?"

"I had to take out his eyes. He could see me, see every move before I made it."

Hondo gave a short nod of approval. "You attacked his weakness. But seriously, dude . . . that was pretty gross."

So I'd found the first soft spot (Puke's overconfidence, his underestimation of me) and I'd landed a blow. I had to admit, I felt pretty proud of myself, despite the fact that I was going to have a killer scar to remind me of the terrible burning pain from those evil little fish with razor teeth. They had only removed half of Ah-Puch's mark, and now it looked like a regular eyeless skull. But at least he couldn't see me anymore.

I went to stand, and that's when I saw my flattened back-pack. I must've fallen on top of it. Quickly, I unzipped it and rooted around for Ms. Cab's eye. I didn't have to pull the baggie out to know. I could feel the mush. I'd smashed her eyeball! She was definitely going to kill me. If Ah-Puch didn't do the honors first.

The boat pitched. A dim light flickered up ahead. Inch by inch we floated toward it until the tunnel disappeared entirely. "Whoa!" Hondo turned in slow circles, taking in the gray jungle around us. Brooks drew in a sharp breath, leaning over the boat's edge.

Broad trees stretched toward the cloudless sky, their branches drooping with the weight of spiderwebs that were choking the life from them. It was a strange world—dull, like all the color had been drained from it. The trees, the sky, the earth were all different shades of gray. Other than the dried leaves rustling in the slow breeze, the place was as silent as an old graveyard.

"It's . . . it's eerie," I said, not sure what I was expecting.

"The Old World," Jazz whispered, all awestruck, as if it needed to be named. Yeah, emphasis on *old*. As in one foot in the grave.

Hondo grimaced. "Place looks dead."

"Not dead," Jazz said. "Asleep. It has been eternal night here ever since the gods abandoned it."

Two small moons inched across the sky in perfect synchronicity.

"Hang on!" I said. "Ah-Puch gave me until the third moon, but the moons here are always present!"

"Maybe he meant in *our* time zone," Hondo said.

Brooks blew a stray curl from her face. "Puke doesn't care about time zones. All he cares about is winning. Good point, Zane. If the moons here never disappear, he could essentially show up any second."

How could she be so calm about this?

Pukeface had told me he needed time to take care of a few things. I hoped that meant things in our world.

"How do we know what time it is here?" I asked Jazz so I could figure out the time back home.

Jazz smacked his forehead and rolled his eye. "Time? Here? Kid, you've got a lot to learn. Time isn't marked in the Old World." He glanced at the watch on his wrist. "Lucky for you, my watch keeps Real World Time—even when I'm here. It's still morning in Cali."

So I had almost a whole day left. Hopefully. I started breathing again.

Hondo craned his neck to see Jazz's massive silver watch with a dozen dials and buttons. "I know a few things about marketing," he said to the giant. "Maybe we could become partners. Then again, I guess your watch probably wouldn't be that popular, considering no one comes here," he added with a shrug. "But the other stuff, like that scooter? Totally awesome."

"Super Turbo Jazz!" Jazz grunted. "I have lots of inventions.

Some didn't turn out too well, like the dog collar that was supposed to make dogs fly. Ended up burning off their fur instead. I got sued over that one. Lost half my life savings."

"Guys!" Brooks interrupted. "Focus?"

The boat bumped up against an embankment of crumbled stone, where the river ended.

"Time to disembark," Jazz said cheerfully.

But there was nothing cheerful about this sleeping gray place. Only a feeling of dread. And the first thought that crept into my head? *I don't want to die here.*

Jazz shouldered a huge pack and stepped off the boat. We all followed. Adjusting his eye patch, he turned to Brooks. "Is now a good time, Little Hawk?"

He was asking for her permission to interrogate me, so I cut him off at the pass. "Yes, I'm a godborn," I said. There was no point trying to hide it now. It was like a boat with a leak in the bottom—pretty soon it would fill with water and sink.

"You can't tell anyone, Jazz," Brooks said, hoisting her bag over her shoulder.

Jazz looked offended. "You know giants are the best secret-keepers—next to seers, that is." Then he narrowed his eye and inched closer to me. "Wait a second. . . . If you're part god . . ."

*Uh-oh.* He'd figured it out and looked like he was going to blow. Whatever was sleeping here was about to wake up. He clenched his boulder-size fists. "You're the one who set that masochistic, bloodthirsty monster free!"

Hondo stepped between me and the giant, craning his neck to look up at Jazz. "Hang on," he argued. "He didn't have a choice. I mean, he did, but not really. Give the kid a break."

Jazz began to shake. A fat green vein throbbed in his neck. Brooks rushed over with a chocolate drink from her pack, which he guzzled, leaving dribbles down his chin.

"He did it to save me," Brooks said pleadingly. "I would've died if Zane hadn't let him out."

Jazz's gray eye roved between me and Brooks like he was trying to connect more dots. How long would it take for the gods to do the same?

"The gods will kill you when they find out," he said finally. "No way will they let another godborn live." Then he let out a loud burp that reeked of onion and dust.

"Yeah, so I've heard," I said. "But . . . I . . . uh, I need to stay alive long enough to kill Ah-Puch." I'd worry about the gods after that. If there *was* an after.

"You." Jazz smirked. "A skinny kid with a . . ."

"Limp," I finished his sentence.

"I was going to say lopsided head, but okay." Jazz snapped a branch off a tree and handed it to me. I guessed it was supposed to be a walking stick. "Best leave it to the gods, kid," he went on. "They've got a lot more experience with this sort of thing."

"He *is* a god!" Hondo argued. "And a hell of a fighter. He can take down a demon runner in his sleep!"

I love my uncle, but he wasn't helping my case. Jazz didn't look convinced. "Demon runners are shadows of the gods with none of their magic or power," the giant said. "The fact is, we don't know enough about your brand of godborn blood— what it's capable of, or not." He wiped some chocolate off his chin and licked his fingers. "That was the whole reason for the Sacred Oath—to keep things balanced, orderly. Unless you've got some powers greater than the gods', you need to step aside."

"It has to be him, Jazz," Brooks insisted, tugging off her single boot. "We . . . we can't let anyone else get to Ah-Puch."

"I hear an *or else* in there, Little Hawk."

"Or else I die," I said.

"Or else he becomes a soldier of death," Brooks added, tossing her boot away.

"Death would be much better than *that*!" Jazz shrugged like he was used to hearing this sort of thing all the time. "Whatever. You want to get yourself killed? Be my guest. But don't drag Little Hawk into this any more than you already have," he said. Then his eye lit up as if something important had occurred to him. "So that's it. . . ."

"What?" I said. "What's *it*?"

"Your dad," Jazz began. "Whoever he is . . ." He stuck his fingers in his ears. "And don't tell me. The less I know, the better. He wanted you to lure Ah-Puch to this place, because he knew that the gods wouldn't look here. Not at first, anyway. He bought you time to do the deed yourself before all the heavens descend on you like vultures. Not sure if that means he likes you or hates you. I guess you could look at it either way."

"You sure the gods won't come here?" I asked, not sure whether that made me feel better or worse.

Jazz started down a shadowy path. "Look around, kid. No one's been here in eons."

Hondo's eyes cut across the pale world. "Not exactly a

dream destination," he said. Then, "I really need to change out of these threads, but can I keep the suit?"

Jazz smirked, and I figured it was safe to ask him about the Sparkstriker then. "Lightning pounder?" he said. "Yeah, I've heard of her."

"Lightning pounder?" That sounded sort of . . . violent.

"She strikes lightning into seers, giving them powers. She's all women's lib, trains girl orphans who have nowhere else to go, stuff like that. Don't know what your old man would want with her. I mean, unless he wants her to train you, which there isn't time for."

"Right," I said, feeling stupidly small. Why would Hurakan send me to an ancient lightning pounder who trains orphan girls? Last time I checked, I wasn't an orphan or a girl. What if this lightning pounder couldn't help me?

Jazz grunted. "Let's get a move on, kid. You've got a god to kill."

# 33

**"Where are we going?"** Brooks asked, trailing Jazz.

"Being a giant has its advantages, like being able to see things from far away."

"What did you spot?" I asked, trying to keep up and totally failing, even with the walking stick.

"You'll see," Jazz said excitedly.

The air was cold and flat. Nothing slithered or breathed or stalked or flew. It was like the place had been abandoned by every living creature. Except one that *had* to be here: the White Sparkstriker.

"We can't just walk aimlessly," Hondo said after we'd trekked for what seemed like a mile through the dense jungle.

"We're not," Jazz said. He had to duck every so often to avoid slamming his head into a branch. "We're going to Puksí'ikal."

"Come again?" Hondo said.

Brooks ran-hopped to keep up with Jazz's enormous stride.

"It's Mayan for *heart*, the center of the Old World," Jazz said with his booming voice. "A place the gods made together, where they could meet, give counsel, pass judgment. Create, destroy. You know, stuff gods do when they've got nothing else to do." He maintained his pace, swiping at stray branches that were getting in the way. "It's the original place, where the first world was dreamed up. And the second and the third." He took quick breaths. "The oldest and most powerful magic in the universe was born *here*! Man, this is going to do wonders for my career!"

My mind turned quickly. So Hurakan must have been a part of this place, too. He was a creator god, along with Mat. The back of my neck tingled as I thought, *This is where it all began.* The first magic. It made the place feel sort of... sacred. Was Jazz right? Did Hurakan want me to come here just because the gods wouldn't? Something felt off about that. But what it was, I didn't know.

I followed Jazz, walking in step with Hondo, who was slower than usual, which was the only reason I could keep up.

"You have a plan for killing old Puke?" Hondo asked quietly so only I could hear.

"Sort of."

"*Sort of* doesn't get you the gold, does it?"

"I have a plan, okay?" I didn't care about gold. I only wanted to take down Ah-Puch and keep him from crushing the whole world. And if I could stay out of Xib'alb'a, that would be super awesome. The wound on my wrist burned and my head throbbed.

"Now that you've gouged out Puke's eyes," Hondo continued as we walked, "how's he going to find you? Wasn't the whole point to get the Stinking One to follow you here?"

"He knows I'm here in the Old World. Trust me, he'll find me. Unless I find him first."

Brooks fell back and said, "You need to be ready. It could be any time."

The trees parted and we stepped into a clearing as long as five football fields. It was dominated by five enormous pyramids arranged in a semicircle. All the structures looked exactly the same. Each had steep staircases, one on each of the three sides that I could see, leading up to what looked like a square temple at the very top. They reminded me of the one Hurakan had created in the Empty, but these were much taller.

We walked into the center of the clearing. Jazz stared up at a pyramid in awe and said, "This here is sacred ground. Where the council—the five dominant gods—ruled, created, and destroyed." His voice caught and he cleared his throat. "It's true," he whispered.

"What's true?" I asked.

"Each side of each pyramid has ninety-one steps, making three hundred sixty-four total."

Wow! He could count fast. Maybe it was a giant thing.

He continued, "When you add in the step taken to enter the temple at the top, the total comes to three hundred sixty-five."

"The number of days in a year," Brooks said, catching on.

"So the gods can count," Hondo said impatiently. "Congrats."

"This is how the marking of time came to be," Jazz declared. "It was *invented* in this place. The legend says that the gods competed for seats here—that's how the council was formed. Each temple represents a different god of the council: Nakon, god of war, and Ixtab—she's running Xib'alb'a these days—then there's Hurakan, god of storms . . ."

My breath caught in my throat.

Jazz went on, "Ixkakaw, goddess of chocolate . . . I think she overthrew another goddess, maybe Ixchel? She was the goddess of healing—didn't like fighting. And then there's Alom, god of the sky."

"So these gods made themselves kings?" I said.

"And queens," Brooks said.

Jazz was still smiling. "Then one, no one knows who, created time, and the world began. Or at least the third version of it. Man, I wish I had a camera!"

So Pacific had once been on the council—before the gods got rid of her and she was wiped from history.

Brooks gazed up. "Some say the gods lost the time rope. It used to be wrapped around the earth, but it disappeared, and now they can't time-travel anymore."

"Seems like a pretty big thing to lose," Hondo said, shaking his head. "Did you say time-travel?"

Jazz yawned wide. "I'll make a camp at the edge of the jungle. We all need some rest, since any moment could be"— he looked at me—"you know, kill-time and all that."

"Shouldn't we be looking for the Sparkstriker?" My insides were in knots.

"You need rest and sustenance, kid," Jazz said. "Besides, no one *finds* Old Sparky." He pulled magically heated pizza pockets and also bags of gummy worms out of his pack and passed them around. Was this all giants ate? I wondered.

"I'll keep first watch," Hondo said, chomping his pizza pocket. "Hey, speaking of watch, does yours have Wi-Fi?"

Jazz shook his head sadly like he was bummed he hadn't thought of that. "But I've got a log that burns for eighteen hours!" He fished it out of his bag. "Oh, and we might need these." He passed each of us a demon-tormenting flashlight. So *he* was Brooks's supplier.

"What are we watching for?" Brooks wiped some crumbs from her mouth. "We'll smell Ah-Puch before we ever see him."

"Have to look out for other gods, too, just in case," Jazz said. "Gotta make sure your boy here gets to Ah-Puch first."

Brooks's cheeks reddened. "He's not *my* boy," she muttered.

I needed to change the subject, fast. "Anyone have any leftover pizza pockets?" I said, polishing off the last of my own cardboard-like meal. "This stuff's great, Jazz. Good thinking to bring it."

Brooks lay back and covered her face with her arms. "How about you all stop talking so loud? We might as well put up a neon sign telling the gods where we are."

For the next couple of hours, my mind reeled. It reeled while we sat around the fire, and it reeled while Jazz thunder-snored and Brooks and Hondo slept. PS, Hondo was supposed to keep first watch, but I guess the guy was still getting over the whole poison-meatball thing. I changed out of my suit and into my jeans and T-shirt (definitely better for god-fighting) and stared up at the twin moons inching across the starless sky, wondering if I'd ever get to see Hurakan again now that I'd lost the jade. My wrist burned, my short leg throbbed, and I couldn't help wondering how a skinny kid with one good arm and one good leg was ever going to beat the god of death, darkness, *and* destruction. But Hurakan had sent me here for a reason. *Find the White Sparkstriker.* Except Jazz had said that wasn't possible. So what was I supposed to do, sit around and wait for the lightning pounder to invite me to dinner?

Images of ancient wars, supernatural creatures, angry gods, and old magic spun through my mind, and all the while I kept thinking, *Is this real? How* could *it all be real?* The night dragged on, heavy and dark. I tried to psych myself up, convince myself that I was braver than I really was. But to be honest, I was scared. Scared and outmatched. I wished Rosie were here, so I could scratch her head and listen to her soft breathing. But I knew she was somewhere she didn't want to be, either, and it tore me up to think she was scared, too.

Somehow I drifted to sleep.

I was jostled awake by a scratching sound. *Rosie?* I thought sleepily. I turned over on the hard ground, my sweatshirt balled under my head for a pillow.

There it was again, like a very light foot stepping on twigs at the edge of the tree line a mere fifteen feet away. I sat up and peered into the dark.

A masked figure stood in the shadows. Staring at me.

# 34

**The figure wore a long red robe, and its match-**ing mask was smooth and flat with only slits for eyes and a mouth. And at its side was a stone ax. Replace the red with black, and the ax with a scythe, and you'd have the Grim Reaper.

*Crap!*

Slowly, carefully, I rolled to my feet. My chest was as tight as dry leather. I wasn't sure what to do. Walk over casually and start a conversation? *Hey, creepy red mask, are you the Sparkstriker? What brings you out this time of night?* Okay, bad option. So I waited, unmoving and staring. But definitely trembling.

The sky was as black as Ah-Puch's eyes, which made everything dark except for the fire. The figure lifted the ax and, with a single thrust, slammed it into a tree. I recoiled as the blow rang out through the forest. Jazz, Hondo, and Brooks kept sleeping like hibernating turtles, which was pretty amazing considering it had sounded like someone had taken a giant sledgehammer to church bells.

The tree vibrated and hummed like a guitar string. Its cobwebs trembled, falling from the branches and trunk to reveal...I blinked. It was like in my dream—a metallic tree, and in it I saw my warped reflection. Tall kid with a left lean, messy dark hair, square shoulders, and wide-set eyes that looked afraid. Definitely not the guy you'd bet on to take down the god of death. But you want to know the weird thing? My reflection had something in his hand—not a cane, but something else. I couldn't quite make it out.

Flakes began to fall from the sky, slowly twisting to the ground. I caught some and smudged them between my finger and thumb. Ash. I looked up. There was a hairline crack running across the black sky. What did that mean? Was this world going to fall apart like the twins' world had?

I took a step closer to the masked figure and just as I did, it darted away. I went after it. And you know what I was thinking the whole time? *I really shouldn't be chasing this thing. Shouldn't. Shouldn't. Shouldn't.*

He, she—it—was quick. I tried my best not to fall behind. Every once in a while my short leg would make me stumble and I'd fall, landing on sticky cobwebbed leaves.

Then the figure slowed and looked over its shoulder like it wanted to make sure I was following. Was this some kind of trap? "Hey!" I called, getting to my feet for the third time. "Who are you?"

A girl's voice bounced off the trees: "Pick up the pace, Obispo."

How did she know who I was? I already didn't like her.

We came to a small glade. She stopped about ten feet away, keeping her back to me. I was glad for the chance to catch my breath. "Are you ... are you the Sparkstriker?" I huffed, bent over with my hands on my knees. Fortunately, I remembered in time something Jazz had told me while we were walking to Puksí'ikal: *No one can look at her face without their eyes burning out of their head.*

I heard a grunt-sigh, then she turned and asked, "Do I *look* like the Sparkstriker?"

"I wouldn't know," I said honestly. "I don't know what the Sparkstriker looks like."

"And you don't look like a hero *or* a god, Obispo."

With a shrug, I said, "How do you know? Do you know a lot of heroes or gods?"

"If you're going to be a warrior, you better learn to listen. You got it?"

Then she went silent. Was I supposed to be listening for something? After a minute or so I got bored of her little game and said, "So?"

"So what?"

"Are you the Sparkstriker?" I asked impatiently.

"I'm nobody."

"Fine, No-*body*," I said, emphasizing the last syllables. "Do you know where I can *find* the—?"

"You're the hero, Obispo," she cut in. Her hand went to her mask. "You tell *me* where the Sparkstriker is."

This girl was seriously annoying. Slowly, she began to peel the mask back, but before I could see her face, she transformed. Shifted the way Brooks did. But this girl didn't turn into a hawk. She became a giant eagle with a broad white

chest speckled with chocolate spots, golden-flecked brown
eyes, razor-sharp talons, and a wingspan of twenty feet. She
let out a loud cry, then took off into the night.

"Wait!" I called after her. Why bring me all the way out
here just to fly away? I rushed over to the mask she'd dropped,
picked it up, and hollered into the dark, "You forgot your mask,
Nobody!"

It was a flimsy thing made of thinly woven silk, so plain
most people would toss it in the trash. Two bits of screen-like
material covered each eye. I looked guiltily around the small
glade, feeling like I was doing something wrong, and tried the
mask on, praying it wouldn't melt my face.

Nothing happened. No face-melting. No magic, no superpowers. Nothing cool.

I tugged it off and stuffed it in my back pocket. That's when
I noticed flecks of shimmering cobwebs floating to the ground.
I looked up to see a massive tree. My eyes traced the trunk
down to thick gnarled roots that snaked through the dark.
They led to a giant hole in the ground, where I thought I saw
a glint of light.

I went to the edge and dropped to my knees to get a better look. About fifty feet down there was a pool of water surrounded by tall stone walls. Beneath the surface were flashing
lights—sudden bolts of energy that made the water ripple and
sizzle and steam.

"What the heck?" I muttered in amazement.

Next to the pool was a cave opening where sparks were
flying out in bursts. After each flash I heard the sound of

metal clashing against metal. My curiosity was definitely piqued, and the thick rope on the ground near my feet looked like an invitation. It was tied around the tree's trunk. There was a narrow edge around the pool that I could follow to the cave if I could get down there. That was a big *if*.

I gave the anchored rope a quick tug, testing its strength. My left wrist still burned and ached. Could I descend with the strength of only one arm? What if I fell? It was a long way down, and who knew what was in that glowing water.

My palms were sweating.

"Put on the mask, stupid!"

I looked up to find Nobody the eagle circling the pit.

"I was going to!" I lied as I jerked it free and placed it over my face. What was so great about this mask anyway? It's not like it *did* anything. Except make my face feel sticky and hot.

I said a couple of Hail Marys, then, gripping the rope with my good hand and looping it around my wrist for a stronger hold, I belly-scooted down over the ledge until my feet were planted against the stone wall below.

Okay, so far, so good. One inch at a time I made my way down the wall, grasping the rope so tight it burned my palm. My arm muscles screamed. The eagle continued circling above. I could feel little puffs of air every time she flapped her wings. So obnoxious!

"Maybe I'll catch you if you fall," she said. "*If* I'm fast enough. On second thought, you better not fall."

I tried to ignore her annoying voice as I slowly rappelled down, and a couple minutes later, I made it to the pool's edge.

Gingerly I picked my way toward the mouth of the cave. Light crackled and sizzled under the water. Maybe there were a bunch of electric eels down there.

I headed straight for the cave.

# 35

**First things first: there was a woman in the**
cave. Second, she was short—as in shorter than my mom. She
wore a red robe like Nobody's and stood on a rickety wooden
stool with her back to me. In her hand was a hefty—no, make
that *huge*—stone hammer that she was pounding into something I couldn't see from where I stood. Sparks flew.

I ducked as one sailed over my head and into the pool.

"Better get out of the way," she said with a grunt. *Slam.*
Another whiz of light.

"You're the Sparkstriker!" She had to be. I couldn't believe
I'd found her! Okay, so maybe Nobody wasn't too bad after
all. Then I remembered I was wearing that stupid mask.

When I went to take it off, the woman said, "I wouldn't do
that if I were you. Could be calamitous."

What? Did she, like, have eyes in the back of her head?
"You mean bad?"

"I mean this light will fry your eyes out of your sockets."

Definitely left the mask on.

Her red hair was all ratted out like a nest, and there were
teeny tiny silver trinkets—bells—woven into the knotted
strands. She turned to me. Her face was uneven in places
where it shouldn't have been. Her nose was bent a little too

far to the right and her right eye sagged an inch below her left. Her forehead had a lump in the center that looked like a giant mosquito bite. "I thought you'd never get here," she said.

"You're . . . you're the—"

"Yes, yes," she said impatiently. "Now hurry over here so I can make sure this fits."

"Fits?"

She rolled one of her eyes. The other one stayed in place like it was glued there. When I drew closer, I peered down at the stone table she was working from. It looked like it could double for a body slab. Right in the middle was a cane, and I'm not talking any cane. I'm talking ninja-style, hammered silver with a jade grip. I'm talking the kind of cane that looked . . . *cool.* Like if you saw me walking down the street with it, you might stop and ask me where you could get one, too.

"Well, don't just stand there. Pick it up!" She shook her head, but strangely, the tiny bells didn't ring.

As I reached for the cane, it started to hum. Then, when I closed my fingers around it, the thing went silent. I don't remember exactly, but I think I was holding my breath, because it felt like a really big moment. Like whatever happened next would matter a lot. Carefully, I picked up the cane. It was light as air and felt warm to the touch. I could swear it pulsed in my hand. I set its tip on the ground, turned, and took a step with it. The cane was . . . incredible!

*Wait a sec. That can't be right,* I thought. My limp was . . . it was gone! My eyes bugged out and my heart rolled over. Then a slow smile spread across my face.

"A few more steps," she said, eyeing me as I took another turn.

I seriously could have cruised around like this all day. "How...? It's...it's amazing!"

"Of course it is," she said. "It's more than it appears. It's also a spear and will do as you command."

I inspected it more closely while she went on about its magic.

"How do I turn it into a spear? Is there a hidden button or something?"

"Do you tell your legs to walk, your arms to move?"

Was that a real question?

She snorted and added, "It's connected to you now. I've pounded it with lightning, bound it with old magic, and infused it with the blood of the gods. Or more specifically, your father's blood. It's indestructible, Zane Obispo."

"My...father's blood?"

"First time he's ever given a drop," she said. "Mighty powerful stuff, too, considering he's *the* creator god."

(Sorry, Mat. I'm totally sure she meant you, too.)

"Now for the grand finale!" she said. "Go choose a bolt."

I looked around the little cave for the first time. The rocky walls jutted out sharply, making the tight space feel even tighter. There were no other tools around, no screws or bolts. "I, um...I don't see any bolts."

"*Lightning* bolts." Her voice rose so loud it shook the stone walls. "The pool?"

I looked over my shoulder then back to her with a

*you've-got-to-be-kidding* expression. "You want me to touch one of those things?"

"You must choose one in order for this to work," she said, holding the hammer over her shoulder like she was ready to use it—on me. "Now hurry up."

*For* what *to work? The cane?* She must've registered my reluctance to stick my hand in the water and touch a lightning bolt.

"Do you think I'd go to all this effort, pound lightning like I haven't done in centuries, just so I could watch you fry your puny brain?"

Point taken.

I went over to the pool and squatted down. The bolts zipped through the water like racer fish. As I reached in, she yelled, "WAIT!"

"Wha—what?" I stumbled back.

The Sparkstriker stepped down from her stool. "Do you have any allergies?"

*"Allergies?"*

"To lightning? Electricity? White-hot energy?"

"Uh—pretty sure I don't." Not that I'd ever touched lightning or white-hot energy.

"That's good." Then, with a nod of her chin, she motioned for me to continue.

I dipped my right hand into the pool. I felt a burst of heat on my skin, but it didn't scald me. The bolts zipped past, weaving through my grasp. Then they went still. Except for one. It slipped into my hand and I lifted it out of the water.

It was like holding a warm, tinfoil-wrapped burrito fresh from the oven, except this pulsed like a living thing. I went back to the cave and handed it over to the Sparkstriker. She examined it then muttered, "It'll do." As if each bolt was unique. Maybe they *were*. . . . Stepping onto her stool, she said, "Well, climb up here."

I didn't like where this was going. "What for?"

"So I can pound this into your leg."

I swallowed, did a double take, and almost laughed. "Are you kidding? You want to pound my . . . my leg with lightning?"

"That's what I said, isn't it?"

"I—I don't think that's such a good idea. I mean, my leg, it already doesn't work too good and—"

"This is why gods and humans don't mix! Never can tell what you're going to get." She set down her hammer. "Zane, your father is the Heart of the Sky."

"Yeah, I know."

"He's very powerful."

"Uh-huh." Already knew that, too.

She looked down at my bum leg, then back to me. "He's also the Serpent Leg."

"Yeah and he passed it on to me," I said, swinging my bad leg.

She smacked her skinny lips together. "A typical human *would* assume that a serpent leg is useless. But in a god, the power of the serpent is unparalleled."

"You're trying to tell me my bum leg is powerful?"

"Your leg," she said slowly, "is the *most* powerful part of you, not the weakest. It's the doorway to your magic, the only clue to your ancestry."

Someone needed to give her a reality check. "Are you going to tell me to run with the storm, too?"

"Why, for the love of all that's holy, would I tell you to run with the storm?"

"Because I'm the Storm Runner."

Her eyes flashed some sort of recognition. "That name was given to you by a goddess."

"Okay..." I said, neither confirming nor denying it.

"The gods' language is... hard to translate for the human mind," she said. "There are many meanings. *Runner* can also mean—how do I say it?—channel, a conduit, power."

"I'm like a *channel* of the storm?" Slowly, the gears in my mind started to rotate. So the demon runners were channels of demon power?

She rapped her knuckles on my forehead. "Are you understanding what I'm telling you, Storm Runner?"

She was starting to irritate me. "Maybe you could just give me the bottom line?"

"You..." She paused. "You *are* the storm. And the storm is you."

Okay, so I wasn't prepared for that. As I opened my mouth to shout *What the holy heck are you talking about?* she held up her hand. "The storm sleeps inside of you. Once I pound the lightning into your leg, it will awaken and race through your blood and bones like a hurricane of magic. It will locate your dominant power."

"Power?"

"Yes, your father—god of storms, fire, and wind . . . Are you even paying attention? Don't give me that sour face. We need to know if any of his strength was passed on to you."

"Fire and wind?"

"Hello?" she said with an annoyed look. "Your father? Heavy-hitter? Creator and destroyer?"

"Fine, the guy's tough, but what do you mean by *dominant*?"

"Hurakan has many powers. Not all of them have been passed to you. Something that epic would kill any human. We need to find out where you're strongest."

*Now* I was following. "So my powers have nothing to do with running?"

She wiped her brow with frustration. "The storm runs *through* you, *in* you. You and the storm must become one, which is why I must pound this lightning into you. But let's not get ahead of ourselves." She shook her head and again the bells in her hair shifted but didn't ring. "You could also possess nothing of true value. Storms need a place to spend their power, and you may be a terrible vessel with no ability to control any of it."

*Nothing of true value? Terrible vessel?* Well, that would officially stink!

"Now, do you want to know the truth of your ancestry?"

I nodded slowly.

"Then let me do my job. Up you go."

I climbed onto the stone slab and lay back as she gripped both the bolt and the hammer.

"Wait!"

"What?"

"Is it going to hurt?"

She set the glowing thing over my leg and raised her hammer. "More than you know."

# 36

**Note to self: Never ask someone if it's going to** hurt unless you're 100 percent prepared for the truth. And no way José was I prepared for the Sparkstriker's answer.

My leg felt like a million branding irons were being pressed into it. The pain was so awful I couldn't even scream. The world exploded in a brilliant stream of white, like I was being shot through a meteor shower. I had to close my eyes. Heat spread through me. Then everything went quiet and still.

I was in the Empty. But how? I no longer had the jade. . . .

I was in an open temple on top of a pyramid. I blinked and looked down at my body. I had spotted paws again, and muscular jaguar legs. With a deep breath, I shook myself and started searching.

"Hurakan!" My voice echoed across the plaza below, ricocheting between the stone buildings. There was no answer. I bolted to the other side of the temple, calling for him. The sun was setting over the sea and the Empty felt exactly like that—deserted, abandoned.

"Hurakan!" I yelled again. "Could use a little help about now!"

I paced across the temple, scanning the jungle below.

Maybe he was mad I hadn't listened to his advice about the twins. Did he need me to tell him he'd been right about them not helping me? That I'd made a huge mistake?

His voice found me first. "I knew you'd show up." Then he materialized in the same black panther form. Yeah, I sort of wanted to nuzzle the guy, but only because I was relieved to see that he was actually there.

"You didn't tell me I was going to get lightning pounded into my leg!"

"No sense worrying you," he said. "Sometimes it's better not to know what's coming."

Mm-hmm . . . So *not* comforting! I sat back on my haunches. The sun was setting and everything—the trees, the sky, the sea—looked tranquil, like they were all taking a deep breath. "I lost the jade."

He nodded slowly but didn't say anything. His eyes blazed a brilliant green.

I stood and walked closer. "So how am I here?"

"The ceremony the Sparkstriker is performing would have brought you to me."

*Ceremony?* That was an interesting word choice. Me? I'd have used *torture*.

"What power is she going to find?" I asked.

"*She* isn't going to find anything. The lightning bolt you chose, that chose you—*that's* the source that will uncover the truth." He stalked closer. "But you already know the answer, don't you?"

"Er . . . pretty sure I wouldn't be here if I knew the answer. Maybe I'm simply here to avoid the *I'd-rather-die* pain."

"I want to show you something."

We headed down to the shore and stood beneath a group of tall, leafy trees. The sand was white, soft, and warm. The sun was a ball of fire, lowering itself into the water slowly.

Hurakan said, "Close your eyes."

"What? Why?"

He gave me a look.

I closed my eyes.

"What do you see?" he asked.

"Darkness."

"Try again. Imagine yourself on the table, imagine the lightning coursing through your blood. Imagine the lightning as a part of you."

I did what he asked. And as I did, my fingertips tingled like before. A terrible heat started to rise in me, so hot I imagined it was the surface of the sun. It raced through my blood. Like before, it felt too big to contain. I opened my eyes and whispered, "Fire."

If a jungle cat could smile, it would look like the expression Hurakan gave me. "Ah," he said. "The Son of Fire. Surprising."

When someone tells you you're the Son of Fire and it's your dominant power, you sort of want to pump your fist/paw in the air and holler *Awesome!* So, yeah, I did. Total impulse. Then, "Wait. You said *surprising*. Why?"

"As the Sparkstriker told you, not all powers of the storm can be passed to you without killing you. I would have predicted wind or rain—something less moody."

"What do you mean 'less moody'?" I didn't know elements had bad days.

"Fire is my least favorite element, the most challenging."
His tail swished through the air.

"Challenging?"

"Not easy to control and highly unpredictable. I don't like
unpredictability."

"Okay, so fire is my power. Do I, like, throw flames at
You-Know-Who? Barbecue the guy? Will that do the trick?"

"First you have to open the gateway in your leg."

"How?"

"Do you feel it? The pulsing? The energy bound there?"

I focused on my bum leg. Hurakan was right. When I
isolated my thoughts to this one part of me, a strange energy
pulsed through my entire body. It was amazing!

"Now feed the flame with your life source and . . ."

"And what?"

"You need a source of heat." He motioned toward the sun.
"Draw on its power." I was about to ask *How the heck do I do
that?* when he added, "Call it to you."

I remembered the way I had felt that night at Jack in the
Box. How some external force had found its way to me, and
my fingers had tingled with some kind of heat. I inched closer
to the sea. The waves lapped at my feet. Following my instinct,
I drew on the sun and felt heat building in me. Slowly at first,
then fast. Too fast. I couldn't breathe.

Hurakan said, "Let it go."

I raised a paw, thinking maybe I could shoot fireballs out
of it or something. But nothing happened. Except the heat
kept rising. I started to panic.

"Relax, Zane," Hurakan commanded.

"Easy for you to say." He wasn't the one being cooked from the inside out.

"You have the power, Zane. The fire answers to you. Feed it with your breath. Yes, like that. Steady, deep breaths."

Except my breath was smoking right out of my nose! And no way could I relax. I began to hyperventilate. The burning snaked its way through me at unimaginable speed. I started for the water, and with my first panicked stride, I saw that my claws were glowing red. As in iron-forging red.

"Zane!" Hurakan shouted as he blocked my path. "Release it!"

"I need the water!"

"No! If you take the easy way out now, you'll never learn to control it. Trust me!"

The power was building, heavy and strong, and so hot I thought I was going to combust. Puffs of smoke curled from my nose and mouth. I spun, let out a fierce roar, and slashed a tree trunk with my burning claws. The trunk burst into flames that spread to the leaves and then the next tree and the next.

A second later, a huge wave formed, curling taller than a ten-story building. It crashed down on our heads, and I spun blindly under the water. Just as quickly, it receded. I shook my body like a dog, trying to get dry.

Hurakan sighed. "Maybe a little more focus next time."

"*Focus?* It . . . it was burning me alive!"

"It will destroy you if you don't release its power. The energy has to have somewhere to go. Do you understand?"

I nodded, still out of breath, and wondered if I ever wanted to call fire to me again. I thought using my power was going to be easy, or at least natural. "If *you* can't control it," I said angrily, "then how am I supposed to be able to?"

"I never said I couldn't control it. I said fire is very challenging, Zane."

"Yeah, no kidding."

At the same moment the world began to spin wildly, like I was in a dryer on high.

"Looks like the Sparkstriker's done," he said.

"Wait!"

"What?"

"What if I never learn . . . to control it?"

"It's your dominant power—it will yield. Eventually. But you really should be friendlier to it."

I started to ask if I could trade fire for something easier, but I was already flying back.

An instant later, I sat up on Sparkstriker's table with my nose dripping blood. Oh yeah, I'd forgotten about that little side effect of travel to the Empty. I blotted it with my shirt.

"It . . . it's fire," I sputtered.

A slow smile spread across the Sparkstriker's face. Then a bell in her hair gave a small jingle. She looked over her shoulder at the cave opening. "Blasted hounds of hell!"

"Wha . . . ? Blasted what?"

"No more time," she said, shooing me out of the cave. My lightning-pounded leg buzzed with incredible strength.

"But you said *blasted* and *hell* in the same sentence. . . . That can't be good. What did you mean?"

"When my bells ring, it tells me someone's arrived . . . in the Old World."

I knew I wasn't going to like the answer, so I didn't ask the question.

But she told me anyway. "Ah-Puch is here, Zane. Are you ready?"

# 37

**Who could ever be ready to face and destroy** the god of death? I wasn't, even though I was the Son of Fire and had a tricked-out super cane/spear and a lightning-enhanced leg that made me feel like I could scale tall buildings in a single bound.

Everything went berserk. The bells in the Sparkstriker's hair started jingling so loud they made my ears ache. Then her eyes rolled back until only the whites were showing, and her skin vibrated and flapped like loose rubber. No wonder her face was so out of whack. Was I supposed to do something? Call 9-1-1 for the supernatural? Give her CPR? Find some superglue?

"You idiot!" That was Nobody. She swooped into the cave and morphed into her human form. I could see now that she was young—maybe Hondo's age. She had pale freckled skin, shimmering dark eyes, and an upturned mouth that looked like it was on the verge of a sneer. Definitely not a smile.

"I didn't do anything!" I shouted, hoping the Sparkstriker would come out of her creepy, face-morphing seizure any second.

"Get a bolt!" Nobody commanded.

This time I knew what she was talking about. I hurried

to the well and came back with a small piece of lightning. Nobody laid the Sparkstriker on the slab, then took the hammer and pounded the bolt into the Sparkstriker's chest like some kind of defibrillator. The old woman snapped straight up and took a gasping breath. Her nose had shifted another inch to the right and her mouth was so close to her chin I thought it might slide off her face any second.

"Blasted gods! *That* was annoying!" Sparkstriker said, hopping onto her stool. "How dare so many descend at the *exact* same time!" She cursed and pounded her fist into the stone slab.

Nobody began to adjust the Sparkstriker's nose and mouth as though her face were made of wax. "We've got the whole Council of Gods out there," the Sparkstriker hissed. "And Ixtab . . ." She closed her eyes and took a deep breath. "She's hunting for Ah-Puch as we speak."

Why the heck was the council here? They had to be here to hunt down Ah-Puch—or maybe even *me*. Hadn't Jazz said this would be the last place they'd look? The gods were *fast*.

"No!" My voice erupted in a hot panic. "I have to find him first!"

Nobody rolled her eyes. There was something annoyingly familiar about the way she did it with a toss of her head and a subtle tilt of her chin.

The Sparkstriker's gaze hardened. "The Storm Runner's right. Track down Ah-Puch before Ixtab and her hellhounds do. I'm counting on you, Quinn."

"*Quinn?*" My heart came to a stuttering stop. "As in Brooks's sister? As in promised to . . ." Was it Jordan or Bird?

Quinn's eyes cut my way angrily. "I'm a warrior hunt-ress of the White Sparkstriker tribe." She said the words like they were rehearsed. But behind her cold glare, I could see I'd touched a nerve.

"Enough inconsequential drivel," the Sparkstriker said. "I'm not about to lose my warriors to the gods' worthless war. So both of you work together and get this thing done!"

"But Brooks is *here!*" I blurted. "She's been looking for you, Quinn! You're supposed to be—" I was shouting with the panic of someone on a sinking ship.

Quinn held up her hand. "Later. Right now, I've got the Stinking One to hunt down. And you? You better get ready, because you'll only get one shot. And it better be a good one, because none of us are in the mood to die today."

The Sparkstriker turned on her stool, grabbed me by the shoulders, and shook me once. "One shot, Storm Runner. One thrust with the spear should do it. It now has the power of your blood and fire running through it."

"One shot . . . Like in the leg?" I swallowed hard.

"His head or heart would be preferable. And if you fail, I will have no choice but to unleash the gods. Until then my warriors will do their best to lead them away from Ah-Puch's trail. Do you understand?"

Then, because people don't usually help for no reason, it occurred to me to ask, "Why are you doing all this for me?"

"I always try to choose the winning side."

That worked for me. I only hoped she'd made the right choice.

Quinn morphed into her eagle form. "Climb on my back and hold on. It'll be a long way down if you fall."

Everything was happening so fast I thought my head might explode, but Quinn was right about one thing. I had a single purpose: to find Pukeface before any of the gods did and waste the guy.

I clung to Quinn's long, thick feathers as we sailed over the Old World. If it weren't for the fact that there was a high likelihood my life was about to be shortened, I would've thought it was the coolest flight in world history. From up there everything below looked like a miniature cardboard cutout—a game board where everything, even death, is make-believe.

She soared over Puksí'ikal. I saw Hondo and Jazz were still conked-out. But Brooks . . . she was gone. *Ugh!* Someone needed to attach a locator chip to her!

"Where's Brooks?" What if she'd been abducted or something?

"*That's* not your quest. Stay focused!"

"She's your sister!"

"There isn't time."

I was about to ask how one tiny detour could hurt when she lifted her head and snarled, "I've picked up his scent."

A few minutes later, we were flying to the outer edges of the Old World, far from the glassy river at its heart. The jungle grew denser the farther we traveled. Every once in a while, Quinn would rotate her head to look around, then dive close to the earth. Each time I thought *This is it.* But then she'd sail back into the black sky. Up close, the atmosphere looked as thin as crepe paper. A tiny tear ran through its center.

"The sky looks like it's going to rip open," I shouted as we flew higher and higher.

"The gods aren't united," Quinn said. "The world will collapse if they really do go to war."

"Don't they care about this place?"

"Some do, some don't. Some might even want to see the old ways destroyed."

"Is that what you want?"

She huffed and said, "None of your business, Zane Obispo. Get your head in the game! Understand? Because either way, Ah-Puch's going down tonight."

My cane glowed, and its powerful pulse matched my own. One shot. I had only one shot.

I don't know why I told her, but the words tumbled out like marbles. "I'll become his soldier of death unless I'm the one to take him out." I glanced at my arm, peeled the flower bandage back. The wound was better, and the mark—it was gone! Mostly. There was only a faint white outline of the skull. Had the lightning "ceremony" healed me? Even if it had, I knew I was still linked to Ah-Puch.

Quinn's whole body stiffened, her wings spread farther, and she slowed for a split second. "And if the gods kill him?"

"He and I are connected, so I'll die, too."

She flapped her wings, picking up speed. "Not tonight, Zane Obispo. Not tonight."

"Quinn?"

"Why are you still talking?"

"If...if something happens to me, promise you'll find Brooks. Okay?" I couldn't figure why she would've wandered away from camp. Except, she was Brooks.

Quinn didn't answer, because a black owl with gold eyes came out of nowhere and slammed into her. I lay flat on Quinn as she spun into a nosedive.

Muwan sped through the dark after us, screeching.

Quinn righted herself and flew parallel to the ground. But Muwan was faster. She whizzed past, ripping Quinn's left wing with her talons. Quinn let out a piercing cry as she tipped too far to the left. I clung even tighter to keep from falling.

"Jump!" Quinn cried.

Was she loca? Ah-Puch's laughter echoed across the treetops. I jerked my cane/spear free. Muwan zipped overhead, her black wings extended wide, ready to wrap me in their darkness. Quinn was dropping fast. Muwan made a third pass, and this time I knew it was for the kill.

Without thinking, I launched my cane at her chest. "Take that, you mangy..." I couldn't come up with a proper insult in the moment, so I settled for, "You suck!"

As it sailed through the air, I saw that it really had changed into a spear. It struck the target with perfect accuracy. Muwan released a terrible scream and started tumbling through the air. I watched in horror as she crashed into the bare trees below. They shook on impact, their sharp branches splitting her open.

# 38

**Quinn was in free fall.**

We were close to the trees, and I knew the sharp branches would rip us up if she continued at this speed. My eyes darted through the dark. Up ahead, twenty or so yards past the jungle, was a small field, big enough for a safe landing.

"There!" I pointed.

"I can't make it," Quinn cried as she plunged nearer to the branches that might as well have been spikes.

"You're a warrior huntress of the White Sparkstriker Tribe!" I screamed. "And Brooks needs you!"

I could feel her giant eagle muscles struggling, flexing. Down, down, down we went, inches from the trees.

*Just a little father. A little farther.*

With an earsplitting cry, Quinn redoubled her efforts, but not before we grazed the last tree's branches and their sharp tips raked her. We crash-tumbled into the field. White stars danced in front of me. Everything went black for a second, then came the pain that shot up my legs. I was on my knees when I scrambled over to her. She was back in human form. "Quinn!"

She groaned and sat up slowly. "You better be worth all

this trouble," she said, flinching and holding her left side. She was breathing too fast.

"You're bleeding."

"No kidding, Captain Obvious."

"What do I do?" I wasn't exactly trained in nawal first aid.

"Do you mean, will I live? Yeah. I'll be fine." She looked down at the slashes on her left arm. "Nawals have super healing powers, so I'm not going to die tonight. But *you* might, if you don't find that spear."

Yeah, why had I thrown my only weapon?

Because I'd had no other choice. Not that Quinn was grateful for it. . . .

My hand tingled with a strange energy, like I'd slept on it for the last ten hours and it was only now prickling to life. I scanned the dense trees, and in the middle of their darkness, I saw a faint blue light glowing like a dimming candle. That had to be the cane! Sparkstriker had loaded it with a Find My Cane app, I guessed.

I stood up to circle back for the spear, and as I did, I saw a figure running toward us in the moonlight. Brooks! With her glowing eyes, ninja-black clothes, and intense expression, she looked like a barefoot warrior.

Quinn groaned. "She's going to kill me."

I stepped out of the way. I mean, no need to get in the middle of a family squabble. When Brooks reached us, her eyes were on Quinn and Quinn only. She fell to her knees to inspect her sister's wounds. A second later she declared, "You'll live."

Quinn nodded slowly.

"That's good." Brooks narrowed her eyes. "It'll make killing you easier!"

"I should've called," Quinn said. "But I couldn't. This con-
flict is so much bigger than you know."

"I thought you were trapped in Xib'alb'a! How are you
here? *Why* are you here?" Then Brooks's burning gaze turned
to me. "And why are you with *my* sister?"

"How did you find us?" I asked, deflecting her question
with one of my own.

"This. It buzzed all the way here." She held up the jade.

My mouth fell open. "You . . . you found it? How?"

"I went back to the boat," she said, the corners of her mouth
almost upturned as she set it in my open hand. "It was wedged
between the deck and the seat."

So that's where she'd gone. I wrapped her in a huge
bear hug.

"Zane, you're"—she gasped—"smothering me."

I let her go. "Sorry."

"Did you take some adrenaline pills or something?" she
asked me.

"He got pounded with lightning," Quinn said. Then she
stiffened and her eyes went wide as she spotted something.
"We've got company."

A dark shadow rose in front of me. Black, hissing mist
with the familiar puke-and-rotten-fish smell that still made
me gag. Someone really needed to tell Ah-Puch to take a bath
or wear some deodorant. Maybe carry a car freshener in his
pocket. Nah, even that wouldn't help.

"Get out of here," I told Brooks and Quinn.

"Not a chance," Brooks said in her signature stubborn tone.

Ah-Puch wasn't in his nice Hollywood suit this time. Steam rose from his gray body. And like before, I could see worms twisting over his transparent skin, banding together as he rose to his full height. His eyes blazed hot white and he clenched his fists at his sides as his chest heaved. "You'll pay for Muwan," he hissed. His eyes found Brooks and Quinn. "You really do need to find better friends, Zane. Why do you insist on hanging out with pathetic creatures so beneath you?"

Brooks spoke up. "Anyone ever tell you how bad you smell?"

Quinn tugged on Brooks's arm to shut her up. Yeah, fat chance of that!

Ah-Puch's next words to her were pointed, the kind that went in for the kill. "No more talk, worthless half-breed." Then black smoke curled out of his fingertips. Before I could even react, it zoomed toward Quinn and Brooks, knocking them to the ground, one on top of the other. Then the smoke took the shape of giant hands and muzzled their mouths.

Brooks's own hands shot up to the smoke, but she couldn't remove it. Taking advantage of his momentary distraction, I inched back, thinking quickly. I needed that spear, but how was I going to get it . . . ? And then I remembered. *It will do as you command.* It was a long shot, but I opened my hand, which was still pulsing with a strange energy. *Come,* I thought.

The energy wound up my arm, but the spear didn't make its way back to me. I tried again, this time with more concentration, which was pretty hard considering Puke was standing right in front of me in his murderous demon form.

Then I felt it. One hot pulse, and when I looked down, the spear was in my hand. I couldn't believe it!

Ah-Puch let out a wicked laugh. "You think your little lightning spear is going to stop me?"

I glanced down and for a second I thought I heard a voice coming from inside the spear, muffled like it was being smothered under a pillow. I knew launching the thing at Ah-Puch while he was expecting it was lame battle strategy. Hondo always said to catch your opponent by surprise, because if they know the attack is coming they'll prepare a counter-strike. Or in my case, a deathstrike!

The air shifted, turning cold, and a demon runner emerged from the jungle. Then another and another, all dragging their hairy knuckles along the ground. Those guys again?

"Now you must suffer for Muwan," Ah-Puch said to me. "And for removing my eyes." He motioned to my wrist. "I must say, I didn't anticipate that move. But no matter, you'll pay for both. And you will be the greatest prize the underworld has ever seen. Godborn of Hurakan, the great creator."

Brooks roared angrily, trying to get to her feet. But Quinn had her pinned, which only made Brooks lash out more wildly. I swallowed hard. My heart thrashed around in my chest. I was outnumbered, outsmarted, and outpowered.

Ah-Puch kept on. "And when all is said and done, your father will suffer, too."

The demon runners hissed and groaned impatiently.

"Hurakan doesn't have anything to do with this!" I bent my knees and gripped my spear, ready to fight whichever demon came at me. Preferably one at a time. Power throbbed in my legs and I wondered how long it would last.

"Oh, but he has *everything* to do with this. He is at the center of my plan. But enough of that. Let's get your punishment started, shall we?"

"I'd rather not."

The demons bared their nasty fangs.

"Maybe we should begin with your friends," he said.

At the same time, thick ropes of white hair slithered out of the forest, followed by a dozen new demons. These were different from the demon runners I'd seen. Instead of blue skin, theirs was a glistening silver that shimmered in the moonlight, and it was thick, like a shark's. They had long white hair that hung in thick braids down their backs, swinging back and forth like tails.

They shrieked, leaping onto the backs of Ah-Puch's little army with amazing force. Teeth gnashed. Claws ripped. Hair choked.

The black-smoke hands released Brooks and Quinn and rose into the air. They formed ribbons and wound themselves into a long serpent that headed toward the silver demons.

I launched my spear at one of Ah-Puch's guys, testing its accuracy. It incinerated the monster on impact, then zipped back into my hand.

Ah-Puch narrowed his gaze. "Very good. Your little toy can melt demons. But it can never kill me!"

Quinn sat up with a wince. Brooks's eyes were bright as she got to her feet, reached into her waistband, and pulled out her demon-burning flashlight.

Ah-Puch pivoted as a woman with long blue locks materialized from a curtain of fog. Her skin was the color of a white-hot sun, and her eyes burned—with real fire! She shifted her white cape and extended one arm. A single flame danced on her palm and grew into a globe.

Puke's mouth curled into a sick smile.

Then the woman hurled the fireball at him.

"NO!" I screamed, launching myself forward to shove him out of the way.

The fireball hit me in the back, exploding on contact, and it knocked me off my feet, but it didn't kill me. I didn't even feel its heat!

The woman narrowed her fire-eyes at me, smiling murderously. "Godborn," she hissed. Then she launched another fireball, but this time I didn't get up fast enough.

I turned to see the damage. Puke opened his mouth and inhaled the thing before blowing it back out as a stream of smoke.

"Hello, Ixtab," he said. "How's my throne? Did you keep it warm for me?"

Her eyes darted between me and Ah-Puch. "I destroyed it," she said with a wicked grin that showed a mouthful of gray teeth. "How does your new hell taste?" Her long white cape dragged across the ground as she came closer, giving me a better look at it. The garment was made of small bones, and its hem was lined with teeth.

"The demons' hair is a nice touch," Ah-Puch said as he indifferently watched the last of his demons get smothered.

Why was he so calm? So confident?

Ixtab's victorious demons dragged themselves over and circled us like hungry wolves. Quinn and Brooks stood back-to-back as they waited for the first strike.

"Er... Ixtab?" My voice squeaked. I was about to tell her not to kill him when she cut in.

"Shut up, godborn." Ixtab raised her hand to silence me. Her hungry glare shifted to Quinn. "Traitors always pay the highest price. Soon you will be dead." Then, to Ah-Puch, "You'll like what I've done with Xib'alb'a. I have a special little corner waiting for you, my pet."

Ah-Puch snarled. It sent chills down the back of my legs. If I were betting on a winner, I might've gone with him.

Ixtab's eyes blazed.

It was now or never. I had to take advantage of Puke's being distracted. I gripped my spear, preparing to throw...

Then Ixtab stepped closer to me, and as she did, a ten-foot wall of fire rose up behind her. Two beasts walked out of the flames. Huge black hounds, twice the size of lions, with long bared fangs and growls that shook the ground. One had eyes that burned white. And the other? Its eyes flickered, changing from burning red to soft and brown and so familiar.

I gasped, blinking to be sure.

The brown-eyed beast had only three legs.

# 39

**I stumbled back. "Rosie?"**

*No, no, no!* I was dreaming. It was a trick! Then I remembered what Ms. Cab had said: *She'll be changed.*

I fell to my knees. Rosie's eyes switched back to red. She sniffed the air near me. Did she recognize me?

"Rosie?" I mumbled. Her pointed ears pricked.

Ah-Puch scoffed at Ixtab. "You think your hellhounds can stop me?" He looked around at the few demons still standing. "Or your pitiful horde?"

"Zane!" Hondo shouted.

We all spun to see him run into the clearing, waving a flashlight, pointing its flesh-burning beam. Jazz was right behind him, and they were both wearing red masks like Quinn's.

Ixtab raised her hand and said some strange word I didn't recognize. The demons charged toward Hondo and Jazz. Black hair grew out of the demons' mouths at freakish speed. Hondo and Jazz were outnumbered! Why would Hondo be so stupid? Then I realized he wouldn't. No way would my uncle march into battle without reinforcements.

While I was distracted, Ah-Puch blew a hot breath, creating a barred cage of black smoke all around me.

"NO!" I screamed.

"Relax for a while. This should be fun to watch," he said. "Should we take bets? I'm going with the demons."

I rushed toward the smoke bars, thinking I'd pass right through them, but they were as strong as iron and I slammed into them before stumbling back, dazed. I lifted my spear, hoping it could cut through the spell, but when I launched it at Ah-Puch, it bounced right off the smoke.

Panic clawed at my insides. I couldn't let anyone else fight this battle for me.

A great wind blew across the field, hot and dry, spreading Ixtab's flames. Quinn crawled over to me.

I wanted to harness the fire, to draw it in and use it against Ah-Puch. But what good would it do me? First, I didn't know how to control it. Second, if Ixtab's fire couldn't kill him, mine surely wouldn't. And I might end up torching the whole place—and Brooks and Hondo with it.

I couldn't take my eyes off Hondo, who had climbed into a tree and was pointing his deadly red light on the demons below. They writhed and screamed as the beam burned them.

Ah-Puch merely leaned against my cage, watching and smiling. "I really need to get one of those toys!"

A second later, dozens of red-robed warriors raced from behind the trees. The Sparkstriker's trained orphans!

So many things happened at the exact same moment. Shrieks split the hot air. The hellhounds growled and gnashed their teeth. Everyone ran at each other like a stampede of elephants. The ground shook. It was all chaos and hair and fangs and screaming.

Brooks, now masked, took off running into the melee. Jazz fought off three demons while another clung to his back, strangling him with a thick band of hair until his eye bugged out. Brooks aimed her flashlight and burned the demon off Jazz's back. It writhed into a column of black smoke.

The red warriors hurled themselves right into the demons' paths, displaying no fear as they reached into their robes. By the time I realized what they were reaching for, their lightning bolts were already flying through the air, exploding like fireworks. Now I knew why they were all wearing masks. I covered my eyes and waited for the searing pain to come, but it never did. I opened my eyelids, fluttering them wildly. I could still see!

The silver demons screamed, clawing at their faces as their eyes burst into flames.

Ixtab raised her hands toward the field and was chanting something when Quinn scrambled to her feet and rammed a lightning rod into her spine. Ixtab exploded into a tower of white fire.

"Now!" Quinn yelled at me. "The magic will only hold her for seconds."

At the same moment, Brooks morphed into a hawk. I guessed she could do it because Ixtab was out of commission, at least temporarily. Quinn stepped back, her eyes wide as she watched her sister fly at the god of death. Then Quinn dove between Ah-Puch and Brooks.

With a flick of his wrist, he sent them both hurtling over the wall of flames.

"BROOKS!" I shook the smoke bars.

Ah-Puch turned to me and smiled, taking a deep breath. "I just *love* the smell of war. And death. Do you smell its sweetness?"

Hate burned inside of me. "Let me out, you—you disgusting cockroach!"

Don't judge. It was the only insult I could think of in the moment.

"And you'll what? Kill me with your little lightning spear?" He nodded once and the smoke prison disappeared.

I didn't hesitate. I launched the spear at Ah-Puch. It rocketed toward him, a blazing light. But right before it hit, he vanished. I spun to find him behind me, smiling. He twisted me around and gripped the back of my neck, drawing blood with his nails. So much for my dynamo spear. Which, by the way, was now lying on the ground like a dead snake.

The world spun. Colors morphed into each other. Everything churned in a blur of amber light. And at the center of it all, tall towers of thick mist rose from the burning ground. One after the other.

"Let's stick around a bit, godborn. This is going to be fun," Ah-Puch said, gripping me tighter.

Fun? This was *so* not fun!

Five figures walked through the fire. I recognized Mat immediately, and I have to admit I was glad to see him. He was more spiffed up than I'd seen him last, wearing a dark blue pinstriped suit with a white button-down shirt and no tie. Next to him was a burly dude with a long beard and black

circles inked around his eyes. He wore a leather jacket, tattered jeans, motorcycle boots, and a sour expression like
someone had woken him up from a long nap. The other three
figures stood erect. My still-in-shock mind realized slowly
that if Mat was here, then that meant ... Holy smokes!

These were Maya gods!

# 40

**My relief turned into misery when I remem-**
bered that the gods also wanted Ah-Puch's head. Since I
was . . . well, paralyzed, I wasn't exactly in a position to do the
deed myself, and we all know what that meant. I was headed
to soldier-of-death boot camp!

(To be honest, I don't even know why I have to write
this next part since you gods already know what happened.
Whatever.)

Ah-Puch gripped me harder and began to chuckle.
"Ma'alob áak'ab'. Buenas noches, old friends. The council is
all back together. How chummy. So good to see you. And
Ixkakaw, you're looking well these days. Don't look a day over
two thousand."

Straight dark bangs framed the eyes belonging to the goddess of chocolate, who actually didn't look a day over, like,
thirty. She was small and willowy, and she walked more
gracefully than the others. This fact was made even more
obvious by her brown cat-woman-like bodysuit. Her bronze
skin glistened as she narrowed her eyes, then smiled. "And
you're smelling as foul as ever, Ah-Puch."

The burly dude looked me over, then said to Ah-Puch,
"We end this tonight."

"Oh, you mean to send me back to my prison, Nakon?" Ah-Puch said, faking a shudder.

So the burly motorcycle dude was the god of war? Kind of a cliché, if you ask me.

Mat shook his head. "The plan is to kill you, actually."

At about this time, the Sparkstriker's army retreated into the jungle and Ixtab was released from the bolt's power. She shook her head, looked around, and adjusted her cape. "*Some-one* is going to pay for that," she said through gritted teeth.

My eyes roved the trees, where I spotted Jazz and Hondo holed up not twenty yards away. Were Brooks and Quinn okay?

Rosie and the other hound stood behind Ixtab, but Rosie kept looking in my direction. Had she remembered me yet?

Ah-Puch grunted. "Did you all think I'd come here to your little playground unprepared? That I'd just walk into your clumsy trap?"

Is that what this was? A trap with me as the bait?

I searched the remaining two gods' faces, wondering if one of them was Hurakan. I didn't even know what his "human" form looked like. The guy half my size with spiky bleached hair, khakis, and a starched blue button-down shirt was defi-nitely not Mom's type. That left the one on the far end. The one who wouldn't take his eyes off me. He had dark disheveled hair, looked like he hadn't shaved in three days, and was so stiff he could've been made of stone. He wore a dark T-shirt, dark pants, and a leather band on each wrist.

"Let the boy fight him," he said coldly.

Yeah, so that pretty much stole my breath. Nice to see you, too, Dad!

Khaki dude ran a hand through his hair, then said, "Why would we let a mere boy fight our greatest enemy? Let's end this, Hurakan."

"Isn't that why you said we had to come here? Back to this . . . place?" Ixkakaw said, throwing her hands on her hips.

Mat and Dad exchanged a glance. What were they up to?

"He's not a mere boy," Mat said.

With a twisted smile, Ixtab stepped forward. "He's—"

Hurakan silenced her with a glare. He came closer, still staring at me. "He is the prophesied one. He released Ah-Puch."

A hush fell over the jungle. Ixkakaw, burly dude, and khaki guy (who I guessed was Alom, god of the sky) gasped.

"Those were lies," Ixkakaw said. "Told by—" She stopped herself.

Nakon popped his knuckles. "Yeah, well, that would make him a god, and that's not possible, unless . . ." His face turned red, and I thought smoke might come out of his ears. "Which idiot god broke the Sacred Oath?" he roared.

The silence was so loud my ears started to ring. A brief movement in the trees caught my attention and I saw Jazz muscling Hondo, covering his mouth and pinning him in place. *No, Hondo,* I thought. *This isn't a fight you can win.* Jazz was right to lock him down.

"Oooh," Ah-Puch said. "This is getting good. Do tell us, Hurakan. Who broke the Sacred Oath?"

Hurakan lifted his chin and clenched his jaw. "Zane Obispo

is my son, the son of wind, storms, and fire. He has the blood of a creator and a destroyer, and I claim him as my own."

My heart skipped so hard I forgot about Puke's nails digging into me. I forgot about the quest, about becoming a solider of death. I was the son of wind, storms, *and* fire! Holy smokes, that sounded so . . . tough!

Hurakan's voice found me. *By claiming you, here in the Old World before the council, I give you full powers.*

*Full powers? Wait. Is that what Mat meant?*

*I said you would control fire eventually. Today is that day.*

*But . . . why wait? Why now?*

*You needed to be on sacred ground and I had to claim you in front of the council. It's the only way for you to defeat Ah-Puch. Do you accept these powers?*

Was that a trick question?

*Zane!*

*Okay, okay. Yes.*

What happened next is hard to explain, even to imagine—for humans, at least. (Maybe for you gods, too.) Heat exploded inside of me and raced like lava through my muscles, down my nerves, and into my bones. The horrible pain made me want to scream, to fall to the floor and curl into a ball. But I was still paralyzed by Ah-Puch's grip, so no one could see my torment.

Ixtab shifted her cape back and forth impatiently. Then she shrieked, "Nothing happened!"

Ah-Puch laughed and said to Hurakan, "I didn't think you had it in you, old friend. Didn't think you'd give up your own freedom for . . . a worthless human. And it was all for nothing. Look, the boy didn't change. He has *no* dominant power! Maybe your blood isn't so potent."

Hurakan narrowed his glare. He tried to come closer, but he couldn't before red snakes curled around his ankles and wrists and formed chains, shackling him.

With a sigh, Mat shook his head and said to him, "You know the consequences."

Hurakan didn't even flinch.

"You are to be sentenced by Old World laws," Mat said to Hurakan.

I could tell by the look on Mat's face that his heart wasn't in his words. He was going through the motions because he had to. But why not stand up to the other gods? Was he trying to protect Pacific?

Alom said, "What about the boy? The law is the law. He has to die."

Ixkakaw nodded in agreement, as did Nakon.

"If he's going to die anyway," Ixtab said, "then let's use him. Let's see if he can defeat Ah-Puch. No sense in all of us getting our hands dirty if we don't have to."

Hurakan said coolly, "Let him fight."

"Good idea," Ah-Puch agreed. "He wins, and you can all go home. I win, and we can prepare for war." Then, with a shrug, he added, "What beautiful irony, Hurakan. A war with your son fighting at my side!"

Hurakan's eyes changed from gold to black as he searched my face. *You know what to do.*

*No! I don't know what to do, and in case you haven't noticed, I'm sort of paralyzed right now.*

*Find the source.*

No more words were spoken. Instead, there was an image. Had Hurakan put it in my mind, or had I conjured it up?

I couldn't move, couldn't fight, couldn't do anything. But I had the jade. I understood what I had to do.

As Puke's grip tightened around my neck, I heard a low growl behind us. When Ah-Puch turned, Rosie released a mouthful of fire. I drew it to me as I envisioned the Empty.

# 41

**· ·**

**·**

**I didn't know if it would work, if I could travel** to the Empty *with* Ah-Puch, but it was my last option. I floated in emptiness, spinning in a void of black. Then came a long tunnel of white mist. When I felt a familiar bounce, I opened my eyes. The sea, the pyramid, the jungle were all there, exactly as I'd left them. I sprang to my jaguar paws. I'd made it!

I didn't celebrate for long, because Rosie's fire burned hot inside of me and because I heard a sickening *hiss* coming from inside the temple. I instinctively crouched. From the moonlit shadows came a monstrous blackish-green snake the size of Jazz. Of course Ah-Puch would inhabit the body of a giant snake when he spirit-jumped here. Whitish liquid oozed from between its scales, and when it dripped to the floor, it...it turned into maggots. Writhing, slimy, disgusting maggots. No wonder the guy reeked!

"Little godborn," Ah-Puch hissed as he slithered toward me. His slitted eyes blazed red. His yellow fangs glistened in the moonlight. "You think you're very smart, don't you?"

Man, I was so hoping he'd turn up as a lizard or maybe even an ant. I inched back, remembering what Hurakan had said: that the Empty was his creation, made of *his* power and *his* magic. A place where the other gods' powers couldn't follow.

Ah-Puch's nostrils flared. "Do you like my chosen form?"

"A goat would've been better."

He reared up, showing me the maggoty red scales of his underbelly. "If I had hands, I'd applaud you, little godborn. I mean, it *was* a clever plan to bring me here." His forked tongue flicked, like it was sniffing the air. "Is that it? You think you can *trap* me in this place?"

"Maybe," I said defensively, hoping his tongue couldn't sense my lie. Trapping him here wouldn't be enough. It wouldn't break our connection. "You can't destroy the real world from here." I backed up slowly, my senses on fire, but definitely more controlled.

"Is that what you think?" he sneered. "That it's me and me alone? Do you really believe I'm the only one who wants to destroy your pathetic world?" He let out a cruel laugh that echoed across the stone buildings. "You're so naive, just like your father. He thought I didn't know he was trying to undermine me at every turn. But here's a little secret, godborn: *You* are the catalyst! *You* are the reason the world will end."

It felt like the black sky was pressing down on me. "Wha... what're you talking about?"

"Even if you defeat me, the gods will never allow you to live. They'll never allow a new race of gods." He lowered his head to the stone floor, coiling his tail slowly. "It threatens our powers, creates unbalance. So I used *you* for my own gain. Imagine what a wonderful surprise it was for me to discover that you're a godborn. You really think I couldn't detect your father's power racing through you?"

He paused, as if he thought I would respond, but I had nothing to say to this snake.

He continued, "Those on my side appreciated knowing there was a godborn among us, but I kept your identity to myself. I claimed I had no idea who your parent was, because that would sow mistrust, fighting, and paranoia among the gods. And once I'd created that little breeding ground, they did all the heavy lifting. I simply had to sit back and watch. So you see, Zane Obispo, you were the most glorious surprise of all."

An angry growl erupted from my throat as my back paws came to the edge of the stairs. I took deep breaths, trying to restrict the heat inside my veins that was threatening to explode any second.

"So, Zane, whether you keep me here or not," he added, "the gods will kill your father. Do you want to know what happens after that?"

"You turn into a cockroach at midnight?"

His eyes hardened. "You should be thanking me for not revealing your secret. But I didn't do it for you. I figured I'd put those powers to good use, because in the end, Zane, they won't help you defeat me. You see, you're a little half-breed nothing now. You need training, guidance, a god to teach you. But with your old man on death row, and the other gods wanting you dead, that training will be hard to come by. Join me and I'll help you attain more power than you ever imagined."

I teetered on the edge of the stairs, thinking I'd had enough of everyone's deals. "I've got a better idea," I said. "How about you release me and I won't have to kill you?"

He let out a twisted laugh and inched closer. "Spoken like a true weakling. Once Hurakan is dead, this place will die, too. And with nothing left here to trap me, I'll head off to the underworld and I'll take back what's mine. So, any way you look at it, I *win*."

I crouched lower, thinking about all the insults kids at school had thrown at me: *Uno, McGimpster, Freak*. How I'd hidden out at home because I didn't want to face them. *Weakling*. I thought about how the gods had been manipulating me this whole time. *Little half-breed nothing*.

Then I pictured all the people who had my back—my family, my friends both new and old—and how they deserved my loyalty and protection. These thoughts expanded like the fire burning inside of me until I couldn't contain it all anymore.

I knew Ah-Puch's blind spot. The one thing he hadn't considered. "You've overlooked something," I growled.

"What's that?"

"I am Zane Obispo, the Storm Runner. I didn't bring you here to trap you." My voice thundered. "I came here to *kill* you!"

Before he could react, I struck the first blow, launching myself onto his neck as we hurtled over the step's edge, down, down, down. We spiraled through a muddle of thick jungle and black skies. As I sank my teeth into his slimy scales, I prayed that he didn't bleed maggots.

He did.

They poured into my mouth as he screamed.

At the bottom, we came apart. Me spitting up vomit-flavored worms, him coiling tightly, getting ready to strike. Before he lunged at me, I leaped up, and his open jaws chomped only air. As I came out of a midair spin, he wrapped his tail around my back legs and pulled hard, slamming my head against the ground. Shock waves rolled over me. He was too big and too strong. Even without his god powers.

I slashed his tail with my claws, still resisting the urge to use fire. He released me and retreated. In one swift move, I catapulted over him and took off running. I was as fast as the lightning shredding the dark sky. Flashes of white lit up the Empty.

"*Run*, little godborn. But I'll catch you no matter how far you go!"

I heard Puke slithering behind me. It would've been so easy for me to go back to the Old World and leave him here. But what was the point? One way or another I would eventually have to face him.

Then Hurakan's whispering voice found me. *You have the blood of a destroyer. Destroy him, Zane.*

Oh sure, easy for him to say, Mr. Destroyer himself. "I didn't exactly take God Destruction 101!" I shouted into the night.

The fire burned so hot inside me I thought I might explode. Ah-Puch was only a few feet behind me, and his monstrous hiss seemed to come at me from every direction. I didn't stop running. *Couldn't* stop.

There! Through those trees, a small clearing. The rippling air of the void was just beyond. All I had to do was get to the edge of what looked like an ordinary cliff from here. Increasing my speed, taking giant leaps, I finally reached my destination and spun to face the god of darkness, death, and destruction.

Ah-Puch's giant body heaved. His eyes blazed with so much hate I thought it might swallow me whole. He slithered toward me confidently as I backed up slowly, balancing on the edge of the abyss with perfect precision. It was like walking on the rim of the Beast back home.

"Join me, Zane. I can show you the full extent of your powers."

"How about *I* show *you* my power?"

He bared his fangs and hissed, "You will always be pathetic and weak!"

"And you'll always be one step behind!"

He sprang. All my instincts told me to pivot out of his way, let his momentum hurtle him into the abyss. But to break our connection, *I* had to be the one to end him. It had to be by my hand—or in this case, paw. I held my ground, waiting for the precise moment. I said a silent good-bye to Mom and Brooks, Hondo, and Rosie. The moment his razor-sharp fangs sank into my shoulder, I grabbed hold of him and launched us both into the black hole.

There was biting, snarling, and clawing. A terrible pain radiated through my whole body.

"Do you like my venom?" Ah-Puch hissed. I started to black out as his tail coiled around my back legs. We plummeted into a bitter pool of nothingness. I looked up at the moon that was getting smaller and smaller.

Ah-Puch constricted further. If I didn't stop him, I'd be overpowered in a matter of seconds. I let out an earsplitting roar, so loud it shook the abyss. Tighter and tighter he squeezed, crushing my ribs, smothering my lungs.

I'd always hoped my last thoughts would be of something good, like the first time I saw Brooks's smile, or the way Rosie's brown eyes shone even in the dark. But when you're about to die, all you can think about is not dying. Or, in my case, how rotten it was to be choked by a giant maggot-breeding serpent in a black hole.

*The fire will do as you command.*

My skin burned. Embers glowed right beneath the surface. Finally I released it. Massive flames engulfed me.

Ah-Puch screamed, and his grip loosened, allowing me to suck in a huge gulp of air. I slipped a front leg free, then my whole upper body. With one last roar, I swiped fiery claws across his scaly face, slashing his eyes. He drew back and I managed to corkscrew out of his grasp. With all the strength I had left, I thrust him downward with the power of my back legs.

"Adiós, Puke," I snarled.

The last thing I saw was a fire-eaten monster serpent spiraling into the vortex, hissing, "I'll come for you."

# 42

••
••

**I woke up lying on a stone slab in a cold dark** chamber. There were rusty iron bars on the door, and beyond that was a gloomy hall that smelled of moldy cheese. Wall torches cast long flickering shadows across the darkness. The clanging of metal on stone rang through the place, along with moans, groans, and an occasional *Kill me now*, which was followed by *You're already dead*.

Crap! Was I dead? This had to be Xib'alb'a.

As if I'd summoned her with that thought, Ixtab appeared in front of the bars, holding a piece of paper and a pen. "Stand in the presence of a goddess!"

I got to my feet awkwardly. "What . . . what happened? Where am I? Where are my friends?"

"Shut up and listen," she said. "You're my pet now. This is your cell, and once you've paid your penance to the gods, you'll join the others in pounding stone day and night until your bones turn to dust."

"Penance? But . . . I—I killed the Stinking One!" I cleared my dry throat. "Shouldn't that count for, like, early release or something?"

She grunted, then slipped the paper through the bars. "You will write your pathetic little story on this, and it will serve as a warning to all the gods. About what happens to those who break the Sacred Oath. And to any human who chooses to defy the gods. Don't try to lie. The paper will know if you are telling the truth or not."

Magic paper. Great! Would it know if I exaggerated a little? "And if I don't feel writing anything?"

"You'll be fed to the hellhounds, one piece at a time."

Hellhounds! Was Rosie around here somewhere?

"Could I see my dog, at least?"

She thrust the pen at me. "Get to work."

I took the pen and the tissue-thin paper. "It's kind of a long story—could take a while." I wasn't in any hurry to start pounding stone until my bones turned to dust.

"You have one day."

I looked at the flimsy paper. "This . . . this is just one sheet. I guess you want the SparkNotes version?"

"The paper will multiply as needed. It comes from Itzam-yée'."

"Itzam who?"

"The Serpent Bird."

That triggered my memory. "He has something to do with the World Tree, right?" Maybe she'd be impressed with my mad Maya history skills.

With an annoyed exhale, she said, "He sits on top of it, can see all of creation, and is the greatest master of sorcery and magic this world has ever known."

"Right, *that* serpent bird," I said. "Just wanted to be sure."

My heart sank. This wasn't how it was supposed to end. I'd killed the worst god of all time, and this was how the gods thanked me? And what about Hurakan and Brooks and Hondo and—

Ixtab turned to walk away.

"Wait!"

When she looked over her shoulder, I said, "If I'm in Xib'alb'a . . . does that mean . . . ?"

She gave me a wicked smile. "Yes, Zane Obispo. You're dead."

*The End*

# POSTSCRIPT

**Don't panic. That's not how my story ends. But** I couldn't write any more down, because I would've had to lie to protect myself, and the magic paper would have...Huh. I'm not sure what it does when you try to make stuff up.

Anyway, everything up until now is absolutely true. So's this next part. But I can't let the gods see it. They can never know the whole story.

When I was finally done writing, Ixtab took me from that cell down a putrid-smelling corridor and into a small living room with gold-papered walls, expensive-looking paintings, a black leather wingback chair, two gray velvet sofas, and a glass coffee table covered in fashion magazines.

"Congratulations, little godborn," Ixtab said, smiling. "You actually *did* it!"

Confused didn't even begin to cover it. "What...what are you talking about? I thought..."

"Well, quit thinking!" With the wave of her hand, Ixtab changed, as in went from creepy goddess of death to magazine cover model. She wore leather cargo pants with too many zippers to count, a white silk blouse, and a Maya medallion on a long gold chain. Her hair morphed from demon-blue to honey brown with streaks of blond. Even her nasty gray teeth were a sparkling white. Definitely an improvement!

She sat down in the wingback chair and spread her arms wide. "Do you like it? It's one of my private chambers in Xib'alb'a. It used to be so drab and depressing, but I've really livened it up, don't you think? The gold wallpaper is all the way from India. And see that skull painting? O'Keeffe, from your neck of the woods."

"Uh-huh," I said, still feeling dazed. *Good enough for HGTV,* I thought, looking around. That's when I noticed blueprints on easels set up on the other side of the room. There were swatches of fabric, paint samples, and photos attached to the boards with big block lettering: PHASE I, PHASE II, and so on. I started again with the most obvious question: "What happened to my having to pound stones and—"

"Calm down. You're not dead," she said too casually. "I snatched you out of that fire pit you created. Thankfully, you being part god, the snake venom didn't kill you."

She raised her brows expectantly.

"Er . . . thanks?" I said.

"Don't you see? I had to give you a good ending. Or, I should say, an ending the gods would approve of. This way they think you received your just reward by dying in battle."

My heart skipped to a quick little beat: *not-dead, not-dead, not-dead.* Okay, so now that that little detail was out of the way . . . "I don't get it. Wha . . . what happened?"

"Well, you managed to rid the world of You-Know-Who, and the war god, Nakon, rounded up Ah-Puch's little pawns, including the Yant'o Triad. And when the gods found out about the hero twins' manipulation and lies? Well, let's just say those boys are getting their just deserts." She sighed.

"Don't worry, Ah-Puch's groupies can't try anything without his power. So it looks like we averted a war. For now—which is a good thing, because this renovation is taking much longer than I expected."

No war. Bad guys caught. Puke spinning in darkness forever. So far, so good.

"Where . . . where are my friends and . . . Hurakan?"

The sounds of jackhammers and electric saws started up right outside the massive wood doors. "Pardon the noise," Ixtab said, raising her voice. She ignored my question and motioned for me to hand over the manuscript. "By the way," she said, flipping through the pages, "Itzam gifted you this paper from the World Tree."

"Yeah, you said that before. But why would this Itzam dude want to help me?"

"His sole purpose is to keep balance and peace. He doesn't want to see the gods go to war."

"Do you really think my story will convince the gods I'm dead? I'm not the world's best writer. . . ."

Ixtab tossed the stack of papers onto the coffee table. "Don't worry," she said. "It's only one piece of evidence. There are more."

"Yeah?" I asked, not sure I wanted to know what they were.

"When you disappeared with You-Know-Who," Ixtab said, "your body was left in the Old World. No pulse, no movement. A little sack of bones. Pathetic, really."

"That's because Pukeface paralyzed me!"

"Yes, well, he did you a favor without even knowing it,"

she said, twisting a diamond ring on her finger. "And of course my hellhound sealed the deal."

*Hellhound.* "You mean *my* dog?" Anger gripped me when I thought about everything Rosie had been through. "You turned her into a monster!"

Ixtab dismissed the accusation with a wave of her hand. "Oh, please. She's had quite an adventuresome life here with me. And I couldn't have her going around the underworld looking like Bambi, now could I? She needed to be fierce if she was going to be a hellhound. So she got training and a little makeover."

"She's *not* a hellhound!"

At that moment a trail of smoke appeared, and Rosie walked out of it. Yep, that's right. My dog just materialized! She was twice her normal size and I have to admit, pretty intimidating. She sniffed in my direction. My throat tightened and I might've stopped breathing. She was black instead of brown, and she looked like she could murder a dragon in her sleep with those fangs, but she was Rosie. My Rosie.

"Hi, girl," I choked as I kneeled. I had to force my tears to stay back.

She swayed sheepishly and when Ixtab nodded permission, Rosie came over, sniffed me, then began nuzzling me like old times. I thought my heart would burst open. I tugged her closer, burying my face in her neck. "I'm sorry, girl. So sorry."

She let out a little whine.

"Not to interrupt your reunion and all," Ixtab said, "but we have a lot to cover and there isn't much time."

"Where are my friends? Brooks and Jazz and . . . my uncle?"

"Home, safe and sound."

I felt a sense of relief. Then I wondered which home Ixtab was referring to? Did Brooks even have a home? Was she back in Venice Beach with Jazz? Was she with Quinn?

Rosie lay down and turned over so I could scratch her belly, which made Ixtab roll her eyes. Then she said, "Rosie saved you."

"Saved *me*?"

"The hounds only go to the deceased—they *never* acknowledge the living—so when Rosie sniffed your motionless cold body, the gods believed you were no longer their problem. It was very kismet, if you ask me."

"Kis . . . what?"

"Never mind. The point is, the gods think you've passed on, which is how you ended up here, but of course you can't stay here, because you're very much alive."

"How'd Rosie end up with you anyway?" I asked as I scratched my dog's head.

"Any animal that belongs to a god—or in this case, a godborn—is sacred," she said.

Rosie wagged her nub and grunted. Smoke came out of her nose. Huh—so we had fire-making in common.

"And it's rare for animals to come here," Ixtab said, "so when Intake saw her, they called me immediately. I knew that she was something special and you'd need her for what is coming next."

"Next?"

"You asked about your dad."

A sour feeling rose in my stomach. He'd sacrificed every-thing to claim me, to give me a fighting chance against Ah-Puch. I held my breath, hoping he wasn't . . .

"He's in prison," Ixtab said. "A teeny-tiny prison, I must say, but at least he's alive. The council isn't stupid enough to kill him. They might need his powers someday."

A booming voice came over a loudspeaker in the ceil-ing: "New soul on level three. Thinks he's Shakespeare. Only speaks in iambic pentameter, and I'm getting ready to smash in his face."

Ixtab shook her head and talked into a microphone on her lapel. "Take him to level five for a brain soak. Then give him two days at the spa." She turned back to me. "Now, where were we?"

"My dad? In jail?" Mental double take. *Did she say* spa?

"Oh, yes. I suppose I should start at the beginning. But listen carefully, because I don't have time to repeat myself." Ixtab went on to tell me how she'd been working undercover with my dad for weeks. Keeping up evil appearances, because the paranoid gods were watching *everyone*. And when Brooks came to help negotiate Quinn's release, Ixtab saw the magical opportunity.

"Opportunity?" My head spun. "Brooks said you sent her to find and bring back Ah-Puch."

"I knew she wouldn't be able to achieve such a feat, but you needed help from someone who understood the Maya legends and gods, and someone you could rely on. She was a true gift."

"Wait a minute. . . . You took away her shape-shifting

magic," I said, remembering. "And you tried to kill us at Jack in the Box!"

"That was good, wasn't it?" Her eyes flashed electric blue. "I sent my best actors for that one, because I knew the gods had spies everywhere. And I *had* to take away her power. She was drawing too much attention to you. The gods would've started asking why a supernatural was hanging out with some human kid."

My mind raced. "You sent that little . . . that monster, the alux. He *wasn't* faking. He wanted to tear my head off!"

"True, but he went rogue. It happens sometimes. Especially the little ones—always trying to make up for their stout nature. If Brooks hadn't killed him, I would've, trust me." She straightened a few magazines then turned back to me. "You want to know the worst part?"

"Worse than being attacked by blue demons and crazy rogue monsters?"

"Having to look like a hideous hag!" She clenched her fists and shook her head.

"Why would you have to look like—?"

"Because it's expected of someone sitting on the throne of death. But if I were a man . . ."

"Okay, I get the whole creepy death god costume, but that doesn't explain why you held Quinn prisoner."

"She was *never* a prisoner. She was in training as a spy for a very old, very secret . . ." She hesitated. "She was working undercover the whole time."

Great! So the gods have a spy network? "Does Brooks *know* her sister was a spy?"

She straightened a black-beaded pillow. "She knows *now*, which could create a problem for Quinn's cover."

Rosie turned in circles before finding a cozy place to settle on the floor. I didn't want to say anything, but man, did she need a bath. Or two. She smelled like singed hair.

"Hang on, didn't Quinn...er, stab you with a lightning bolt?"

"She had to..."

"To make it look good." I nodded, catching on. "I get it."

My mind raced through everything Ixtab had done, everything she'd been responsible for. All her answers added up. Then I remembered Ms. Cab. "You turned the seers into chickens!"

"You're a little slow for a godborn, you know that?" she said, annoyed. "Think about it. We couldn't have a bunch of seers running around knowing what we were up to, now could we? For this all to work, it had to be flawless. We had to get you to the Old World, so your dad could claim you in front of the council if you were to have half a chance at defeating Ah-Puch."

"Puke could've killed me!"

"That was a risk we had to take."

"Yeah, because it wasn't your head!"

Rosie crooned in agreement.

"Why?" I asked. "Why would you risk so much to help my dad, to help me?"

"We..."

"Who's *we*?"

She turned away, paused, then looked back. "Your father's not the only one who broke the Sacred Oath."

*Oh. Ohh. OHHHH.*

"There are other godborns. *Were* other godborns."

Yeah, wasn't expecting *that* little tidbit of information. "Wha...what happened to them?"

I thought I saw her wipe off a tear, but she turned too quickly. "We don't know....We sent them away—to hide them—but they all died. It was like their blood couldn't hold the power."

*They all died?* My breath whooshed out of me. The whole thing was too depressing. "Then...does that mean I'm going to—?"

She shrugged then spun back around with a deep frown. "You seem to have defied the odds. Who knows why you survived? Maybe because you're Hurakan's..." She shivered. "I shouldn't be telling you all this. It's ancient history. Right now the important thing is that you disappear. Do you think you can play dead?"

Rosie got to her feet and roared like a lion. Fire spat from her mouth and her eyes. I fell back. "Whoa!"

"Oops," Ixtab said. "She's trained to go into hellhound mode on the command *dead.*

"Steak!" Ixtab commanded, holding up her hand. Rosie settled back into her non-demon mode.

"*Steak* is the command for stop?" I asked.

"Unless you want her to rip your enemy to shreds before she barbecues them."

"You said something about my playing d—" I looked at Rosie. "You-know-what?" I said, getting back on topic.

"You can't go home."

"Why not?"

"First, because it's no longer there. Had to sort of destroy everything in a huge flood, a good excuse for why you all had to leave so suddenly."

The room spun. "Where am I supposed to go, then?"

"You'll see. But I've cloaked you with powerful shadow magic so the gods can't detect you. It's quite perfect, if I do say so myself."

"But what if... what if the gods come knocking on the underworld's door and I'm not here?"

"Remember the demons I sent that looked exactly like you?"

I couldn't help it. I smiled. She was a serious mastermind! "And what about my mom and Hondo and..."

"They're waiting for you."

Relief spread through me. "Where?"

"You'll see."

"But it's not like some deserted, awful place with no internet or tacos, right?"

"Tacos you can get. Internet? Maybe not. And under no circumstances can you use your powers outside the shielded place I'm sending you to. If you do, the gods will pick it up on their radar, and they'll hunt you down and murder you in your sleep. Do you understand?"

I really didn't want to think about getting murdered in my sleep. "Wait a sec. What am I supposed to do with my powers? Don't I need some kind of training?"

She shook her head. "Too dangerous. Go to the movies. Eat tacos. Read books. Do what humans do. Live a normal life."

"Normal? I'm *not* normal!"

Wow! Before, all I'd ever wished was to be like everyone else, and now? I actually liked the way those words made me feel.

I didn't even mind the fact that I still had one shorter leg. Yeah, Sparkstriker's lightning-bolt surgery hadn't permanently fixed it. I kind of thought my limp would have disappeared now that I was a claimed godborn who could control fire, but I guess magic doesn't work that way. Still, it didn't bother me. It didn't seem like a weakness anymore, just part of who I was. And besides, it connected me to my dad, ole One Leg.

That reminded me. "What about Hurakan?" I asked Ixtab. "Can he come, too? I can't let him rot in prison."

"Don't worry about him. He'll be fine. He's suffered much worse, believe me," Ixtab said. "Now, do you want to see your human family or not?" She looked at her watch. "Hurry, we have a cab to catch."

"There's cab service from Xib'alb'a?"

"Of course. At least until I can get Uber to negotiate with me."

# POST POSTSCRIPT

**The cabdriver was a skeleton decked out like** Elvis in a white jumpsuit, sideburns, and all, and he belted out "Jailhouse Rock" the entire ten-minute drive. We couldn't take any roads—especially the heavily watched cosmic ones. So we only had one option: we cruised the ocean. Under the waves, that is. Thanks to Pacific speeding up time for us, it was like being on a roller-coaster submarine, which meant everything whizzed by in a blur. Although I'm pretty sure I saw a two-headed shark.

This was Pacific's "parting gift" to me. She had to find a new hiding place. The gods would read my story soon enough, and everyone I'd been trying to protect would be revealed. Even Mat wasn't safe. Stupid truth paper!

"We're here," Elvis said, bursting through breakers. Imagine going through a crazy car wash at Mach ten. That's what this was like. He pulled to a stop on a white sandy beach lined with swaying palms.

"Where . . . where are we?"

"Isla Holbox, Mexico," Ixtab said. "Very secluded, and surrounded by water, which is the most important part."

"Why does the water matter?"

"Messes up signals, wavelengths, the gods' ability to see clearly. Plus, it's protected by—"

"Your shadow magic."

"Precisely."

I ducked to peer through the windshield. "Whoa!"

I couldn't believe what I was seeing. A luxury vacation house—the kind you only read about in adventure books or see in those fancy travel magazines. The place was tucked under tall, willowy palms, had two stories, a palapa roof, and thick timbers holding up a massive back porch where hammocks swung in the afternoon sun. A quick glance down the shore in both directions told me we were pretty secluded, with the next house at least two football fields away. Rosie barked, whined, and pawed at the car door.

When I went to open it, Ixtab grabbed my arm, reached into her pocket, and removed a silver letter opener. "I almost forgot. This is for you."

"Er...what's this for?" I thought it was a weird parting gift.

"You know, for someone who's part god and has seen ancient magic, you really are lacking in the imagination department," she said. "It's your cane-slash-spear. I had to hide it somewhere." She tapped the end and the cane popped out.

I took it from her. It was just as cool as before. "Does the spear still work?"

Ixtab rolled her eyes and stepped out of the car. "Ándale," she said. "I don't have all day."

Leading with my warrior cane, I stepped out of the cab.

"One more thing." She pointed to the right, past the house and across the jungle.

I blinked. Once. Twice. "Is that what I think it is?"

"Yup."

Rosie hunkered low and covered her eyes with her paws, groaning. Some things hadn't changed. I patted her on the head reassuringly and asked Ixtab, "But how the heck did you move a whole volcano?"

"It was your father's idea." She played with the gold bangles dangling from her wrists. "It wasn't a bad one, either, I have to admit. We couldn't simply leave it in New Mexico—it had too much magic left over in it. So Mat replaced it with a replica, and I, of course, did all the heavy lifting to bring the real one here."

"And the people on this island didn't wonder when a volcano sprang up out of nowhere?"

Ixtab shrugged. "It happens sometimes."

I couldn't take my eyes off *my* volcano. I almost threw my arms around Ixtab's neck but stopped when I realized she might strangle me.

"You obviously approve," she said.

"Approve?" Grinning, I ran my hands over my hair. "It's . . . it's amazing!"

"I created a portal inside that leads to Xib'alb'a. You may use it in case of emergency," Ixtab added. "*Extreme* emergency."

"Emergency? Why would I have an emergency? You said this place is safe."

"I said your family and friends are safe. Nowhere is ever entirely safe for someone like you."

I clutched my cane. "Then I guess it's a good thing I have this. And Rosie." The dynamic duo was together again!

Rosie barked in agreement.

Ixtab looked down at her. "I hate to give her up. She would have made a wonderful hellhound." Then she ducked back into the cab. "I'll be seeing you again, Zane Obispo. It's inevitable." As she closed the door, I swore I heard her tell the esqueleto, "Now take me to that dreadful Aztec king."

As soon as the cab had disappeared, I saw Mom running barefoot from the house toward me. Her dark hair blew across her face. I hurried over and hugged her. Either she'd shrunk or I'd grown, but either way it felt great to be home. Yeah, I know it wasn't New Mexico, but home is where my family is.

Hondo was right behind her. He shook his head and socked me in the arm "Diablo! You did it. You actually did it. Well, I helped, but still!"

"*Diablo?*"

"Your new nickname! You earned it by killing the god of death! Totally perfect, right?"

"Yeah. No!"

Mom was crying, hugging, crying, mumbling, naming every santo in the universe. She wiped her face and said with a smile, "I bet you're hungry. We're grilling steaks. ¿Tienes hambre? Maybe something to drink?"

Rosie half groaned, half whined. Mom blinked and looked down at her for the first time. "Hey, girl." She knelt down and scrubbed her neck with both hands. "You're even more hermosa than the last time I saw you!" Rosie danced in place, fish-tail wagging her body. That's what I love about my mom. She always knows the exact right thing to say.

We started for the house and I looked around. Hondo knew who I was searching for.

"She hasn't been here."

Oh. I waited for more, but Hondo didn't say anything else about it.

My heart sank. I mean, wouldn't yours? Not that I liked Brooks (as in *like* her) or anything. It for sure wasn't like that between us. Brooks barely tolerated me most of the time. I just wanted to talk to her about everything that had happened. You know—say good-bye on the right note. I mean, she was annoying, and brave, and controlling. And she was complicated, and smart, and amazing. I definitely didn't... Never mind.

A few minutes later I was sitting under the palm-covered porch, eating flautas (heavy on the salsa) with Mom and Hondo. I filled them in about everything that had gone down with Ah-Puch and Ixtab. Hondo told me that he and Jazz and Brooks had been sent from the Old World back to Venice Beach. Apparently Jazz had sold his shop there so he could open a new company, AGE: Advanced Giant Engineering. And Brooks was with him, wherever he was. The good news was that once the gods read what I had to say (and hopefully they're slow readers), they might give Jazz a pass, since he was in the dark for so long. But Brooks? No chance. She had aided and abetted a wanted criminal. For sure, they wouldn't forgive that. Which meant she would always be in danger.

"And Quinn?" I asked.

"You mean the gorgeous sister who nailed Ixtab with a bolt?" Hondo asked with a wide grin.

"Okay..."

"Haven't seen her. Not since we got back to Venice."

Mom reached over and grabbed my hand. "We have so much to talk about."

Yeah. Like Dad. But there was plenty of time to catch up about him. And everything else.

I grabbed another flauta and set it on my plate. "I, um... I'm sorry I dragged you guys into this."

"This?" Hondo looked around. "Yeah, it's a real hellhole."

"But...what will you guys do for work? Like, I know how much you loved New Mexico, Mom, and now it's all gone."

"I can learn to love anyplace as long as we're together." Mom let out a light laugh. "This beautiful house is a gift from Ixtab, and Hondo and I have decided to open a bike and surf shop. Doesn't that sound fun?"

"Like Jazz's?"

"With a few tweaks." Hondo crossed his arms and leaned back. "I'm going to offer wrestling lessons for tourists' kids. Total *Nacho Libre*! And you're going to love the island. Population sixteen hundred, and twenty-six miles of white beaches." Then his face fell. "There's only one downside."

"Too many people?" I teased.

"No cars allowed. Only golf carts," he said. "You know how slow a golf cart is?" He shook his head. "It's tragic."

Familiar footsteps sounded and when I turned, you wouldn't believe who I saw waltzing through the house. Mr. O and Ms. Cab! Thankfully, she was in human form again.

Mr. O grabbed me and pulled me into a tight hug. "Héroe."

"Everyone was a hero," I said, turning to Ms. Cab.

Ms. Cab lifted her chin. "You're lucky all the seers went

back to normal, because if I had to be a chicken one more day..."

"Good to see you, too," I said, with a pang of guilt, as I realized that her cover would soon be blown as well.

Ms. Cab reached into her dress pocket and pulled out a handful of...birdseed? She tossed some into her mouth. I figured my own mouth must've been hanging wide open, because she shrugged and said, "An acquired taste."

Mom stifled a laugh and Hondo made a disgusted face.

"Mr. Ortiz took wonderful care of us while you were away," Mom said.

Ms. Cab sighed. "I suppose. Old fool followed me here just because I told him I'd have dinner with him."

Mr. O's face lit up when he looked at Ms. Cab. Any guy who could still love someone who'd been a cranky chicken and ate birdseed out of her pocket was a champ in my book.

"I couldn't let you get away, amor," he said, to which she huffed. "We will be very happy on this isla."

"In separate huts!" Ms. Cab reminded him.

Turning to me, he raised his bushy brows and asked, "And La Muerte? Did she work?"

I recalled the pepper's effect on Jordan. "Definitely took out a bad guy," I said.

Mr. O beamed while Ms. Cab popped more birdseed into her mouth and mumbled, "Idiots."

I laughed. It was her way of saying she cared about us.

"And one more thing, Zane," she said.

"Yeah?"

"You owe me an eyeball."

After everyone went inside, I headed down to the beach. Rosie raced after me, yelping and jumping in the waves. Being in Xib'alb'a hadn't really changed her. Sure, she looked different on the outside, but inside she was still the dog I had rescued. And now she had rescued me.

The sun was melting into the water and everything had an orange glow. If I had to hole up somewhere, this seemed like a pretty good place. But shadow magic or no shadow magic, I knew I wouldn't stay here forever.

Laughter spilled out of the house. I sat on the sand and stared at my legs. My shorter one was a clue about where I'd come from and what I could do. I mean, if I hadn't had a limp, the Sparkstriker would never have been able to find my dominant power.

I laid back and closed my eyes as Rosie settled next to me. "Tomorrow," I said, "we can hike the Beast again."

Rosie whined.

Then I felt something blocking the sun. I opened my eyes to see a hawk circling overhead. "Brooks!" I shouted, bolting upright.

She landed nearby, kicking up some sand. Which I totally thought she did on purpose. Like I said, she can be annoying.

Rosie barreled into her as Brooks shifted back into a human. What, were they like BFFs now? Brooks fell back laughing as she rubbed Rosie's ears. "Hey, girl."

I got to my feet, pulled Brooks up, and squeezed her in a bear hug. Man, she smelled good. Like coconut oil and fresh towels.

"Okay," she said, pushing me back. "I can't breathe."

"Wha...what are you doing here?" I was so excited, I had a hard time standing there without hugging her again. "Hondo said you were with Jazz, and he didn't know where—"

She rolled her eyes. "Get real, Zane. You think I wasn't going to get the whole story from you? Besides, I'm a fugitive now."

"Yeah. Me too."

She tucked her hair behind her ear and straightened her short black jacket. "So give it up. All of it. And don't leave out any details. Start with you killing Ah-Puch. Oh, and don't leave out waking up in the cell and the story you had to write for those evil gods."

"How'd you know?"

"I have friends in low places," she teased. She meant Ixtab.

We plopped onto the beach and I spilled all the details. Brooks listened intently, tracing her fingers through the sand, nodding every few minutes like she could see the images my words painted.

"I wish I could've lied," I said. "To protect people from the gods' wrath."

She shoulder-bumped me. "So when do I get to read this tell-all?"

My throat tightened. Brooks? Read it? How about never?

"What about Quinn?" I asked, wanting to change the subject.

"Her cover was blown when she took your side. She couldn't go back to Xib'alb'a, so she's in a protection program until she can be reactivated. She's fine with it—she didn't like being with all those dead people anyway."

Rosie's eyes shot flames at the word *dead*.

"Meat!" I yelled. "I mean, *steak*!"

My dog settled back down, licking her chops. I was definitely going to have to come up with a better command or she might barbecue anyone in her path.

"You and Rosie are a perfect flame-throwing pair," Brooks said as she stroked Rosie's neck.

I laughed.

"So what now?" Her amber eyes glittered in the setting sun.

I took the jade from my pocket. "You're not going to like it."

"But you're going to tell me anyway."

"I have to bust my dad out of prison."

"*Another* prison break? Ugh!" She got to her feet. "Ixtab will kill you for breaking your promise. . . . And the gods will have your head on a spike if they find out you're alive."

"I don't have a choice. He risked everything for me. No way am I going to let him rot in some speck of dirt somewhere."

Brooks stared out at the ocean with a deep scowl. "I say we lay low for a while."

"What if it were Quinn?"

She threw me a glare. "I'd storm the castle."

"Then I guess I'll storm the castle."

"You really are a pain, you know that?"

"So I've been told."

"Fine." Brooks lifted her chin. "But you so owe me!"

"It could be dangerous."

With half a smile, she said, "I was built for danger."

"You're going to have to learn to swim," I told her as the waves crashed to the shore.

"No."

"Yes."

Pulling her knees into her chest, she shook her head. "Not doing it, Zane."

Rosie ran into the water like she was demonstrating that it was safe to go in.

Brooks grabbed my hand. *I'm glad you didn't die.*

*Me too.*

*If you ever leave me behind again, I'll kill you.*

I stood and backed into the water slowly. "You'd have to catch me first. And in case you forgot, I'm a godborn."

With a sigh, she shrugged. "In case *you* forgot, I can fly."

Grinning, I launched myself into an oncoming wave. When I came up for air, I shook the water from my hair and looked toward the shore. Brooks was gone. She'd shifted into a hawk and was soaring over the sea, wings spread wide, their tips glistening in the sunlight. There was still so much I had to tell her, but it could wait. I watched her fly, thinking she was meant to be a hawk. And I was meant to be a godborn. Like Mr. O had said, destiny comes knocking, and *if you don't open the door, she will come in through the window.*

That's important, because if you're reading this, you have a bigger destiny than you ever knew.

Remember when Ixtab said all the other godborns died? I'm not so sure I believe her. Why would I be the only one left?

And if there's even a tiny chance you're out there, I *need* to know.

If you can read this, you've got magic in your blood. Only another godborn would be able to see the words on these last few pages. Which is why I took the risk to write down the whole truth. I was hoping to find you. Hoping I could trust you with the secret.

If you wait long enough, your destiny will come knocking. Take it from me—someday, when you least expect it, the magic will call to you.

*El FIN*

# GLOSSARY

## Dear Reader:

This glossary is meant to provide some context for Zane's story. It in no way represents the *many* Maya mythologies, cultures, languages, pronunciations, and geographies. That would take an entire library. Instead, this offers a snapshot of how *I* understand the myths and terms, and what *I* learned during my research for this book. Simply put, myths are stories handed down from one generation to the next. While growing up near the Tijuana border, I was fascinated by the Maya (as well as the Aztec) mythologies, and I was absolutely *sure* that my ancestors were related to the gods. Each time I've visited the Maya pyramids in the Yucatán, I've listened for whispers in the breeze (and I just might've heard them). My grandmother used to speak of spirits, brujos, gods, and the magic of ancient civilizations, further igniting my curiosity for and love of myth and magic. I hope this is the beginning (or continuation) of your own curiosity and journey.

**Ah-Puch** (*ah-POOCH*) god of death, darkness, and destruction. Sometimes he's called the Stinking One or Flatulent One (Oy!). He is often depicted as a skeleton wearing a collar of dangling eyeballs from those he's killed. No wonder he doesn't have any friends.

**Alom** (*ah-LOME*) god of the sky

**alux** (*ah-LOOSH*) a knee-high dwarf-like creature molded out of clay or stone for a specific purpose. The creator of an alux must provide offerings to it. Otherwise it might get mad and take revenge on its owner. Sounds kind of risky, if you ask me.

**Bakab** (*bah-KAHB*) four divine brothers who hold up the corners of the world, and all without complaining about having tired arms

**Ceiba Tree** (*SAY-bah*) the World Tree or Tree of Life. Its roots begin in the underworld, grow up through the earth, and continue into paradise.

**Hurakan** (*hoor-ah-KAHN*) god of wind, storm, and fire. Also known as Heart of the Sky and One Leg. Hurakan is one of the gods who helped create humans four different times. Some believe he is responsible for giving humans the gift of fire.

**Itzam-yée'** (*eet-sahm-YEE*) a bird deity that sits atop the World Tree and can see all three planes: the underworld, earth, and paradise. Imagine the stories he could tell.

**Ixkakaw** (*eesh-ka-KOW*) goddess of the cacao tree and chocolate

**Ixkik'** (*sh-KEEK*) mother of the hero twins, Jun'ajpu' and Xb'alamkej; also known as the Blood Moon goddess and Blood Maiden. She is the daughter of one of the lords of the underworld.

**Ixtab** (*eesh-TAHB*) goddess (and often caretaker) of people who were sacrificed or died a violent death

**Jun'ajpu'** (*HOON-ah-POO*) one of the hero twins; his brother is Xb'alamkej. These brothers were the second generation of hero twins. They were raised by their mother (Ixkik') and grandmother. They were really good ballplayers, and one day they played so loudly, the lords of the underworld got annoyed and asked them to come down to Xib'alb'a for a visit (no thanks!). They accepted the invitation and had to face a series of tests and trials. Luckily for them, they were clever and passed each test, eventually avenging their father and uncle, whom the lords of the underworld had killed.

**Jun Jun'ajpu'** (*HOON hoon-ah-POO*) father of the hero twins, but nothing more than a severed head

**K'ukumatz** (*koo-koo-MATS*) (also known as Kukuulkaan) one of the creator gods. He is said to have come from the sea to teach humans his knowledge. Then he went back to the ocean, promising to return one day. As Kukuulkaan, he is known as the Feathered Serpent. According to legend, he slithers down the steps of the great pyramid El Castillo at Chichen Itza in Yucatán, Mexico, on the spring and autumn equinoxes; festivals are held in his honor there to this day. El Castillo is definitely a cool—but also hair-raising and bone-chilling—place to visit.

**Kukuulkaan** (*koo-kool-KAHN*) see K'UKUMATZ

**Ma'alob áak'ab'** (*MA-ah-lobe AAH-kab*) a Mayan *good evening* greeting

**Muwan** (*moo-AHN*) a screech owl that Ah-Puch used to send messages from the underworld (Good thing she couldn't text!)

**Nakon** (*nah-CONE*) god of war

**nawal** (*nah-WAHL*) a human with the ability to change into an animal, sometimes called a shape-shifter

**nik' wachinel** (*nikh watch-een-EL*) a Maya seer, a diviner who can forecast the future

**puksí'ikal** (*pook-SEEK-ahl*) Mayan word for *heart*

**Saqik'oxol** (*sock-ee-kh-oh-SHOLE*) the White Sparkstriker; a being that lives in the woods, wears a red mask, and dresses entirely in red. The Sparkstriker pounded lightning into the first daykeepers (diviners).

**Sipakna** (*see-pahk-NAH*) an arrogant giant who was killed by the second generation of hero twins when they dropped a mountain on him

**Xb'alamkej** (*sh-bah-lam-KEH*) one of the hero twins; see JUN'AJPU'

**Xib'alb'a** (*shee-bahl-BAH*) the Maya underworld, a land of darkness and fear where the soul has to travel before reaching paradise. If the soul fails, it must stay in the underworld and hang out with demons. Yikes!

**Yant'o Triad** (*yahn-TOE*) three evil deities who happen to be brothers: Yant'o, Usukun (*ooh-soo-KOON*), and Uyitzin (*ooh-yee-TSEEN*). Also referred to as Good, Bad, and Indifferent, they love nothing more than to see human suffering. Hmm . . . where's the good in that?

# ACKNOWLEDGMENTS

I can't begin to express my gratitude for all the hands and hearts that played a role in bringing Zane's story to life. I'm so grateful to Rick Riordan and Disney Hyperion for not only honoring diverse voices, but for building the stage from which to share our stories. (PS: Rick, you're also a keenly aware reader/editor! You'd make Athena proud.) And speaking of editors: I hit the lottery with Stephanie Lurie. You took a leap into the volcano with me, trusting that I knew my way out. Your tremendous brainpower, generosity, sense of humor, and gift of chocolate made the trip all the better.

My deepest appreciation to my fierce agent, Holly Root, who sent me a perfectly timed e-mail one day that unearthed Zane's story. Your Ixtab-worthy tenacity, confidence, and wit were the waves that carried me to shore.

Thank you to both Catherine Rhodes at the University of New Mexico's Department of Anthropology, and Judith M. Maxwell, Ixq'anil, the Louise Rebecca Schawe and Williedell Schawe Professor of Linguistics and Anthropology at Tulane University, for your linguistic expertise. And to Erin Jerry—thank you for reading Zane's story through the lens of a special-education scholar and advocate. A bouquet of thank-yous to Julie Romeis. Your thoughtful guidance made all the difference in getting this writer over the hump.

For my dear friend, and fellow bruja, Aida Lopez. Thank

you for always seeing beyond the horizon and journeying with me to the shaman's house. And for Lucia DiStefano, a beyond brilliant writer and reader, thank you for being "swoonishly in love" with this story. Your text came at the exact right moment.

A nod of solidarity to the legendary Rocky Balboa (yep, the boxer), whose story inspired a young girl and a stubborn heart.

I would be remiss if I didn't acknowledge the generations of women in my family both past and present. You gave me the fire and the bones.

Thanks to my wonderful parents, who read the earliest versions of this book when it was still a baby manuscript and loved it anyway. Mom: they *are* real. Dad: I hope your "Maya roots" text comes true.

And of course, to my familia: I know living with a writer can be maddening, especially a writer on deadline. Your love and support are my sustenance and strength. For my husband, Joseph, thanks for buying a ticket into my world and loving my crazy imagination. For my amazing daughters: Alex, your streetwise insights, excessive exclamation points when I got it wrong (they really were excessive), and music expertise brightened Zane's long journey. (PS: The cape looks good on you.) Bella, your infectious humor and daily snaps recharged my batteries. And of course, the unexpected SO GOOD text that told me I'd *really* aimed right. Julie Bear, my partner in all things magic. You get it. You always have. Even if you didn't like the soggy bread.

And finally, I thank God for the immeasurable blessings. I promise to use them well.

*Coming in Fall 2019*
*from J. C. Cervantes*

**The Fire Keeper**